"WHAT ARE YOU DOING HERE?"
ROSS DEMANDED

He was moving toward her, and there was no way Hope could avoid him. Fighting back a sense of panic, she tried to decipher the expression that crossed his face, but all was lost in a blur as he came to stand only inches away.

One thing about Ross Adair was certain: his masculinity. Hope felt as if her entire body had suddenly been turned to molten lava.

Slowly, deliberately, he enfolded her in his arms. Her senses swam as his lips descended on her mouth. The kiss was brutal, but it was also exciting, and the momentary pain of its impact was stabbed through with intense pleasure.

"Is that what you came here for?" he asked, his breath hot against the softness of her skin. "Is that what you wanted?"

MEG HUDSON
is also the author
of these SUPERROMANCES

These books may be available at your local bookseller
or by writing to:

WORLDWIDE READER SERVICE
1440 South Priest Drive, Tempe, AZ 85281
Canadian address: Stratford, Ontario N5A 6W2

MEG HUDSON

TWO WORLDS, ONE LOVE

A SUPERROMANCE FROM
WORLDWIDE

TORONTO · NEW YORK · LONDON

Published September 1983

First printing July 1983

ISBN 0-373-70079-2

Printed in Canada

CHAPTER ONE

THE DISTANT MOUNTAINS were cloud brushed, their peaks wreathed in filmy rings of haze. As she left Asheville behind her and drove toward the massive, green gray shapes that dominated the far horizon, Hope said their name aloud: "The Great Smokies." And in a magical sort of way it seemed as if the mountains were summoning her, luring her toward adventure, excitement....

She smiled rather wistfully. Although she certainly was looking forward to these next few weeks, she very much doubted that either adventure or excitement would play a part in them. She would be going on a painting trip with a fellow art teacher, Lorna Evans, and it promised to be a rather prosaic experience. But that was enough for the moment. All she really wanted just now was a change of pace, some new scenery and the chance to relegate old, traumatic memories to the past, where they belonged.

She had not been given that chance during her recent visit to Asheville. In fact, her stay in the gracious North Carolina city had been entirely too painful. She had been forced to remember Lewis and the desperate unhappiness he had caused her.

And the ghosts of old family troubles had arisen, too....

Hope straightened her shoulders and set her chin resolutely. The tense session in Asheville with her mother's elderly cousin, Emily Standish Collingworth, was now a part of the past, thank God. She'd fulfilled a difficult family obligation—that of breaking the ice with a relative whose communications had been few and far between. She had gritted her teeth and endured Cousin Emily's questions, her curiosity and her criticisms. Now, at least, she would never have to pay Cousin Emily a return visit. And, with effort, she had managed to leave on a reasonably pleasant note that morning, keeping the smile fixed on her face while she ignored Cousin Emily's final, pointed comments.

Because she had been anxious to get away as soon as possible, Hope had bypassed the chore of having her old Volvo checked out at a local service station, promising herself to put the car in a garage for a going-over after she joined up with her friend Lorna in Gatlinburg. She suspected that it was going to need some work done, since the trip down from Concord, Massachusetts had done nothing at all to alleviate its already audible complaints. Luckily, Lorna had suggested they use her car on their trip, since it was a much newer model.

The clouds that had been skirting the mountains were getting closer, Hope noticed, and the atmosphere seemed to have reached its saturation point. Mist turned to drizzle, and drizzle to a fine-falling rain. She switched on the windshield wipers, which creaked reluctantly across the glass surface, as if protesting the need to perform at all.

Fortunately, the rain was not heavy thus far, so her visibility was not seriously restricted. She felt, in fact, as if she was traveling through a rather lovely drenching mist, which made the mountains surrounding her appear green all of a sudden, rather than charcoal, as if they'd decided to don June's bright, still-new foliage despite the darkness of the weather.

The previous day, when she had stopped at a gas station to fill up the Volvo's tank, the attendant had given her a road map of the area and in answer to her query had suggested that the most direct route to Gatlinburg would be via Route 19 to Route 441, then through Newfound Gap. Later, glancing again at the map, Hope had noticed that the two highways junctioned at the town of Cherokee. This was a distance of about forty miles, so she'd surmised it could easily be covered in an hour or less.

The rain, of course, was slowing her down. But even as she was about to search out a service station where someone could take a look at the creaking windshield wipers, they seemed to correct whatever problem had been possessing them and began to swing back and forth in a pleasantly reassuring tempo. Hope sighed with relief. She'd had enough problems lately. She didn't need something even as small as a malfunctioning windshield wiper to further plague her.

She shrugged, determined not to lapse into a bout of negative thinking, and reminded herself that the whole idea of taking a trip south and going painting in the Great Smokies with Lorna Evans had been to cast off the old and make an entirely new beginning. Maybe after a summer away from New England she'd even go so far as deciding not to go back to teaching art at the Abbott Academy in Concord come fall.

Hope chuckled at the thought, then sobered quickly because the weather was forcing her to concentrate on her driving. The rain was getting heavier and she was glad that the traffic on this weekday afternoon was light. The road was hardly a super-highway, and there was a fair share of curves in the bargain. Peering ahead, she saw a road sign and noted that at this point Highway 19 either veered south to join 19A or else continued straight ahead. Without a second thought, she continued on Route 19.

After a few miles, she realized she was definitely getting into the mountains, climbing one moment and descending the next. Briefly, she wished for sunshine. It would have made her present task easier, and she knew the countryside would have been gorgeous on a sunny day. The mountain laurel and the rhododendrons were in bloom, lending splashes of vivid color through the grayness. Yet she soon appreciated the fact that even under the best of weather conditions there would have been little chance to do much scenery surveying. A mountainous road like this one demanded all the skill a driver possessed.

Hope passed through the resort area of Maggie Valley, which she'd heard was a popular place for skiing in the winter. She could easily see why. There were plenty of slopes to choose from in the vicinity. And beyond Maggie Valley the way became even steeper and more difficult, until at moments it seemed as if she and her Volvo were literally clinging to the edge of a very precipitous Earth.

She was conscious of tumbling mountain streams, forests that were impenetrable to light, hairpin curves in the road that took her breath away and precipices that came much too close to her wheels for comfort, giving her the awful sensation that she was surely going to plunge over the rim of one of them at any second. Then, when it seemed as if she must have come to the top of everything, the Volvo began to protest in earnest.

Although she had never been mechanically minded, Hope realized very quickly that this was not a problem the elderly car was going to be able to fix by itself, as it had done in the case of the recalcitrant windshield wipers. No, the car was in trouble...and so was she!

Then, ahead of her, she saw a sign at the side of the road and just managed to make out the words, "Entering the Qualla Boundary." This was followed by something about the area being a Cherokee Indian Reservation, and she frowned. Until now it had not occurred to her that there might actually be Cherokees living in the town of Cherokee. She wondered if she would even be allowed on an Indian reservation. These were private preserves, after all—or so it seemed to her—and she imagined that the Indians who lived on them would probably also be very private people and might consider her an intruder.

Her heart sank as she came to a second sign. It pictured a truck going down a near-perpendicular decline, and with it were the words, "Steep Downgrade for the Next Five Miles."

This warning, Hope decided a few seconds later, had been definitely understated. She fought to control the balking car as the road started downward in a series of hairpin curves that blocked her visibility and gave no idea at all of what might lie ahead at the next blind bend. She found herself praying that she didn't meet anyone coming the other way, because it didn't seem possible that she'd be able to give someone else the right of way—even if she wanted to.

Her luck held until she was almost at the bottom. Then, as she rounded an especially tricky curve, she found herself nearly bumper-to-bumper with a pickup truck just starting upward. She gasped aloud, but the truck driver seemed to have no problem at all avoiding her.

Hope had only a glimpse of him as he went by, but she was almost certain he was an Indian, although the black, broad-brimmed hat he was wearing shielded his face too much to be sure. The drizzle hampered her vision, anyway. Then she emerged into a narrow valley and saw yet another sign to the side of the road. This one proclaimed the fact she'd actually arrived in the town of Cherokee.

A moment later she was dazzled by a stretch of motels, shops and restaurants. The roof of one motel was ornamented with three wigwams, and in the doorway of a shop billed as a "trading post" just across from it she saw a rather elderly man dressed in full Indian costume, complete with a long, multifeathered headdress, evidently taking refuge from the rain.

So this was Cherokee. Hope found it difficult to believe that she was actually within a genuine Indian reservation. This particular area, at least, seemed to have been staged purely for tourists.

The Cherokees. Hope tried to remember some of the facts she'd learned about these people long ago in school, then gave up, temporarily, because now that the Volvo had come to relatively level ground it was obviously in the throes of something she could only pray was not going to prove to be a terminal mechanical illness!

Finding a service station became the first order of business, and after driving two blocks Hope saw the reassuring sight of a stand of gas pumps on the right side of the road. She managed one final turn, pulled off the street and came to an involuntary halt a few feet sooner than she'd intended to, for at this point the Volvo simply quit.

Fortunately, this was a fairly large service station, obviously geared for repairs. There were two service bays to the left of the central office area, both of them open and both of them occupied. In one bay there was a car that looked to be about the same vintage as the Volvo, but no one was working on it at the moment. The car in the other bay was an expensive sports model, sleek, black and shining.

Hope's attention became riveted on the long, denim-clad legs that protruded from underneath the sports car. As she watched, the possessor of the two legs wriggled his way out of the restrictive space and stood up. For a moment Hope forgot her own problems as, despite herself, she stared at him.

He was tall, very tall. Definitely slim, too, yet there was a latent sense of power about him. His broad shoulders were encased in a vivid red shirt, which was unbuttoned halfway down his chest and tapered to a slender waist cinched by a wide black leather belt with a heavy brass buckle.

Hope felt as if her throat had suddenly gone dry. This man was almost flagrantly masculine, and just looking at him made her uncomfortable in a peculiar sort of way. It had been a long while since a man had affected her sensually, and although she really didn't want to look at hid any more closely, she could not keep her eyes from sweeping upward. In another instant they'd reached his face, and the sight of that jolted her totally.

He was Indian. There could be no doubt at all about his bloodline. And it seemed to her that all the pride she would have associated with the Cherokees was stamped into his face. It was a rugged face and looked as if it might have been chiseled from a granite outcropping on one of the mountains surrounding this valley. Hope decided, in fact, that this man was the prototype of an Indian chief—an extremely handsome Indian chief.

Something seemed to snap inside her as she realized that he was watching her in return. He was standing at the side of the sports car looking across at her, and she felt herself rocked by his gaze. His eyes were as black as some gemstones she'd bought once out in Colorado—Apache's Tears, they were called—and just now they looked equally hard. Hope sensed that he was assessing her, but then he turned away casually, having evidently decided, to her chagrin, that she wasn't worth further attention.

She was conscious of a profile averted, and it was an astonishing profile. His nose was perfectly formed, almost aquiline in shape, his lips were full and generous and there was a smoothness to the slant of his cheeks.

Impatient with herself because of the impact he was making on her, Hope waited for him to approach so that she could discuss the problems of her car with him. She was completely unprepared when not only his profile turned away from her—*he* turned away from her, making his way toward the door that led into the service-station office.

While she watched, he inserted some coins into a soft-drink machine and a moment later came out with a bottle held to his lips, quaffing thirstily, evidently oblivious to her presence.

Hope had been having a bad day, and this was the kind of final touch to it that she didn't need. Anger flared, and she fought for self-control. As far as she knew, this might be the only service station in town. At least, it was as far as she was going to be able to get. She disliked the thought of doing business with this rude stranger, but she didn't have much of an alternative.

He was standing next to the shiny sports car, surveying it in a manner that Hope could only consider critical, and in a way this was a relief. Maybe he simply didn't like anything very much. Then to her astonishment he reached inside, and after a moment music from the car's radio filtered out, a popular new-wave beat that she usually liked but that now made her grit her teeth.

She watched as the tall, arrogant stranger put aside his soft-drink bottle and slid back underneath the car again, effectively shutting Hope out of sight—and probably sound, as well, with the radio blaring in his ears.

Indignation took over. Hope stomped across to the sports car and coughed loudly.

Nothing happened.

"Excuse me," she said. Obviously he didn't hear her.

Incensed, she decided there was only one thing left to do. Sharply, she nudged the foot nearest her, noting as she did so that it was shod in what looked like a very expensive leather boot.

There was a moment of absolute stillness. Then slowly he emerged, pulled himself into a sitting position and looked up at her.

Hope could not help but wonder how she must appear to him and found herself wishing that she'd paid more attention to her makeup that morning. The previous spring she'd been ill with the flu for a time, a siege that had taken its toll. May in New England had been cold and wet, and June, up until her departure, hadn't been much better. There had been no opportunity to get out in the sun and put a tinge of needed color in her cheeks.

Because she was so pale, her violet blue eyes looked even larger than usual. In fact, they seemed almost oversized in her piquant, heart-shaped face. Wanting to leave Asheville as quickly as possible that morning, she had simply brushed her ash-blond hair down around her shoulders, not bothering to arrange it in any sort of style.

The man opposite her seemed to dismiss her appearance with a simple, uninterested glance. Then he asked, "What is it?" His face remained so impassive that she couldn't help being daunted by it.

"Well," she began, finding her voice with difficulty, "if you don't mind, I would like some service."

"Oh?" Very dark eyebrows rose to crease a perfect forehead. Watching, Hope's eyes traveled on to see that his hair was quite beautiful. Thick and absolutely black, jet velvet rather than satin. Again she felt that strange, dry sensation in her throat and was disgusted with herself. There was no reason to let this...this rude individual provoke any sort of emotional reaction in her except distaste, she told herself firmly.

Suddenly he stood up, towering over her. Still inscrutable, he appraised her with a thoroughness that was totally disconcerting. Again Hope found herself wishing that she'd paid more attention to her makeup and had been more careful about arranging her hair. But at least the clothes she had on were becoming. She had an excellent fashion sense and long before had learned how to satisfy it with far more ingenuity than money.

She was wearing a Greek crocheted blouse, eggshell in color, that had loose-fitting bell sleeves. It was banded at both the cuffs and the V-neck with a contrasting crocheted pattern in the same shade. Around her slim waist she wore a raspberry macrame belt that picked up the tone of her linen slacks. And just now she knew there was an added note of color in the picture. She could feel herself flushing as this man continued to stare at her steadily.

"What kind of service were you looking for?" he asked with a politeness she at once found suspicious. She also discovered, to her surprise, that he spoke like a Southerner. His wasn't a pronounced Southern accent, but it was there, soft enough and different enough to be interesting.

Hope swallowed hard. "There's something wrong with my car," she said lamely.

Those ebony eyes were disconcertingly grave, and he sounded almost solicitous as he said, "That's too bad."

"What?" Hope echoed.

"I said that's too bad," he repeated obligingly. "Anything serious, do you think?"

"Yes, I think it's serious," she retorted. "But it's up to you to find out!"

His shrug was very slight. "Why me?" he asked reasonably.

"Why you?" Hope stopped only because she couldn't continue. Words literally failed her, so she drew a long breath. Then she managed, trying not to sputter, "Because it's your job, after all!"

"My job?" Hope saw his mouth twitch with suppressed amusement, which only intensified her growing resentment. Then he said, "Oh..." as if some great revelation had suddenly come to him. "You think I work here...."

"Don't you?"

He shook his head. "No, I don't. The proprietor is a friend of mine, though. Randy Youngdeer. He's out on a road call, but he should be back soon. Will you wait?"

"I don't have much choice," Hope told him.

"I could take a look under the hood if you like," the tall stranger suggested, a shade too indifferently.

"Thank you, no," Hope replied shortly, not bothering to be gracious about it. Again she saw that fleeting hint of amusement cross his face, and again resentment came with its sting. She didn't feel that anything was funny in the least...nor did she relish being a target for what he must consider some sort of joke. She added tersely, "I'll wait for Mr. Young...what did you say his name is?"

"Youngdeer."

Hope was spared a reply because at that moment a slightly battered yellow truck careened into the service station and came to an impressive stop almost too close to her feet for comfort.

The man who climbed out was obviously Indian, too, though he was quite different from the tall, rude stranger. He was shorter and sturdier in build, with a broad, well-developed chest. Hope could imagine him as a professional football player. His nose was broad rather than aquiline, and his black hair was straight and worn rather long. He was not overwhelmingly handsome, but he definitely looked friendlier, and there wasn't a trace of mockery in the smile he flashed at her.

"Hope I haven't kept you waiting too long," he said in an accent that was also definitely Southern. "Hey, there, Ross," he teased, addressing the other man. "You could have helped her out, couldn't you?"

"I wouldn't have wanted to venture a diagnosis," the man named Ross said, and those Apache's Tears eyes swept Hope again, complete with that hint of cynical amusement that was so disconcerting. "I offered to take a look under the hood, but the lady wasn't interested."

Randy Youngdeer had already moved to the Volvo and lifted the hood. He was peering inside, his back to both of them. His voice was muffled as he asked, "Which way did you come, miss?"

"Highway 19 from Asheville," Hope said.

"You must have held your breath when you hit some of those downgrades."

"I did," she admitted. "And I knew when I pulled in here that it was definitely the end of the road."

Randy Youngdeer nodded, straightening. "You can say that again!" he agreed. "You drove all the way down from Massachusetts with this old baby?"

"Yes."

"Miracle she didn't conk out on you long before

you got here. I'd say," he added with a frown, "that she's got her share of problems. But nothing that Youngdeer's Keep-'Em-Young-Forever service can't fix. You planning to be around for a few days?"

Hope was appalled. "Absolutely not! I have to meet a friend in Gatlinburg this afternoon."

The service-station manager shook his head. "No way, lady," he told her flatly. "For one thing, do you realize what sort of country it is between here and Gatlinburg?"

Hope sagged. "Hilly, no doubt," she ventured.

"Hilly's not quite the word for it. You go straight through the heart of the Great Smokies, via New-found Gap. You hit some of the highest elevations in the Eastern United States. Fine, if you've got a car that's in shape—which yours certainly is not! Look," he continued with a scowl, "I wouldn't let you drive out of here in that baby. Not the way she is now."

A low chuckle broke through the silence that fol-lowed this announcement, and Hope became aware that the disdainful Ross had been listening to this whole interchange with obvious amusement.

He said, still chuckling, "Watch it, Randy, or the lady's apt to get the law on you. You seem to forget that women don't like to be told what to do these days."

Involuntarily, Hope raised her eyes. As they meshed with his, the resulting impact shocked her. No man had a right to be so attractive and so dis-agreeable at one and the same time.

To her surprise she saw him stiffen, and she had the satisfaction of knowing that the impact had not been entirely one-sided. Suddenly this picture seemed to become cemented in her mind and she knew that it was one of those life scenes that would always be a part of her. She would forever be able to summon instant recall so that she would mentally re-live this June day in a North Carolina Indian village, with a tall, provocative Cherokee standing against a background of slanting gray rain, while in the misted distance the green slopes of the Great Smokies rose toward the north. She had the odd sense, in a way she couldn't fully understand, that this man and the mountains were united when it came to such qualities as strength and endurance. The thought even crossed her mind that it would not be too difficult to be told what to do by a man like him. For if he loved a woman—if he ever were to love a woman—he would have only her best interests at heart.

Randy Youngdeer, looking worried, said, "I'm not trying to tell you what to do, miss."

"Please," she protested. "I didn't think you were. Obviously, if the problem with the car isn't something that can be fixed immediately I'll have to make other arrangements."

"Well, I have some work scheduled this after-noon I've got to handle first. It's promised. But I can get to your Volvo right after that, and if you check with me later on I can tell you exactly what we're facing."

"There's no chance you could solve the problem tonight?"

Randy Youngdeer shook his head regretfully. "No chance." His grin was appealing. "Look," he said, "Cherokee's not a bad spot for a stopover. Matter of fact, tourists come here from all over the world. We've got a lot of attractions hereabouts, wouldn't you say, Ross?"

"I'm opinionated," Ross said casually.

"Gets kind of crowded this time of year," Randy Youngdeer added, ignoring the comment. "But I happen to know there's a vacancy in the Three Wigwams up the street. You can't miss it. It's the motel with the three wigwams on the roof. My sister and her husband run it."

"Thank you," Hope said. "I'll walk on up there."

She hesitated, because the rain was coming down very heavily now. She had a raincoat and scarf in the car, but the thought of lugging her suitcase up the sodden street was not a pleasant one.

Randy Youngdeer said, "I'll call over to be sure they don't give the room to anyone else, okay?" Then he added, "You finished with that black beauty of yours, Ross?"

The answer came monosyllabically. "Yes."

"How about running the lady over on your way, then?" Randy said, to her dismay. "Your name, miss?"

"Hope Standish," she said reluctantly.

"Okay, Miss Standish. They've got a good little coffee shop at the motel. I'm sure you'll be comfortable. And I'll get to the Volvo as soon as I can—that's a promise. Now, what do you want to take along with you?''

Randy Youngdeer was moving to the trunk of the car as she spoke and in another second had it opened. Hope pointed to the suitcase that held most of the things she'd need for an overnight stay, but instead of putting it on the ground so that she could pick it up herself, Randy Youngdeer handed it directly to the man called Ross.

Hope bit her lip. There was no reason at all why this man should drive her up the street to the motel. Without meaning to, the friendly gas-station manager had put them both in an awkward position. One that Ross would probably like to wriggle out of as much as she would, she imagined.

But there was also no reason why she should get soaking wet just to assert her independence. As she walked over to the sleek black sports car, Hope tried to tell herself that this was the only reason she was going with him.

CHAPTER TWO

IT WAS A VERY SHORT DRIVE, yet it seemed eternal to Hope. As they pulled up in front of the Three Wigwams Motel she geared herself to get out of the car quickly, thank the man named Ross, then reach for her suitcase and escape into the now welcome sanctuary of the motel office.

Her involuntary chauffeur, however, had other plans. He'd donned a bright yellow slicker with an attached hood that reminded her of coastal New England's traditional foul-weather gear, and as he turned to Hope he thrust the hood up to cover his thick, black velvet hair.

"I'll check to see if Penny Raincrow really does have a room for you," he said. "Randy tends to be something of an optimist."

The name struck her. "Penny Raincrow?" she echoed.

His eyebrows rose mockingly, but he only said, "If you stay around Cherokee for a while you'll come across a lot of names that will seem strange to you. Names...and many other things, as well."

"I'm sure...."

Ignoring her response, he continued, "Some of the old-timers around here say that Indians used to have just one name. The legend goes that in older times a baby was named for the first thing a mother saw that made an impression on her after the birth. Let's say she looked out the window of her traditional Cherokee log house and saw a partridge. She'd name her new baby Partridge. Or she might see a running deer or a wolf or perhaps a laurel in full bloom."

"That's fascinating," Hope said sincerely. "What a charming custom!"

"I suppose it could be considered so," Ross conceded. Then he opened the car door a crack and shrugged. "I might as well make a dash for it," he said, and before Hope could protest that she was perfectly able to handle the matter herself of whether or not there was a room available, he'd got out of the car and was dashing through the steadily falling rain.

She sighed. The truth of the matter, she had to admit to herself, was that she hadn't forced herself to protest nearly as quickly as she could have—had she wanted to. And this didn't make sense to her. There was absolutely no reason to prolong what had been entirely a chance encounter, and not a pleasant one at that. She tried to tell herself she didn't like Ross any more than he seemed to like her, and that, she decided grimly, was very little indeed.

She was startled when he suddenly appeared on her side of the car, tapping impatiently on the window. The rain was slanting in her direction so she lowered the glass just enough to hear him say peremptorily, "Unlock your door."

She did so, but her fingers were fumbling as she pulled up the door lock. No doubt about it, this man really unnerved her.

He opened the car door for her, clearly impatient, then said in the manner of someone accustomed to giving orders and having them instantly obeyed, "Leave your suitcase and come along. Your room hasn't been made up yet, but Penny says it won't take too long. Meantime, we can get a drink of something hot in the coffee shop."

He didn't wait for her reply. It was clear that he expected her to follow him. Hope was tempted to tell him that she could perfectly well wait in the lobby, but to protest now would mean speaking to the back of his head, already a fair distance in front of her.

It was past the lunch hour, and there was no one else in the small coffee shop. Hope hesitated in the doorway. The thought of sitting down at a table in an empty room with her reluctant chauffeur was enough to give her butterflies. The little restaurant was pleasant, though. It was pine paneled, with bright floral-printed curtains framing the windows. There were copper accents in the candlesticks on each table and in the plant holders used lavishly along the walls. The decorative focal point, though, was a large portrait of a man wearing a turban fashioned of strips of colored cloth. He was holding a thin-stemmed pipe between long, slender fingers, and his face was very unusual. There was a gentleness, a wryness about him. Had Hope not been in a place that made it seem likely he must be a

Cherokee, she could not possibly have guessed his nationality.

Her "host" had crossed the room to a table at the far side, which overlooked a small garden at the back of the motel. There was also a rectangular swimming pool and a set of swings for children, all quite vacant at the moment.

"Sit down," he suggested, although he did not offer to draw out a chair for her. Then, when he saw her studying the portrait, he said, "That's Sequoya. You might call him the patron saint of the Cherokees. As close to one as we have, at any rate."

"Sequoya was a Cherokee?" Hope asked, surprised. "I thought the name originated in California."

"The giant redwoods?" he asked. "They were named after him, yes, but Sequoya was a Cherokee. I should say, to be more accurate, that he was half Cherokee. His father was an Englishman. You see that medal he's wearing in the portrait? The one suspended by a ribbon around his neck?"

"Yes."

"It was given to him by the Cherokee Nation in appreciation for his having invented the Cherokee alphabet. As far as is known, he's the only man in the history of the world who managed to invent an entire alphabet without being able to either read or write in any other language. He was a remarkably wise man in many ways."

A woman entered the coffee shop through a swinging door from the direction of the kitchen.

Short and stocky, she had a broad face with rather flat features that reminded Hope of Randy. She wore her gray hair fashioned into a bun at the nape of her neck, and even though her dress, a blue cotton, was faded from many washings, and the leather moccasins she wore had seen better days, there was an air of dignity about her that Hope instinctively responded to.

"Well, Ross Adair," she asked, "what are you doing out on a day like this?"

"Randy let me use the garage to do a little work on my car," Ross answered amiably.

"Bad weather for the tourists," the woman frowned, peering out at the deserted swimming pool, where the raindrops were pitting the surface of the light blue water.

"The summer's young," Ross told her casually. "Mrs. Brook, this is Miss Standish." He turned to Hope. "It is *Miss* Standish, isn't it?"

"Yes," Hope managed to reply.

"Randy's got her car in for repairs, so she'll be staying at the motel for a while," Ross volunteered.

"You've checked with Penny?"

"Yes. She's fixing up a room now."

"She must have had a cancellation," Mrs. Brook observed. "It's a good thing you came in today, Miss Standish. There are a couple of busloads of tourists coming in tomorrow, and they'll take up most of the rooms—one of those tour groups here to take in the drama, among other things. Penny might be able to arrange an extra ticket if you want to go along."

"That would be very nice," Hope said quickly, "but I expect I'll be leaving first thing in the morning. As soon as Mr. Youngdeer can finish with my car, anyway." She had no idea what the drama might be that Mrs. Brook was referring to. Something widely known, evidently, if whole tour groups came to see it.

"Got any pie left, Mrs. Brook?" she heard Ross ask.

"There may be a piece or two of blueberry."

"Who made it?"

Mrs. Brook smiled. "Minerva Lightfoot," she said. "She bakes pies for us twice a week now."

"Then I'll have a slice, and I'd recommend it to you, Miss Standish."

Hope, on the verge of refusing, found herself nodding assent instead. She also went along with his suggestion that they both have coffee.

When Mrs. Brook had left them, he said, "Sorry I can't offer you a cocktail or a glass of wine first. You'll find that they don't serve any alcohol in Cherokee."

Hope enjoyed wine occasionally, but the matter of whether or not she had anything alcoholic to drink was one of relative indifference to her. Still, it was strange to go anywhere where drinks weren't offered, so there was genuine surprise in her voice when she asked, "Oh?"

"Alcohol is forbidden on an Indian reservation," he told her. "At least, you won't find it served in public places."

"Really?" This time her surprise was even more

pronounced. "Is it against religious beliefs?" she asked.

"No," he answered, thoroughly serious now. "Alcoholism is a leading health problem among American Indians."

Despite herself Hope flinched, for the subject of alcoholism was one she avoided, and she had no intention of getting involved in a conversation about it with Ross Adair.

He was waiting for her to say something, though; she sensed that. It seemed impossible to change the subject without a comment, so she said, "Alcoholism, I'd say, is a universal problem," and was prepared to go into something else when he interrupted.

"I didn't mean to imply that we stand alone insofar as alcoholism is concerned, Miss Standish," he said levelly. "But according to statistics, Indian alcoholism is estimated to be much higher than the national average for white people. That doesn't mean, may I add hastily, that all the old myths about Indians and 'firewater' are true. But some studies have shown that Indians actually do stay drunk longer than Caucasians." He added with a wicked grin, "Though I can't say I've ever tried to prove it, one way or the other."

When Hope didn't answer this, he looked across at her, much too perceptively. "What is it?" he asked, and she was surprised to look into ink-black eyes that were not making fun of her now. In fact, they were quite devoid of mockery.

She found herself stammering as she answered, "N-nothing, really."

"Is someone close to you an alcoholic?" he persisted.

"My father was an alcoholic," she admitted heavily. "It...it killed him."

"He died of alcoholism?"

"No. He went swimming late one afternoon when he was drunk...and he drowned," she said, not able to camouflage the bitterness. "He was a wonderful man, but he...had a weakness. And when things went wrong for him he'd...take another drink. I loved him very much, and watching him go to that bottle was like...like living in a constant nightmare. A horror story. If my mother had tried to help it might have been different, but she didn't. She was the one with all the money—inherited money. She comes from an old Boston family. Dad was an English teacher in the same school where I teach now. Shakespeare, especially. That was his forte. He'd always wanted to be a Shakespearean actor, and he looked the part. He was very handsome in a way that was...well, he had delicate features for a man, and there was a certain whimsicality about them."

Hope glanced toward the painting at the end of the room. "Rather like your Sequoya," she said, for it was this quality in the face of the portrait that had struck her immediately.

"Like Sequoya?" Ross Adair echoed.

Hope nodded. "Yes. You can see the compassion and tolerance in Sequoya's face, can't you? Well, you could see it in my father's face, too."

"How long ago did he die?"

"Three years ago. Then I was offered a teaching job in the same school...."

"You teach Shakespeare?"

"No. I teach art."

They were interrupted by Mrs. Brook's arrival with the pie and coffee. Watching the Indian woman serve them, Hope suddenly became overwhelmingly aware of the confidences she had just volunteered to this total stranger. A feeling of intense embarrassment came over her and she wished she could somehow vanish without having to say another word to him. What had possessed her? She, who was normally such a private sort of person when it came to revealing the things that really mattered to her. She'd never before spoken so freely of her father and what she considered his affliction—not even to her closest friends. Yet she had unburdened herself to this man as if he was some sort of confessor.

"Good pie, isn't it?" he said between bites, and it occurred to Hope that he might very well want to change the subject they'd been discussing as much as she did.

"Yes," she agreed. Then his next statement made her realize what a mistake it was to take anything about him for granted.

"Where is your mother now?" he questioned.

This was the last thing she had expected him to ask, and her chin instinctively tilted defensively. But almost as quickly her innate sense of fair play took over. After all, it was she who had brought up the subject of her parents in the first place.

"She lives in Boston," Hope said, "or at least that's her home base. She has a condominium overlooking Boston Harbor. A penthouse, really. I must admit the view is gorgeous. A good bit of the time, though, she travels. Just now she's visiting friends in England, then she'll be going to the Algarve. I think she plans to spend the balance of the summer on the French Riviera. She has a lot of . . . connections, shall we say."

"A very wealthy lady, eh?"

"Yes, I suppose she is," Hope said defensively.

"Yet," he observed, "you drive a rattletrap of a car that is clearly on its last mechanical legs."

Hope's chin tilted higher. "I make my own way, Mr. Adair," she said firmly. "I ask nothing of my mother, and I expect nothing from her. She left my father two years before he died, so I—"

She broke off at this point, aghast at herself because the conversation was becoming so personal. She could not believe she was volunteering this kind of information. She'd never been one to pry into the private lives of others, and she'd always resented any attempts at intrusions into her own. That was one reason why being with her cousin Emily in Asheville had been such an unpleasant experience. Emily—her mother's first cousin, actually—had never had any use for Hope's father in the first place, and even now that he was dead she still made this very clear. She had prefaced her remarks about the late Hilary Standish by saying that she had always prided herself on her own lack of hypocrisy. Listening to this elderly relative, Hope had seen nothing commendable about this particular character trait of hers. She would have much preferred Cousin Emily to have kept her opinions to herself.

Also, via some sort of family grapevine, Emily had learned about Lewis. This was especially annoying because Hope was an only child and she really didn't have many relatives—just a variety of aunts and uncles and cousins, none of them very close to her. She had found it difficult to believe her ears when Lewis's name had first come up in conversation, and soon after she found out that Cousin Emily was not about to be dissuaded when it came to discussing him.

The fact that it had proven to be a very one-sided conversation had not helped. Cousin Emily had taken it for granted that Hope's heart had been damaged beyond repair because of Lewis, and she had gone to great pains to relate her own life experience, this supposedly proving that even the best marriages were not necessarily those made for love. No, Cousin Emily had been "madly" in love, but the romance had been broken up by her family. Now she claimed she could look back and admit that they had been right. Her lover would not have been suitable as a husband, not suitable at all. And in due course she had married Gerald Collingworth and moved to Asheville, where they'd lived what she termed a "marvelous" life. Gerald had become a judge and had died a very wealthy man, which made Cousin Emily a very wealthy widow.

"I never want to be a wealthy widow!" Hope

said now violently, then found to her horror that she had spoken aloud.

"You're thinking of your mother?" Ross Adair asked politely.

Hope stared at him, totally mortified. "No," she choked, picking up her coffee cup in an attempt at diversion. She intended to sip the hot beverage, but instead she managed to jostle the contents so that creamy brown liquid spilled out directly onto the middle of her portion of blueberry pie.

She reared back as if she'd been stung, and this time she almost dropped the entire cup. Fortunately she was able to rally, steadying the cup and placing it back on its saucer. Then she had the horrible feeling that if she didn't get tight control of herself very soon she was going to burst into tears.

She didn't know what sort of reaction she expected from Ross Adair, but she wasn't prepared for his sympathy. He said quickly, "I'll have Mrs. Brook bring you another piece of pie."

"Thank you, no," came the answer swiftly. "I've really had enough."

He had finished his own pie and most of his coffee. "Whatever you say," he agreed, then glanced at his wristwatch.

It was a heavy gold watch, Hope noticed, with a digital face. It looked decidedly expensive, but then so did the belt with the wide brass buckle.

She said, surprisingly loath to bring this moment with him to a close, "I must be keeping you from something."

His impatience was barely concealed. "Is that a

question or a statement, Miss Standish?'' he asked her, then before she could answer continued, ''Never mind. You're not keeping me from anything, except possibly settling down with a good book, which is always a pleasant thing to do on a rainy afternoon like this. I'm not going to work until tonight.''

She deliberately refrained from inquiring as to what sort of job he had because she was determined not to get into any further personal conversation with him. Nor did he offer to tell her. And it was with a decided feeling of anticlimax that she watched him stand up and reach for his wallet.

Briefly she wondered if she should offer to pay for the pie and coffee, especially since she'd wrecked the better part of hers. But she was almost sure that this would bring a scathing glance that she didn't feel up to coping with.

Although he was unaware of it, his questioning of Hope had probed four painful wounds: the subjects of her father, his tragic death, her mother and perhaps especially the matter of Lewis, revived during the tense visit with her cousin. These were a quartet that belonged locked in Pandora's box forever as far as she was concerned, and she did not thank Ross Adair for having caused her to open that symbolical box, no matter how inadvertent his intentions might have been.

Mrs. Brook appeared and Ross quickly settled the bill. Then he said, ''Your room should be ready by now, I'd say.''

This time they went through the connecting door

into the motel, and Penny Raincrow was at the desk. She looked very much like her brother and was equally friendly.

"We'll take good care of Miss Standish, Ross," she said, and it seemed to Hope that Penny Raincrow had got the impression Hope was in Cherokee because she was a friend of Ross Adair's. If this were so, it was something that Hope would have to correct!

"You have room 112, Miss Standish," Penny Raincrow informed her, "and you don't have to walk around in the rain to get to it. Just take the inner corridor. Fourth door on the right."

Hope took the room key from her and picked up her suitcase before Ross Adair could make a move for it. Not that he necessarily would have done so, she thought dismally.

Just then the phone behind the desk rang. Penny Raincrow excused herself to answer it, and Hope was left to face Ross alone. He looked very tall—and very forbidding.

"Thank you," she said to him, trying to keep her voice low enough so that it wouldn't be overheard.

"My pleasure," he replied, and there was something especially intriguing about that soft Southern tone.

Hope's thoughts involving him threatened to race off again, and she forced herself to rein them in tightly. Ross Adair was staring down at her again with that remarkable lack of expression she found so disconcerting.

"I realize that you were somewhat conned into driving me over here..." she began.

"No trouble," he assured her, and she decided that she really liked him better when he wasn't being so polite.

"I'm sure Penny will make you comfortable here," he continued, "and you can be certain Randy will have your car fixed up as soon as possible. He's an excellent mechanic."

"Yes," Hope said a bit feebly. "I'm sure he is."

"Then," Ross Adair continued, as if she hadn't spoken at all, "you'll be able to get on your way again without any more...detours. Watch out driving that car of yours across to Gatlinburg, though. Even Randy can't perform miracles."

"I will," she promised dully.

"Goodbye, then," he said, but he seemed oddly hesitant. For one emotion-boggling moment, Hope had the feeling he was going to take her in his arms and kiss her.

It was such an intense impression that she nearly reeled toward him, and only the further shock—the shock of knowing how much she wanted to do this—saved her. Incredible though it was, she also knew she wanted him to kiss her. She wanted to feel his arms around her, she wanted to savor the pressure of those mobile lips molded tightly against her own.

Thoroughly jolted, Hope managed to thrust out her hand in an effort to maintain her dignity. Ross Adair took it gently, his fingers pressing slightly as they encircled hers. His touch was warm, there was strength in his grip, and an unprecedented rush of feeling swept over her, so swift, so sharp that she was sure she must be conveying at least some semblance of it to him.

She glanced down at their hands clasped together. His dark skin contrasted sharply with her fairness. She shivered, strangely thrilled by this. Like everything else about him, she found the rich tone of his skin impossibly attractive.

Time seemed suspended as he held her hand, and she had the heady feeling he might be about to ask her if he could see her again before she left Cherokee. But this wasn't to be.

As if he were actually thrusting something away from him, Ross Adair said again, "Goodbye." Then he added unexpectedly, "Have a pleasant summer."

"Thank you," Hope answered. And with that he nodded and turned away.

The phone rang again and she was conscious of Penny Raincrow's voice in the background. But this was a dim sort of consciousness. Primarily, Hope was filled with the sight of Ross Adair.

She watched him through the rain-streaked picture window as he walked over to the shiny black sports car. This time he had not bothered to throw the yellow hood up over his head, and even though his sleek black hair was getting wet, he appeared oblivious to the rain.

She wondered what he was thinking about and more than half feared that she was already gone from his mind. Would he consider her simply a stray vacationer who had happened into Cherokee because she had car trouble? Would he remember her only as someone to whom he had given a lift and offered a cup of coffee?

As she unlocked the door to her room, Hope knew that although Ross Adair might have the ability to push a mental delete button as far as she was concerned, it was going to be a long, long time before she would be able to forget him.

CHAPTER THREE

HOPE PHONED the service station shortly after five o'clock only to discover that Randy Youngdeer had been called out on yet another breakdown job. A girl answered the phone and offered to take a message, but in response to Hope's question as to whether or not the Volvo was ready, she hesitated.

"I don't think so," she said. "Randy mentioned something about having to order a part. . . ."

This was very bad news for Hope. She left the message that she'd call back first thing in the morning or would walk over if the rain let up in the meantime. But the thought of being stranded in Cherokee was immediately depressing. She hadn't planned for anything like this to happen.

She ate dinner by herself in the coffee shop and found that every time someone entered the little restaurant she was looking up much too anxiously, hoping it might be Ross Adair. But this did not happen. In fact, there wasn't a single Indian patron in the room. The dinner guests were obviously tourists, most of them middle-aged.

Evidently Mrs. Brook had the evening off, and in her place was a young redheaded waitress. She suggested fresh rainbow trout, a specialty of the region, and Hope was not disappointed in choosing it. The fish was delicious.

Having finished dinner, she headed back through the office on the way to her room. There was a man at the desk now, an Indian. Hope was becoming accustomed to seeing Indians wherever she turned, which was logical enough, but there was still an unreality to it. Until now, Indians had been a part of American history familiar to her primarily from remembered illustrations in grade-school textbooks. She envisioned stern and stalwart men wearing feathered headdresses. More often than not they were seated atop white horses, staring moodily toward an invisible distant horizon.

The description, she decided, fitted Ross Adair. Or it would if he had a feathered headdress and a horse.

She tried to smile at the idea of this, but the smile wouldn't quite materialize. Why did this man have the power to affect her so, she wondered.

She was aware that the man at the registration desk was watching her curiously, and now he asked, "Did you want something, miss?"

There was that Southern accent again. It seemed so strangely misplaced, yet it was very pleasant. "No," Hope said hastily. Then she amended, "I will be wanting to make a long-distance call from my room, though."

"Go right ahead," he invited. "Make as many as you'd like. They'll just be added to your bill," he finished with a smile.

Hope returned the smile as she continued past the

desk, and she wondered if this man might be Penny Raincrow's husband. She also wondered if Penny or her husband was related to Ross Adair, or, for that matter, if most of the Indians in Cherokee were related to one another. Her interest was piqued, but once back in her room she momentarily put her conjectures about the Cherokees aside while she placed the call to Lorna Evans in Gatlinburg.

Lorna was obviously disappointed, as Hope had imagined she would be, but she was also audibly annoyed.

"I've been here waiting for you since noon," she reminded Hope. "And I wouldn't have come down from Knoxville in the first place and booked our reservations at this lodge if I'd known there was the slightest chance you weren't going to make it."

Hope remembered then that her friend was currently teaching in Knoxville, but still she fought back a surge of annoyance as she said levelly, "I didn't plan for this to happen, Lorna."

"You shouldn't have tried to make a trip like this in a car that's in less than perfect condition," Lorna pointed out. "The Great Smokies are extremely rugged. I know that road into Cherokee, and it's a wonder you didn't smash up along the way. Honestly, Hope...."

"I'm sorry, Lorna," Hope said, and at this late date she began to recall certain things about Lorna that she'd forgotten, things from the days when they'd gone to art school together. She decided whimsically that there was surely truth to the old adage about distance lending enchantment to a relationship. She and Lorna got along beautifully when they limited themselves to letters and an occasional phone call, but now Hope remembered that Lorna had always been one to take offense easily, and she often criticized others bitterly if things did not go her way.

What would it be like to go on a painting trip with her in the mountains for two weeks? Humor faded as Hope faced the fact that it might be trying in a number of ways. For one thing, Lorna had known Lewis, and she was almost certain to attempt to pry out all the details, which Hope had no desire to discuss. It was enough that Lewis had left her with a bitterness and a sense of caution toward men that surfaced much too frequently. She recognized her wariness in her encounter with Ross Adair, for instance, and she wondered if she'd ever be able to place her trust in a man again, to give him her love without retaining terrible reservations.

A man like Ross Adair, for example. . . .

Hope sighed. She had been looking forward to this trip in the Great Smokies for so long. She had been saving for it all year, and that hadn't been easy to do. In the months before his death her father had incurred a staggering number of bills, and she was still trying to get them paid up. The family lawyer had advised her that this was an obligation she could escape; legally she was not responsible for her father's debts. But Hilary Standish hadn't left an estate—nothing of any tangible value, anyway—and Hope had felt that paying those people he owed was necessary to clear his honor. Now she wondered dimly if she'd been a fool about that, as she'd evidently been about so many other things.

Lorna said impatiently, "Hope, when do you think you can get here?"

"I don't know, Lorna," Hope admitted. "I'll get back to you as soon as I can."

Lorna had to be satisfied with this, but as she hung up the receiver Hope knew that her "friend" was not going to wait for her very long in Gatlinburg, nor could she blame her. As it was, she'd have to send Lorna the money for her part of the room rent. There was that question of honor again. And since she really couldn't afford the double tariff of a room in Gatlinburg and the one in this Cherokee motel, as well, something definite would have to be decided as soon as possible.

Hope shrugged. There wasn't anything more she could do about the situation tonight, she told herself, so she switched on the TV, hoping for an escape. And when a frantic chase scene in a cowboys-and-Indians movie flashed across the screen she actually burst out laughing as she espied a chief wearing a feathered headdress astride a white horse. Then, with the thuds of stampeding hooves ringing in her ears, she collapsed onto the nearest chair, and in another instant her laughter had changed to sobs and she was crying, the tears streaming down her cheeks. Like a bewildered child, Hope found herself wishing that Ross Adair would come stalking into the room to take her in his arms and hold her close to him as he kissed her tears away.

This was such a ridiculous thought that it forced her back to sanity. Feeling very tired, she got up and switched off the TV. Then she showered, put on a thin blue cotton nightgown and got into bed. But it was a long time before sleep arrived to erase her troubled thoughts.

RANDY YOUNGDEER CALLED the next morning before she had the chance to walk over to his gas station.

It was not yet eight o'clock and she was about to go to the coffee shop for a light breakfast when the phone rang, and she heard his low, Southern drawl.

"Is the car ready?" she asked eagerly.

"Sorry to say, no," Randy told her. "And I hate to tell you this because I know you're in a hurry to get on your way, but... I'm afraid it's going to take a while. This old baby of yours has seen her best days, no doubt about it, and one problem is that she's a foreigner in the bargain. It's hard to come by parts for an old Volvo hereabouts."

"What needs to be replaced?" Hope asked with a sinking feeling.

"The universal joint," Randy said. "It helps connect the drive shaft to the rear axle, and needless to say the car can't move without it. I don't know why the old one didn't fall apart right in the middle of the road, to tell you the truth. It was totally shot. Anyway, it's not a part you can get that easily, but I've got feelers out in Sylva, which is the nearest place where I could expect to come up with anything like that. If not there, we'll try both Knoxville and Asheville. Whichever, Miss Standish, it's going to take a couple of days.''

"But it can't!" Hope protested. "Oh, I know you're doing all you can, Mr. Youngdeer. But I absolutely have to leave here today.''

For more reasons than one, she thought silently. If she stayed around there she risked running into Ross Adair again, and heaven only knew what that would lead to! But if she didn't see him, it would almost be worse. She'd be looking for him behind every tree....

"One thing you can't do is make a car go when it won't,'' Randy Youngdeer said practically. "Like I told you, I've been on the horn already to a place in Sylva. The people I talked to will get back to me as soon as they come up with something. Meantime.... Look, I know it isn't any of my business, but couldn't you just kind of relax and enjoy a stay here for a couple of days? We like to think we've got some pretty beautiful country here in Cherokee, and there's plenty to do.''

"Within walking distance?" Hope asked gloomily.

Randy chuckled. "That depends on how much of a walker you are,'' he conceded. "Actually, there are lot of things like the Indian Museum and the Qualla Cooperative that aren't that far away. You could even walk up to the Oconaluftee Village. But I admit that having a car does make getting around easier.''

"Only until they break down,'' Hope said grimly.

"Well, for selfish reasons I'm glad that happens from time to time. I wouldn't be making much of a living if they all ran perfectly," Randy said cheerfully. "Look, Miss Standish, I've got an idea...."

"Yes?"

"A week or so ago I bought an old heap from a guy who needed some quick cash. When I'm finished with it you can bet it's going to be a genuine antique auto. Meantime, though it isn't in much better internal condition than your Volvo, it would be safe enough to drive around town. If you didn't go too far I could always come and help you out if she decided to act up."

"I don't know, Mr. Youngdeer," Hope said doubtfully, thinking of her budget. From what he was saying to her it sounded as if the repairs to get the Volvo going again could amount to quite a bit, and if this was going to be the case she certainly didn't have enough surplus cash to rent a car, even temporarily.

"Look," Randy said, "it'll do the old girl good to be driven around a little bit, and it'll give you wheels. I wasn't thinking of charging you, by the way. You can pay for the gas you use, and that's it. Part of Youngdeer's service policy," he added warmly.

For the first time in longer than she liked to remember, Hope's spirits lifted. "Thank you, Mr. Youngdeer," she said. "I accept your offer."

"Good! I'll get her over to you as soon as I have a chance to leave here for a few minutes."

"Please don't bother doing that," Hope said

quickly. "I'll walk over right after I've had some breakfast."

The coffee shop was featuring wild-blueberry muffins, and although Hope seldom had much appetite early in the day she ate two of them. Almost immediately she felt better, and as she stepped out of the motel her eyes inadvertently traveled upward to the hills surrounding the town. In the morning light they looked as if they'd been washed by the previous day's rain. She'd never seen so many fresh and glorious shades of green, colors from the palest chartreuse to a spruce that was almost black. The sky was equally intense, a raw-silk canopy in a deep shade of blue, and the air was clear, pure and distilled.

Randy Youngdeer was talking to a young Indian who was sitting at the wheel of a pickup truck, evidently just having had it filled with gas. The man looked at Hope with an expression of approval that was universal in its meaning, and she was glad that she'd gone back to her room after breakfast to refresh her makeup and brush out her long blond hair, which she'd swept back and tied at her neck with a bright purple scarf that matched her skirt. She was also glad to realize that not all the men in Cherokee were as stern and stoical as Ross Adair seemed to be, nor as indifferent to her presence.

And yet he hadn't really been indifferent—not all of the time anyway, she reminded herself. She'd told him all sorts of things she'd never told anybody before. And he had listened to her with grave attention. In her mind's eye she could see him now, that dark head inclined slightly, those jet eyes watching her intently.

She forced the image away and greeted Randy Youngdeer, who was looking at her with an approval of his own that was warming. Then she saw that he'd parked her Volvo at the far end of the service station, where it would be out of the way for the moment, and her spirits faltered. There was something so absolutely despondent looking about the little car.

Randy, following her gaze, said, "Don't worry. I can't say she'll be like new when I get her fixed up, but I promise you she'll be drivable and safe. I know that Swedish cars are supposed to last forever—and I have to admit that they're excellently engineered—but you should consider going for a new model as soon as you can. Meantime...that's Betsy." He gestured toward a car parked on the other side of the gas pumps, and Hope gasped.

It was a convertible and of a vintage she couldn't begin to determine, for she had never been a car buff. But it looked as if it should be in a movie. It was shining red, and the chrome gleamed proudly. A real conversation piece.

Randy grinned. "Something, isn't she?" he said enthusiastically. "By the time I get her in shape she's going to be gorgeous, let me tell you. A fair bit to reckon with under the hood, but no problems we can't solve. Like I said, she'll be fine if you just drive around this area. No taking off into the mountains, okay?"

"Randy," Hope protested. "I mean, Mr. Youngdeer...."

"Randy will do fine," he told her.

"Then please call me Hope," she returned. "Randy, I can't possibly drive that car. If I dented it I'd never forgive myself. It's...it's beautiful," she finished sincerely, and this was certainly something she had never said before about a car.

"She's already got a couple of dings here and there and I'm going to have to do some body work on her anyway," Randy said. "So, like I told you, don't worry. Take her and enjoy yourself. You've got a great day for looking around. The nicest we've had in a couple of weeks."

Hope nodded, because obviously this was true. Nature could not have been more generous in endowing a day with beauty. How could Hope refuse to explore Cherokee and its environs now that such a magnificent vintage car had been placed at her disposal?

"What should I see first?" she asked curiously.

"I've got a couple of pamphlets in the office," Randy said. "There's a visitor-information booklet about the village and another about the drama, stuff like that. I think maybe you might go through the museum first, though. I don't know how much this sort of thing interests you, but if you want to get a broad idea of the Cherokees and their history the museum is the best place to start."

"It interests me very much," Hope found herself saying. Not only was this absolutely true, but there was a reason behind the truth. For all the while she had been standing there talking to Randy Youngdeer she had been wishing that a low black sports car would swing into the service station and....

"The drama has just opened," Randy continued. "You might want to take in a performance. It's pretty colorful, and sometimes I think half the people in Cherokee play some kind of part in it." He grinned, that friendly grin that came so easily to him. "Seasonable occupation," he said, "like the fellows in Indian regalia outside the trading posts up the street. I think they get a kick out of it, and so do the tourists. Not too authentic, though. The Cherokees never wore a lot of feathers like that. In fact, none of the Eastern Indians did. Those long headdresses you see are usually Sioux war bonnets. From the Western Indians, at any rate. But I have to admit they're eye-catching."

Hope had to laugh. "Do you ever play a part in the drama?" she asked.

"I did one year," Randy confessed. "A girl I know got me involved in it. I had a part that mostly required standing around the stage and looking very tough and brave. One night, though, I tripped over my own feet, and that, I'm relieved to say, was the end of my theatrical career!"

Hope found herself laughing with carefree abandon, something very unusual for her. But she had only a few seconds to enjoy the feeling. The sound of an engine revving and gears whining turned her head around, and the sports car she had been thinking about swung off the road and came to a screeching stop alongside the gas pumps.

Hope thought her heart had stopped beating.

Ross Adair, behind the wheel, was dazzling this morning in a bright green shirt open at the throat.

"Forgot to fill her up when I left here last night," he told Randy, and then nodded to Hope. She nodded back, unable to say so much as good-morning to him. The expression on his handsome face was totally uncompromising. There was not a vestige of friendliness to it. Ross Adair looked polite enough...but totally uninterested. She chided herself for being a fool in thinking that she might have stirred him a fraction as much as he had stirred her.

"Good morning," he said coolly. "Have you come to get your car?"

Randy, busy with the gas pump, answered for her. "The Volvo's going to take a while," he said. "Needs a universal joint, among other things. Hopefully I can get one from Sylva, though I may have to go farther. Meantime, Miss Standish is going to play tourist here in Cherokee."

"Oh?" Ross Adair asked, his dark brows arching. Hope had the decided impression he was not pleased by this information, which was puzzling. Why should it matter to him whether or not she stayed in Cherokee for a couple of days? The town was big enough to hold both of them.

"I'm loaning her Betsy," Randy Youngdeer went on, with a glance toward the red convertible.

To Hope's surprise, Ross Adair registered astonishment at this bit of news, but he only said, his voice suspiciously mild, "You don't say." Then he addressed Randy directly. "Put the gas on my tab, will you, Randy? I'm in a hurry." And with the briefest farewell wave he was off again.

Hope, looking after him, found herself wishing that this encounter had never happened. She also found herself wishing she could avoid his path for the rest of her stay in Cherokee. There was something so very upsetting about the man. His attitude, perhaps. She wouldn't go so far as to say he actually *disliked* her—in fact, for a time the previous night she'd thought very much the contrary. But now she had the feeling that he really had been anxious to get away from her, as if he wished to avoid any further association with her—and this stung.

She went into Randy's small office in an effort to get control of her emotions, which threatened to become too turbulent, and gathered up a handful of pamphlets about the area attractions he had mentioned to her. But when she went outside again Randy glanced at her swiftly, and she knew she hadn't fooled him.

"Don't let Ross get under your skin," he counseled, his smile wry. "He tends to be something of a loner, I guess you'd say."

Randy left it at that and turned his attention to the red convertible, patiently instructing Hope about a few of Betsy's foibles. Minutes later she was on her way out of the service station, thrilled to be driving the big old car. It handled beautifully, and it wasn't long before Hope had rumbled over the small bridge across Soco Creek and was heading toward the Cherokee Indian Museum.

The museum itself was a surprise. Starkly

modern, the architecture made eye-arresting use of stone and slate. Inside, an attractive Indian girl presided at the ticket desk. She accepted the entrance fee from Hope, then gave her an explanatory folder directing her to the various parts of the museum.

Lavish use of primary colors had been made in the spacious interior, which was divided into informal sections, each depicting various aspects of Cherokee history and Cherokee life. There were six mini-theaters, glass dioramas in front of which one sat to watch a video display and listen, at the same time, to a taped story of the Cherokees' history. The story began in prehistoric times and culminated in the present.

Hope decided to bypass this and look first at the displays. There were many of them, ranging from impressive collections of arrows and other artifacts—arranged in huge showcases that were, themselves, arrow shaped—to clothes, cooking utensils, striking handwoven baskets and a variety of ancient stone weapons, all of these authentic items that the Cherokees had used over the centuries.

In the Hall of the Honored Cherokees she found the slogan "Peace to their ashes and sorrow for their going," and she stared with awed reverence at the beautiful stained-glass windows high in the wall. Each window was a glowing portrait of an Indian who had made a major contribution to the fascinating Cherokee Nation.

There was Sequoya, with his turban and pipe, who once again reminded her in a strange way of her own very Anglo-Saxon father. But now Sequoya also brought to mind the face of Ross Adair. Forcing aside thoughts of that particular Cherokee, Hope hastily went on to something else. She became enraptured by several charts that showed the written Cherokee language Sequoya had invented. Then she tested out the "hear phones" that permitted one to listen to the language being spoken. Each time a character was pronounced, a symbol in the chart was electronically illuminated. Familiar English texts like "Mary Had a Little Lamb" were translated into Cherokee, and Hope listened, absolutely fascinated, to the somewhat guttural yet oddly musical sound of this language.

Having absorbed this, she returned to the mini-theaters. She sat down in front of the first window, pressed a button and found herself listening to a story that went way back in time, when the world was a very ancient place. Then, as she progressed from window to window, the story gradually moved forward. And suddenly Hope felt herself being gripped by intense emotion.

She'd never had any particular illusions about the history—or the fate—of the Indians in this country, which had first been theirs. But the story of the Cherokees was especially poignant to her. She felt a surge of anger against her own ancestors, frontiersmen who had literally stripped these proud people of their land and heritage and forced them on a march across the mountains, which had nearly led to their extinction. She appreciated the fact that these new Americans had been facing dreadful dilemmas of their own, but the thought of how they had dealt with the indigenous population was appalling.

The Trail of Tears. Everything terrible that had happened to the Cherokees since the white conquerors had first taken arms against them had culminated in the Trail of Tears, when, in 1838, they had been ousted from the lands they owned in Georgia and North Carolina and ordered to take up new residence in Oklahoma. Tribe members who did not want to leave their land had been forced to do so—at gunpoint, if necessary.

This military maneuver had been called "The Removal," and the human trail across the mountains had been one of sickness and death...except for those Cherokees who had resisted the army order to move, escaping into the forests and mountains, where they had lived in hiding until public opinion changed.

Finally, due largely to the efforts of Colonel William Thomas, a man the Cherokees had called their "white chief," the land now known as the Qualla Boundary, the reservation surrounding the town of Cherokee, had been set aside by the United States government and put in trust for the Cherokees. In this way it would be theirs for all time, and under a charter given to them they could live together there and govern themselves in peace.

Hope felt as if she'd been wrung out emotionally by the time the last of the mini-presentations was over. Subdued, she moved on to a small room where a movie showing a meeting of the local Tribal

Council was in progress. From this she discovered that Cherokee was governed today by a bona-fide Indian chief, duly elected by his people. But the actual proceedings of the council meeting were a parallel of local government meetings in towns all across the United States.

Finally she wandered into the gift shop and bookstore and, despite the limited amount of spending money she had with her, could not resist buying a number of booklets that dealt with various aspects of Cherokee life and legend. These included an account of the Trail of Tears removal written by one of the soldiers involved in enforcing that grim edict.

As she left the museum, blinking into the blazing sunlight of the bright June day, Hope found herself surprisingly eager to learn all she could about these fascinating people of whom she had been so unaware—until yesterday.

Would knowing more about the Cherokees lead to a real understanding of them, she wondered. Perhaps learning about Ross Adair's people and making him aware of her empathy would erase the indifference he seemed able to turn on her so easily.

Why was she even *thinking* about Ross Adair? Hope walked back to the red convertible, which she'd parked a discreet distance down the lot so there would be no danger of anyone running into it.

Why, indeed?

CHAPTER FOUR

HOPE HAD SPENT so much time in the Indian Museum that a noon whistle was blowing somewhere as she slid behind Betsy's wheel, and she found to her surprise that she was hungry. It must be the mountain air, she thought to herself, for she seldom felt hungry and had needed to put on a few pounds since her recent illness.

She stopped for a hamburger and a thick milk shake, and as she ate she glanced through the folders she'd picked up at Randy's service station. There were several attractions around Cherokee that would be worth taking the time to visit. The Oconaluftee Indian Village, for one. A sign by a road near the museum had indicated that the village was only a short distance farther up the mountainside, and the same road also led to the outdoor theater where the drama, "Unto These Hills," was being presented.

Before delving further into Cherokee history, though, Hope decided to familiarize herself a bit more with her surroundings, especially since the venerable Betsy seemed to be performing very well. She reminded herself that she must tell Randy he could be really proud of his red convertible.

Thinking of Randy made her wonder whether he'd had any word about the part he needed to fix her Volvo. She found herself close to hoping that he hadn't. If he managed to fix the car over the course of the afternoon there would be no reason why she couldn't drive on to Gatlinburg the first thing the next morning. And if that turned out to be the case, it would mean that this would be her only day spent in Cherokee. As Hope contemplated this a strangely disconsolate feeling came over her.

She told herself she wanted to know more about the Cherokees. If she was to be honest with herself, she had to admit that Ross Adair was the main motive for this "wanting." Randy Youngdeer and Penny Raincrow also intrigued her, and she had become entangled in the web of Cherokee history, as well. She really wanted to read the literature she'd bought at the museum, for once she understood a little more about the Cherokee Nation, exploring the area would be that much more interesting. She wouldn't be able to explore everything, of course—that would be impossible. She could hardly follow the Trail of Tears on foot, as the Indians had during that terrible, long-ago "Removal." But even a visit to the Oconaluftee Village would mean more to her if she did a little homework first.

The thought occurred to her that even if Randy managed to get her car fixed by the day's end, should the part be available in Sylva, there was no real reason why she shouldn't stay over in Cherokee one day longer. She could manage to stretch her finances that far. She'd simply be more prudent during her time in the Great Smokies with Lorna, that was all. And Lorna was not exactly a great spender, so this wouldn't prove to be too difficult.

When she called Lorna she would simply have to fib about the reason for her delay. She could say the car still needed more work. Thinking of doing this made Hope feel like a schoolgirl contemplating playing hooky, and she discovered that the feeling was both heady and pleasant. Lorna was already annoyed with her, and there was no doubt that she'd be explicit enough about this once they were together. One extra day wouldn't make that much difference. And chances were that the part wouldn't arrive today anyway...so, as Randy Youngdeer might have put it, "when you got down to the basics there really was no problem!"

Before she'd driven away from the service station in the big red convertible, Hope had been struck by the idea that she might want to do some painting, so she had got her old wooden paint box and a few canvases out of the Volvo's trunk, along with a portable easel. Randy had been occupied with a customer at the time or he might have commented on it. She'd come to the conclusion that he didn't miss much, nor was he shy about asking questions. Yet his curiosity and his friendliness seemed so natural and open that it was impossible to resent either.

Actually, getting out the paints and taking them with her had been more or less a matter of habit. Hope usually did this, just as a photographer customarily took along a camera. There was no way to tell when a view or some other subject might be stumbled upon, and it was always frustrating when something presented itself unexpectedly and the equipment wasn't handy.

The thought of doing any serious painting in Cherokee hadn't crossed Hope's mind. Up until now her energies had been absorbed by her broken-down old Volvo—and a strikingly handsome Indian man. But suddenly the inspiration struck her, and she became possessed of the desire to do something, if only a few charcoal sketches that could later be recreated in oil. She wanted something that would give her a personal memento of this place, a personal memory of this experience. She wanted something she couldn't buy at a trading post.

She pulled out the small map of the town that came with the visitor-information booklet she had picked up at Randy's and studied it, using the museum as her point of reference. Highway 441, the road she had intended to follow up to Gatlinburg, ran directly in front of the museum. It was bordered on the east by the Oconaluftee River. The Qualla Cooperative, where Indian crafts and other native products were sold, was directly across from the museum. And next to the cooperative the road started up the mountainside and passed by the theater and the Indian village.

The whole area seemed to be built on levels because of the mountainous terrain, and Hope had glimpsed a number of attractive homes scattered along the hillsides. Wild flowers pinpointed bright splotches of color against the ever present shaded greenery, and the rhododendrons, almost at their peak, were a glorious color—rich lavender pink, she'd call it.

She decided that she'd like to capture a vista of the mountains in a painting, plus at least a touch of the color of the rhododendrons. If she could get the basics down she could finish the work at a later date.

For a time Hope drove around aimlessly. Finally she crossed the bridge over the Oconaluftee, which was only a shallow stream at this time of year. Its pale turquoise water splashed gently over the rocky riverbed. There was a picnic grove on the far side of the river, but the grass needed mowing around the redwood tables and benches, and Hope wondered if it was used very much. Possibly it was still too early in the season for picnics.

She turned back toward Highway 19, following it in the opposite direction than she had come from the other day but proceeding cautiously. She had no desire at all to find herself suddenly on a curving mountain lane again. The road was full enough of curves even here. It swept past the large Leisure Inn complex, one of a famous chain, the sign out front looking rather surrealistically familiar in this setting. A short distance past the inn she took a turn to the right. Almost immediately the road started upward, and Hope realized it would be impossible to get very far away from the town of Cherokee without encountering hilly roads.

She decided to find a turning place and go back,

but this didn't prove to be easy. Finally she came to a bisecting road farther up the hillside. It was little more than a dirt lane, though, and it wasn't long before Hope realized she was following someone's driveway. Soon she came to a circle that marked a dead end, and directly in front of her, atop a slight embankment, she saw a low, attractive house built mainly of stone. It seemed to blend with the terrain, flowers blazing around the entrance and spilling out on either side of a flagstone walk. It was the most attractive house Hope had seen thus far and surely the loveliest possible setting for a home. She could imagine that the view from the front windows must be spectacular—a panorama of mountains and valley.

She sighed. There was a terrace in front of the house on which several comfortable reclining chairs and pretty, round tables had been scattered about, and it seemed to Hope that nothing in the world would be more refreshing than to sit in one of those chairs and give her eyes a visual feast. The owner of this place was indeed lucky.

Reluctantly she turned back, but this time she discovered a very narrow lane that veered to the right, and on an impulse she decided to follow it. The view wasn't quite as good as it would have been from the terrace of the house, but she should still be able to capture the essence of the countryside. Anyway, it was certainly worth a try.

Finally the lane became too difficult to traverse with ease, so Hope parked. She didn't want to take any chances with Randy's car, nor did she want to find herself in the position of having to back up for two miles.

Gathering up her painting equipment, she started her search for a good place to set up, but there were so many trees to contend with that it was quite a while before she found a spot that satisfied her. Then she unfolded her easel and started to sketch.

She outlined several scenes in charcoal, using quick, sure strokes, and after that she couldn't resist trying to capture some of the green tones in oil. It took a few minutes to squeeze the ribbons of paint out onto a paper palette, then she picked up her brush and became completely immersed in her work.

Hope loved to paint and would have done nothing else as a career were it not for the need of money. Her paintings had been exhibited on occasion at small showings and she'd even sold a few of them. But each time one sold she missed it terribly, as if the painting was a child who'd been given away to strangers. Also, the financial rewards had been few and far between and had certainly not provided her with enough money to live on.

And her art, like everything else in her life, had suffered a setback because of Lewis. There had been a setback because of her father, too, primarily during those last months that had led to his tragic accident. But Lewis was responsible for the most part. He had lied to her so terribly, and she had believed in him so completely. Again, she wondered if she'd ever be able to find it in her heart to put trust in a man. And again, inexplicably, this made her think of Ross Adair.

Then, suddenly, she jumped. As if some magical kind of extrasensory perception had been put into play she heard his voice call her name. The rich depth of his tone, that Southern slur. . it *had* to be his voice, she told herself, although she didn't believe in this sort of coincidence.

For a moment she actually wondered if she might be hallucinating, then he spoke her name again. "Miss Standish," he said, and Hope swung around, paintbrush in hand.

The sight of him was such a shock that she instantly dropped her brush. She didn't know where he'd been swimming, but that was obviously what he'd been doing. He was wearing white trunks that fitted him like a tight glove and were particularly graphic against the deep natural tone of his skin, that exciting skin now gleaming with moisture. Unlike a temporary summer tan, his was an even color that covered his entire body—all parts of it, she concluded weakly—and it was very difficult to keep her eyes from following her thoughts. It was almost impossible not to dwell upon certain visible accents of his physique that were tangible evidence of a definitely blatant manhood.

"Miss Standish," he repeated, very peremptory about it this time. Hope, trying to answer him, found she had no voice at all and could only nod.

He was not pleased to see her. He was not at all pleased to see her, and it was clear he had no intention of camouflaging this fact. The impatience in his voice was barely leashed as he demanded, "What are you doing here?" Then, almost at once, he answered his own question. "Trying to paint something, I see."

Hope bent to pick up her paintbrush and felt her cheeks flame. Then, to her further dismay, she found that the bristles were now full of pine needles, the whole thing making a smeary mess.

Anger made her voice come back. "Do you object?" she asked icily.

"Yes, I do," he said bluntly.

"Oh?" Hope managed, her own sarcasm brimming.

"Oh!" he mimicked. "Like a lot of other visitors you seem to have the idea that because this area encompasses an Indian reservation the whole place is public property. That isn't so, Miss Standish."

"Just what is your point, Mr. Adair?" Hope surprised herself by asking, stung by his tone.

"My point is this," he said levelly. "The Cherokees own their own homes here just as other people do elsewhere. And just as you would not like to have someone come in and set up a workshop in your front yard, wherever that might be, so do we frown on such a practice."

Hope stared at him, unable to believe what he was saying. Ross Adair was both ridiculing and belittling her, and the effect was devastating. She said, choking over her words, "I wasn't aware that this was your property."

"I didn't say it was," he returned. "Nevertheless, I have the right to be here—and you don't!"

He was moving toward her, and there was no way Hope could avoid him without tripping over her easel. Fighting back a sense of panic, she tried to decipher the expression that crossed his face, but all was lost in a blur as he came to stand only inches away. One thing about Ross Adair was certain—his masculinity. Even the smell of him—a distracting combination of earth scents and the fragrance of pine—was so completely male. Hope felt as if her entire body had suddenly been turned to stone. Yet just as quickly this stone was becoming lava, a molten lava that flowed through her erotically as she stood rooted to the spot.

Slowly, deliberately, Ross Adair enfolded her in his arms, and Hope knew at once that she would be powerless to resist him...even if she wanted to. He pulled her so close to him she could feel the dampness of his swim trunks. She could feel....

Her senses swam as his lips descended on her mouth. The kiss was brutal, but it was also exciting, and the momentary pain of its impact was stabbed through with intense pleasure. Then he paused to ask, "Is that what you came up here for?" His hot breath caressed the softness of her skin. "Could I be right about that? I've sensed a certain invitation from the very first moment I laid eyes on you."

His mouth was descending again as he spoke, but it was his tone that rang in her ears. She realized his actions were only that—actions, unmotivated by desire. Even worse, they were actions of contempt. Hope managed to look up into two dark eyes that stared back at her dangerously, and yes, the same contempt that filled his voice sparkled in their depths, and she hated the fact that she felt as if she could drown in their blackness.

Something suddenly snapped inside her, and with all the force she could muster she pushed him away. "Oh!" she sputtered then, lashing out at him. "You're full of nothing but hate, aren't you?"

Not waiting for an answer and determined not to look at him again, Hope turned away, and instantly hot tears came to fill her eyes. *Don't let him see you cry,* she told herself sharply. *Don't let him see you cry!* Keeping her back to him she thrust the dirty paintbrush into her paint box even though she knew that it would be a mess to clean up later. Then she began gathering up the other equipment she had so joyfully unpacked only a few minutes earlier, but her fingers fumbled nervously, making the task that much harder. Finally, she had everything together, and folding up her easel she turned to face the devastating man who seemed so bent on tormenting her. But he had left her in just the same way he had come upon her—quickly and silently.

It was then she saw the path. It wound its way up the hill through a grove of slanting trees. Letting her gaze follow it, Hope could see one side of the stone house that had intrigued her so. Simultaneously, she heard a splash. Realizing there must be a swimming pool somewhere up there, she knew that Ross Adair had just dived into its waters.

Hope gritted her teeth fiercely and started back up the lane toward the spot where she'd parked Betsy.

Arrogant, miserable, conceited, opinionated!

These and a number of other adjectives tumbled over one another in Hope's mind as she drove back down into town. Nor did she wander this time. She headed straight for Randy Youngdeer's service station. Regardless of her previous thoughts she decided that if her Volvo was in even reasonable condition to drive she wouldn't wait until morning to leave Cherokee. She'd put this place behind her as quickly as she could get back to the motel, settle up her bill and get her things packed.

"THEY HAD THE PART in Sylva," Randy said jubilantly, "and believe it or not, a fellow who was driving over this way brought it along on his truck. Won't take me more than a couple of hours to put your Volvo back together."

"That's great, Randy," Hope managed, forcing a smile in an effort to convince him of her enthusiasm. Obviously, leaving the town of Cherokee today was out. "Would you say I'll be able to get off first thing in the morning, then?" she asked quickly.

"If I have to work all night," Randy promised solemnly. "Though I wish you weren't so anxious to leave."

"I have a commitment with this friend of mine," Hope explained, "and she's already annoyed with me because I got delayed."

Randy grinned. "She?"

"Yes," Hope said a bit stiffly.

"Well, you could hardly help that! Anyway, did you make it up to the village?"

"No, I didn't. But the museum was fascinating. The story of the Cherokees really moved me. Especially the part about the Trail of Tears."

Randy nodded, but he didn't seem inclined to linger on the subject of the injustice done to his people. "If you didn't already plan something for tonight, you could take in the drama," he offered practically. "Just speak to Penny. I'm sure she can get you a ticket."

"Maybe I'll do that," Hope agreed.

"Incidentally, did you get to the Qualla Cooperative?"

"I'm afraid I didn't, Randy," Hope answered. "And I really wanted to. If you could let me take Betsy out just for...."

"Betsy seems to be thriving on it," Randy said. "So please, go right ahead. You'll find that the prices at the cooperative may seem pretty high, but one thing that can be said for the stuff they sell is that it's all authentic. There's none of that cheap fake stuff that's so easy to come by."

"Good. That's exactly what I want to avoid."

"I know what you mean," Randy replied. "Anyway, some of the pottery's pretty affordable, and some of the smaller baskets, too. The big ones cost quite a lot because they take so long to make."

"I can imagine."

"It really is too bad you couldn't get to the village. They do most of the work right there. The beadwork, too."

"Maybe I'll be able to come back another time," Hope said, but this was merely a placebo of sorts.

Once she had put Cherokee behind her, she had no intention of ever returning again!

"I hope so," Randy said cheerfully, then turned to greet a customer who had just pulled up to the gas pumps.

Hope drove out of the gas station and toward the museum again, and at one point was almost sure she spied a familiar, sleek black car up on the road ahead of her. But by the time she had reached the intersection of Route 441, it had disappeared. Then she warned herself about the danger of having visions involving Ross Adair and of seeing phantom black sports cars, and the memory of his rebuff came to sting again.

Randy had said that Ross was a loner. That was for sure, Hope decided. And she wondered what had ever happened to make him that way.

THE QUALLA COOPERATIVE was a large, low building, which blended well with the architecture of the neighboring museum. The spacious interior was open in design, with collections of different Cherokee "specialties" displayed together in groups.

Hope was immediately attracted by the woven baskets. They were beautifully made in bands and patterns of varying colors, all of them earth tones. Remembering Randy's admonition about the prices she checked a tag before letting herself be carried away by her enthusiasm. He was right. The large basket that had caught her eye cost four hundred dollars, which she simply didn't have. But it was easy to appreciate the craftsmanship that had gone into its making.

She sighed and turned away. It would be nice, just once, to yield to impulse and buy something she liked but really didn't need. Glancing up, she caught the eye of a young woman standing behind a large center counter. She smiled sympathetically at Hope, and Hope responded, her own smile edged with ruefulness.

Business was slow at the moment. There were a couple of people browsing around the cooperative but no obvious buyers, and with a slight shrug the woman came around from behind the counter. She glanced toward the basket Hope was still looking at and said, "Nice...but they do cost a mint, don't they?"

"Yes, they do," Hope agreed.

"Of course, they're all handwoven," the woman pointed out. "Double woven, actually. It's an old and rather complicated technique that takes quite a bit of time and effort. Only original Cherokee designs are used and the materials are all native, all gathered right on the reservation. The dyes, too." She smiled again. "I'm not giving you a sales pitch," she said. "I just thought you might want to know why the price is so high. A lot of our people make a living by plying these old crafts. At least, it augments their incomes. But I think I can safely say they'd rather wait for a sale than cut their prices or shortcut the work itself. They're really proud of the things they make."

"They have reason to be," Hope said sincerely.

She noticed that this young woman, too, spoke with a soft, Southern accent. She was very attractive. She was certainly a Cherokee, her features straight and fine, more like Ross Adair's than Randy Youngdeer's. She wore her glossy black hair shoulder length, and she used just a trace of makeup. Hope had noticed that most of the Indian women didn't seem to wear any makeup at all.

She was also quite tall. As tall as Hope anyway, who was slightly above average height. And she was as friendly as Randy Youngdeer. Thinking about this gave Hope a warm feeling. Thank goodness not all Cherokees were as unpredictable as Ross Adair!

"Are you on a tour?" she asked Hope.

Hope shook her head. "My car broke down on my way into town yesterday," she said. "It's being fixed."

To her surprise, the Indian woman laughed. "You must be Randy Youngdeer's favorite Yankee," she said. "I spoke to you on the phone, as a matter of fact. I'd stopped over at Randy's, and when he had to go out on a road call I stayed around and sort of kept an eye on things. You're staying at the Three Wigwams," she concluded.

Hope was used to small-town New England, so the fact that news could travel quickly when it concerned strangers wasn't too surprising to her. "That's right," she admitted. "I'm staying there through tonight."

"Oh? Randy thought you'd be around a few days," the Indian woman commented.

"So did I. But he managed to get the part for my

car this afternoon. He said he'd have it fixed for me by tomorrow morning, so...."

"Well, it's too bad you have to leave so soon. That is...." She hesitated. "What a busybody you'll think I am! I'm Wonder Owl, incidentally."

Wonder Owl. It was difficult to accept some of these intriguing names without revealing an interest that could easily be misconstrued. Hope said carefully, "Pleased to meet you. My name is—"

"You're Hope Standish," Wonder Owl said easily. "Have you managed to get to the museum and the village and all?"

"The museum, yes. I'm afraid I'm going to have to miss the village. But when I get back to the motel I'm going to see if Mrs. Raincrow can get me a ticket for the drama tonight."

"Oh, you really should see it," Wonder encouraged. Then she giggled impishly. "I have a small part in it myself. As Randy may have told you, lots of us take part in the drama every year."

"As a matter of fact, he did tell me that," Hope said, laughing at the memory of Randy's description of his theatrical experiences. Then sharing what he'd told her, she added, "He indicated that he just about fell over his own feet."

A smile flitted across Wonder Owl's face, though it was not exactly a happy smile. "Yes, Randy does have a tendency to fall over his own feet at times," she said slowly. "One thing is for sure. He was never cut out to be an actor."

She might have said more, but she and Hope were interrupted by the arrival of a busload of tourists.

Two other Indian women came out from a back room to help Wonder take care of the eager customers, and Hope went back to browsing among the woven baskets, the pottery and the beadwork. There was also a lovely display of silver-and-turquoise jewelry of Indian design, but she knew without being told that these pieces came from the Western United States and were probably Navaho in origin.

She wanted a remembrance that was purely Cherokee, and she finally decided to splurge on a woven basket that could double as a summer handbag. Having made this decision, she found herself feeling surprisingly carefree.

It was good to be a little reckless once in a while, she told herself, and almost immediately the vision of Ross Adair came back to haunt her.

She was annoyed at herself for even thinking of this man who had been so abominable in the way he had treated her. His icy politeness earlier that day had masked a flagrant rudeness, and she thoroughly resented his having made her feel like a gauche intruder, a parody of the tourist type favored by cartoonists.

She couldn't repress the thought that Wonder Owl probably knew Ross Adair. Cherokee was a small place and most of its permanent residents must be acquainted. And the majority of them also had the further bond of their Indian blood. Wonder seemed very different from Ross Adair in her attitude, though, as did Randy Youngdeer. Certainly, neither of them was a "loner."

Another impulse possessed Hope, and she decided to add a pair of earrings to her purchase. They were beautifully beaded in tones of deep blue and turquoise and would go perfectly with her favorite summer dress. And although she knew her budget would have a definite dent in it as the result of this spending, Hope felt considerably happier than she had in a long time as she went up to the counter to pay Wonder Owl.

Wonder, having just finished with a customer, turned to Hope immediately, and there was genuine warmth in her smile. "You've chosen well," she complimented her.

"Thank you. I wanted something that is really... Cherokee."

"Well, both of these items are 'really Cherokee,'" Wonder assured her. "By the way, do you think you will be going to the drama tonight?"

"Yes...unless Mrs. Raincrow can't get me a ticket."

"Penny will manage," Wonder said confidently. "What I was thinking is...well, I thought maybe you'd like to meet me for coffee afterward. We could go up to the Leisure Inn. They have a folksinger there at the moment who is pretty good."

"I'd love to," Hope said, a bit surprised by the invitation but also delighted by it.

"You'll be driving Betsy, of course, so suppose we meet in the lower parking lot," Wonder suggested.

"I'll drive up to the theater with my brother. He's in the drama, too." She hesitated. "Randy might join us at the inn," she said then. "And—"

She was interrupted again by one of the bus passengers—a woman who really was a cartoonist's prototype of a tourist, Hope thought with some resentment—and so she didn't complete the sentence.

After a moment Hope managed to interject herself between the questions the customer was asking Wonder to say that she'd wait for her in the parking lot after the drama. As she left the Qualla Cooperative, though, she was puzzling over what Wonder had been about to tell her. If Randy Youngdeer joined them for coffee, was he going to bring along a friend?

It suddenly occurred to her that perhaps the friend might be Ross Adair.

CHAPTER FIVE

IT WAS A BEAUTIFUL EVENING. As Hope started out from the Three Wigwams she could not suppress the feeling that this was a night for romance, and a bittersweet sense of loneliness assailed her.

Tonight she was conscious of being young. She was even aware of her beauty, in a modest sort of way. Her mirror had not lied to her, and for the first time in many months she had taken special pains with her appearance, as if she were setting out for a deliberate rendezvous. She had decided to wear her favorite summer dress, and the Cherokee earrings were the perfect accompaniment. The dress was made of a natural cotton fabric that had been hand dyed in tones of blue, lavender and turquoise. It had a full skirt, and with it she wore banded lavender sandals with slender heels. The total effect, admittedly, was very becoming. Hope only wished that there was someone around to appreciate her in the way she wanted to be appreciated. But there wasn't apt to be anyone, she told herself sadly as she slid behind Betsy's wheel. Then she laughed ruefully as her eyes were drawn skyward to the perfect third-quarter moon suspended at just the right angle against a night that could have been painted with Indian indigo dye.

Hope had brushed her hair into a pale gold mass that curled around her shoulders, and tendrils of it escaped into the caressing wind as she drove along in the big red convertible and passed the river. Then she turned left and continued up the steep road that led to the Mountainside Theater. As Wonder had suggested, she parked her car in a lower-level lot and followed the crowd up toward the theater entrance.

Hope loved drama, and the stage gripped her as neither television nor the movies ever could. Tonight was no exception, and she found herself responding fully to this play about the Cherokee people, acted out under the star-studded sky that canopied the home of the descendants of those who had managed to escape from exile at the time of the Trail of Tears.

There was a moving scenario of the sacrifice of the brave Tsali, who had been martyred so that a few of his people might escape into the hills and in that way preserve the Cherokee tradition forever. And once again Hope was impressed by the versatility and knowledge of the great Sequoya.

It seemed to her that every person in the cast of one hundred thirty truly belonged in the play. There was a total involvement, more so than anything she had ever seen before in a theatrical production. And the musical score augmented the play beautifully. It was extremely stirring, and the fact that it had been written by Jack F. Kilpatrick, a nationally recognized Cherokee composer, provided an added significance. The consciousness of heritage, Hope realized, went especially deep in all these people of Cherokee blood.

She was sitting between two elderly couples, both of them members of a tour group. They were pleasant enough and included her in their conversation between acts, but her dreadful sense of loneliness still persisted. The more she became gripped by the story of the Cherokees—as tragic as it was triumphant—the more she yearned to have someone at her side who could share this experience with her.

She fought away the thought of this "someone" being Ross Adair, yet the whole performance would have meant ten times as much to her if he could have been here with her. A surge of emotion swept through her as she thought about him, and she knew that she would have been sharing much more than just the drama. She would have been trying, via the story of his people, to understand him better.

She started to remonstrate with herself about wanting to understand him at all, only to give up quickly. She couldn't keep denying that she was fascinated by him. He thoroughly intrigued her, and she realized it would be only too easy to let that intrigue get to the point where it would be impossible to forget him. In that case, she told herself sternly, she'd better start protecting herself right away.

The drama came to an end, and Hope wiped away a tear. She was not the only person to have been moved, she saw. The setting itself was so unusual—an amphitheater against a backdrop of those same Great Smokies that had played a central part in the play's denouement. Spellbound for the moment, Hope sat still when the people on either side of her showed no indication to move hastily. And actually this was wise. There was such a mob around the exits that it would have been futile to rush for them.

During the course of the drama, Hope had tried to identify Wonder Owl among the many young women on stage, but she had failed. For one thing, the distance to the stage was substantial. Stage make-up also made a difference, and she'd imagined she'd seen Wonder Owl at least a dozen different times.

She suspected it would take a while before Wonder Owl could come out and join her in the parking lot, so there was no hurry. And when, finally, the couple to her left decided it was time to move, Hope followed slowly and made her way up to the theater entrance. Then she began walking along the road that curved down the hillside, but the going was still very slow.

Suddenly she remembered seeing a series of steps on her way up that led from one level to the next and would certainly offer a shortcut. Now Hope saw that quite a number of others were electing to take the steps instead of walking all the way around. She joined them and was halfway down the first flight when she thought she heard her name being called. Thinking that it could only be Wonder Owl, she swiftly turned to look.

Disaster struck with shocking speed. The heel of Hope's sandal caught firmly in the chink of one of the stone steps, and losing her balance completely, she felt herself go flying out into space.

She was dimly aware of hearing a woman scream and of seeing hands trying to reach out and clutch her, but it was as if her body was trying to elude their grasp. As she plunged into another dimension a blur of terror, blended with fright's purest essence, took possession of her senses. Then in another instant she was swept to the ground and veiled in a curtain of total blackness.

HOPE DIDN'T WANT to come back to reality. A hidden voice was telling her that reality would mean pain, and if she could stay in this netherworld all the mortal afflictions of the flesh would forever be alleviated.

Then she heard a voice command sharply, "Look at me!" And even though everything within her was protesting against doing so she heeded that voice, because she knew to whom it belonged. Still, she responded very slowly, working her way through a haze of pain and then carefully opening her eyes, as if afraid of what she might see.

She was thoroughly aware of the man leaning over her before she noticed anything else at all about her surroundings. She was so aware of him, in fact, that she drew her breath in sharply, causing an immediate resurgence of pain.

He said in a tone considerably more gentle, "Take it easy, Miss Standish." But this was an impossible request. It made Hope want to giggle and she actually choked back something between a laugh and a sob. How could she ever "take it easy" when he was around?

Then she found herself focusing upon him, and she drew her breath in for another reason. She was in a hospital—that much was obvious—and she was lying on an examining table in the center of a very sterile-looking room. Cautiously lifting her head, she quickly surveyed the spotless equipment, the gleam of metal instruments and the lights that were so bright they hurt her eyes.

But the shock of knowing where she was became eclipsed by the realization that he—Ross Adair—was a part of this scene. He was wearing a white coat, which made him seem all the more formidable to her. There was no doubt at all that he belonged here. He had enough natural dignity as it was, but the coat invested him with an added aura of authority.

Pain seared through her neck and she reluctantly eased her head back down. What sort of hospital was this, she wondered silently. For that matter, where was it? And what sort of position did he have there? She supposed that Ross Adair must be a technician of some sort. Yet she couldn't help but have the feeling that he was, at least at this moment, very much in command.

Then someone else came within her line of vision, a middle-aged Indian woman wearing a white uniform. A nurse. She said something Hope could not quite hear, then added, "Dr. Adair." These last two words were quite audible.

Dr. Adair!

"That's all right, Thelma," he nodded casually. "I'll check the X rays again later, myself." Turning back to Hope he said, "I've given you a shot that should take the edge off the pain. And...I've decided to admit you."

"Admit me where?" Hope asked fuzzily.

"To the hospital," Ross Adair told her with a slight but very frosty smile. "The Cherokee Indian Hospital. You were brought here by the rescue squad."

Hope tried to struggle to a sitting position, but a bolt of pain shot through her, forcing her backward.

"I wouldn't do that if I were you," Ross Adair advised her, which only added to her mounting resentment. "You've fractured your clavicle, but at that you lucked out. By the account of several witnesses, that must have been quite a spectacular fall you took. You could have been injured very seriously. As it is, you suffered a simple fracture, no nerve or vascular complications, so if you'll behave yourself you should be as good as new in just a few weeks."

"A few weeks?" Hope echoed the words, appalled by them.

"That's what I said," he told her imperturbably. "It's not a serious injury in itself, Miss Standish, but something like this does take time to heal properly. It will be necessary to immobilize the shoulder—your left shoulder, by the way—which we can do by means of a simple strap device that will keep your shoulders pulled back. You'll also be required to wear a sling on your left arm. In fact, it would be advisable to wear the sling even after the three- or four-week preliminary period is over. Unless, of course, you really need to use your arm. But I can give you further advice about that later.''

''Please,'' Hope said, struggling to sit up again despite his warnings.

''Let me help you,'' he said unexpectedly, and very carefully he eased her into a sitting position. Not only were his arms strong, she discovered, they were surprisingly gentle, and he held her until she'd swung her legs over the side of the examining table.

Even then, Ross Adair did not release her at once. Nor did Hope want him to. True, her legs were still too wobbly to walk on, but that wasn't her reason. It was rather that there seemed a safety, almost a sense of sanctuary, to being held in his arms.

Carefully, because it hurt to move, she pressed close to him without really being aware of what she was doing. And suddenly she was conscious of a warm feeling, slowly mounting, that traveled through her body, arousing the strangest sensations in its wake. These tremors, she was astonished to realize, left very sensuous echoes. And these ''echoes,'' she knew only too well, would become akin to a dormant volcano coming to life again if her treacherous body were not suffering from an entirely different sort of trauma.

Fortunately, the shot Ross Adair had given her was starting to have its own effect. It was dulling the pain, as he had said it would, but it also made Hope feel groggy, and she said accusingly, "That must have been a blockbuster!"

Carefully, he released her. Was he, too, expressing just a bit of reluctance about taking his hands away from her, or was she only imagining this? Then he stepped back. "What must have been a blockbuster?" he asked. "Your fall?"

"No, whatever it was you gave me...."

"You can trust me when it comes to dispensing medication," he said coolly. "Or to do anything else involved in the practice of medicine." He paused and inhaled deeply. "Now, we'll get you into the contraption you'll be wearing, and then Thelma can take you along to your room."

The "contraption" was definitely restrictive. But common sense told Hope that it was necessary to inhibit the movement of the afflicted shoulder and arm. At least Ross Adair—*Dr*. Adair—hadn't insisted on putting her in a cumbersome cast. It might be awkward driving with this shoulder harness and a sling on one arm, but somehow she'd manage, she decided woozily. She found herself saying aloud, "I have to leave as soon as possible."

Ross Adair had picked up her chart and was reading it. "What?" he demanded, raising his eyebrows questioningly, his expression so totally disconcerting it almost overrode the effects of the drug.

"I was...thinking to myself," Hope said lamely.

"What were you thinking, Miss Standish? Where must you go so quickly?"

"No place, I guess. What I mean is...I have to leave Cherokee as soon as possible."

"You're not still thinking of making your pilgrimage across the mountains in that relic of a car of yours, are you?" he questioned.

"That's exactly what I was thinking," Hope said, her speech somewhat slurred now. "My friend is still expecting me in Gatlinburg and there's no reason why I—"

"There is every reason," he cut in abruptly. "But we're not going to discuss it tonight. Fortunately, there is an available room for you here in the hospital."

"Fortunately?"

"Miss Standish, I should tell you that this is an Indian facility, and normally we do not admit non-Indians. In fact, we do not even treat outsiders, except when it's an emergency. Needless to say, your case is an emergency, and I don't want to transfer you to Sylva or Bryson City tonight. I think it's more important that you remain somewhat immobile for the present. Thelma can take you along to your room now, and I'll check in on you later."

At that moment the nurse who had spoken to Ross Adair earlier entered the room. She was pushing a wheelchair, and there was nothing Hope could do but let herself be helped into it. Soon she was gliding along first one shining corridor, then another. Near the end the nurse stopped. She reached inside an open door, flipped on a light and then carefully guided Hope through. There were two beds, both empty. "I'd take the one next to the window, if I were you," the nurse said. "There's a nice view, as you'll see come morning."

"Thank you," Hope said dully. At this point she was grateful to let the nurse help her into bed, and as her legs practically collapsed under her weight she found herself muttering abjectly, "Where has my strength gone?"

"You had a bad shock, falling like that," the Indian woman said sympathetically. "Your strength will come back just as quickly as it left you, though. Now get some rest."

Left alone in the hospital room, Hope was at first certain she wasn't going to be able to get any rest at all. Not only was there a pain in her shoulder and an ache in her head, there was the stunning realization that Ross Adair was a doctor.

But nature's own method of healing augmented the powerful medication he had given her, and it wasn't very long before Hope was conquered by sleep. It was a deep sleep, filled with dreams she would not remember. Yet she felt sure that Ross Adair must have come in to stand by her bedside during the course of that sleep. He had told her he would look in on her, and she had no doubt he had kept his professional word. And when she finally awakened, sunlight was streaming through the window by her bed and she found she was looking out over a vista of mountainside covered with beautiful laurel and rhododendrons.

Another Indian nurse brought Hope a breakfast tray, but the doctor who came in to see her that morning was not an Indian. He was a balding, middle-aged man with a pleasant, low-paced manner and a decided Midwestern twang in his accent, all the more pronounced against the soft, Southern drawls to which she'd become accustomed.

She wanted very much to ask this man about Ross Adair. She yearned to know who he was, and how he fit into the scheme of things here at the hospital. But something kept her silent, and after the older doctor had examined her she slipped back into sleep.

It was almost noon when Hope woke up again. She was just finishing the tuna-fish salad and corn bread that had been brought to her for lunch when Ross Adair arrived. He came into the room as she was raising a glass of iced tea to her lips, and she paused in the midst of the gesture as if she were posing in a tableau. He was wearing tan slacks and a royal blue knit shirt, and he looked rested and virile and very much in command of himself.

"Finished with that?" he asked as Hope put the iced tea back on the tray. Even though she wasn't completely, she nodded and let him remove the tray and set it aside. Then he sat down on the side of the bed and surveyed her with an interest that was clearly professional. She imagined he must look at slides under a microscope in precisely the same manner.

"You seem to be doing well enough," he concluded after this inspection.

"What is that supposed to mean?"

"Just what I said. No complications that I can see. You have a simple closed fracture of the clavicle, with no displacement of the fracture ends. In other words, a nice clean break, which means that time is the only thing required for you to heal. The bump on your head may ache some, but it's not serious. So...follow orders, and you'll have no problems.''

"And what might the orders be?'' Hope inquired suspiciously.

Ross Adair folded his arms firmly. "For one thing,'' he said bluntly, "you'll have to forgo your plans to drive around the Great Smokies. Maybe in two weeks or so you'll be fit enough for riding in a car, though certainly you won't be able to take the steering wheel yourself.''

"You can't be serious!''

"I'm quite serious, Miss Standish. And I talked to your friend Lorna Evans, by the way. She called the motel last night to find out when you were going to be able to meet her. Penny Raincrow put her through to me here. I told her about your accident, and she decided to go back to Knoxville.''

Hope hesitated, not really surprised by this bit of news. Then she said, "Dr. Adair?''

It was the first time she had used his name in any form, and she saw that hint of amusement lurking in those jet eyes again. But he only said, almost too politely, "Yes?''

"Frankly, I can't stay here in Cherokee, if that's what you're indicating. I...I just don't have the money,'' she added, hating to have to admit this to him. "I allowed myself enough for the trip, but that didn't include anything like the daily rate of the Three Wigwams! I'm only hoping that my medical insurance is adequate to cover these hospital expenses.''

He considered this for a moment, then he said coolly, ''It will take us several weeks to get your bill in order, so I would put that out of your mind for now, if I were you.'' He hesitated, then added, ''You told me your mother is a very wealthy woman.''

''That has absolutely nothing to do with me!''

''You and your mother have no rapport?''

''Very little,'' Hope said bitterly. ''I think I pretty well told you that, too.''

''Yes, you did. I might add that I had the feeling you regretted those confidences the moment you'd spoken them. Am I right?''

''Well, wouldn't you have?''

Ross Adair almost smiled. ''Maybe,'' he said. ''Curious, isn't it, how one sometimes feels impelled to pour out such things to a total stranger? I was surprised that you chose me. For that matter, I was flattered.''

''You? *Flattered?*''

''Does that seem so impossible to you? I'm capable of being flattered, after all. Most people are. But we're digressing. I assume what you're saying to me is that you refuse to ask for your mother's help?''

''Absolutely,'' Hope said firmly. ''And although you're right, although I do regret having said all those things to you, I somehow think that you're able to understand why I feel as I do.''

''Understand? I don't know,'' Ross Adair told

her slowly. "I've never had a similar experience. My mother died when I was only a few months old...so obviously I never knew her. Therefore I can't really judge how I'd feel if I were in your position. Though I'd like to think...."

"Yes?"

"I suppose I'd like to think that my relationship with my mother—had she lived—would have been closer. Not that I have any reason to think it would have been. But all of that is beside the point. I advise against your traveling for the next two weeks, at the minimum, so if you can't stay any longer at the Three Wigwams, we'll have to come up with some other arrangement." He rose as he was saying this, speaking as matter-of-factly as if the issues involved were already faits accomplis. Then he added, "You'll be here through tonight, in any event. You can get up when you wish or walk around or sit in the armchair. I'll ask the nurse to bring you something to read. Reading may be a bit awkward for you, but I'm sure you'll find a way to manage."

"Depending on my ingenuity?" Hope suggested wryly.

"Yes, depending upon your ingenuity," he said, totally unruffled. That dark, impassive gaze swept her face. "A lot of what we accomplish depends upon our ingenuity, Miss Standish—or suffers from the lack of it."

She couldn't resist it. She said, "You're quite a philosopher, aren't you, Dr. Adair?"

"I've never considered the matter," he rejoined. "It isn't very relevant at the moment, anyway. I think it's more important for you to realize that your healing process will be faster if you don't re-sist...being here quite so much.''

Had he been about to say that she'd get over this accident sooner if she didn't resist *him*? Hope pondered this, and although her heart lurched at the thought she warned herself against this kind of fantasy. Yet it was obvious he'd made a definite effort to come in to see her just now. He'd told her when they first met that he worked at night, and unless his schedule had been changed, it seemed likely that he wouldn't be going on duty again for several more hours.

The thought that he had made a deliberate safari to the hospital just to visit her was unexpectedly heady. She nearly said something to him about it, then decided it would be wiser to hold her tongue. Ross Adair had a way of twisting phrases!

"I bought some books and pamphlets at the museum the other day that I'm anxious to read," she said. "Would there be anything similar in the hospital library, do you think?"

He frowned. "What kind of books and pamphlets did you buy?"

"A variety, actually. Mostly about the Cherokees...."

Once again she would have sworn that she saw that flicker of amusement cross his face. But it was quickly suppressed as he asked, "You're so eager to learn about the Cherokees?"

"Interested, yes," she supplanted.

"Well, then," Ross Adair said with a wicked

smile, "perhaps you should enlist the help of a Cherokee to teach you!"

LATER, HOPE WAS GLAD they'd been interrupted by a nurse coming in to perform the routine chore of checking her temperature and pulse. Later, too, she thought of many things she might have said to Ross Adair in answer to his provocative suggestion. Clever things, things that might even make him a bit ashamed of himself for mocking her genuine interest in the Cherokee people.

Thinking of the Cherokees made her remember both Randy and Wonder Owl. Probably by the time Wonder had arrived in the theater parking lot Hope had already been whisked off by the rescue squad. But Betsy still would have been there. What must Randy have thought to find his cherished old car abandoned like that? Or had Ross Adair filled him in on what had happened?

The middle-aged nurse who had been on duty when she'd been brought into the emergency room the previous night stopped in during the middle of the afternoon and, to Hope's surprise, brought the supply of literature she'd purchased in the museum.

Thanking her, Hope said, "I'm afraid I don't even know your name. But this was a very nice thing for you to do."

"I'm Thelma Saunders," the woman told her. "Penny Raincrow got your material together for me, and she said to tell you she hoped you wouldn't mind her rummaging among your things. Dr. Adair suggested it."

"No, I don't mind at all," Hope said quickly, somewhat thunderstruck by the nurse's statement that Ross Adair had asked Penny Raincrow to get these things together for her. She hesitated, thinking about this, then said, "Miss Saunders, would you happen to know Wonder Owl, the young woman who works in the Qualla Cooperative?"

"Of course," the nurse replied. "I saw her earlier today and she's quite concerned about you. She wanted to come and visit you this afternoon, but Dr. Adair insisted that you have no visitors until tomorrow. He feels that peace and quiet are the most important things for you right now."

There were many responses she felt like making to this statement, but she only asked, "Do you know Randy Youngdeer?"

Mrs. Saunders nodded. "He sends you his very best wishes, and he told me to tell you not to worry about Betsy. He said she's back at his place, and she's fine." A curious look suddenly crossed the older woman's face. "Now it's my turn for a question," she said. "Who, may I ask, is Betsy?"

Hope managed a weak laugh. "Betsy is Randy's antique automobile. He...he loaned her to me." At this she swallowed hard, and before she could help herself the emotional toll of the accident came to consume her. Tears filled her eyes, and she stammered, "Everyone h-here has been v-very kind to me."

"And why wouldn't we be?" Thelma Saunders asked softly. "Wonder said to tell you, incidentally, that the date for coffee at the Leisure Inn is still on as soon as you're up to it. And Dr. Adair said to tell you he'll be picking you up first thing in the morning.''

"Dr. Adair will be picking me up?"

"I believe he's found a place for you to stay. He doesn't want you to leave Cherokee until you're really on the mend.''

Mrs. Saunders was moving toward the doorway, obviously about to leave, and although there was no point in blaming this woman because Ross Adair was being much too high-handed, Hope had to detain her.

She said, ''Would you ask Dr. Adair to stop by to see me as soon as he comes on duty, please?''

"Well, I would," Mrs. Saunders answered, "but he won't actually be on duty again—on call, that is—until the end of the week. Anyway, you'll be seeing him yourself well before then.''

"But he's on the staff of the hospital, isn't he?'' Hope persisted.

"Not in the usual sense, no. Dr. Adair is on the staff of the Joslin Clinic in Boston.''

"The Joslin Clinic!'' Hope repeated, incredulous.

"That's right. Since you're from Massachusetts, you probably know that the clinic is a major diabetes center. Dr. Adair specializes in the treatment of diabetes, and he has come back to Cherokee because—with the exception of alcoholism—diabetes is the greatest health problem among our people. He's here under two grants, one from the National Institute of Health, the other from the Diabetic

Research and Training Center. But because we're somewhat short staffed he has volunteered to take charge of the emergency room for us two nights a week. Most of his time is spent in research, though. Some very specific research, I might say.''

Thelma Saunders hesitated. ''We're very proud of Ross Adair,'' she said then, simply.

Hope could only nod, for she was staggered by the information she'd just been given. Ross Adair, on the staff of a leading medical facility located right in Boston!

Thoughts whirled, and Hope remembered with some chagrin how she had at first assumed he was a garage mechanic. She also remembered how angry he had made her when he had ignored her while blithely continuing to work on his own car. And when she got right down to it, she had to admit that the memory still rankled.

Ross Adair might be a very distinguished physician, she conceded, but he had a few things to learn about manners when it came to being a man.

CHAPTER SIX

THE NURSE ON DUTY the following morning had obviously been given her instructions. She moved into the room briskly and produced some of Hope's clothing, which she rather vaguely said had been "sent over."

The choices, Hope had to concede, were good. There was a lilac sweat shirt that she would call casual but chic, and considering the shoulder harness and sling she would be wearing, its loose raglan sleeves would be quite comfortable. In lieu of slacks, her favorite wraparound skirt had been selected. It featured the same lilac of the shirt plus tones of turquoise and copper, an arresting color combination. Finally, whoever had picked out this outfit had thrown in Hope's string sandals. They added the perfect touch.

As soon as Hope had finished with her breakfast the nurse helped her get dressed, and she was shocked to discover how awkward even this simple task was. Dimly, she could begin to accept the fact that Ross Adair had been right when he'd said she wasn't ready to travel.

It was exactly ten o'clock when he came walking into the room, and Hope could not help but feel that all the freshness and vitality of the outdoors had come in with him. He looked glowingly fit today, wearing snug-fitting jeans and a bright yellow sport shirt, which, as most things did, enhanced his dramatic coloring.

"Ready?" he asked pleasantly enough.

"No," Hope said shortly, and saw those disconcerting eyebrows quirk upward.

"Oh?" he said, then added with a touch of humor, "Something holding you up?"

"A lot of things. For one, I don't know what you have in mind. Mrs. Saunders said you'd arranged a place for me to stay, but she didn't say where,"

Hope hesitated. "It isn't that I'm unappreciative," she told him, anxious to find the right words to say to him. "But you shouldn't have bothered to do that. Anyway, I've already told you I can't stay here. I did some phoning yesterday afternoon and it seems my best course is to get a bus to Asheville, and from there I can either take another bus back to Boston or perhaps fly."

"You have relatives in Asheville?"

Had she told him about her mother's cousin Emily? Hope couldn't remember, so she said only, "A distant relative, but I don't intend to see her. I don't intend to stay in Asheville, for that matter."

"You really are antifamily, aren't you?" he observed.

"No! It's just that I—"

"You don't get along with the Asheville relative, either?"

"Really, Dr. Adair—"

He nodded. "You're right. It isn't any of my business. I'll admit that before you point it out to me. Now let's get along, shall we?"

Hope shook her head. "No," she said, wishing that just being around him didn't make her feel so ridiculously weak. "I've already told you I can't go with you."

"And you can't stay here," he pointed out. "As I think I already made clear to you, this is an Indian facility."

"Yes, you've made that very clear," Hope said, feeling her cheeks begin to flush. "But I didn't exactly try to become a patient here, you know!"

To her horror, she could feel tears threatening, and the last thing she wanted to do was appear helpless in front of Ross Adair. She could imagine the expression in those midnight eyes if that were to happen. Once again, though, he was unexpectedly compassionate, and this had a dire effect. The tears brimmed over.

He covered the distance between them in one step, towering over her as he sat on the edge of the hospital bed. "Hope," he said, "I'm sorry! I don't know what comes over me when I try to deal with you. I...."

"It's a case of bad chemistry," she sniffed, and was startled to see that he looked as if she'd slapped him.

"Is that what you call it?" he asked in a curiously strained voice. "No, wait. This isn't the time to become personal. You've been under an obvious strain, and I'm not talking about your accident. I'm sure that you've been under a strain since before you came to Cherokee, and I haven't done much to lessen it. Come along with me, and if you don't like the arrangements I've made we'll change them, I promise you that. I'll even drive you to Asheville and put you on a plane to Boston when I feel it's safe for you to travel."

To Hope's astonishment, he reached out a long finger and lifted her chin. She saw that he was smiling. It was a dazzling smile, and the impact of its charm was so totally unexpected that Hope felt her knees grow weak in a way that had nothing to do with her fall. The same warm feeling she'd first felt in the emergency room came to suffuse her again, but this time it was much more intense. This time she was aware of Ross Adair only as a man, not as a doctor.

This man aroused her—just being near him aroused her—and she knew that she could not possibly trust her own emotions, her self-control, around him. There was something so essentially male about him. He could have been Adam—allegorically, at least. And he could easily become the Adam in her own particular world if she let herself yield to the mesmerizing effect he had on her.

In addition to the purely sexual impact of his presence was the rare tenderness of his touch. As he continued to hold her chin with that single finger, Hope felt young and fragile and very vulnerable and discovered to her further astonishment that these could all be extremely pleasant feelings when someone like Ross Adair was gazing into her eyes.

"Trust me, Hope," he said. "Trust me just a little bit. After all, they brought you to me last night . . . and I'm quite proud of my reputation as a physician." Again he had hesitated before completing the sentence, and she had the feeling that this wasn't at all what he had intended to say.

Hope tried to assemble the New England fortitude of which she'd always been quite proud. She said a bit stiffly, "It isn't a question of trusting you. I can't afford to stay in Cherokee. That's the simple fact of the matter, though I don't particularly relish saying it over and over again. Nor do I expect you to drive me into Asheville. I can take the bus."

"No, you can't," he said firmly. "Not until the healing process is considerably more advanced than it is right now. Remember, there's no reason to consider your injury serious—unless you fool around with it. If you take needless chances, you can expect to have complications as a result. I'm not a specialist in orthopedics, but it doesn't take one to know that you could easily suffer more damage if you go jouncing around on a bus in the near future."

Hope shook her head. "I'm afraid I'll simply have to take a chance and . . . and hold myself very still," she said.

The question came so suddenly that she was not prepared for it. "Are you really so afraid of me?" he asked.

The smile had vanished. Once again he seemed impassive, but she was beginning to know that this seeming indifference was not to be trusted. She hesitated, caution's flag waving, yet it was not in her to dissemble. After a moment she said, "No, I'm not afraid of you. I don't understand you, but that's something else again."

"Understanding comes only with time," he said. "We haven't had that much time, you and I."

Hope swallowed hastily, because there was a certain implication to what he was saying that came close to frightening her.

You've been burned by a man, remember, she cautioned herself. Then, knowing that he was waiting for her to answer him, she said, "Regardless of time, I can't help but recall that two days ago you ordered me off private property. You gave me the impression I was trespassing by being in Cherokee in the first place and that you couldn't wait for me to leave." Remembering his searing kiss and the roughness of his embrace, her cheeks flamed again. But she added steadily, "Have you changed so much between then and now because I've become your patient?"

"No," he said, "I haven't changed." Then for a moment he seemed confused as he ran those long fingers through velvet-black hair, which Hope yearned to touch. He was hesitating, and Hope had the feeling he was afraid of saying more than he wanted to. Finally he drew a deep breath.

"Look," he said, "let's just say that it's the physician in me, rather than the man, doing the thinking at the moment. I've already told you that if you don't like the arrangements I've made for you I will defer to your wishes as soon as possible. Now, if you don't mind, could we please get going?

I have a full schedule ahead of me today and I'd like to see you settled so I can start in on it.''

It was a rebuke, and he didn't bother to veil it. Hope suddenly became conscious of the fact that Dr. Ross Adair was, as Thelma Saunders had said, an extremely distinguished physician whose time ordinarily must be at quite a premium.

He was young to be so noted in his field. Hope was sure that he couldn't be more than thirty-four or thirty-five, and insofar as physical fitness was concerned he was surely at his peak. Thinking about this, she knew she was in danger of beginning to wander emotionally again, and she warned herself that she must avoid dwelling on the physical aspects of this man whenever he came around her.

But then, she told herself, he probably wouldn't be around her all that much. It was entirely possible that he would ask one of the other doctors at the hospital to take over her case.

At the thought of this, Hope felt a wave of helplessness that was so strong she was afraid tears were going to brim all over again.

She was so annoyed at herself that she nearly bit her tongue before saying, "I'm ready if you are. If you'll just take my books for me, we can go. I don't have much else here with me."

"I know," he nodded. "I'm afraid the dress and shoes you were wearing the other night have had it. The rest is pretty much on your back, isn't it? The things I had Penny Raincrow pack for you this morning?"

So...even the choice of the lilac top and the

printed skirt had been his! He could be surprisingly thoughtful—and surprisingly perceptive, as well. Hope was close to feeling grateful to him until he insisted upon taking her out to his car in a wheelchair.

"Do you really think that's necessary?" she protested sharply.

"I'll be the judge," he said calmly, and a moment later Hope was being wheeled back down the long corridor toward the hospital entrance.

The day was bright and beautiful. Hope decided it was the loveliest day she had seen thus far, then had to admit that this might very well have something to do with the tall, dark man at her side.

He drove his black sports car with the same expertise with which he seemed to do everything, and she began to wonder if Ross Adair ever goofed. He always appeared to have the upper hand in any situation. She couldn't decide whether this was due to years of training, or whether it was simply a basic facet of his personality. Thinking of the years of medical school and residency he must have gone through, she began to wonder still more about him. What had made him decide to become a doctor? Had some personal experience inspired him to study medicine? Certainly he must have been strongly motivated. How else could he have left these beautiful Great Smokies? How else could he have headed north, to enter what must have seemed like an entirely different world to him?

Thinking about this, she was startled to hear him ask, "Something bothering you?"

"No.'

"It's almost time for your medication, if your shoulder is acting up. But if the pain's really bad I can give you a shot that will work more quickly than the oral dose.''

Hope's arm was definitely painful, but that wasn't what was beginning to affect her. Rather it was his proximity, the scent of that pine-touched shaving lotion he used, the awareness of his warmth. . . .

She said hastily, ''I don't need a shot, really,'' her tone a bit more cool than she'd intended. But this seemed to satisfy him, although his answering nod was curt.

He had taken a left turn onto the road in front of the hospital, and now she saw a sign at the next intersection that pointed to both the hospital and the Mountainside Theater.

"Is the theater near here?'' she asked, surprised.

"Yes,'' he said, seeming equally surprised for the moment. Then he admitted, ''I'd forgotten you were unconscious during that ride with the rescue squad. To get to the theater we would have taken another left just a little way past the hospital. It's only a short distance farther up the hillside. If you had to have an accident you chose a very convenient place in which to stage it.''

"I didn't stage it, Dr. Adair!''

He looked across at her and grinned. ''A figure of speech, Miss Standish,'' he said with elaborate politeness. ''Don't always take me so literally.''

Was that a warning? Even as she pondered this, Hope realized that once again she was, indeed, taking him literally. She had a tendency, in fact, to analyze every word he said. She made up her mind that, if only in self-defense, she was going to have to learn to be more casual with him.

They passed the large Leisure Inn complex, and a short distance beyond it Ross Adair took a side road that wound up into the hills. It wasn't very long before Hope began to experience a definite sense of familiarity. This was one of the routes she'd taken on her exploring trip of the territory a couple of days ago. In fact, it was the very same route that had led to their unpleasant meeting.

Even as she realized this, they came to the circle that marked the dead end of the road, and Hope saw the low stone house ahead of her, the same house that had attracted her so much.

The protest came involuntarily. "No!"

"Why do you say no?" Ross Adair asked.

"This is *your* house, isn't it?" she demanded, a sense of total confusion overtaking her.

She knew that he was watching her closely, and she tried very hard not to look at him. She didn't want to look at him. . .not until she'd got considerably more control of herself. As things stood now, she felt at a total disadvantage. She couldn't understand why he was bringing her here—and she didn't know what she could do about it!

Then she felt that long finger touching her chin again, and Ross Adair was turning her head so that she had to look at him. She caught her breath as her eyes met that deep, dark gaze she found so impossible to decipher.

"This is my aunt's home," he said levelly. "She's a widow, and now and then she accepts a guest to help augment her income. This doesn't happen on any regular basis. Only when someone absolutely requires a place to stay. So, Miss Hope Standish, you will be well chaperoned here...and quite safe...." He did not need to finish with the words "from me." The unspoken ending was as obvious as if he'd shouted it.

Hope was too mortified to answer him. He was treating her as if she were an overly emotional adolescent, and in all honesty she couldn't blame him. She should have acted more maturely. She'd dealt with life on many levels, after all; she'd known all kinds of people. Perhaps too many kinds of people, she thought somewhat bitterly. She had no desire at all to play the part of an ingenue with any man, especially not with Ross Adair. Yet, inevitably, she seemed to assume just that role with him.

Amusement flickered in his dark eyes. That much, at least, she could read without difficulty. He said, "Are you coming along without protest?"

Hope rallied. "Why would I protest?" she countered, and she had every intention of letting it go at that. But temptation made her add, "I have to admit that I can't understand why you've brought me here, though. If I'm not mistaken, it was from a portion of this property that you evicted me the other day. So I can't quite see why you're bringing me back to it now."

"Because it seems the expedient thing to do," he

said, becoming as professional as if he'd suddenly donned his white coat. "Come along."

She took him at his word and was opening her door when he barked, "Don't try to get out by yourself! I'll help you."

He quickly came around and guided her to her feet, putting an arm around her as he did so. And when she felt the taut strength of his muscles pressing through the thin fabric of her blouse, Hope literally rocked.

"Steady," he whispered in her ear. "You'll get your bearings back in a minute."

She was tempted to disagree with him, as she felt the warmth of his breath caress her temple. It seemed unlikely she'd ever get her bearings back. Even were she never to see Ross Adair again after today, she knew she would never forget him.

Was this what was meant by the old cliché about opposites attracting? She and Ross certainly were opposites...in so many ways. Yet he evoked in her a response as old as nature, a response far more consuming than anything Hope had ever known before.

She shivered slightly, and he said, "Take it easy." Perhaps because he thought she was still unsteady on her feet, he continued to keep his arm around her as they made their way up the flagstone steps toward the flower-bordered terrace. At the foot of the steps he looked down at her, and a brief smile etched his arresting face.

"You look like Cinderella," he told her.

At that moment Hope felt like Cinderella. She

had to wonder what role this dark and handsome stranger might be about to play. Prince Charming? Hardly!

There was no chance to speculate further on this. A tall, slender woman had emerged from the house and was crossing the flagstone terrace. Immediately Hope could see the resemblance to Ross Adair, but the woman's black hair was heavily streaked with gray, and it would have been close to impossible to determine her age. She could have been fifty, sixty, maybe even seventy. Yet there was an unusual vitality in her gait, a vitality so reminiscent of Ross.

"I'd begun to wonder if you two were ever going to get here," she said, coming down the steps smiling, her hand outstretched. "Hope, my dear, I'm Loretta Wood, Ross's aunt. I'm delighted that you'll be staying with me for a while. What delayed you, Ross?"

It would be like him to come right out and tell her I hadn't wanted to go along with his plans, Hope thought bleakly. She was relieved to hear him say instead, "A few details to take care of, Aunt Loretta. But Hope is all checked out now."

That was a statement with a double meaning if she'd ever heard one, Hope decided, but she held her tongue. Ross's arm was still around her, and he didn't seem ready to relinquish it. He helped her gently up the steps, and Loretta Wood, addressing him, asked, "Should Hope get right into bed? Or would it be all right for her to sit out here on the terrace? It's lovely in the sun and we could have some iced tea. After all, it won't be too long till lunchtime."

Ross laughed. "To answer your first question first," he said teasingly, "Hope doesn't need to go to bed at all—except, perhaps, to take a rest during the afternoon. She's free to wander around, to sit out here on the terrace or to do as she likes, provided she takes it easy. And I'm going to ask you to make sure she obeys those orders, Aunt Loretta. Hope has a rather definite mind of her own and she doesn't completely agree with my prescribed treatment."

The older woman laughed. "Well, my dear," she said, addressing Hope, "Ross can be a bit high-handed—as you may have already learned."

Indeed she had learned this, but she wasn't about to give him the satisfaction of saying so. As she looked more closely at Loretta Wood, she had the distinct impression that she'd seen her before. She tried to remember if Ross's aunt had been one of the actresses in the drama or perhaps an usherette at the Mountainside Theater. But that wasn't it.

Finally she asked a bit timidly, "Haven't I seen you somewhere before, Mrs. Wood?"

"At the Qualla Cooperative," Mrs. Wood said promptly. "Two of us came to Wonder Owl's rescue the other afternoon when that tour bus arrived."

"Of course."

"Wonder Owl called a while ago, incidentally. She'd like to come over and visit you later in the afternoon. She's working in the cooperative until four, but she'll be free after that. She was very upset about the other night. She got to the parking lot at just about the same time the rescue squad arrived. You can imagine how horrified she was."

"It was such a stupid thing to have happen," Hope said dismally

"It was an accident," Ross Adair said firmly, to Hope's surprise. "Nobody's fault. And in a little while you'll be fine again. That's the most important thing."

Finally he released her, saying, "Come and sit down at one of these tables, Hope. Where's the iced tea, Aunt Loretta?"

"I'll get it, Ross," his aunt replied.

"No, let me," he contradicted. "You stay here and talk to Hope. I'm sure the two of you will have a lot to say to each other."

He left them with that somewhat oblique remark, and Hope wished she knew exactly what he'd meant by it. Did he expect her to start pummeling his aunt with questions about him the minute he was out of sight?

The conceit of the man! The utter conceit of him!

Mrs. Wood said, "Ross tells me you're from the Boston area."

"Yes, I am," Hope nodded. "Concord, actually."

"Did you know him up there?"

She shook her head, puzzled. "No. We met here in Cherokee the other day. In...in Randy Youngdeer's garage, as a matter of fact."

Mrs. Wood was obviously surprised. "That's strange," she murmured.

"I beg your pardon?"

"Nothing, my dear, nothing at all," she said hastily. "Ross isn't one to become acquainted with people so quickly, that's all. When he asked if you could come and stay here I had the impression you'd known each other back in New England, and I'll confess I was glad to think so. It would mean that he finally—"

To Hope's chagrin, the sentence was not finished. Ross Adair appeared in the doorway to ask, "Where do you keep your lemons, Aunt Loretta?"

"In the refrigerator, Ross," Loretta Wood said a bit tersely, and Hope had the feeling that she, too, regretted this particular interruption. The mood of their conversation had quickly become one in which to exchange confidences, but just as quickly it had been broken.

CHAPTER SEVEN

THERE WAS A STRANGE UNREALITY to sitting on a pleasant flagstone terrace sipping iced tea with Ross Adair and his aunt. Hope felt as if she had stumbled into an enchanted garden. The flowers that edged the terrace spilled paths of color down the mountainside, their fragrance mingling with the fresh woodsy scent of the pines, a scent that would always remind Hope of the handsome Cherokee doctor now at her side.

He was being as pleasant, as urbane as if they were at a tea party in Boston, and the three of them chatted about a variety of things, including Hope's own career as an art teacher. Hope didn't mention that she'd been in the act of painting the very scene that now lay before them when she'd been so rudely interrupted the other day. But then, nor did Ross.

Loretta Wood commiserated with her about having to forgo the painting trip through the Great Smokies and suggested that when Ross gave permission she could surely find some interesting scenes to do right around Cherokee.

"We have our full share of local color," Mrs. Wood said with a smile. "You could start right at the Oconaluftee Village. As a matter of fact, a number of prominent artists have gone there to paint. The material is practically endless. The village is a recreation of an eighteenth-century Indian village, so everything the craftspeople do emphasizes the arts and crafts of the Cherokees as they were practiced over two hundred years ago. Basket weaving, bead making, pottery. All of those things are done in the traditional way.''

"Aunt Loretta even takes a whirl at it herself once in a while and goes up and strings beads,'' Ross said, grinning.

"Strings beads, indeed!'' his aunt rebuked with feigned indignation. "I'll have you know that Indian beadwork is an art.''

"I go along with that,'' Hope said. "The designs I've seen are wonderful and the colors are glorious.''

"Often we use Venetian beads, which were among the first trade goods introduced to the Cherokees,'' Mrs. Wood said. "And incidentally, the village isn't just a women's enterprise. The men make dugout canoes using the old method of gouging out whole trees with fire and axes. They also make blowguns out of green river cane. There are regularly scheduled demonstrations of their skill with this weapon, which is purely Cherokee in origin, as far as I know, and they're worth watching.''

"Careful,'' Ross cautioned, still grinning. "You'll have Hope thinking that she's wound up in the wrong place, Aunt Loretta.''

Although he spoke lightly, Hope sensed there was

an underlying significance in his words. It was as if he was determined not to let her forget for very long that they came from two different cultures. She began to think that the implication, in his mind, was that these two cultures could never mix successfully.

Mix successfully! Now *she* was jumping to conclusions. She was reading a meaning into every word Ross Adair spoke—which was foolish, to say the least.

Just because he won't give you a chance doesn't mean that you shouldn't give him one, she advised herself quickly.

She swallowed her tea rather hastily while she thought about this. Then, feeling suddenly that she might choke, she took a deep breath. Neither reaction went unnoticed.

Ros said with a slight frown, "I think we'd better get you to your room so you can rest awhile, Hope. I'd prefer you to keep the shoulder brace on even when you're lying down, at least for the next few days. And before you say anything, I know this isn't the most comfortable thing to do."

"Whatever you say, doctor," she nodded, and was satisfied to see a startled look cross his face.

"Hope is to have the Fern Room," Loretta Wood told her nephew before he could comment on Hope's statement. "If you'll show her to it...."

"The Fern Room?" Ross repeated, obviously surprised.

"That's right," his aunt said steadily. "While you're helping Hope get settled, I'll phone Wonder and tell her it's all right for her to come over later. Assuming that you agree to that, of course.''

"Permission granted," Ross said, coming around to draw out Hope's chair for her. Then he started to help her to her feet, even though she was perfectly capable of getting up by herself. She was tempted to take advantage of this, but the thought of relying on his steadying arm again was much too disturbing, so she started in the direction of the house by herself.

They entered a long living room that had a window wall across the front, facing the terrace. A wide roof overhang shaded the windows, though, so that the interior of the room was subdued and pleasantly cool. The walls were whitewashed, the ceiling crisscrossed with dark-stained beams, and the furniture looked both well used and very comfortable. The colors were bright, and the designs in the curtain fabrics and the throw pillows on the couch were distinctly Indian. It was a charming room, and Hope felt very much at home in it.

Nor did the rest of the house disappoint her. After traversing the living room they went up two steps into the dining area, which was furnished in pine with beautiful woven wall hangings and copper accents. Another picture window overlooked a neatly landscaped backyard and a free-form swimming pool.

Gesturing toward the pool, Ross said, "It's rather slippery out there at the moment, so I'd prefer that you don't try to swim. One fall is all it would take to...."

"Don't worry," Hope replied. "I'm not that

much of a swimmer.'' She spoke somewhat absently, because she was thinking only of the time she'd met Ross Adair in the field and he'd been dripping wet.

They continued down a long corridor to a bedroom at the end that was like a small suite in itself, located in a side ell with its own private bath adjoining.

The room was furnished in green and white, the walls papered in a pattern of beautiful ferns. The bedstead, dresser and chairs were painted in soft white, while the bedspread was in a tone reminiscent of new garden lettuce, banded in wide stripes of deep green and ivory.

Hope stood on the threshold, enraptured. ''It's really lovely!'' she exclaimed.

''Yes, it is, isn't it?'' Ross Adair agreed, and again Hope suspected he was on the verge of saying something more to her but had stopped himself short.

''Most of your things are still at the Three Wigwams,'' he added rather offhandedly. ''I'll stop by later and get them from Penny. Meantime, I put your medication in your handbag. Let's get a pill into you now, and maybe it'll help you get some rest.''

Hope was not about to protest. Nor did she object when he slipped her shoes off her feet and helped her lie down, after drawing back the bedspread. He pulled the spread over her gently and propped pillows behind her so that she'd get support for her shoulder and comfort at the same time.

Hope could not repress a smile. ''You'd make a good nurse,'' she teased him.

He laughed. ''I may ask you to write me a testimonial to that effect—one that I could show to some of the nurses who work with me up at the Joslin," he said. "I have a reputation for being something of a bear on occasion. Rather demanding, shall we say? Anyway, more than once I've heard a nurse mutter behind my back that I should have to do her work and then I'd appreciate it."

"When will you be going back to Boston?" Hope asked.

He had gone into the bathroom to fill a glass with water, and before answering he brought it over and gave it to her with a pill, which he'd obviously taken out of her handbag. She hadn't even noticed him doing this. One had to give him points for efficiency, she conceded.

He put the water glass on the night table and sat down on the bed by her side. Despite her aching shoulder this sort of proximity began to have its usual heady effect on her.

"I've been here since March," he said, "and I'd like to stay around a few months longer, if possible. I'm working under a grant, which is sufficient as far as finances are concerned. It's time, or rather the lack of it, that's the leading factor. I took a sabbatical of sorts to do this. I'm on the faculty at a couple of Boston-area medical schools as well as on the staff at Joslin, so I have work to be done on both fronts. I think I'm on to something in my research, though, so I want to keep going as long as they'll put up with my absence."

"Would it be prying too much to ask just what it is you're working on?" Hope ventured.

He hesitated briefly. Then he said, "Well, among other things it involves studying the effect of insulin on Indians who suffer from diabetes. There have already been some detailed studies done on other tribes. The Pimas, for example, a tribe from the West. It's been shown that Pima Indians who take insulin have a higher incidence of diabetic retinopathy—that's a disease that results in damage to the eyes—than those who are not insulin dependent. The Pimas were chosen for the study I mention because they have the world's largest reported incidence of diabetes mellitus, or what is popularly known as 'sugar diabetes.' And this is despite the fact that they are not a particularly large tribe. They are, in fact, only a fraction as large as the Cherokees, who are actually the second-largest Indian tribe in North America."

"Which is the largest?" Hope asked curiously.

"The Navahos," Ross Adair said. "They number more than 100,000 people, while we number somewhere around 70,000. Anyway, among the many conclusions still to be reached is whether diabetic retinopathy is simply more severe among those Indians taking insulin—which could account for the higher incidence of it in these particular people—or whether there is some other relationship."

He smiled at her somewhat wryly. "What I'm doing, specifically, is investigating eye complications among those of my own people who are taking insulin," he said. "And I think I'm on the right track, but I'm a long way from coming to any conclusions!"

He straightened and added almost apologetically, "Sorry, Hope. I didn't mean to become so clinical."

"Please," she protested. "It's fascinating."

"Well, to me it is," Ross Adair admitted. "Now, my dear, the pill should be helping you in a little while, so try to get some sleep. I don't think I have to tell you that sleep is one of nature's best healing mechanisms."

"True," Hope said. She forced herself to smile. Then, to her surprise, Ross leaned over and kissed her full on the lips. But this was a gentle kiss, its tenderness a complete contrast to the way he had kissed her when he had found her painting on his aunt's property.

He said, as if reading her mind, "Forgive me, Hope, for the way I behaved toward you the other day. I think I was trying very hard to convince myself that you were another avid tourist, motivated by the kind of curiosity I despise. Regardless, though, it was inexcusable of me to act as I did. Would it be too much to ask that we start all over again?"

Hope hesitated. She was not at all sure that she wanted to "start all over again." It seemed to her that despite some rather poor beginnings she and Ross had made progress in their relationship. She saw no need to dismiss this, so she was startled to hear the icy edge of anger in his voice when he said, "I see I'm not to be reprieved so easily. But then I should have realized that you're not the type simply to forgive and forget, are you, Hope?"

Before she could answer, he stood up. And once again she saw the old impassivity back in his face.

"Ross..." she began, but he shook his head.

"No need to get into it any further," he said. "We'll talk again when you're feeling better. Meanwhile, enjoy your visit with Wonder."

He left without waiting for an answer from her, and the sense of loss that lingered in the wake of his departure was acute. But before very long the medication began to work, and Hope dozed off.

She slept deeply. When she awakened she knew she'd been dreaming, but she couldn't remember what her dreams had been about. She was possessed by an overwhelming sense of confusion, and for a moment she had no idea where she was.

Then it all came back to her. And with memory came the realization that she was lucky to be a guest in Loretta Wood's lovely home. True, they hadn't got into the matter of money yet, and that was something she'd have to discuss with Mrs. Wood as soon as possible. But since a convalescent period was mandatory just now, she could hardly have found a better solution to what could have been a considerable problem. She had Ross Adair to thank for being here, this she knew.

She wondered why he had seemed so surprised when his aunt had said that she was to be given the Fern Room. It was a lovely room, a very intimate sort of room. It had been furnished with care for someone very special. Thinking of this, Hope found herself wondering who that special someone might have been.

There was the possibility, of course, that this was Loretta Wood's own room, but Hope didn't think

so. For one thing, there were no personal possessions around at all. No books, no photographs, no
bric-a-brac. Hope decided that perhaps Wonder
could tell her more about the room—and about a
lot of other things, as well. If, that is, they had the
chance to talk alone.

She got up cautiously and made her way to the
bathroom. There she splashed her face with cold
water, managed to get a comb through her hair and
then put on a bit of lip gloss. But there was no question that she looked peaked, and she was discover-
ing that it was rather awkward to achieve much of a
toilette with one arm in a sling and a shoulder brace
restraining her motion.

Her clothes felt rumpled, but she had nothing else
to change into. Then she remembered that Ross had
said he would pick up her things at Penny Raincrow's and—

For the first time, the implication of his words
really hit her.

Did Ross *live* here?

The thought was staggering!

Ross had closed the door to the Fern Room behind him when he'd left earlier. Now there was a
knock on it, and when Hope called, "Yes?" it was
Wonder Owl who opened it cautiously, peering
around the edge.

Her eyes fell upon Hope and she gasped. "Oh!"
she said. "You look like a bird who's had its wing
clipped!"

"That bad?" Hope protested, and Wonder
laughed.

"Actually," she said, "the sling gives you a rather fetching air." She broke off quickly to add, "Hope, I'm so sorry. What a rotten thing to have happen! Ross says that when you began to come to, you kept muttering that I was calling you."

"Well...I thought I heard my name," Hope admitted carefully. "So like an idiot I swung around and caught my heel...."

"It wasn't me calling you," Wonder said, wide-eyed. "By the time I got there they already had you on a stretcher and were putting you in the rescue squad. Fortunately I got a glimpse of your face, so I knew it was you. Otherwise I might have thought that...."

"Thought what, Wonder?"

"Well, that perhaps you'd decided not to keep our coffee date. After all, it was a spur-of-the-moment thing."

"On the contrary," Hope reminded her. "Mrs. Saunders told me that when you called the hospital you said to tell me it's still on, as soon as I'm up to it."

"I meant that," Wonder promised, "and Randy will be the first to applaud. He was really looking forward to it."

This was a rather ambiguous statement. Hope couldn't decide what the exact relationship was between Randy Youngdeer and this lovely Cherokee woman. Possibly they were merely good friends, yet she suspected there was more to it than that. And, remembering the expression on Wonder's face when she'd talked of Randy at the cooperative the other day, she couldn't help but think that it involved some sort of problem.

Wonder was looking around the room. "Isn't it beautiful!" she said. "I was amazed when Mrs. Wood said I'd find you in the Fern Room. I don't think anyone has been in here for years."

"Years?" Hope echoed.

"Not since—" Wonder stopped and bit her lip. "I'm rattling on too much, Hope. Mrs. Wood said to come out on the terrace as soon as you're ready. It's still nice and warm and sunny out there, and we should take advantage of it. The sun tends to disappear over the mountains much too soon around here."

Wonder was chattering on, and Hope had no doubt that this was because she didn't want to get back to the matter of the Fern Room. . . and its previous inhabitant.

MRS. WOOD WAS SITTING OUT on the terrace with a friend whom she introduced as Minerva Lightfoot. The name rang a bell with Hope, but it took her a moment to remember that this was the woman who made blueberry pies for the coffee shop at the Three Wigwams.

The women were drinking frosted root-beer floats, and Mrs. Wood insisted on going into the kitchen and making the same thing for both Wonder and Hope. Wonder protested the calories, but she and Hope were told firmly that they could both use a bit of extra flesh on their bones.

In Hope's case, this was true. She knew she was a

shade too thin. But Wonder, it seemed to her, had a near-perfect figure. In fact, the young Cherokee woman was very, very pretty. Yet there was an air of wistfulness about her that again made Hope think of Randy Youngdeer, and her suspicion that there was some sort of problem between the two of them.

The root-beer float was delicious, augmented by a large scoop of vanilla ice cream. It brought back childhood memories to Hope of times when she and her father had gone to visit her grandfather up in New Hampshire. He'd been a remarkable old man—as strong as his son had been weak, Hope remembered ruefully—and the hours she'd spent with him were very precious to her. There hadn't been nearly enough of them.

She could remember him taking her into town for root-beer floats at a little ice-cream parlor with old-fashioned marble tables and wire chairs. She hadn't had a root-beer float since then.

She said something about this to Loretta Wood and Minerva Lightfoot, and Mrs. Lightfoot said rather sadly, "We can never equal the tastes of childhood. They are very special. That's why wherever the Cherokees travel they never forget the first ramps of spring, or bean bread—although both of these things would probably taste strange to you, Hope."

"Ramps?" Hope asked. "I don't think I've ever heard of them."

"They're one of the first greens we pick in the spring," Mrs. Lightfoot said. "Some people eat them raw, like salad, but there's an old Cherokee recipe that says you only do this if you're not 'social minded.' "

Wonder laughed. "What Mrs. Lightfoot means is that ramps taste good, but they don't exactly improve your breath. They're like garlic. They tend to be on the strong side."

Mrs. Lightfoot nodded. "Usually," she said, "we parboil them first and then fry them in a little grease. I have to admit that for me spring wouldn't be spring without ramps. But it's all a matter of custom—something you get used to." She laughed. "I always freeze some of my ramps, Hope, so I'll fix you up a dish of them one of these days, if you want to try them."

"I'd love to," Hope replied. Then she asked, "Do any of the restaurants in Cherokee serve Indian food?"

"No, they don't," Loretta Wood said. "Not with any regularity, anyway . . . unless there's a new place open I don't know about. I've often thought it would make an interesting enterprise for someone."

"There are annual feasts where Cherokee food is featured," Mrs. Lightfoot put in. "And actually, we eat a lot of Cherokee food ourselves. People are always asking me if we really eat the greens, the bean bread and the other things they've read about in some of the publications the museum puts out. I assure them that we do."

"True enough," Wonder Owl agreed. "As a matter of fact, I have a cousin who got married about six months ago, and she's just now learning to make what she considers 'American things,' like spaghetti. Her husband is white, and there's a limit to his tolerance of Cherokee cuisine as a daily diet!''

They all laughed at this, and Hope leaned back, feeling pleasantly relaxed. In the company of Wonder, Loretta Wood and Mrs. Lightfoot she had none of the dreadful feeling that she might do or say the wrong thing at any moment. It was only around Ross Adair that she felt so unsure of herself.

As if she possessed a genie's lamp and had just rubbed it, he suddenly appeared, coming around the side of the terrace and lightly vaulting up the steps.

''Minerva!'' he said first, spotting Mrs. Lightfoot. ''How great to see you!'' Then those disconcerting midnight eyes fastened upon Hope and he asked, ''How's my patient?''

Hope's voice seemed to stick in her throat, and it was Mrs. Wood who answered for her. ''She's doing quite well, I'd say.''

''And I see you're plying her with nourishment,'' Ross teased. ''Just don't spoil your appetite for dinner, Hope. A friend of mine gave me some magnificent brook trout he caught this afternoon, and I've decided I'm going to play chef tonight and cook for all of you.''

''Well!'' his aunt said, obviously surprised by this, but Ross was already turning to another topic.

''I stopped by and got your things from Penny,'' he told Hope. ''Your suitcase is in your bedroom, but I stashed all your painting equipment in the front-hall closet. Don't try to unpack by yourself, incidentally. When you want anything, I'll do it for you.''

"*I* could unpack for Hope," Wonder interposed.

Ross had favored her with a warm smile and a pat on the shoulder upon entering, and now he said, "That's a good idea. Why don't you get the basic unpacking out of the way before we have dinner?"

Hope was on her feet by the time he'd finished saying this, and it was all she could do not to rush back into the house. Wonder followed along behind her, and she had to force herself to slow down. The fact was that she badly needed to put some distance between Ross Adair and herself. And somehow, she told herself, she was going to have to do better than this. It was ridiculous to start virtually dissolving in front of him every time he appeared.

They reached the Fern Room, and Wonder, without being asked, closed the door behind her. Then she asked curiously, "What is it with you and Ross?"

"What do you mean?" Hope hedged.

"Something seemed to come over you right after he got here," Wonder observed. "And he...well, he's certainly trying to put his best foot forward. I have the feeling he painted a smile on his face—and that's not like Ross."

"What *is* like Ross?"

"He's a difficult person to describe, Hope," Wonder said, "or to define. Randy might be able to do a better job of it than I can. He knows Ross better. They went to high school together—the one in Sylva, not the one on the reservation. Aunt Loretta liked the school system there better, and I guess Randy's family felt the same way. Anyway, they used to make the trip every day, and it's a pretty long ride. Then, of course, once they'd graduated Randy came back here and went to work at the service station. He's part owner of it now. Randy has plenty of his own kind of ambition. Nothing like Ross, of course. But I often think that Ross got a good deal of his incentive because of Lamanda.''

"Who's Lamanda?" Hope asked quickly, and then wondered if she really wanted to know.

"Aunt Loretta's daughter," Wonder said. "You may have guessed it...this was her room. The Fern Room."

"Ross's cousin, then?" Hope asked, but Wonder shook her head.

"No," she said. "Lamanda was Ross's wife."

The whole world seemed to go out of focus. With eyes suddenly gone blank, Hope stared at the lovely Indian woman, and her throat was sandpaper dry.

"He was married...to his c-cousin?" she stammered.

"Lamanda wasn't his cousin," Wonder said. "Not really. She was Aunt Loretta's daughter by a previous marriage. Her first husband died when Lamanda was just a little girl. Then, not too long after that she married Ross's uncle—his mother's brother. Lamanda was just a couple of years younger than Ross. You could say that they grew up together. Anyway, Ross's mother had died when he was a baby, so he always spent a lot of time over here with the Wood family. His father never did marry again, and Ross was the only child. A lonely child, too, the way Randy tells it. I guess he always was a...loner. He never seemed to trust people—except for Lamanda, first, and then Randy, once they got to know each other in school.''

"And Ross and Lamanda were...were married?'' Hope had to force out the question.

"Yes. They were just kids. That is, he was in medical school, and she was living back here in Cherokee with her parents. Lamanda always wanted to be an actress. She used to act in the drama every year, but she was never very strong. For one thing, you see,'' Wonder said slowly, "she was diabetic.''

Wonder said this as if it should have some significance, but Hope couldn't fathom what she was getting at and only shook her head helplessly.

"When Lamanda died,'' Wonder went on after a moment, "Ross made up his mind to devote his life to trying to do something about diabetes. He's come a long way in his profession, and we're all very proud of him.''

"But today,'' Hope said, trying to piece all of this together, "he brought me here to his aunt's house and put me in...this room. His wife's room....''

"Yes, that's true. And no one has used it since Lamanda lived here.'' Wonder paused and took a deep breath. "She's been dead for more than ten years, Hope. What I mean to say is, it's been a long time, so Ross....''

Hope found that her legs were trembling, and she sat down on the edge of the bed, wishing she could hide her head in both hands. But just now that wasn't possible because of the sling.

Wonder said, "You look awful, Hope! Ross would thrash me if he knew I'd told you all this. My family always said they should have named me Chatterbox Owl instead of Wonder Owl, and I'm afraid they're right. I should have let Ross tell you what he felt you should know. . . when the time is right."

"When what time is right?" Hope demanded dully.

"Ross would have to answer that," Wonder said practically, "but I'd say he'd want you to know everything there is to know. Obviously you must mean a great deal to him."

"I don't know why you should think that."

"Because he wouldn't have brought you to this house if you didn't. Also. . . well, I hope you won't take offense to my saying this, but I don't think Ross has ever been seen with a non-Indian woman here in Cherokee. I'm sure it's different in Boston. He must have many non-Indian friends there, both men and women. That's where you met him, isn't it?"

"In Boston?" Hope asked. "No. What made you think that?"

"Randy thinks so. He said when he walked in on you two the other afternoon he was sure you knew each other—and were just pretending to be strangers. He said he could feel the sparks flying."

"I'm sure he could," Hope conceded. "But I'm afraid they were sparks of antagonism! Ross did not exactly take a liking to me at first sight. And that really *was* his first sight of me, Wonder."

"Then why did he bring you to stay in his house?"

"I don't know. Maybe it was a sudden overdose of the milk of human kindness."

"From Ross?" Wonder demanded skeptically.

Before she could say anything further there was a knock on the door. Then the subject of their discussion called out, "Are you going to take all night? She couldn't have had that much in one suitcase, even though I admit it was a large one."

"Hope is just getting into something more comfortable," Wonder fibbed, and then added in a voice that approached a stage whisper, "You do have something more comfortable with you, don't you?"

"Yes," Hope nodded. "A caftan."

At this, Wonder got busy with the unpacking and for the next few minutes stashed things in dresser drawers and hung other things in a closet while Hope watched, feeling very helpless. She was also possessed by the sensation that they were intruders, both of them. Trespassers in a room that had belonged to the tragic young woman who had been Ross Adair's wife.

How could she possibly stay here in Lamanda's room, Hope asked herself, and then realized she was confronted by an even more urgent question. How, while still in the grip of Wonder's revelation to her, could she possibly face Ross Adair himself?

CHAPTER EIGHT

THE CAFTAN WAS a hyacinth blue, a lovely shade, close to the color of Hope's eyes. Usually, wearing this color gave her a good feeling. But tonight, she thought morosely, nothing could give her a good feeling about herself or anything else.

Dinner was delicious, though. Her palate told her that, although she wouldn't have cared, really, if she'd been eating sawdust. Ross had broiled the brook trout to succulent perfection, and with it they had fresh greens and a delicious spoon bread baked by Mrs. Wood.

Minerva Lightfoot had left, but Wonder had been invited to stay to dinner, and for this Hope was grateful. Anything to prevent having to be alone with Ross...or having to go back to what she now regarded as solitary confinement in Lamanda's room.

To her surprise, Ross served a chilled white wine with their dinner. It complemented the fish perfectly, and when he moved to pour her a second glass she did not protest. She was aware that he'd noticed her expression when he'd first put the bottle on the table, and his eyebrows had arched in a devastatingly cynical manner.

Nevertheless, because of Ross's discussion with her about alcoholism and the fact that the sale of alcoholic beverages was forbidden on the reservation, she had assumed that Indians did not drink, generally speaking. Actually, she had imagined that drinking alcohol was considered to be an illness, rather than something one did socially.

She broke her thoughts off midway, aware that Ross was giving her what she could only consider a long, hard look. And as if to mock her, he raised his wineglass and said, *"A siyu!"*

Hope thought for a moment that Wonder was going to choke, but she herself was interested by just the tone of these two words, obviously a toast. Ross added another phrase that she couldn't distinguish at all, but again there was an unusual cadence to it. The words he was saying were somewhat guttural in intonation, and yet they sounded very pleasing. Where had she heard something similar before? The answer came to her as quickly as the question had: at the Cherokee Museum, when she'd plugged in a headset and listened to the recording of "Mary Had a Little Lamb" in Cherokee.

"I'm afraid I don't understand you," she said now with a faint smile.

"I was speaking in Kituhwa," Ross answered. "It is the middle dialect of the Cherokee language, which is the tongue used by my people."

"The middle dialect?"

"There were originally three Cherokee dialects," Ross explained. "The Eastern one, called Elati, is now extinct. The Western one, Atali, is spoken by the Cherokees who live in Oklahoma. You may re-member that they were the ones who did not manage to hide in the mountains at the time of the Trail of Tears,'' he added.

This time, Wonder actually did sputter and cough. "Honestly, Ross," she protested.

"What is it, Wonder?" he asked with deceptive mildness. "You must realize that Hope has a great curiosity about us. Like all other Indians, Hope, they now say that the Cherokees—I should say our ancestors, of course—came to this continent from Asia, making their pilgrimage over a narrow strip of land that has since been covered by the waters of the Bering Strait. The Cherokees and the Iro-quois—who settled in the North—are brothers under the skin. That's to say that originally we were all part of the same general tribe.''

Wonder was looking at Ross curiously. "Aren't you going to tell Hope that both the Cherokees and the Iroquois were known for their terrific phy-siques?'' she teased. "The men, I mean! They were taller than most Indians and very strong.''

"True," Ross nodded, refusing to be ruffled. "The Cherokees came south and established their hunting grounds over territory that now comprises eight states. Theirs became the greatest empire of all the Southeastern Indian tribes. De Soto was the first white man ever to visit these parts, and when he came into Cherokee country in 1540 we had a population of approximately 25,000.''

"25,000 people...in 1540?" Hope reflected.

"That's right. And I might say that de Soto's invasion of our world marked the end of many things even before the famous Trail of Tears. There was disease, to give one example. Nearly half of the entire Cherokee population died from smallpox in 1738."

It was Loretta Wood who protested this time. "Really, Ross!" she said sharply.

Ross stood. "I shall have to leave you ladies," he said, at least feigning regret. "I'm a bit behind in my work and I'll have to burn some of the old midnight oil to get caught up."

"Don't push it too hard, Ross," Wonder said unexpectedly.

He was sliding his chair back into place at the table, and he paused to ask, "Push what, Wonder?"

"Your work, of course. What else?"

Ross didn't answer. He moved to Loretta's side and bent to kiss her lightly on the forehead. Then, as he straightened, he looked directly at Hope, too quickly for her to avert her gaze.

Their eyes meshed, and Hope felt as if he'd clutched her physically. Those dark eyes of his were so compelling that it was as if she were being drawn by a strong magnetic force, and she found she could not look away. She could only stare back at him weakly, and suddenly an unsolicited tremor of sensation coursed through her body so acutely that she actually reached out and grabbed the edge of the table.

When he spoke, though, it was to say in an entirely level tone of voice, "I think you should call it a day, Hope. Time for your medication, I'd say."

"I want to help with the cleaning up first," she told him. "Then I'll take it and go to bed."

He shook his head firmly. "Now," he contradicted, with an authority that was obviously accustomed to being obeyed without question.

"Ross...."

"Now!" he repeated.

Loretta Wood laughed. "You might as well go along with him, Hope," she said. "Wonder will help me, won't you, dear? And anyway, there isn't that much to do. The dishwasher does most of the work."

"Come along," Ross said, and to her consternation he came around to her side of the table and helped her to her feet before she could protest.

As they walked down the hall to the Fern Room together, Hope was so intensely aware of his nearness that she felt as if every nerve in her body was quivering. He was walking slightly behind her, but he was so close that if she stopped she knew they'd bump into each other, and the mere thought of this happening caused her to shudder. The idea of him touching her, touching her in any way, was so provocative that—

Hope tried to block out these conjectures, these fantasies, but proximity to Ross Adair was stirring her to a sexual awareness she'd never experienced with Lewis.

Lewis. There was nothing overwhelming about the story of Lewis and her. Hope was only now beginning to realize that. It was no great tragedy, though she'd been hurt deeply by him. She and her father had been visiting friends on Cape Cod the weekend her father had drowned, and Lewis had been renting a cottage farther down the beach. It was he who had dragged her father out of the water. He knew cardiopulmonary resuscitation and had started in immediately in an attempt to resuscitate the older man, and for that Hope would always be grateful. It was comforting to know that everything that could have been done for her father had been done.

Later Lewis had driven her to the hospital—they had followed the local rescue squad—and had been with her at the terrible moment when she'd been told that her father was dead. Over the next few days, he had been wonderful to her. He had stayed by her side and had helped her through so much that it seemed impossible he was virtually a stranger and that she knew almost nothing about him.

The funeral had been in Concord, and Lewis had driven her up from the Cape. Afterward they had gone back to the Colonial-style house where Hope and her father had lived. She'd been consumed by loneliness and had invited Lewis in, and later that night it had seemed perfectly natural when Lewis had suggested that he stay with her. It also had seemed natural to go into his arms in the small hours of the morning, expending her grief in tears, a torrent that had threatened to go on forever. She had been surprisingly inexperienced in her relationships with men, she could see that now. But Lewis's expertise had made up for both of them. He had been gentle, and looking back she had to admit that she'd put up little resistance, even though she'd experienced the minimum of pleasure in the resulting act.

Lewis was the first man in her life—the only man in her life to date, she thought wryly. The week after her father's funeral she had gone back down to the Cape with him at his insistence, and she had lived with him for the next five days. This period remained a blur in Hope's mind. She had been so grief stricken that it had been easy to be grateful to Lewis and to respond to a little kindness.

Lewis was a writer, working on his first novel, and at his suggestion Hope had read a couple of chapters of his manuscript. She'd found it dull and lifeless and had been hard pressed to compliment him about it. Looking back, though, she realized that Lewis had been possessed of enough conceit that it really hadn't mattered what she'd said. He'd simply wanted an audience.

On the sixth morning, his wife had walked in the front door and down the hall and into the bedroom...and Hope would never forget the shame that had come to infiltrate every pore in her body. Lewis had carried off the situation much better than she had. So had his wife, for that matter. To Hope, the degradation had been complete, and she could not wait to get away, to catch the first bus back to Boston.

For the next month, Lewis had phoned her and tried to see her, but she had refused to listen to his explanations. He had written her, saying that he and his wife had already separated before he'd gone to the Cape. They had a "business arrangement," he'd said. She'd been financing him while he wrote his novel, and that was all there was to it. It was over between them now, and they were going to get a divorce.

But Hope had been too stung to believe this. Many times during that dreadful period she had thought of calling her mother. She'd even thought of going to see her and telling her the whole sordid little story. But Barbara Standish would not understand—of that her daughter was sure. Barbara Standish had little compassion for weakness. She had proved this decisively in the case of her own husband. No, she would never understand. She wouldn't allow herself to understand. Even to Hope, the affair with Lewis had uncovered a weakness in her own character that she'd never suspected and that appalled her. She couldn't blame her mother if she reacted in the same way.

Fall came, and she started teaching art in the same school where her father had been a literature teacher. So the months went by, one year passing into another. But she still felt clouded by the memory of her affair with Lewis, brief though it had been.

"Hope!" the man at her elbow said urgently. "What the hell are you thinking about?" He had moved up so that they were side by side, and he was frowning as he peered down into her face.

"Nothing," she fibbed.

"A strange sort of nothing," he said tautly. "You look as if you're in the throes of a nightmare. What is it?"

"Nothing, really," she said again.

"None of my business, is that?" Ross growled. "You have a very lofty way of trying to put someone in his place, haven't you?"

"I wasn't trying to put you in your place at all."

"No? Well, I'm sure I don't know *what* it is you're trying to do to me, Hope. But we won't get into that. If you wanted to stay up longer all you had to do was say so. It's just that I didn't want you fooling around in the kitchen trying to help Aunt Loretta with that arm of yours. All you'd have to do is stumble on something and—"

"I don't usually fall over my own feet, Ross," she said coolly.

"You merely trip over your own tongue, is that it?" he countered.

They had come to the end of the hall. Turning to face him, Hope was surprised to see that he was obviously tense. For a moment she could only stare. Then she said slowly, "I wasn't aware that I've been tripping over my own tongue."

"It's been for a good reason," he told her ironically. "You've been so afraid of saying the wrong thing that you've bottled your feelings up. Are you always like this? I mean, is it some sort of neurosis with you? Or is it merely the way you react to this environment you find yourself living in?"

Hope tilted her chin defiantly. "Neither," she said. "Doesn't it occur to you it might be because you're so perverse I don't know what to say to you?" She expelled a long breath as she finished this statement, then straightened as if to do battle with him. But again he surprised her.

"You make quite a warrior in that caftan, with your arm in a sling," he chided lightly, that glint of humor in his eyes. "I think you'd better wait until you can use both hands before you get yourself in a real conflict with me! In the meantime, why don't we try a symbolical peace pipe instead?"

Ross's tone was oddly husky as he finished speaking, and he drew Hope to him very gently, careful not to press against her injured shoulder. As their lips met, the depth of his kiss sent a rocket of desire soaring not upward but inward. Fireworks exploded inside her in secret places she'd never known about, and Hope, silently surrendering, gave herself up to him...not as she would have wished to, because of the cumbersome arm, but with a spirit that transcended her present physical limitations. Without even realizing what she was doing she raised her good right hand and touched the midnight velvet hair that intrigued her so. It was as soft, as wonderful to feel as she had imagined it would be. Then she cupped her hand around the back of Ross's head and drew him toward her again, this time inviting him with her own lips until the resulting kiss between them became fired with promise.

It seemed to Hope that she drowned in the kiss that followed, nor did she ever want to come up for air. She was immersed in Ross Adair, the pinewood scent of him, the strong resilient strength of him. Yet after a moment he stepped back, and gripping her good arm he looked down at her. Desperately she tried to read his face and couldn't. Then he sighed, and for just an instant she saw unexpected sorrow in his eyes and a weariness that struck out at her.

They were at the door of the Fern Room, and it was impossible not to remember Lamanda. In fact, Hope couldn't imagine how she had managed to forget Lamanda. Yet she had. For a few minutes she had forgotten everything except Ross Adair—and the tantalizing passion he evoked in her.

She sagged, and again he was too discerning. "What is it, Hope?" he asked quickly. Then he added, accusing himself, "I've hurt you!"

"No, Ross," she assured him. "You haven't hurt me."

"Well, at the least it's time for you to quit," he said unsteadily. "And for me to get to work."

Hope drew a deep breath and tried to veer away from the personal. "Where do you work? At the hospital?" she asked him.

"Some of the time, yes," he answered. "But I've set up a study here in the house for most of the paperwork. It does very well. Just a question of making myself get down to details," he added wryly.

Was he implying that she was a distraction to him? Hope wondered about this, quickly deciding that even if it were true, she could not feel in the least guilty. Rather, she wished she had the power to distract him totally from everything else in his world for a long, long time.

Quietly he asked, "Need some help getting ready for bed?"

Hope shivered as she thought of what might happen should she accept this offer, but when she didn't answer him immediately he said with a trace of irritation, "I wasn't going to suggest that I undress you personally. Or. . . ." He paused, and she knew he was being deliberately provocative. "Would you like me to?"

Hope tried to be cool as she faced him. "What am I supposed to say to that?" she asked. "One minute you accuse me of being so afraid of saying the wrong thing to you that I trip over my own tongue, and the next minute you try to provoke me into—"

"Into what, Hope?" he interrupted.

"Oh, Ross!" she exploded, and was caught short when suddenly he smiled. The impact of his smile, in fact, was too much for her. It caught her midway between laughter and tears and she turned toward the door of the Fern Room, knowing only that she had better get away from him. No more sparring, not tonight. Neither physically nor emotionally was she up to it.

Ross started to say something, but he didn't get very far. Evidently he thought better of whatever it was, because before he even uttered the first word, he shrugged. "Look," he said, "I'm going to get Wonder to come and help you. You'll be able to manage in a few days, but right now I realize it's a bit difficult to function on a one-armed basis."

"Yes, it really is," she answered.

He nodded and leaned toward her. "Good night, Hope," he murmured. "Try to sleep well."

His lips brushed her forehead swiftly but with a tenderness that brought stinging tears to her eyes. She turned away without speaking, not wanting him to see the tears, for she was afraid that if he did he might follow her into the Fern Room, and right now she couldn't bear the thought of being in this room with him. It was Lamanda's room. It would always be Lamanda's room.

Hope sat down disconsolately on the edge of the bed. Her shoulder was aching, and the brace was awkward and constricting. Ross was right. It would have been miserable to attempt to embark on a long bus ride wearing this thing.

But as it was, she felt so helpless. . . and this was a feeling she detested. She had yielded to helplessness only once before in her life, when she had turned to Lewis for solace. She'd got solace—and a lot more than that, she thought bitterly. She'd learned a lesson about men that she would never forget.

Yet common sense surfaced to tell her that just because Lewis had been dishonorable didn't mean that every other man would act as he had.

It was Lewis who really had been the weak one in their relationship. Hope was only now beginning to see this, and she could also see that Lewis had indeed taken advantage of her in the fullest sense of the old cliché phrase, reaching her in a highly emotional moment when she'd felt totally alone in the world and was reaching, herself, for warmth, compassion and affection.

How different it would have been if Ross had been there, she found herself thinking.

"You wanted me?" Wonder asked, coming into the room.

Hope jumped, startled. "Oh, it's you, Wonder," she said, trying to smile. "I'm so awkward with this brace. If you could just help me get the caftan off...."

"No sooner said than done," Wonder promised, and in very little time Hope had changed into a nightgown and washed her face and brushed her teeth. Then she sat on a straight-backed wooden chair while Wonder brushed out her hair with slow, even strokes.

"It's like spun gold," Wonder said admiringly.

Hope laughed, and she found herself saying, "Ross's hair is like black velvet. Yours is more like satin. But—" She broke off abruptly, horrified at herself.

Wonder stopped brushing, and there was a moment of silence between them before she resumed stroking. Then she said, "You're right. Ross does have gorgeous hair. But then, he's a pretty gorgeous man, wouldn't you say? As you can imagine, there was a time when half the women in Cherokee were after him. Or looking for a significant glance in their direction, at the very least. I'm afraid that went for me, too," Wonder admitted. She giggled. "I have a cousin who was madly in love with Ross when they were in high school together," she confided. "She's a nurse at the Cherokee Hospital now, and she says that whenever she's on duty and he's around her heart still does a flip-flop, even though she's been happily married for years. I'm younger, of course. I was in grade school when Ross went off to college. But I remember the whole thing. . . with Lamanda, that is.''

There was that name again, a gentle ghost hovering between them. "Was Lamanda very beautiful?'' Hope asked.

"She was lovely,'' Wonder said honestly. "She was half Cherokee—Loretta's first husband was white. So Lamanda had Indian features but gorgeous gray eyes. Quite an arresting contrast. I was only fourteen when she died, but I can remember what a dreadfully sad time it was. Deep winter. Ross was at the medical college in Richmond, Virginia, and of course he came home for the funeral. He was like a stone man walking around. He didn't speak to anyone. He didn't even seem to see people. His father was alive then, but he never could reach Ross. They were never close to each other. But his uncle—this is Loretta's second husband I'm talking about—was alive then, too, and he and Ross were always very close. We all called Mr. Wood 'Uncle Cal.' I guess he really was a distant cousin of mine on my mother's side, so I suppose you could say Ross and I are related, as well.

"Anyway, it was Mr. Wood who had a lot to do with Ross's upbringing, because Mr. Adair was always very much involved in council affairs. He used to go to Washington for different causes the Cherokees were dealing with, that sort of thing. Mr. Wood taught Ross how to fish and how to track through the woods. He taught him a great deal about nature, and as you know, our people have always been very close to nature. We have a great respect for everything that lives, everything that grows.''

"Ross's father never married again?" Hope asked.

Wonder shook her head. "Never. His wife had left him for another man just before she died, and even though Ross was only a baby when it happened, I think his father managed to instill a distrust of women in him that I don't think even Lamanda was able to make him forget.''

Wonder put the hairbrush on the dresser and then hung up the caftan Hope had been wearing. "Well," she said, "would you like anything before I go home? Want me to bring you in a glass of milk or something?''

"No, thanks," Hope said, her thoughts spinning. But she managed to add warmly, "You've been terrific, Wonder. I really appreciate it.''

"I'll be back tomorrow," her friend promised. Then, at the doorway, she stopped. "You know I told you my family is always saying I talk too much. I think maybe I've talked too much to you tonight about...about certain things. Maybe we should have taken it in easier installments! Anyway, Hope, keep one thing in mind, will you?''

"What's that?"

"You're good for Ross," Wonder said. And with this she went out, closing the door behind her.

Hope was very tired. For one thing, the accident and its aftermath had taken quite a toll on her. And Wonder's revelations about Ross and Lamanda had been a lot to handle in her present, much too precarious emotional condition.

So although she craved sleep, it eluded her for most of the night. She was conscious of moonlight filtering through the windows, etching the graceful patterns of ferns on the wallpaper. She'd never placed much stock in ghosts, but now she wondered if, sometimes, spirits did come back to haunt the living, and the idea made her shiver.

How would Lamanda feel about her?

Hope knew that if Ross Adair were *her* husband she did not believe she could ever let him go, either in life—or in death. And if there was such a thing as love beyond the grave, theirs would survive. It would last through eternity.

She thought of eternity as a long, rose-lined tunnel that went on and on and on. And as she started to wend her way through it, negotiating maze after maze and turn after turn, she finally fell asleep.

CHAPTER NINE

WHEN HOPE AWAKENED the next morning the first thing she was conscious of was the fresh pine fragrance that wafted through the open windows, and the association she made with the scent was inevitable. For that matter, although she couldn't remember exactly what her dreams had involved, she knew that Ross Adair had been a central figure in all of them. She also knew that they had not been happy dreams. Even now, facing the glory of this new June day, she felt an oppressive sense of sadness.

The house was very still, and she wondered if Ross was already at work in his improvised study. She also wondered how she could face him again and be casual about it. This effect that he had on her was totally unnerving, and she only wished that she could match a fraction of the cool front he seemed able to don whenever he wanted to.

She'd heard that sometimes people who'd suffered a great tragedy were never able to really love again. Would Ross ever love another woman the way he'd evidently loved Lamanda? Certainly her death must have had a tremendous effect on him. Its impact had been so great that he had decided to devote the rest of his life to studying the disease that had killed her.

As Hope slowly dressed, it seemed to her that there was an innate loneliness to Ross's quest. Even the thought of him at work in his study, doing research well into the early hours of the morning, presented the picture of a very solitary figure.

Yet Wonder said it had been ten years since Lamanda had died. In the meantime, Ross had lived out his twenties and now was almost in his mid-thirties. Was it possible his emotions had never really been touched by another woman during all those years?

Such conjecture was really pointless, Hope told herself curtly as she managed to brush out her hair to a semblance of order. She then added a touch of pink gloss to her lips, and although her mirror told her that she was still very pale, she didn't look nearly as wan as she had yesterday. A good night's sleep here in this lovely room had done quite a bit to restore her.

And there had been no ghosts. Nothing had interfered with her slumber except for those dreams of Ross, which had been as disturbing as everything else about him. Hope wished she could remember exactly what had taken place in them—if only to better understand herself. She had no illusion about her dreams giving any clue as to how she might better understand Ross Adair.

She opened the door slowly and started down the hall, noticing that the other doors were all closed. One of them, certainly, must lead to Ross's room, for although no one had actually said so, Hope was sure that he was living here at present. What would be the point to working in Loretta Wood's house and then leaving at all hours to go somewhere where only a bed for the night was offered.

Unless there was someplace here in Cherokee where Ross was being offered more than just a bed! Hope thought about this and frowned. Maybe he had revived a relationship with someone he'd known years ago. A Cherokee woman, perhaps. It would be a likely thing for him to do, wouldn't it?

Such thoughts will get you nowhere, Hope warned herself sternly. And as she continued on her way down the hall she turned her attention to the matter of Ross's relationship with Wonder Owl. There seemed to be a genuine affection between the two of them, but Ross acted more like a brother to Wonder than a potential lover. And Wonder, although she admitted to a childhood crush on him, hadn't displayed even the trace of a desire for anything more than friendship.

No, Wonder Owl was involved in some way with Randy Youngdeer. The more Hope thought about this, the more she was sure of it. But there was obviously some sort of stumbling block in their path.

Now you're becoming downright psychic, Hope nearly spoke the words aloud as she walked into Loretta Wood's lovely living room. She felt irritated with herself for not being able to get Ross Adair—and everyone who touched upon him—out of her mind.

Despite the quiet in the house she more than half

expected to find Mrs. Wood in the living room or else on the terrace, visible through a row of windows. But both were empty, so Hope retraced her steps to the kitchen and immediately spied a note, which had been propped up on the counter where she could hardly fail to miss it.

Loretta Wood had written:

I've gone up to the village to do some of the beadwork Ross was teasing me about yesterday. Ross left early this morning to have some on-the-spot sessions with some of the people who live in the more remote areas of the reservation, so we probably won't see him for the next couple of days. You'll find wild-blueberry muffins keeping warm in the oven and coffee in the percolator, and Ross suggested that you spend the morning lying out on the terrace and taking it easy. Wonder will be over to fix lunch for you.

Ross left early this morning...so we probably won't see him for the next couple of days. Those were the words that seemed to leap out from all the rest, and Hope felt a pang of loss that was astounding. Why did the fact that she wouldn't be seeing someone for a few days, someone who was still a stranger to her, bother her so much?

But Ross wasn't just someone, and the thought of his absence did bother her. It bothered her acutely. Why hadn't he mentioned to her last night that he'd be going away for a while? He could have told her, if only so that she'd have her medical instructions to carry out in his absence.

"Child!" Hope did say this aloud, and then added silently that she'd be apt to start pouting if she kept pursuing her present line of thought. So she set about putting her breakfast together, which was fairly easy to do. Loretta Wood had wrapped the blueberry muffins in foil, having buttered them first, and it was a simple task to pour a cup of steaming hot coffee and add a little cream to it. The wonderful smell of the coffee alone was enough to perk up her spirits.

Hope settled in at the round kitchen table and was again surprised at her appetite. She knew that the mountain air was partially responsible for this, but also she seldom had such fare as fresh-baked muffins and "real" coffee. Living by herself in Concord she'd come to rely on instant coffee and convenience foods, even though she liked to cook when she could find the time—and the inspiration.

She had a sudden vision of preparing a gourmet dinner for two in a romantic, candlelit room. *Just for me and Ross Adair,* she imagined dreamily, and had to laugh at herself because she was thinking like an adolescent schoolgirl.

Breakfast finished, she managed to wash the dishes without breaking anything. It was hard to be other than clumsy these days. Then she went back to her room and gathered up some of the literature she'd bought at the museum. Carrying this with her good arm she went out on the terrace, anointed herself with some suntan cream and let the peace of the place wash over her. The scent of the flowers and the fragrant pines was almost overwhelming, as was the sight of those magnificent mountains, forever in the background.

The Great Smokies. Hope viewed them with a new appreciation, having been enlightened about their history. A long time ago, those mountains had harbored the Cherokees who had managed to escape from their captors during the terrible Trail of Tears. Ross's ancestors had been among those Cherokees, and but for their daring and their ingenuity in keeping body and soul together as they hid out in the mountains, there would be no Cherokees in North Carolina today. Very likely, there would be no Ross Adair.

This was an overwhelming thought, the kind of thought that led from one idea to the next in an attempt to make sense of the complex threads that weave together the tapestry of life.

Hope selected one of her booklets and was soon absorbed in this account of the Cherokees. Four thousand of them, she learned, had died during the course of the Trail of Tears from 1838 to 1839. Several years later a white man, an Indian trader named Colonel William Thomas, befriended those Indians who had lived in hiding in the Great Smokies. Hope remembered his name from one of the presentations at the museum. He bought land for various individuals and held it in his own name for them, and he continued to hold this land for the Cherokees while they lived on it and developed it. Then, when he was elected a United States senator, he became instrumental in getting laws passed through Congress whereby the Cherokees were granted United States citizenship. After that, they were legally entitled to own land of their own.

This wasn't the end of their problems, though. Hope read on, appalled by the many unfortunate things that had continued to happen to these people over the years. It was not until 1875 that the Qualla Boundary was established and the Cherokee lands were really secured, and not until 1889 that the rights of the Cherokees were legally established by the North Carolina legislature, and the Eastern Band of Cherokees was formed. In the meantime, life for the Cherokees had been a constant struggle.

In more recent years, Ross's father had evidently been very active in civil matters involving the Eastern Band. Hope remembered Wonder saying something to this effect. Just as Ross was putting his energy—and his heart—into medical research, so had his father put all of his effort into bettering conditions among his people.

Still, there were many, many gaps to be filled in about the Cherokees, about Ross and about his family. Hope also wished she could learn more about Lamanda without being openly curious. This was a subject she could not bring up with Loretta Wood, even though Loretta was obviously a warm, open-minded person. Lamanda, after all, had been her daughter. Her only child, in fact. To ask questions about her might only incur the danger of opening up some very painful emotional wounds.

Hope put aside the booklet she was reading and

closed her eyes. There was a great deal to think about, so much that she wanted to know and understand. In comparison, giving up the trip through the Great Smokies with Lorna Evans did not seem very important. Even the memory of that awful time with Emily Collingworth in Asheville could be dismissed under the heading of one more chapter in life she didn't want to repeat. And Lewis—well, memories of Lewis, she realized with some surprise, could be relegated to that same category.

HOPE HAD NEVER been one for taking naps, but this morning she was lulled into sleep by the beauty of her environment. That, plus the natural toll sudden trauma takes on the human system. She slipped into a light sleep and awakened only when she heard Wonder Owl say, "You're going to be as red as a lobster if you don't watch out!"

Hope opened her eyes to see Wonder standing next to the deck chair she was lying on, looking down at her anxiously. Wonder wore blue denim shorts today and a white blouse with very colorful embroidery on it, the outfit emphasizing her lovely figure. She also wore a broad-brimmed straw hat tilted back on her head, and the whole effect was totally charming.

The thought crossed Hope's mind: *how can Ross Adair keep himself from falling in love with her?*

"Really, Hope," Wonder said. "If Ross comes back and finds you burned to a crisp Aunt Loretta and I will both get the full brunt of his wrath, which can be considerable, let me tell you. I made up my mind some time ago that I never want to be in the way when Ross flies off in a rage!"

Hope could not repress a smile. "That bad?" she asked.

"That bad," Wonder said firmly. She took off her hat and held it out. "Here," she said, "put this on. At least your face will get some shade. The hat will look better on you than it does on me anyway."

"I doubt that," Hope said sincerely. Nevertheless, she did what the Indian woman asked.

"Definitely, it looks better on you," Wonder decided, nodding. Then she added, "I'm going in to get us both some iced tea."

Left alone, Hope could not help but speculate about what Wonder had just said. Why would Ross be so angry with her and his aunt if they allowed Hope to get sunburned? Certainly his professional reputation wasn't at stake. If a patient were so foolish as to lie out in the sun too long, it would hardly reflect on the doctor on the case.

She suspected that Wonder was of a somewhat romantic turn of mind. But then it did seem to her that both Wonder and Loretta Wood were glad to see Ross interested in her. The implication was not only that Ross had always tended to be a loner but that—since Lamanda's death, perhaps—he had led a very lonely life, despite his professional success. With his good looks, though, and the charm he obviously could summon quite readily when he wanted to, the kind of life he was leading must be of his own choice. Ross, Hope felt sure, could lead any kind of life he wanted to. He must have deliberately chosen a solo path, and obviously he didn't want a woman at his side on any permanent basis. It was as if he inherently distrusted women. Or was it that he had been so "burned" by at least one of her sex, Hope wondered, that he had become deeply embittered?

Wonder was carrying a tray on which there were two frosty glasses of iced tea and a plate of molasses cookies, and as she put it down she asked, "Why so glum? Is your shoulder bothering you very much?"

"Not really," Hope answered, which was true enough.

"Boredom setting in, then?" Wonder asked sympathetically. "I know it's hard to be inactive. Forced leisure is never much fun. When Ross gets back, though, maybe he'll let you broaden your horizons a bit. I'm sure Randy would let us borrow Betsy, and I could do the driving. There's nothing all that exciting here on the reservation, but there are some pretty places I can show you. And we could visit the village and some of the other things around here that you haven't seen yet."

"Perhaps the reservation isn't exciting to you," Hope pointed out, "but it is to me. How big is it, anyway?"

"I can tell you that exactly," Wonder said with a smile, "because the figure impressed itself on my mind when I was in grade school. I think I learned it because I was never too good at math, and I had the idea that memorizing statistics might help. Anyway, the reservation encompasses 56,573 acres. And most of them, as you know from driving around here, are very mountainous."

"And the Cherokees themselves own the land?"

"The Cherokees hold what are called 'possessory rights' to the land," Wonder explained, "but actually the federal government holds the deeds. They're kept in trust for us, and I should tell you that there is nothing arbitrary in their doing this."

"Why's that?" Hope asked curiously.

"Well," Wonder continued, "in 1924 the Tribal Council petitioned Washington to do this for our own benefit, and the effect is very much the same as if we held the deeds ourselves. For instance, we can buy and sell property among ourselves, although we have to have the consent of the Tribal Council to do so. The main thing is that non-Indians can't buy property on the reservation. That's how we're protected. Of course, other people can lease from the Cherokees and run businesses here. In fact, quite a few of the local businesses are operated by non-Indians."

"And that works out well?"

"It works out fine," Wonder said. "In a small place like this you'd hear about any trouble, believe me."

"I know," Hope agreed. "It seems a lot like New England!"

Wonder laughed. "That's not the only thing that might remind you of New England," she said. "Take the Tribal Council, for example. The way the Tribal Council works is very democratic, and basically it goes back to the kind of government we've always had among ourselves. The chief of the tribe is elected every four years, and the members of the council hold two-year terms. There are regular meetings, just like in any government organization, and from what I learned in school of your New England town meetings I'd say our ways aren't too different. The Federal Bureau of Indian Affairs works very cooperatively with the Tribal Council, and then we also have the Cherokee Indian Agency. It has jurisdiction over the administration of affairs here on the reservation, it maintains the school system, and so on. Incidentally, that date I'm planning at the Leisure Inn for you and Randy and myself involves a fourth, as you might have guessed.''

Hope almost asked if the fourth was going to be Ross, then was glad she hadn't spoken when Wonder went on to say, "He works at the Bureau of Indian Affairs office. A very nice guy. About our age, maybe a couple of years older. He's from California.''

"An Indian?" Hope asked without thinking.

Wonder looked faintly surprised, but she said only, "No, he's white. His name is David Ford. I think the two of you might get on well together. But again, Ross—''

Wonder didn't finish whatever it was she had started to say about Ross because just then a telephone inside the house started pealing, and she went to answer it.

When she came back she was frowning. "A call for Ross from Boston,'' she said.

"His hospital?" Hope said quickly.

"No. At least, I don't think so. I asked if I could take a message and she said she'd try again. She didn't even give me time to tell her that I don't know just when Ross is planning to come back."

She! Hope felt a dull thud echo in the general region of her heart and tried to fight off the ridiculously unhappy feeling that threatened to engulf her.

"Does Ross often go off to other parts of the reservation like this?" she inquired.

Wonder shook her head. "No, he doesn't. I think this is the first time, matter of fact. I'm sure he's had it on his agenda, though. Ross is very meticulous about his work. And of course this study is something he's really dedicated to. He'll do a good job on it." She hesitated briefly. "He wants to reach some of the older people who live in really remote places. Would you believe that some of them—not very many, but some—don't even speak English."

"And Ross speaks Cherokee that well?"

"Yes," Wonder nodded. "He speaks it quite well. He and Uncle Cal used to rattle off to each other in Cherokee when they wanted to tease me. It always made me furious."

"You don't speak Cherokee, then?"

"Very little," Wonder admitted. "Frankly, not too many of the younger people are much for keeping up the language. Every now and then, attempts are made to revive it. They talk about teaching Cherokee in the schools, and if I'm not mistaken they've actually tried to do so from time to time. But the interest really isn't there."

"That's too bad," Hope said impulsively.

"I suppose it is, in some ways," Wonder conceded. "The thing is, though, that like young people everywhere we don't want to be hidebound by the traditions of the past to the point where we feel smothered by them. And primarily we're Americans. That's my opinion, anyway. And I'm not alone in feeling the way I do. You should talk more to Aunt Loretta or to Ross about this, because I've noticed that you really seem to be interested."

"Is that so surprising?"

Wonder smiled. "I mean *truly* interested, Hope. Not just curious. A lot of the tourists who come here are curious enough, but I don't sense any deep and genuine interest about the Cherokees on their part. In fact, they tend to make me very much aware of the differences between us—in ways that are not always what one might call flattering."

"I can imagine," Hope said dryly. "Nevertheless, from just the little that I've seen and learned since I've been here, it's obvious you have a rich and wonderful tradition and it shouldn't be allowed to die out. The wisdom and courage of the Cherokees has really affected me—although I think I can understand your wanting to be a part of the age you're living in without feeling 'hidebound' to the past, as you put it."

Hope paused and laughed a rather helpless little laugh. "Listen to me!" she said. "Wonder, you've every right to tell me I don't know what I'm talking about."

"But perhaps you do," Wonder said. "Ross

should hear you. He'd be very much in agreement with what you're saying. Even though he's lived away from here for a long time and I'm sure he'll never come back on a permanent basis, I don't think a day ever passes when he doesn't remember he's Cherokee.''

Wonder laughed. "Enough talk," she said. "I hope the molasses cookies haven't taken the edge off your appetite for lunch—though I notice you've only eaten one of them. Aunt Loretta hard-boiled some eggs for us before she left this morning and I'm going to make up some egg-salad sandwiches. Also, I'm going to whip up a milk shake for you. Ross said milk will be good for you just now."

"What about yourself?" Hope asked.

"I'm watching my calories," Wonder said with a smile, and with that they turned to talking about other topics, topics that were not so interesting as Ross Adair but were a lot safer.

When Wonder decided it was time to make the sandwiches, Hope opted to go in the house with her. Lovely as it was on the terrace, even she had to admit she'd had enough of the sun for one day.

The kitchen was cool, pleasantly shaded by the large maples just outside the windows on that side of the house. Wonder refused to let her do anything to help, so Hope sat at the big round table and they continued to talk about a variety of relatively innocuous things. Finally, though, she began to feel as if Wonder was deliberately keeping the conversation low-level.

Wonder seemed a bit abstracted when she eventually sat down at the table, and as they began to eat their lunch Hope thought that maybe the time was right for asking the pretty Cherokee girl a few careful, exploratory questions about Randy Youngdeer. She felt she knew her well enough so they could both be honest with each other, but before she could make up her mind about this Wonder said suddenly, "I have a favor to ask of you!"

She blurted the words out with such intensity that Hope froze right in the middle of taking a bite of her sandwich. "What?" she asked quickly, leaning forward.

"Well," Wonder said slowly, "it involves my brother. I don't know what Ross may have said to you about him, but...."

"Ross hasn't said anything to me about him."

"That doesn't surprise me," Wonder said a bit cryptically. "Though I thought he might have because...oh, I don't know."

Hope noticed that Wonder had barely touched her own sandwich, and her second glass of iced tea was still full. Now she said gently, "What's the problem, Wonder?"

"Well...Stan has been in trouble," Wonder said softly, her head bowed. "And not just once, either."

"Please, Wonder. You don't have to tell me anything unless you really want to."

Wonder looked up and inhaled deeply. "I really want to, Hope, and...it's important. Stan's two years older than I am, and when he was going to high school in Sylva he got a girl in trouble and...well, they got married. But there were problems right from the start, and when the baby was only about a year old this girl divorced him. Then she took the baby with her and moved to Florida. The last we heard she was married to someone else. The whole thing is especially hard for Stan because he never gets to see his own child. So to top things off, he started drinking. He got in trouble with the Tribal Council and everyone else over that. Poor Stan, he's one of those people who never seem to have anything go right for them."

"I'm sorry," Hope said, not knowing what else she could say.

Wonder sighed. "He's been living back home the past year or so," she went on. "Before that he was working around Knoxville. Different places, you know. Then he was on this construction job when he had an accident, so they laid him off. After that he came home, and we thought he would just stay around till he was well again. But now...well, he's on unemployment and he's very depressed. For one thing, it's almost impossible to get a job around here if you have a history of anything even touching on alcoholism. It's a real strike against a person. I'd swear that Stan hasn't done any serious drinking since he's been back, but I have the feeling that at any moment he's going to drop right off the deep end. I try to do what I can, like getting him to take a bit part in the drama, things like that. But it isn't enough."

"Has anyone else tried to help him?" Hope asked.

Wonder hesitated again. Then she said reluctantly, "Randy gave him a job for a time, but it didn't work out. They had words and Randy fired him. Now Randy says he has no use for Stan, which I consider...very unfair. But the thing is, you see, I don't think anyone around here has ever understood Stan."

"What about the rest of your family?"

"Well, my father died several years ago, and there are three younger kids at home. One is still in grade school, and the other two are in high school. My mother is really artistic—she does beautiful weaving and she dresses handmade dolls. You may have seen some of her dolls at the cooperative. Anyway, Stan inherits his talent from her. There's no doubt in my mind about that. He does watercolors, and I think they're very different. There's a certain...twist to them. It's kind of hard to explain. But I know he could do well in art, maybe commercial art. He's that good, I just know it. I mean something like illustrations for magazines, or maybe...."

Wonder stopped at this point, looking so unhappy that Hope took matters into her own hands.

"You want me to look at his work, is that it?" she prompted.

"That's exactly it," Wonder admitted wryly. "But I almost hate to ask you to."

"Why, for heaven's sake?"

"Because it seems to me you have enough problems of your own right now. And...I don't know what Ross would think of my putting Stan in touch with you."

"Ross," Hope said evenly, "has nothing to do with it. Wonder, you've got to get over the idea that Ross has some sort of authority over me. Just because he happened to be on duty at the hospital when they took me in there doesn't mean that he. . . that he has anything at all to say about what I do or don't do!"

Hope hadn't intended to sound quite so defiant, but the expression that came to Wonder's face was plainly one of shock.

"It isn't that I don't appreciate Ross's kindness to me," Hope amended hastily. "I do. He didn't *have* to bring me here. It was very gracious of him. But. . . ."

Unexpectedly, Wonder smiled. Then she said, "You don't have to explain, Hope. But—about Stan. . . ."

"I'll be glad to look at your brother's work," Hope told her. "You've got to make it clear to him, though, that I'm no authority. I teach art, true, and I try to do some painting myself when I have the time. But that doesn't give me the kind of expertise one needs to be a bona-fide art critic."

"I think you would know whether or not Stan shows any promise," Wonder said. "I only ask that you be honest with him. The worst thing any of us could do for Stan would be to raise false hopes."

A moment later Wonder switched the subject, and they began to discuss the drama and other things. Strangely, the matter of setting a time and place for a meeting between her brother and Hope was not even brought up, and Hope was left with the distinct and disturbing feeling that nothing was going to be determined until Wonder had first talked about this to Ross Adair.

CHAPTER TEN

WONDER LEFT during the middle of the afternoon, and shortly afterward Mrs. Wood came home. She and Hope had a quiet supper together and spent the evening watching television.

The next day Mrs. Wood stayed home, and when she and Hope sat down to lunch together she explained that this was Wonder's day to work at the cooperative. She added that she thought Wonder also had something she had to do in the evening.

It had clouded over, and Hope was reminded of the day when she'd first driven into Cherokee from Asheville. Again, the mountains merited their name. They were definitely smoky today, and as she looked out at the hills surrounding this narrow valley she wondered if Ross was somewhere up there in the mountains, living in someone's primitive home. Maybe he was even staying in a wigwam!

She wondered if any Cherokees still lived in wigwams or, for that matter, if any of them ever had in the first place. Probably they had, she thought, since the motel where she had stayed her first couple of nights was called the Three Wigwams.

It was not a day to sit out on the terrace, and Hope grew sleepy after lunch. When Mrs. Wood suggested a nap, she was more than willing to agree. Once propped up on the comfortable bed, though, she turned her attention to her collection of literature on the Indians. She soon learned that the Cherokees had never lived in wigwams. Like the elaborately feathered headdresses, wigwams had originated with the Western Indians and, in fact, had been used principally by the Plains Indians. They afforded a simple, portable home for those tribes who were wanderers by nature.

The Cherokees had always been a more settled people. They had established themselves alongside the rivers that ran through the mountain valleys, and usually they lived in houses. These were made basically of wood, with cane woven to make basket-like walls. Later, when white settlers moved into their area, the Cherokees copied the log houses they built, adding interesting innovations of their own.

In addition, each family had constructed a special hothouse in which they slept during cold weather. It was made of a framework set over a broad hole dug into the ground and covered with earth. A fire was kept burning during the day so that the structure would be warm enough for comfortable sleeping at night, and benches around the outer rim served as beds.

Thoughts of this communal type of bedroom and the warmth of a fire on winter nights, nights which undoubtedly would be very chilly up here in the mountains, made Hope sleepy, and she dozed. It was dusk when she awakened and went out to the kitchen to see if she could help Mrs. Wood with their dinner. But she found that Mrs. Wood had prepared an essentially one-course meal, which she said was called *Tsi-Ta-Ga A-Su-Yi Se-Lu.*

Ross's aunt smiled as Hope tried to say this after her, then went on to explain that it was a distinctly Cherokee dish, really a stew made with chicken and "skinned corn," to which she usually added beans, as well.

"The beans are optional," she said. "Just a little salt and pepper for seasoning, and that's all there is to it. I let it cook through a good bit of the afternoon so that the flavors mix together. It's the long, slow cooking that makes things like this good," she added.

They also had a fresh watercress salad tossed with a tart French dressing, which, Mrs. Wood had to admit, was not Cherokee in origin.

"But I would still call this an authentic Indian meal," she told Hope. "I wanted to cook something that is really native to us, because you've expressed such interest in our food…and in so many other things about us. Which reminds me, Minerva Lightfoot came over for a little while when you were asleep, and she says that as soon as Ross pronounces you fit to travel, she wants you to come over to her house and she'll show you how to make bean bread."

As soon as Ross pronounces you fit to travel. Hope frowned, but she didn't try to correct what was very definitely a mistaken impression.

Hope thoroughly enjoyed the Cherokee chicken stew, and she was grateful to Mrs. Wood for going to the trouble to make it for her. Once again they watched television together, and both were yawning by ten o'clock.

"I'm just not used to this mountain air," Hope said apologetically.

"Well, dear, I would say that nature's healing process in action has more to do with it," Mrs. Wood told her. "For you, that is. For me...let's just call it the onset of old age!"

They bid each other good-night, and Hope made her way to the Fern Room with a warm feeling. Mrs. Wood really seemed to enjoy having her here for her own sake, not just as a favor to Ross Adair. At least she hoped this was true. In such a short time she had come to be fond of the older woman, just as she was of Wonder.

Thinking of Wonder almost instantly led to thoughts of Randy Youngdeer. He had not yet come over to visit her, and she wondered if this was because he hadn't been granted "permission" by Ross. She frowned again at the thought of Ross's seeming assumption of authority. She was going to have to speak to him about it. There was no reason for him to feel so responsible for her.

Finally she drifted off into sleep, thinking of the talk she must have with Ross when he came back and wondering how she was going to manage it.

ALTHOUGH SLEEP HAD COME easily enough, Hope did not stay asleep. In fact, she awakened with something of a start and realized she'd been having a bad dream, though she couldn't remember what it had been about.

She sat up in bed carefully, positioning herself against the pillows so that she'd be as comfortable as possible with the shoulder brace on. There was no moonlight streaming through the windows tonight. In fact, there was a stillness and heaviness to the air that made her think the rain was about to pour down at any moment.

Maybe it was thinking of cool, silver rain that did it, but Hope began to realize that she was thirsty, and hungry, as well. Nor could she dismiss either sensation, and she soon knew that unless she did something about both, she wasn't going to have a prayer of capturing any more sleep tonight.

She got out of bed and reached for her dressing gown. It matched the nightgown she was wearing, which was fashioned of a fairly sheer cotton sprigged with blue and yellow flowers. Then, barefoot, she started down the hall for the kitchen, certain that Mrs. Wood wouldn't mind if she did a bit of midnight refrigerator raiding.

Almost immediately she saw that the second door on her right was open and yellow light was streaming out into the hallway. She assumed it was Mrs. Wood's room, and she prepared herself to explain what she was doing if her hostess was awake.

As she passed the threshold, though, she stopped completely still, rocked by such a surge of emotion that it was physically unsteadying. She felt that her heart had leaped into her throat and she should try to reach up and catch it with her one good hand.

The room had probably once been a bedroom but was now transformed into a study. A large wooden desk dominated the center of the room, with two file cabinets along one wall and a long table heaped with papers and journals along the other. There were a couple of functional metal chairs and two or three lamps, all of them turned on, including a powerful one beamed at the stack of papers piled on the desk where Ross Adair sat working. Just above its cone of light, his hair glistened like ebony velvet. A slim silver pen was balanced between his long, graceful fingers, and he was wearing dark-rimmed glasses that were astonishingly attractive, though they gave him a professional air that made him seem much too remote.

Hope's approach had been soundless, and at this point she was more than willing to suffer both hunger and thirst if she could escape without being seen. But she was not to be so lucky.

She wasn't aware of the sound her movements had made, but against the stillness of the night it was enough. Ross looked up swiftly, his pen still poised, and in another instant whipped off the glasses that he obviously used only for close work.

"Hope!" he said, and he seemed so startled that she wondered if he'd forgotten she was living here.

He pushed back the papers he'd been working on and stood up, seeming taller than ever to her. He was wearing slacks that were so dark brown they were close to black, and a white shirt that made an arresting and extremely provocative contrast to the rich tone of his skin. He'd unbuttoned the top two buttons of the shirt and had rolled up his sleeves, and all Hope could do was swallow hard as she stared at him helplessly. Why did he have to be so attractive and so difficult at one and the same time?

There was an oddly husky note to his voice as he asked, "What are you doing up at this hour?"

"I...I don't even know what time it is," Hope confessed.

He smiled briefly. "Past two," he told her.

The words came before she even thought about them. "You shouldn't be working so late!"

"Oh?" he asked, his eyebrows upraised quizzically.

"I mean, you must be tired," Hope said quickly. "You've been traveling and...."

"Traveling?" he questioned, his tone teasing. "Yes, I suppose I covered all of eight miles between my last place of call and this house. I've been here on the reservation. You did know that, didn't you?"

"Yes," she conceded. "Both your aunt and Wonder told me."

"Aunt Loretta also knew that if you needed me she could have me reached through the hospital. They knew where I'd be...they had the addresses of the people I intended to visit, that is."

Hope wrested her eyes away from him and tried to pull her emotional reins together, but even this attempt at control took a tremendous effort. Then she said, "Ross, I appreciate your concern. But there's no reason why I should have needed you."

She had not realized how this was going to sound.

The words thudded into the space between them, and Hope imagined that she actually saw him flinch. Then he said in a voice so quiet she had to strain to hear it, "No. I suppose not."

Involuntarily she moved into the room toward him, desperately anxious to make amends right now, for she had no desire to cause any further misunderstandings between them.

"Please," she said. "I didn't mean it the way it sounded. It's just that your aunt and Wonder and...and even Mrs. Lightfoot all seem to think that I shouldn't move an inch without your permission."

"I see. And that violates your spirit of independence, right?"

"Well, yes, I suppose it does," Hope admitted somewhat reluctantly. "What I really mean, though, is that there's no need for you to concern yourself about me in this way. It isn't as if I were your responsibility. You have so many more important things to...." Hope swallowed awkwardly, possessed now of the dismal feeling that with every word she spoke she was only making things worse.

Ross came around the desk and leaned against the front of it. Then he folded his arms and surveyed her with that total inscrutability she found so unnerving. He said levelly, "No, you're not my responsibility, are you, Hope? Thanks for reminding me. I suppose I *have* been letting things get a bit out of hand. Mentally, at least."

She stared at him helplessly, and the words were wrung from her. "I'm sorry," she said.

Curiosity edged his voice as he asked, "What are you sorry about?"

"I don't know," she groaned, that odd sense of helplessness coming over her again.

"There's no need for you to be sorry if it involves me," Ross said, becoming as professional as if they were in a consulting room, he the doctor and she the patient. "I took matters involving you into my own hands because it seemed necessary at the moment. Or should I say expedient? Either way, I think it's actually worked out rather well at that, though you may not agree. Your being here, I mean. You will be able to convalesce as you should, and I think having you here is definitely beneficial to Aunt Loretta. I can already see the evidence of that."

"Beneficial to your aunt?" Hope asked, astonished by this.

"Yes. She's needed to have a young woman in the house...for a long time."

Hope didn't know how to answer this. To comment at all would mean that she already knew about Lamanda, and she simply wasn't ready to confront Ross with this knowledge. She wasn't ready to see the look on his face when his dead wife's name came between them.

Suddenly he straightened, and Hope had the feeling that he was casting away a shadow. Then a brief smile etched the curve of his lips, and he said, "You still haven't told me what caused you to get up at this hour."

"Nothing, really," she hedged.

"Oh, come on, Hope," he teased. "You're not the type to do something without a reason!"

She didn't know how to take this remark, either, and again decided that it was the better part of wisdom not to pursue it. She said frankly, "I was both hungry and thirsty. Probably if it had been just one or the other I would have been too lazy to get up. But as it was...."

"So I've been keeping you from raiding Aunt Loretta's refrigerator, is that it?" he asked, the smile deepening.

"Honestly, Ross...."

"Don't protest. Come to think of it, I could use a bite to eat myself, so let's go and see what we can find."

Ross started toward her as he said this, and Hope inadvertently backed away from him. He was acting like an indulgent uncle, she thought bitterly, while she did not feel in the least like a recalcitrant niece. Then it seemed to her that his eyes darkened, and an expression she could not fathom came to lurk in them. But he said nothing more. He merely led the way toward the kitchen and beckoned her to follow.

Once there, he made her sit down at the round table while he foraged in the refrigerator. Emerging after a few seconds with ham, green peppers, onions and eggs, he announced cheerfully, "I'll make omelets for us."

"But that's too much trouble," Hope protested.

"Not at all," Ross assured her. "Anyway, I could use something substantial. I had an early dinner with the people I was interviewing, but that was about eight hours ago. Also, it was groundhog stew, which doesn't happen to be my favorite dish. So...how about a glass of sherry to sustain you while I'm putting things together?''

He was already getting out wineglasses and pouring amber-colored sherry for both of them while he spoke, and as he handed her wine to her their fingers inevitably touched. Hope could feel a quiver that was the essence of sensuality sweep through her, and at that instant their eyes met and held... and the world seemed to stop for Hope. The entire globe became suspended in orbit for a timeless interval during which her pulse began to thud so hard that she could feel its beat echoing as if she were hollow inside.

Ross said very softly, ''You know, Hope, the Indians never smoked peace pipes. At least, the Cherokees never did. That's a white man's term. But if we had invented such a thing, I'd suggest that you and I smoke one now. I think we both need peace between us, wouldn't you agree?''

She could only nod at him, unable to take her eyes away from his. She knew how intensely vulnerable she must appear to him, yet there was nothing she could do to change this impression. Before she could rally, he smiled at her, a smile of such sweetness that it transformed him completely, erasing all the harshness from his face. His lips brushed her forehead, and he said, ''Agreed, then.'' Hope was still looking up at him, her lips parted, as he turned away and started taking various bowls and pans from the kitchen cabinet.

After a moment, the world began to revolve on its axis again, and Hope's pulse slowed somewhat, but she felt as if she'd been through a transcending experience with Ross, as if somehow they'd climbed together to a new and different plane. Maybe, she told herself, they could come closer to understanding each other on this level. Maybe, for that matter, he already understood her better than she thought he did. As for him. . . well, he was still a mystery to her. But never in her life had she wanted to unravel a mystery so much.

So often, when she'd been with him, there'd been a sense of unreality to their being together. And now, in the early hours of the morning, this feeling returned as she sat at the table in Loretta Wood's kitchen eating the delicious omelet Ross Adair had concocted.

Hope tried to study him covertly while they ate, but she was reasonably sure he knew exactly what she was up to. She'd never met a person so fully aware of everything—and everybody. Ross Adair, she told herself, would be a very difficult person to fool.

She wanted to ask him about so many things—his work, for one—but she couldn't quite bring herself to pose questions of this sort to him for fear she might be rebuffed. Finally, as a safe topic, she hit upon Wonder's visits and the fact that she was going to look over some of the artwork Wonder's brother had done.

Ross's reaction was instantaneous. He was finishing a third piece of toast when she told him this, and he put it back on his plate and frowned. Then he said bluntly, "I'd rather you didn't do that."

It was her turn to frown back. "Why not?" she demanded mildly.

"Stancil Owl already has enough crazy notions spinning around in his head," Ross said. "He's been in trouble in one way or another ever since he was a kid. You'll be doing the whole family a disservice if you encourage him in something he'll never possibly follow through on."

He spoke so flatly that she could not help but be annoyed, even though the last thing she wanted to do just now was get into an argument with him. But she couldn't simply give up on this because Ross Adair was voicing his disapproval. She'd promised Wonder, and she was convinced that this matter meant a great deal to her newfound friend. She said, trying not to sound too defiant, "I don't agree with you, Ross. I wouldn't think of encouraging Wonder's brother unless he truly merited encouragement."

"And suppose you find that he does?" Ross asked sardonically. "What do you propose to do then?"

"What do you mean?"

"Are you going to take Stan under your wing and become his sponsor?"

"Oh, please," Hope protested.

"Look, Stancil Owl has quite an eye for women," Ross said in a tone that was so level it was close to deadly. "He could become a leech to you if he were given even the slightest opportunity. I don't really give a damn how much talent he has! A lot of people have talent in the various creative fields, but it takes more than talent alone to succeed. I should think you would know this, if you're as professional as you pretend to be."

This statement evoked an instant response. "I haven't pretended to be anything!" she told him hotly.

"All right," he shrugged. "Excuse me for my poor word choice. I think you know what I'm saying. It's a mistake to encourage people you can't follow through with, especially when you know they can't follow through on their own."

Hope answered him without even thinking about the possible effect of her words. "Someone must have encouraged *you*," she said. "Someone must have helped *you* out, or you would never have made it to medical school."

The silence in the kitchen became acute. Ross had turned to put the milk and eggs back in the refrigerator, and now he shut the refrigerator door with a thud. He swung around to face her.

There was no tenderness in his face, nothing but sheer hostility. Hope flinched from his expression, but she knew that there was no going back, no trying to reclaim those hastily spoken words.

He said flatly, "You don't know what the hell you're talking about!"

She swallowed hard. "All right," she said. "I'm sorry. I shouldn't have put it that way. But—"

"But you can't imagine how a Cherokee like myself could have gone off to medical school except by the benevolence of some kind patron, is that it?'' he asked caustically. "Hope, I think it's about time you learned that things are not always as they seem. You shouldn't vent instant opinions or leap to instant conclusions about matters you know nothing about!"

"Ross..." she began, and to her distress her voice broke on his name.

The look of scorn he gave her was like a whiplash. "Please," he said ironically, "spare me the feminine ploys."

This was too much. Without even thinking about her injured shoulder, Hope got to her feet so suddenly that she was thrown off balance. She literally rocked, and for a moment she thought she was going to fall. Then, as she reached out to grab the nearest surface, a spasm of pain clenched her and made her cry out despite herself.

She was sure Ross couldn't have taken more than two giant steps as he crossed the room to her. He reached out quickly to steady her, but his eyes were like coals, and the line of his jaw was rigid.

"You can't even take care of *yourself*," he told her coldly, "to say nothing of people like Stancil Owl!"

Tears surged. Hope felt as if she'd gladly give ten years of her life if she could keep herself from crying right now, but this proved to be impossible. She wrenched herself away from him, and as more pain flamed through her shoulder she turned blindly toward the door. She was intent on only one thing, and that was to get back to the Fern Room and lock herself inside. To do anything, in short, that would keep Ross Adair away from her.

But her escape route was blocked.

Ross moved to stand directly in front of her, and to her astonishment he said, "Take it easy, darling." The grin he gave her was a crooked one and so endearing that she gasped from its effect. Then he asked, "What happened to that symbolical peace pipe we were talking about?"

"How can you even...even speak about such a thing?" she sputtered. "How could anyone possibly smoke a...a peace pipe with you...when you carry on so about Wonder's brother? Someone I...I don't even know!"

"Let's say that I overreacted about Stan Owl for reasons of my own," Ross said, plainly trying to make light of this.

"What reasons?" Hope asked suspiciously.

"Could you believe I might be jealous?" he suggested.

"No!" she scoffed.

He laughed. "Well, then," he said, "let's say that I want you to take another puff on our symbolical peace pipe as a kind of preventive medicine."

"Preventive medicine, indeed!"

"There are other forms of preventive medicine that might be more effective," he conceded, and before she realized what he had in mind he moved closer to her and very carefully enfolded her in his arms.

He held her gently, clearly mindful of her injured

shoulder, but there was nothing at all gentle about his kiss. His lips came to claim her mouth in a manner that spelled total possession. Then, as he held her even closer against him, his tongue began to probe. The sensation this created was overwhelming, and Hope involuntarily responded so intently that suddenly forks of desire's lightning were stabbing both of them. Ross leaned her back very slightly, so that her left side was nestled in the protective hollow of his arm. Then his left hand began exploring the folds of her gown, thrusting it back until his fingers found the low-plunging neckline of her nightdress, moving on to play a searing arpeggio across her flesh. Next, he was touching first the roundness of her breasts and then the upthrust tips of her nipples, tautened by a passion she couldn't hide.

His own arousal was obvious to her, and the tangible core of his sexuality drew her even closer to him of her own accord. A strange thrill ran though her as she pressed against this tantalizing evidence of his maleness, causing her to want Ross as she had never wanted a man before. She was, in fact, shocked by the blinding strength of her desire, so fiery in itself that even the pain in her shoulder couldn't distract her from it.

But Ross was conscious of her injury. He groaned, then said, "Oh, my God, Hope! We *can't*, darling. Not until you've healed more than you possibly could have by now."

Very slowly he pushed her away, and through the haze of her own passion Hope became well aware that this was taking all of his fortitude. Nevertheless, she felt as if she were being robbed of something ultimately precious, and the fear possessed her that having come so close with him and then being forced once again to separate might mean that a moment like this would never come to them again.

Ross said gently, "Off to bed with you, beautiful lady." The kiss that swept her lips now was brief but almost excruciatingly tender. "I'd tuck you in," he added, "but frankly I couldn't trust myself with you tonight. Will you be able to manage by yourself?"

Manage by herself?

It was a question Hope didn't even want to think about, let alone answer.

CHAPTER ELEVEN

Mrs. Wood, Hope soon discovered, was a busy woman, volunteering at the Qualla Cooperative, lending a hand at the Oconaluftee Village and working closely with the Cherokee Historical Society, among other things.

With Ross back from his tour around the reservation, his aunt no longer seemed to feel that she had to be a nurse companion to Hope, and Hope found herself on her own in the house from time to time. Mrs. Wood was as solicitous as ever, but it was evident that she looked to Ross as the one in charge, and Hope found that the simplest thing to do was to accept this.

After all, she told herself, she would not be in Cherokee much longer. Probably in a couple of weeks she'd be free to go. But...to go where? Back to Concord, she supposed, and the thought was more than a bit dismal.

In the meantime, there was nothing for her to do but rest. The day would no doubt come when ''her physician'' would tell her it was safe for her to start being more active, but thus far he still suggested she limit her activities to the house and the terrace.

Ross was also busy with his work again. He

usually came home for dinner, but on those nights when he was helping out in the emergency room at the Cherokee Hospital, Hope didn't see him from one day to the next. And whenever this happened, the extent of the emptiness she felt was staggering. She told herself she'd better get used to being without him, but this didn't do any good, either. Instead, she found herself waiting for him to appear, and it always seemed magical when he did.

She noticed, though, that he was looking more and more tired with each day that passed. He seemed to be under a decided strain. She wondered if perhaps his research was not going well and wished that an opportunity to ask him about this would present itself.

Wonder dropped in regularly, even though she, too, was busy with a variety of things, but she still seemed quite preoccupied. With Randy Youngdeer, Hope wondered. Randy finally made it over to the house one evening, and Hope was really pleased to see him again. She considered Randy to have been her first friend in Cherokee, and she felt a special warmth toward him.

Nothing further was said about Wonder's brother showing Hope his artwork, and she imagined that Ross had probably told Wonder to keep Stancil Owl away from the house. The thought was disturbing, but Hope decided to say nothing about it for the present. She had no wish to get into an argument with Ross. Anyway, chances were that he was right. Even if Wonder's brother proved to be very talented—and Hope's experience warned her that this was unlikely—she really had no right to encourage him. For one thing, she didn't have that many connections in the art world herself, despite the fact that she both taught art and did paintings of her own.

One afternoon as her stay at the Wood house began its second week, Hope found herself home alone. She'd eaten a solitary lunch at the round table in the kitchen and was feeling quite lonely as she dutifully sipped the glass of milk Ross had prescribed as a regular accompaniment to her meals. With this finished, she managed to wash up her dishes "one-handed" and then took some of her Cherokee booklets and wandered out onto the terrace.

It was a perfect summer day, the kind of day that cries out to be shared with a good friend...or a lover.

A lover. Ross had come very close to being her lover. Hope looked down at the sling on her arm and grimaced, only too aware of the treacherous warmth that suffused her whenever she thought of the feeling of his body against hers and the touch of those long fingers tantalizingly probing her breasts.

Resolutely, she turned her attention to an account of the old Cherokee legends and became absorbed in one about how the Earth had been created.

It seemed that in the beginning all living creatures had lived together in the "sky vault," which was called Galun'lati. Finally, though, the vault became overcrowded with animals and people, so something had to be done. Far beneath the vault the ocean could be seen, and the people wondered what might lie beneath it. Then one day a brave little water beetle offered to venture forth to see if he could find out.

The beetle flew down to the surface of the water that spread beneath Galun'lati and searched in every direction, but he couldn't find any place where he could rest. Finally there was nothing else to do but dive to the bottom of the sea and bring up some mud, so this he did...and magically the mud began to grow. It grew and grew, according to the Cherokee legend, until at last the island known as Earth was formed....

Hope had got this far and was about to turn the page when a long shadow fell across the book. Completely startled, she looked up to see a strange man standing at the side of her chaise longue, staring down at her.

For a moment she knew the feeling of pure panic. He was a shabby-looking person, his jeans faded and frayed, his light orange T-shirt stained with grease. He needed a shave and a good shampoo, as well, but it was primarily the expression in his eyes that daunted her. They were as black as Ross Adair's eyes, but there any similarity ended. These eyes were dull as charcoal, and there was a gauntness to the man's face, a bitter twist to his lips.

The words came involuntarily, and Hope knew that she was actually shrinking back in obvious fright as she uttered them.

"What are you doing here?" she snapped, realizing that her pitch was definitely higher than usual.

"I was invited," he said flatly.

"By whom, may I ask?"

"You may ask," he said, and to her horror he pulled up a nearby camp chair and sat down in it. "By you. I'm Stancil Owl."

Wonder's brother! This dissolute-looking individual couldn't be Wonder's brother! This was the first thought that came to Hope's mind, and she sensed that he was aware of it as clearly as if she'd spoken aloud. His smile was purely derisive, but though he still frightened her, she wasn't about to let him off easily because of this. She said frostily, "You might have phoned first. Or at the very least, you could have announced your arrival."

"With what?" he asked. "A fanfare of trumpets, maybe? Is that the way your guests usually announce their arrivals?"

"Well, they don't just creep up on people!" Hope said defiantly.

"It's an old Indian custom," he told her. "Creeping around without making any noise, that is. Comes from stalking deer through the forest. Or enemies. . . or whatever."

He laughed shortly, and Hope realized that Stancil Owl definitely was going to be a problem. She could not repress an audible sigh. It was enough to deal with one sensitive Cherokee, let alone taking on two.

Sensitive. She had not thought about this word before in connection with Ross Adair. Arrogant sometimes, yes. High-handed, too, and even rude. Aloof, yes. And he could also be loving, tender, a very caring person despite that outer shell of inscrutability he seemed to don so easily. But she'd never stopped to think until this very moment that at least some of his attitude was due to an extreme sensitivity. This was what accounted for his awareness and the aura of understanding and compassion that tended to escape despite the stoical camouflage he tried to adopt.

Was Stancil Owl's derisive attitude also a form of camouflage?

She shouldn't care whether it was or not, Hope warned herself. As a matter of fact, she should make sure that he left before Ross found out he'd been there at all. Yet her curiosity was stirring, and she knew very well that she couldn't simply dismiss this man without further conversation, even if she were able to persuade him to leave.

He was leaning forward, his hands clasped between his knees, staring off somewhere toward the mountains as if she wasn't even around. This was a shade better than facing an expression that had been close to a sneer, but Hope had to break in on whatever it was he was thinking about—nothing very pleasant, to judge from the expression on his face.

"Does Mrs. Wood know that you were coming over here this afternoon?" she asked.

He shrugged. "I didn't tell her, if that's what you mean."

"And...and Dr. Adair?"

He grinned, a downright nasty grin. "Dr. Adair, eh?" he jeered. "Sounds high-and-mighty, doesn't it, but prick his skin and you'll find out he's just like the rest of us. To answer your question, though, no. Ross doesn't know I was planning to call on you, Miss Standish. For that matter, Wonder doesn't know, either. I guess that's what you were going to ask me next. She said the other night that you'd offered to look at some of my stuff, but I wasn't much for it. Then yesterday she told me the offer was off. That made me curious. I thought I'd come and see for myself what made you change your mind."

His words left Hope with no doubt at all that Ross had contacted Wonder after the conversation they'd had about Stancil Owl and his artwork. He'd probably warned Wonder to keep her brother away from the house. Despite her determination to avoid conflicts with him while she was still a guest in his aunt's house, this thoroughly annoyed her.

Stancil Owl was watching her closely, and now he said, "I can see you've thought it through. Okay, we both know that Ross didn't want me to meet you. I suppose he's protecting you."

Hope was sufficiently irked by this to say stiffly, "I don't need that kind of protection."

"You didn't call off the idea of looking at my stuff yourself?"

"No," she said. "I did not."

"You talked to Ross about it?"

She hesitated, then decided there was no point in denying this. "As a matter of fact, I did."

Stancil Owl nodded. "He's got no use for me," he said, as if he were talking about something as casual as the weather. "Randy Youngdeer doesn't, either. Randy gave me a job because of Wonder, but I blew it. I guess you know that, too. Yes, I see you do. Anyone ever tell you you've got a mighty transparent face?"

He, too, spoke with a soft Southern accent, more pronounced than Ross's accent. But then Ross had spent quite a bit of time living in the north in recent years. Nevertheless, Stancil Owl's voice reminded her of Ross, though certainly nothing else about him did. But the vocal reminder was enough. She felt an odd sort of ache and knew that for the rest of her life she'd have the unhappy ability to feel lonely in a crowd every time she remembered him.

Stancil Owl asked conversationally, "Ever play poker?"

The question startled Hope, and she frowned. "A few times, yes," she allowed. "Why?"

He laughed. "You'd be hard put to bluff anyone out," he told her.

"I'm not interested in trying to bluff anyone out."

To her surprise, he nodded. "I can believe that," he said thoughtfully, "now that I've seen you. And if I'd seen you sooner I'd have known this had nothing to do with you. About not looking at my stuff, that is."

Before Hope could answer, Stancil Owl rose slowly and stretched, like a man just awakening from a long sleep. Then he stood silently for a moment and ran his long fingers over the stubble on his chin. A second later he smoothed back his rumpled hair with the same hand.

"Look," he said then, "I'm sorry I scared you."

"You didn't scare me," Hope began, but he stopped her with a laugh.

"I did scare you," he contradicted her. "On purpose, for that matter. I guess I wanted to see what kind of stuff you were made of."

"And did you find out?" she asked, unabashed.

He didn't answer at once. Instead, he stared down at her intently with a bleakness in his dark, opaque eyes that made her shiver. Then he said, "Yes, I think I found out. Thanks for the offer in the first place, anyway. And good luck to you. I hope you'll be back on your feet soon."

He nodded abruptly and turned away, moving back across the terrace toward the steps at the far side with a tread that was, indeed, as noiseless as that of an Indian stalking prey through the forest. And Hope found that she couldn't let him go quite so easily.

Her voice rang out clearly. "Mr. Owl!"

He stopped in his tracks, then slowly turned to face her. "Yes?"

"I would like to look at your work."

Stancil Owl shook his head. "It wouldn't do," he told her flatly.

"Why wouldn't it do?"

"It would only get you in trouble with Ross," he said, "and there's no need for that."

"Isn't there?" Hope asked him. "Look, Mr.

Owl. Dr. Adair has been very kind to me, and it's true that I'm staying here in his aunt's house, probably for the next week or so. But that doesn't mean that he's my...my keeper!"

The word emerged with more indignation than she had intended, and Stancil Owl grinned.

"You mean to stand up to him, is that it?"

"It isn't a question of standing up to him. I like your sister very much, and she asked me to do this." Hope paused. "Also, now that I've met you I want to do it."

"Now that you've met me?" Stancil Owl echoed incredulously.

"That's right."

He came slowly back toward the chair he had vacated and sat down. "Look," he said then, "Wonder isn't any art critic, know what I mean? She's stuck with me through...well, through a lot of things, because she's my sister and a...a good kid. She thinks the stuff I do is great, but that's just her opinion, you know what I'm saying?"

"I'm not an art critic, either," Hope said levelly. "I know what I like, and that's about all I can tell you. I told Wonder the same thing, and I also told her that I don't have any particular clout in art circles. I know a few people, but that's about it. So there's not much I can offer you, really, just by looking at your work, except maybe some encouragement if you're good—and an honest opinion if you're not."

"And you'd give it to me, wouldn't you?" he asked her with a faint smile.

"What do you mean?"

"That honest opinion if I'm not good."

"Yes," Hope answered. "Yes, I would."

"Well," Stancil Owl said, "that's what I'd like to know. Whether I'm just fooling myself and Wonder, too, or whether I should...keep on trying." He drew a long breath. "You're the first person either of us has met who knows anything about art at all," he said. "Wonder tells me you teach in an art school up North."

"It's not an art school," Hope corrected. "I teach art in a girls' school. There's quite a difference."

"Okay." He hesitated, and she sensed that something was troubling him. "Say what you will about Ross," he said then, "but he'd be mad as hell if he found out I was here, to say nothing of if I came back and showed you my stuff. If you're going to be living under the same roof with him there's no point in putting you through that."

This was not the first time that Hope had been warned of the potential fury of Ross Adair's anger, and she stiffened. She was damned if she was going to be intimidated!

"I'll worry about that," she said firmly. "Okay?"

"Whatever," Stancil Owl replied. "You usually alone here in the daytime?"

"I never know for sure," Hope admitted. "It depends what Mrs. Wood is doing. And Ross's schedule also varies, but he hasn't been around much lately."

This was only too true.

"Mostly at night, I guess," Stancil Owl said a bit cryptically.

"What do you mean?"

"Wonder mentioned that except when he's at the hospital he's been going out to talk to different people on the reservation in the daytime. Getting their family histories, I think she said. Then he comes back here and 'works until dawn,' the way she puts it. I guess Aunt Loretta is worried about him and she's been talking to Wonder about it. As if Wonder could do anything with Ross. Maybe Randy could, I don't know."

This bit of information was oddly disquieting. The thought that Ross Adair was working in his temporary office—just two doors down from her own bedroom—caused Hope literally to tremble from an emotion that she knew only too well was entirely treacherous. She had a vision of him sitting at his desk bent over stacks of paper, wearing those dark-rimmed glasses that made him seem so remote, and she shivered.

"Something wrong?" her companion asked.

Hope shook her head. "No. Look, I don't see any reason why we should be secretive about this. Come over tomorrow and bring your work, and we'll look at it together, all right?"

He stood again. "Fine," he said, "with one understanding."

"What's that?"

There was a bitter edge to Stancil Owl's grin. "I've had my share of trouble," he acknowledged, "so I don't go out looking for it, know what I mean? If I bump into it that's one thing—I won't run away. I'm not asking for it, that's all."

"You're speaking of Ross, of course."

"Right now, yes. Just don't mention I'm coming over with my stuff, okay? If he walks in on us, that's something else again. You know what I'm saying?"

"Yes, I know what you're saying," Hope told him. "Just come tomorrow, and for now we'll let it go at that."

IT HAD BEEN EASY ENOUGH for Hope to be decisive sitting out on the terrace with Stancil Owl at her side. Wonder's brother had struck a strangely responsive chord in her.

Once he had departed, though, she began to have second thoughts. She didn't know how having Stancil around the premises would affect Loretta Wood, but she did realize full well that if Ross were to discover what she was about to do he would be absolutely furious.

Nevertheless, Hope had no intention of going back on her promise. But she had to admit to herself that she wished she hadn't made it quite so quickly. It would have been wiser to have given the matter—and how to handle it diplomatically, with the fewest possible reverberations—considerably more thought.

After a time she went back into the house and tried to take a short nap, but sleep eluded her. Her shoulder was aching, for one thing, and she was growing very tired of both the brace and the sling.

She got up and changed into her caftan, having found that this was the most comfortable kind of dress for her to wear toward the end of the day, when she really wanted to feel relaxed. The past few nights Mrs. Wood had let her help set the table and do a few other things that she could manage comfortably, and right now she needed activity of any sort, even limited activity.

She opened her bedroom door, intending to go and find Mrs. Wood and ask if she could expand her horizons a bit and maybe help with some of the cooking, as well. Then she stopped short. Ross was standing only a few feet away, turning the knob on the first door down the hallway, which led to the room directly next to the Fern Room.

All of the doors along the hallway were usually kept closed. Hope had discovered that one led to a spacious linen closet, one to a bathroom, and she knew that the second door on the right opened into Ross's office. It was bad enough to think that he was this close to her when he was working, but she'd had no idea that the room in which he slept literally touched upon her own bedroom, wall to wall.

He, too, stopped short when he saw her, and she had the unpleasant feeling that this was an encounter he'd hoped to avoid. The thought wasn't very flattering, nor could she imagine why he wouldn't want to see her. In her opinion, that symbolical peace pipe they'd smoked had left a decidedly mellowing effect upon her. But evidently Ross didn't feel the same way.

She found herself scrutinizing his face, and she had to frown at what she saw. Ross looked strained, terribly strained. There were deep lines of fatigue around his mouth, and his eyes were as shadowed as if they'd been brushed with a charcoal pencil.

Definitely he must be working too hard, she found herself thinking. He was probably anxious to finish his research project and get back to Boston. What he needed was a woman in his life to make him rest when he should. Someone to make him take care of himself. He was going at entirely the wrong pace and one day it was all going to catch up with him.

A woman in his life! Hope could not help but imagine what it would be like to be the woman in Ross Adair's life, to share with him both his triumphs and his troubles. To love him. . . .

To love him! The phrase, centered on that all-important word, seemed to beat at her. *Love!* She was besieged by the sudden realization that she loved this man standing before her. She loved him with an intensity that swept thoughts of Lewis, and anyone else who had ever touched upon her life, into oblivion. There had never been anyone for her but Ross—and there would never be anyone else. Yet he didn't see her in the same light. He didn't see her in the same light at all. She was sure of that.

Hope was swept by a sadness so intense that tears actually came to fill her eyes, tears that stung terribly.

"What is it?" Ross asked, seeing the tears and seeming to be thoroughly startled by the sight of them.

"Nothing, ' Hope said quickly. "I was . . . thinking, that's all."

"Very sad thoughts, I'd say," he commented. "What causes them? Not me, I hope. I've tried to keep out of your way. When I began to think about what so nearly happened between us the other night, it seemed to me that the wise course for both of us would be to avoid being alone together. I admit that it's a long time since I've had a woman. Perhaps it's an equally long time since you've had a man. And God knows we attract each other—that way! I think we're both adult enough to admit it. But I also think that involvement of that kind wouldn't do either of us any good."

"Oh?" Hope questioned, but she spoke almost absently, because she was concentrating on those lines of weariness in his beloved face. She also had the feeling that he was deliberately trying to put her off with his statements, trying to make her want to keep herself at arm's length from him.

Her question was almost gentle. "What is it with you, Ross?" she asked him. "Has something gone wrong with your work?"

"My work?" he echoed, seeming genuinely surprised. "What makes you think anything has gone wrong with my work?"

"Sometimes when things don't go right in one area we take it out on the first person we encounter in . . . in another area," Hope said, trying to keep her voice steady.

Ross's laugh was rough. "And what area do you think you fall into, Hope?" he asked her. "The sphere of pleasure, pure pleasure? Well, that's true to a point. But it's also an oversimplification. I'm not saying you couldn't gratify me, Hope. There's little doubt in my mind that you'd be all any man could ask for, in that respect. But there's more to it...."

"What are you trying to say, Ross?"

The slightest of smiles came to curve his lips. "I suppose you must know," he said then, in a tone as casual as if he were merely making idle conversation, "that I've fallen in love with you. But I'm fighting it like hell!

"It isn't easy," he went on, "to be so close to you and yet so far away. I'll be frank about it. I think bringing you here to this house was a mistake. A mistake for both of us."

A mistake for both of us. Each word was like a bitter pill, to be swallowed down without water. Hope could feel her throat burn, and she was suffused by a mixture of sorrow, shame and intense disappointment. It wasn't love that Ross was talking about. He wanted her, yes. She believed that, just as she wanted him. But what he was speaking about was—what was that dreadful word for it—carnal. An entirely carnal feeling. Whereas love....

Desperately anxious not to say the wrong thing at a moment she felt was close to critical, Hope held her tongue. And by the time she could have framed a reply, it was too late. Loretta Wood appeared in the kitchen doorway to say cheerfully, "Ah, there you both are! Dinner's about ready, and I thought you might like a glass of sherry first."

The spell—or whatever had been looming between them—was broken, but it soon became apparent that Ross was going to continue to keep his distance from Hope. He included his aunt in the dinner table conversation, refused dessert and then left them with the statement that he had a lot of paperwork to get done tonight or else he'd be hopelessly behind schedule.

Loretta Wood didn't say anything until she and Hope both heard the door down the hall close and knew that Ross had gone into his study. Then she sighed and shook her head.

"He's working much too hard," she said. "Of late, he seems almost possessed by what he's doing. Ross has always put a great deal of energy into anything he has set out to accomplish, but I've been trying to tell him that no one can work around the clock without its taking a pretty severe toll after a while. As a doctor, he should have the sense to know that, but...."

It was a moment when Hope might have been able to bring up the subject of Lamanda, since it was her tragedy that had inspired Ross to do this sort of work in the first place. But she let the moment pass. Tonight she wasn't up to coping with anything else that involved Dr. Ross Adair.

CHAPTER TWELVE

HOPE HAD WONDERED whether or not Stancil Owl
would actually show up again, and she more than
half suspected that if he did decide to show her his
work at all he would do so via Wonder. But she was
mistaken. History repeated itself in only twenty-
four hours, as he loomed up at her side while she
was out on the terrace reading, but at least this time
he didn't sneak up on her. He said, "Hi!" in a surprisingly friendly fashion.

He also looked much more presentable. He'd
shaved and had washed his hair and was dressed in
immaculate khaki trousers with a matching shirt.
He still looked haggard, though, and the lines of
dissipation still creased his face, but he was no
longer a person from whom one would flinch.

He was carrying a large cardboard portfolio.
Placing this on the glass-topped table between
them, he took the same chair he'd sat in the day
before.

"How's the arm doing?" he asked in a tone that
made Hope suspect he was putting off the moment
when the portfolio would be opened. To Hope, this
indicated that Stancil's artwork meant so much to
him he might actually be afraid of her verdict, and

this in turn gave her misgivings. She couldn't help but think Ross Adair had been right. It wasn't her business to encourage or discourage Stancil Owl, for either course could be dangerous, but she'd gone too far now to back off.

"It's my shoulder that was injured, actually," she said, "and I guess it's coming along quite well. Ross wants new X rays in a day or two, then we'll know more definitely."

"And if you've healed up sufficiently you'll go along home?"

Hope didn't let herself think about this. "Yes," she said, then added quickly, "All right, let me see them!"

Stancil Owl's smile was sheepish. "So, okay, I'm a coward," he admitted with a frankness that made him a lot more appealing. "This stuff is important to me, but don't let that make any difference to you. Do you know what I'm saying? I don't want you to soft-pedal anything with me."

"Don't worry," Hope said firmly. "I may not be an art critic, but I do know enough about the subject to have a fair idea of what's basically good. Anyway, it's hard enough to just get by in a profession that involves creativity—even if you have talent. So, if I really feel you don't have any talent at all I'm going to tell you right out. Is that agreed?"

"Agreed," Stancil Owl nodded.

Despite this, Hope was hesitant as he handed the portfolio to her, for now that the moment was at hand she could almost feel his apprehension. Then, as if by silent mutual consent, they further stalled for time when Hope found it difficult to untie the strings that kept the package together and had to turn to him for help. His fingers fumbled, too, but finally there was nothing more to do except turn over the first of a stack of papers. When she did so, Hope gasped in honest surprise.

She didn't have to say anything. Stancil Owl had already told her she didn't have a poker face and she knew she was proving that now. She also knew that he was watching her so intently that he was not apt to miss even the slightest nuance of expression.

She turned from one to another of his paintings in absolute delight. Most of them were watercolors, though he had a few pen-and-ink sketches interspersed. But all were executed in a style that she could only call unique. Wonder was right when she had suggested that her brother would make a good magazine illustrator. In fact, Hope was ready to concede that he would make a superb illustrator. It was certainly a way in which he could make a living, and probably a very good one, but his talent went far beyond what was necessary for commercial art, in Hope's estimation.

Cherokee and various phases of its scenery, its life and its people formed the subject matter for his work. He had captured the very essence of it all in a style that was completely his own. There was nothing photographic about his art, nothing that could be called conventional, yet on the other hand he was not really modern. Nor was he abstract, although at moments he did approach something like fantasy.

No, he was...he was simply Stancil Owl, Hope thought, feeling a certain humility as she looked up at him.

She said slowly, "You are very, very good."

For a moment he looked at her as if she'd struck him. Then he sat back slowly and expelled a long breath, and a wry smile crossed his face. "I was afraid to hear your verdict," he confessed.

"You've nothing to be afraid of at all, Stan," she said sincerely. "May I call you Stan?"

"Yes, Hope," he said with a touch of humor. "You may indeed call me Stan!"

"What you've done is very...exciting," she told him, trying to find the right choice of words. "New and different, as old as time, as contemporary as today, as advanced as the next century. And your use of color is nothing short of sensational. Really, I—"

"Stop!" he protested, holding up his hand. "My head will be too big for my shoulders!"

A strange expression flitted across his face, and Hope didn't have to be told that there hadn't been very many times in Stancil Owl's life when there'd been a chance of his head becoming too big for his shoulders. She thought of his ill-fated marriage, the child taken from him, his brushes with the law and his bout with alcoholism, and she knew she was perhaps reading too much into some of this—she was mentally going beyond what Wonder had told her. But Stancil Owl had traveled down a rough road. It showed in his face.

Because she knew how important this was to him,

Hope deliberately tried to dim some of her own enthusiasm for his work and forced herself back to basics.

She said carefully, "You have a lot of talent, Stan...but that doesn't mean that you're assured instant fame and fortune. I think you know that."

"Only too well," he said ruefully.

"The thing is to put you in touch with the right people," she went on. "I have a few contacts in Boston, and you may be sure I'll get in touch with them as soon as I'm back in New England. I only wish that I knew more people who could help you along. My feeling is that all that's needed is for your work to be seen. I mean *really* seen. The right kind of exposure, the right kind of publicity. I'm not an expert at this, and I don't have the perfect connections...or any clout of my own. I told you that much yesterday. But I'll really try to get something going for you, and we'll keep our fingers crossed."

Stan nodded gravely. "If you didn't do another thing for me, I'd say you've already done more than enough."

There was a warmth to his expression as he looked at Hope, a warmth that made her faintly uncomfortable. The last thing in the world she needed just now was any sort of emotional involvement with Stancil Owl. Nevertheless, she meant what she'd said, and to show his work to someone who might be able to help him more than she could was certainly going to be her first order of business when she got home.

She said tentatively, "Do you suppose you could

let me take a few of your things back north with me?"

He shrugged. "Take the whole portfolio," he suggested.

"I won't need all of it...and I'd be terrified to take it, anyway. I'd never forgive myself if it became lost or damaged along the way."

He smiled. "I can't really believe it would be any great loss," he confessed.

"Stop thinking so negatively, Stan," Hope found herself saying. She tried to make light of this by adding, "If my crystal ball is right, there are going to be a lot of good things in your future."

He didn't answer this, and she turned back to his paintings and finally selected four to take back to Boston with her. To make any selection at all was difficult. All of the paintings were excellent, but these four showed the versatility of his considerable talent.

Once he'd left, she took the paintings back to the Fern Room and laid them flat on the bed. Her next task, she told herself, would be to find some sheets of cardboard—something, at least, that would protect them adequately. Then she'd wrap them securely and put them in a safe place—the closet shelf, probably—until her departure.

Again, though, she was interrupted. This time, the focus of attention was the kitchen door. Someone was knocking on it as Hope made her way toward the front of the house, so she changed her route and went to open it.

To her surprise, she found Randy Youngdeer on

the threshold. He came in at her invitation, but he seemed uncomfortable, restlessly shifting from one foot to the other. His usual, cheerful grin was absent, and this was so unlike Randy that Hope was puzzled.

"Something wrong?" she asked him.

"Nothing more than usual," he said glumly, and such a statement wasn't like Randy, either. Then he murmured, "It's about your car."

Randy had sent word to Hope right after her accident that she wasn't to worry about the Volvo, and he'd assured her that it would be ready and waiting for her whenever she wanted it. This sentiment had been reiterated the other day when he'd come to visit, along with the suggestion that she not pay him a cent until she'd seen the car and was satisfied. Hope had been appreciative of his kindness and had told him so.

Now she wondered if the problem might be that he wanted the money for the Volvo after all. Randy, she knew, would hate to come out and ask her for it under the circumstances, even though he did have it coming to him. But it was a bill she was going to have to pay sooner or later, regardless of the fact that it would further dent her already damaged financial state. And certainly that was her problem, not his.

"Randy," she said, "for heaven's sake, give me the bill! If you need some ready cash for something there's no point in not coming right out and saying so!"

"Oh, it isn't that," he told her hastily. "I have a

buyer for the Volvo, that's all, and I wondered if you'd ever thought about selling. The price is pretty good, considering."

"Really?"

"Really," he repeated, naming her a figure that was indeed very good. It was a lot more than she would have expected anyone to offer for a car that had definitely seen its best days.

She must have looked puzzled because Randy said, "This guy's a foreign-car buff. Works on them himself. Takes a part from one and puts it in another, that kind of thing. And he's got the money to spare."

"I see."

"Look, Hope, I'm not trying to twist your arm."

"Please don't," she said wryly. "I'm having enough arm trouble as it is."

Randy's answering smile didn't quite reach his eyes, and this convinced Hope that something really was bothering him. Something connected with her Volvo? That didn't seem likely.

As if to assuage her fears, he said, "Look, I told you the car's ready and waiting, and that still goes, okay? I just promised I'd convey this offer to you, that's all. If you don't want to sell, just say so. But...."

"But what, Randy?" she prodded.

"I'd hate like hell to see you start north in that car with your weak shoulder and everything," he said. "Ross mentioned that after a period of inactivity like this it's going to take you a while to work up the strength in both your shoulder and your arm.

He said something about your maybe needing therapy treatments. I guess he's talked to you about it.''

"He hasn't said anything definite about therapy," Hope answered, "but if I need further treatment I'll get it in Concord or Boston. Anyway, I'm going to have to start north in something, Randy, and I don't really want to take the bus or plane for the pure and simple reason that I'm going to need a car for transportation when I get home."

"You could take the money from the sale of the Volvo and either get something secondhand with it that would actually be better than what you've got now or else make a hefty down payment on something new," Randy suggested practically.

"I wouldn't even think of getting a new car right now," Hope assured him. "My finances just couldn't handle it, to tell you the truth. I think you're right, though. With the money from the sale of the Volvo I could find something that would give me adequate transportation, at least."

"A lot better transportation than you've got now," Randy repeated seriously.

Hope considered the matter carefully. "I'm almost positive I'll take the offer," she replied after a moment, and was surprised to see Randy's look of relief. "But I'd like to take a day or two to think about it, then I'll get back to you. There's a condition, though. You've got to accept a fifteen-percent commission right off the top!"

"No way," Randy said firmly.

"That's ridiculous!" Hope sputtered, and was further disconcerted when her exclamation was echoed by a very familiar voice somewhere behind her.

"What's ridiculous?" Ross Adair asked, turning her statement into a question.

"I got an offer for Hope's Volvo today," Randy explained. "But she's only willing to sell it if I take a cut, and I'm not about to do that."

"Oh?" Ross queried laconically. "Business is business, Randy."

"Not when..." Randy began, then evidently thought better of what he was going to say.

Hope caught a glance exchanged between the two men but couldn't decipher it. Nevertheless, she felt herself snared in the middle of something.

"If you won't take your cut, Randy," she said, "I definitely won't sell. And that's final."

There was a taunting quality to Ross Adair's smile. "Take it, Randy," he suggested.

"Oh, hell," Randy said, resigned. "If you're going to make a big case out of it, Hope, all right. Just let me know when you make your final decision and I can have the money for you right away...and thank you."

"Thank *you*," Hope repeated. She stared after Randy's departing figure, surprised for more reasons than one. She had the feeling that he'd been reluctant to come here today in the first place, and now his desire to rush off seemed equally obvious.

It was too much to fathom, especially under Ross Adair's watchful eye, and Hope sighed.

Immediately he asked, "What's the matter? Shoulder hurt?"

"Yes," she admitted, which was true. Her heart, though, was aching even more.

"When did you last take your medication?" he queried.

"About four hours ago."

"Time for another pill, then," he said authoritatively. "Sit down and I'll get it for you."

Hope nodded and sat down at the round table, still puzzled by Randy's odd behavior. She also wondered why Ross had come home so early this afternoon and was glad that he hadn't arrived any sooner. It would have been disastrous if he'd walked in on her meeting with Stancil Owl.

Stancil Owl! Hope sat up, appalled, realizing that she had forgotten all about the paintings lying in full view on her bed.

She tried to tell herself that there was a chance Ross wouldn't see them. It was fairly dim in the room at this time of day, and the medicine was in the bathroom cabinet. Possibly he'd go directly into the bathroom and wouldn't even get near the bed.

But she was not to be so lucky—as she knew the moment he stalked back into the kitchen.

He was holding the paintings as if they'd been dipped in poison, and the expression on his face was enough to intimidate anyone.

"How the hell did these get on your bed?" he demanded.

Hope shrank away from him, her face going white. Ross was towering over her, savagely angry. Then suddenly her defenses rallied. With one swift gesture she reached out with her good hand and wrenched the paintings away from him.

"Just who do you think you are?" she demanded evenly, spacing the words out slowly.

"Would you like to find out?" Ross taunted, moving toward her.

Instinctively Hope shied away, backing up so that she stumbled against the chair she'd been sitting in, and in the next second was sprawling out into space.

The pain that shot through her shoulder was so intense that she screamed, so devastating that momentarily she blacked out, as nature dispensed a share of mercy. But this reprieve was only a temporary one. She seemed to swim her way back into consciousness, only to find herself on the verge of drowning again in the depths of those midnight eyes.

Ross scooped her into his arms with such gentleness that it was as if he hadn't moved her at all. Then he carried her down the hall without saying a word and deposited her on the big comfortable bed in the Fern Room.

Despite the pain, the confusion and the anger that she'd felt for him just then, the thought crossed her mind that this was his dead wife's room he was bringing her to. This was his dead wife's bed!

Had he ever shared this bed with Lamanda?

Hope opened her eyes to see that he had left her, but he was back again almost immediately, this time carrying a black medical bag. She saw him grab an object out of it and recognized a hypodermic syringe, which he quickly filled with something extracted from a vial. Then he said briskly, "Here, your left arm. Please...don't try to hold it out. I'll take care of it."

The needle plunged, but Ross was very good at what he did. She felt only the merest prick. Then he was propping her against pillows, arranging them so that her injured side would have maximum support. "Take it easy for a few minutes," he said. "Once the shot takes effect I'm going to take you up to the hospital for an X ray."

"That isn't necessary," Hope protested. "I'm not all that fragile, Ross. I can assure you I haven't broken anything else!"

"I didn't say you had," he rejoined. "But you may have added insult to injury as far as your original damage is concerned. In any event, I already told you I wanted you to have another X ray shortly."

"But not this soon."

"It doesn't matter. Look, Hope, this is one time I'm going to have my way!" There was a coldness to the way he spoke that struck at her far more than his words did, and she retaliated.

"What is it with you?" she demanded. "Do you simply like to push people when they have their backs to the wall? Is that what you did with your wife?"

The question catapulted into the room, then reverberated back around Hope's own ears so that she cringed from the sound of it. But still she was not prepared for his reaction.

Never before had she seen such agony in a man's

face. She'd inflicted pain on a raw wound, a wound that would never heal, she told herself bleakly, and she knew that she would give anything in the world to be able to take back what she'd just said. But it was too late. Much too late.

The words were wrung out of him. "What do you know of my wife?" he stammered. "Who told you about Lamanda?"

"Lamanda?" It was a woman speaking, and Hope tore her eyes away from Ross Adair's tormented face to see Loretta Wood standing in the doorway.

This could not have been worse. It was bad enough to have said such a dreadful thing to Ross, but now she was opening up another wound—the sorrow of a mother for a daughter who had died long ago.

"Oh, my God," Hope said simply, wishing that she could disappear from the face of the earth.

Mrs. Wood came into the room and looked from one face to the other in bewilderment. "I heard your voices," she said. "It sounded as if something was wrong so I came to see...."

"It's all right, Aunt Loretta," Ross said quickly, but Hope knew him well enough to realize he was not nearly as calm as he was trying to appear to his aunt. "Hope had a fall...it was an accident. I'm going to take her over to the hospital for another X ray and she doesn't particularly want to go, that's all."

"But what about Lamanda?" Mrs. Wood persisted.

"Hope asked me about Lamanda and I wondered how she knew about her," Ross said evenly. "I should have realized that the two of you had probably spoken of her. I should have realized that."

"As a matter of fact, we haven't," Mrs. Wood said. Then she added almost abjectly, "I didn't know whether or not she knew that...."

"That Lamanda and I were married?" Ross finished, smiling so sadly that Hope wanted to cry out for him. "Well, she knows. And it's all right. So... Hope and I will get going. It shouldn't take very long, but don't start anything for dinner, okay? Unless the X rays indicate that Hope should rest in bed, I'm going to take you two lovely ladies out to dinner."

Hope could not have been more astonished. Mrs. Wood seemed happy about this, though, and she left the room with a pleasant little wave of her hand.

After a moment Ross said, "Come along with me without making it any more difficult for either of us, will you? Later we can talk about Lamanda... or anything else you want to talk about. But I think you'll agree that we both need a cooling-off period first."

He looked at her as if she puzzled him, his handsome brow furrowed. Then he said, "I don't know what it is you do to me, Hope. I don't usually let my temper take over so easily. Now it seems that I owe you an apology. You had every right, of course, to look at Stancil Owl's paintings."

Hope, unable to speak, had no idea how eloquent

her lovely face was. Ross started to say something more, then, as if issuing a warning to himself, said, "Later." He was very gentle with her as he helped her get ready. In fact, inexplicably, Hope felt a new kind of closeness to him and was actually glad that Lamanda's name had finally been mentioned between them.

THIS WAS THE FIRST TIME that Hope had approached the hospital in daylight and she was immediately struck by its unusual architecture. It was very modern in concept, built predominantly of stone and concrete. The earth-covered sloping sides had been planted with small shrubs, and there were openings every so often into which the windows had been discreetly set. The entire structure had been thoughtfully integrated with the land surrounding it. The hillside plunged away in front, the mountainside loomed behind and the hospital itself barely broke nature's contour.

Ross drove up under the main porte cochere this time, instead of using the emergency-room entrance, and carefully helped her out of the car. Once inside, he was recognized and greeted by everyone they met, and there could be no doubt that he was held in very high esteem by the entire personnel. Finally, he left Hope alone with the X-ray technician, a pleasant young Cherokee who was openly admiring in a way that was refreshing.

By the time Ross appeared at her side he had already checked the X rays, and he said, "You really lucked out. There doesn't seem to be any damage from today's mishap, and the original injury is healing quite well.''

Hope nodded mutely, suddenly feeling shy before him, perhaps because she was not used to seeing him in his professional milieu. She was aware that he was studying her revealing face much too intently.

He said in a tone that was surprisingly gentle, ''We can go now, Hope. Unless you'd prefer to stay here.''

She glanced up instantly and was surprised to see a hint of amusement in those dark eyes.

''Come along,'' he said, without waiting for her answer, and then pushed a small step stool over to the examining table and helped her climb down. But he made no move to take her arm as they went down the corridor, and when they reached his car she quickly tried to open the door and get in by herself.

Ross swiftly forestalled her. ''Take it easy, will you?'' he cautioned, laying a restraining hand on her good right arm. ''You tend to leap much too quickly—especially to conclusions.''

There was nothing that Hope could dare say to this at the moment. She felt Ross slide into the front seat beside her and wondered if she could possibly bear this kind of proximity right now. What, for example, would she do if he suddenly drew her into his arms? She asked herself this and at once knew the answer. She would melt into his embrace to meet his desire with a passion of her own, a passion that was already beginning to rise at only the thought of his touch. And this time she was certain that regardless of what he had said about such a union on their part, neither her injured arm nor anything else would stop them from continuing to a culmination that was beyond her power to imagine.

She stirred, moved by a tide of utter sensuality. And this was only accented by the faint scent of the after-shave lotion that wafted across to her as Ross reached out to switch on the ignition.

Then the moment passed, and Hope realized that the last thing in the universe Ross Adair was going to do right now was take her in his arms. As if to prove this, he shifted into gear in a way that seemed even more emphatic than usual and accelerated down the hospital driveway.

CHAPTER THIRTEEN

THEY WERE SILENT on the drive back to Loretta Wood's house, and this time Hope opened the door and got out of the car before Ross had the chance to come around and help her. She felt awkward and suffered a twinge or two, but anything was preferable to having him touch her just now. She was too vulnerable before him.

Loretta Wood was waiting for them in the living-room doorway, and she caught her breath in sharply when she saw Hope. "You're so pale, my dear," she said. "What happened?"

"Nothing happened," Ross reported easily before Hope could say anything at all. "Hope had her X rays and she's doing fine. No damage from the fall as far as we could see. In another week she should be able to dispense with the shoulder harness, unless she does something especially awkward in the meantime." His smile took the sting out of the words as he said this.

"I'm sure Hope didn't fall down deliberately, Ross," his aunt protested.

"No," Hope put in. "Very definitely, I did not!"

Ross grinned. "I don't remember making an accusation," he pointed out.

Unexpectedly, Mrs. Wood said, "I think this calls for something stronger than sherry."

"Bourbon and branch water," Ross agreed. "Same for you, Hope?"

"I don't think so."

"What if I prescribe it?"

"All right. . .if you say so," she agreed.

"I'll fix the drinks in a minute," Ross told his aunt, and she nodded.

"I'll see if I can conjure up some appetizers," she decided, and to Hope's dismay went out to the kitchen, leaving her alone with Ross. She wasn't ready to cope with him, but she knew she wasn't about to be let off, either.

Once again a long finger came out to tilt her chin upward, and she met eyes as dark as night. Now, though, they looked softer than velvet.

"Dearest Hope," Ross said gently. "You take everything so damned hard. When something bothers you, why don't you ask me about it? About Lamanda, for example?"

Hope avoided this and countered, "I did ask you about Stancil Owl. . . ."

"And you completely ignored what I told you, didn't you?" Ross rejoined, shaking his head at her. "All right, I admit I was wrong. I can't say I'll ever be enthusiastic about any other man coming around you." He smiled, a disturbingly tender smile. "Also," he told her, "I'll surely never be able to question your spirit. I've never met a woman quite so strong willed. And in such a deceptively fragile-looking package, too."

"I'm not fragile!"

"Just now you appear to be," he contradicted. "You're white as a sheet, your arm's in a sling and your eyes seem so sad with those dark shadows underneath. Just looking at you makes me feel like a miserable heel. Does that satisfy you?"

It was she who had been feeling like a heel because of the dreadful thing she'd said to him about Lamanda, so she was taken aback by this admission on his part. She said quickly, "It's not a question of satisfying me!"

"Isn't it, though?" Ross retorted wickedly, with such obvious meaning that she felt herself flushing. But before she could think of a suitable reply he gently propelled her toward the kitchen door and said, "Come along. Maybe you don't need a drink, but I could certainly use one!"

"Frankly," Hope said, "I'm not sure I really want a drink. I'm tired and...."

"Yes?" he prodded.

Hope had no desire to get into an analysis of her conflicting emotions so she said evasively, "Principally, I'm tired."

"You can rest later," Ross told her succinctly. Then he added, "Both you and my aunt seem to have forgotten that I invited you two out to dinner, provided you were well enough. Since you're okay, I think it would do you good to get out of the house."

"Not tonight," Hope repeated, but Ross didn't even seem to be listening to her. He was striding toward the kitchen, and a moment later she heard him say something to his aunt.

She followed slowly and, looking at Loretta Wood, felt certain that the older woman didn't want to go out to dinner any more than she did. She said quickly, "I've told Ross I really am quite tired and I'd much rather go to bed than go out to eat. I'm not even hungry, to tell you the truth."

Loretta Wood nodded. "Neither am I," she admitted. "I was so afraid that you'd been seriously hurt again . . . well, it gave me quite a start."

"I'm sorry, Mrs. Wood," Hope said impulsively.

"It wasn't your fault, dear."

Surprisingly, Ross agreed. "If anything it was mine," he said darkly. Then he added, "Where, may I ask, have you hidden that bourbon, Aunt Loretta?"

"I haven't hidden it anywhere, Ross," she told him. "It's in the cabinet in the dining room, where such things are always kept."

"Will you join us?"

"Thank you, no," she said. "Just now I'll settle for a cup of tea. As a matter of fact, I think I'll take it to my room and lie down for a while. I'm reading a good book, and half an hour of relaxation is what I need at the moment. Then we can think about having a simple supper that will suit all of us. Which reminds me, Minerva Lightfoot made some mushroom soup yesterday. She even gathered the mushrooms herself. She gave me a big jar of it and a loaf of her chestnut bread, as well, because she wanted Hope to try both."

"What?" Ross demanded, incredulous.

"You heard me, Ross," his aunt told him calmly.

"I've been making a few Cherokee dishes for Hope, myself. She's interested in our food, in case you didn't know it. Minerva's going to teach her how to make bean bread, as soon as Hope can get out and do some visiting. Minerva said it would be easier for her to do it in her own kitchen."

Hope nearly laughed aloud at the expression on Ross's face. But he only said, "You're not about to try groundhog stew or possum on her, are you?"

"You know that I don't like opossum because it's so greasy," his aunt reminded him. "Of course, a good groundhog stew can be delicious."

Mrs. Wood, Hope saw with admiration, did have a poker face. Then their eyes met, and Hope saw a decided twinkle in those midnight ones, so much like Ross's. She smiled back, knowing that in some respects, at least, she and Loretta Wood had achieved a full rapport.

Ross said dryly, "I stand corrected. I suppose you've also instructed Hope about the nutritional value of Cherokee foods. Especially that of the greens we eat, which most people don't know anything about at all."

Mrs. Wood folded her arms. "Well, I started to," she said, "but there are so many. Sweet grass, ramps, poke and angelica are only a few of them. Then there are all the things that we use to make tea, like sassafras and spice wood. Incidentally, Hope, Minerva meant to bring me some of the ramps she has in her freezer. She promised to save them for you."

Ross literally threw up his hands. "I give up," he

said in mock despair, and bolted for the dining-room cabinet in which the whiskey was kept.

Once he'd left the room, Loretta Wood moved across the floor with surprising speed and said in a low voice, "Hope, don't judge Ross too harshly. He's been through so much, he's suffered far more than he should have for someone his age. He's worked very, very hard to get where he is today. And...he's a very fine person, loyal and good."

Before Hope could recover from this confidence, Ross's aunt was over at the stove putting on a kettle of water for her tea, and Ross returned brandishing the bottle of bourbon.

"I think I'll go on a rampage," he announced. "Anything to preserve my sanity! And I insist that you *do* join me, Miss Hope Standish, for at least the first drink. Doctor's orders!"

Hope didn't try to protest again. She watched as Ross made drinks for both of them with his usual efficiency, but she was unprepared for it when he put the two glasses on a tray, instead of handing her one. This left him with a free hand, and he came over to her and took hold of her elbow.

Instantly his touch sent desire flaming through her. Hope drew a deep breath, and when he said, "Let's go in the living room with these," she could think of nothing else to do except go along with him, even though the very last thing she wanted just now was to be alone with him. She was too apt to reveal herself entirely to him.

"I'll put the soup on low so it'll be ready when

you want it," Mrs. Wood called after them "You can fix up the chestnut bread, Ross."

"Chestnut bread, indeed," he muttered.

Hope tried to choose a chair where Ross would have to sit a fair distance away from her, but this didn't work, either. He simply pulled up another chair, so that he was only a few feet in front of her. Then he reached out to click her glass with his, and he said, "To a better understanding between us." He sipped, and added ruefully, "I'm still working on it."

"So am I," she replied under her breath.

To her surprise, the bourbon went down well. Ross had been right. At the moment, the drink had a certain medicinal quality—at least it seemed so. She wished that it would also give her the ability to steel herself against Ross, unlikely though this was. The smile he was favoring her with was so disarming that she felt herself melting, despite her intention to achieve control of her soaring, dangerous emotions and somehow keep the upper hand.

After a moment, Ross said quietly, "There are quite a few things to be resolved between us, aren't there?"

Were there? That depended, of course, on how much he wanted to include her in his life. Hope had no real illusions on that score. She knew very well how easily he'd be able to shut her out, just when she thought she had a toe in the door.

"Aren't there, Hope?" he repeated, and she decided to answer the question as honestly as she could.

"I don't know," she said.

"You don't know, or you don't care?" he asked.

"I don't know."

"I suppose Wonder's told you all sorts of tales," he persisted, then went on without waiting for her answer, "and I'm not saying that she's necessarily been overly inventive about them. But Wonder is definitely a romantic."

"And you're a pragmatist?"

"Is that a question or a diagnosis?" Ross asked, leaning back in the chair, his long legs stretched out.

Hope couldn't answer at once, because she was much too conscious of his highly disturbing physical attributes. In addition to being strikingly handsome, Ross Adair exuded vitality—and virility. The combination was emotionally lethal.

She searched for her voice with effort, found it and said carefully, "I would never venture a diagnosis about you, Ross."

"Not ever?" he teased. "Come now, Hope, am I that difficult?"

"Sometimes," she admitted.

He was holding his glass of whiskey between his hands, and now he gazed down into its amber depths and said with a deliberateness that made her know he was controlling himself with effort, "I suppose that, partly at least, our problems are due to an age-old barrier. Remember those famous lines—Kipling, wasn't it—about East being East and West being West, with the conclusion that the twain shall never meet? It amounts to the same thing, doesn't it? For that matter, the Cherokees, like all American Indians, came from Asia originally."

She stared at him. "For an intelligent person," she finally sputtered, "you are sometimes absolutely idiotic!"

"Am I, Hope?" he asked. "Idiotic about you, maybe. I'd have to plead guilty to that. But don't think I haven't spent a few sleepless nights trying to work it all through about...about us. Haven't you noticed that just when we seem at the point of...of an understanding, something tends to happen to shake it?"

"Yes," she said, "I've noticed. But I don't think that our respective backgrounds, or the differences between them, should be blamed. I don't have any problems with your aunt or with Wonder or Randy Youngdeer or...."

"Or Stancil Owl?" he prompted.

"Please," Hope said. "Let's not bring Stancil Owl into this."

Ross laughed. But then he said, "The business with Stan Owl, I admit, brought me close to the end of my patience!"

Hope could not repress a smile. "I gathered that," she said dryly. "But may I say that your patience has the shortest fuse I've ever seen."

"That's not true. I'm extremely patient...about some things."

"Medicine, maybe?" Hope inquired.

"What?"

"Your work, Dr. Adair. I can imagine that

you're very patient about your work. But in your personal relations...."

"You don't know anything about my personal relations!"

Hope's grin was impish. "I'm finding out!" she retorted.

She was teasing him, actually teasing him. She wouldn't have thought she could ever do such a thing with Ross, and the idea that she could be this lighthearted where he was concerned gave her a giddy feeling.

She laughed out loud when she saw the bewildered expression on his face. Watching the bewilderment merge into confusion, then into a smile laced with humor, she wondered how she could ever have thought that his face was expressionless.

"Well," he said, seeming very pleased, "I've discovered something else about you. You do have a sense of humor after all! You've taken everything so damned seriously that I'd begun to wonder."

His smile became so tender that she stirred, fearful that her love for him was going to be much too transparent. Then he said softly, "Will you make me a promise, Hope?"

Instantly she was on guard. "What?" she asked.

"You've looked at Stan Owl's paintings. Now will you promise me not to see him again?"

Hope was thoroughly taken aback by this, and she responded instinctively, without pausing to wonder why he should make such a request of her.

"No," she said. "No, I won't promise you that."

Ross literally drew back and said stiffly, "I don't think it's much to ask. I know considerably more about Stan than you do."

She shook her head. "You're prejudiced," she told him.

He stared at her. "*I'm* prejudiced?" he demanded. "Look, Hope—"

"Listen, Ross," she countered. "In the short time I've known her, Wonder has become a friend of mine. I'm genuinely fond of her. I told you that I made her a promise because she's very concerned about her brother. And now that I've seen his work I think there just may be a chance that I can help him. If I had better connections of my own in the art world, I know there'd be a chance. As it is, I intend to do the best I can for him. So under the circumstances, I can't possibly promise you that I won't be in touch with him again. I shouldn't think you'd even suggest it, if you'd stop to think things over first."

"Then you're mistaken," Ross said. "Stan Owl has been nothing but trouble for years—to everyone he's touched. I see no indication that he's changed, despite the efforts of any number of do-gooders to rehabilitate him." Ross didn't attempt to hide his bitterness as he spoke. "You must realize that Wonder and Randy are very much in love with each other, if you've got all that close to Wonder."

"I had a feeling they were," Hope admitted.

"Well, what do you think is keeping them apart? Randy's tried to help Stan not once but several times. Twice he's given him a job and had to let him go because Stan got drunk and insulted the customers. One day he even stole some money out of the cash register. Wonder's blindly loyal to her brother and...all right, I can admire that to a point. But there is also a different kind of point, a point of no return, and where Stan Owl is concerned it was reached a long time ago.''

Hope surveyed him steadily. ''Did you know his ex-wife?''

Ross's eyebrows jerked upward. He seemed slightly shaken by this question, but finally he said, ''Yes. What's that got to do with it?''

''Was it she who turned you against Stan?''

He shook his head impatiently. ''Hell, no! Nothing 'turned' me against Stan except Stan himself. As for his...ex-wife, she was a sweet kid, if you must know. He had no business fooling around with her. And she got nothing but grief from him.''

''I'd say that's one side of the story,'' Hope said carefully. ''It seems to me that she gave him a fair measure of grief, too. And she ended up taking their child away from him completely.''

''A damned good thing,'' Ross muttered. ''What chance would she have had with Stan? Not to mention the chances of a little baby! God, Hope, you've seen him for yourself. You *have* seen him, haven't you? I presume he came here with those paintings of his?''

''Yes, he came here,'' Hope said, her chin held high. ''He's been here twice. The first time we just talked. He hadn't brought any artwork with him, so I asked him to come back.''

Ross stared at her in disbelief. "You *asked* him to come back?" he repeated.

"Yes, I did. And when he returned he'd shaved and had washed his hair and put on some clean clothes."

"Spare me the platitudes," Ross said wearily. "You should be a missionary! Why waste your time teaching art to rich preppies when you have this latent talent for reforming all mankind?"

Hope could feel her cheeks burning, but she refused to let herself be daunted by his sarcasm. She said, "As a matter of fact, Stancil Owl is very talented. And I do mean *very* talented. If he's given the opportunity to have his work seen in the right places I think you'll find that he's been misjudged by many people. Certainly by you."

"Thanks a lot," Ross said bitterly.

The symbolical peace pipe had vanished, Hope knew, and in its place a symbolical chasm came to yawn between them. Across it, Ross sat rigidly, and although he was only a few feet from her, he seemed completely unapproachable.

He had finished his drink and now he rose, glass in hand, and said, "I'm going to make myself another. How about you?"

"No, thanks," Hope replied almost too hastily. Ross sensed this and stopped abruptly. Then he stared down at her, the old inscrutable mask firmly in place again.

"What's the matter?" he asked. "Afraid the firewater will get to me and I'll break the place up?"

His tone was so caustic that she felt herself

burned by it. But she managed to make her own tone calm as she replied, "That sort of question doesn't deserve an answer."

"Hope..." he began after a tension-filled pause, his voice hesitant.

She shook her head. "No, Ross," she told him. "Let's not get into anything else. There are times when you and I don't seem to be able to agree about anything. I think this is one of them. Anyway, I really am tired. And even though it's rather early, I think the best thing to do would be to go to bed—"

She broke off, because there was a double meaning to that phrase "go to bed" that she was sure would not elude him, and she tried to prepare herself for another sarcastic comment. But whatever Ross might have said to her was destined to remain unspoken, because just then the telephone rang.

Hope watched him cross the room to answer it, a tall, graceful man who seemed slightly weary at the moment, although this did not in the least diminish the powerful attractiveness that was such an integral part of him. She heard him say hello pleasantly enough, but at his next words she stiffened.

"Well, hello, love," Ross was saying in a voice that was warmer than any she'd ever heard him use before. "You're back in Boston? Yes, my aunt told me you'd called a couple of times, but there just hasn't been a right moment when I could get back to you."

He was making no attempt to lower his voice, and Hope wondered if he actually wanted her to hear him speaking to this other woman in that caressing tone. But she wasn't about to listen. She got up quietly and made her way down the hall, and once in the Fern Room she turned the key that dangled in the lock.

If Ross Adair came looking for her later—doubtful prospect though this was—there was no way that he was going to get in.

CHAPTER FOURTEEN

THE DAYS PASSED SLOWLY, and finally the time came when Ross told Hope that she could dispense with the shoulder harness, although it was imperative that she continue to wear the sling. But when she suggested that she should now be able to travel without waiting any longer, he flatly stated that this was out of the question for at least another week.

"I will want a final X ray before I can release you," he said formally, very much the doctor about this. "Then the therapist at the hospital will show you how to do a series of simple exercises that will help strengthen your arm and shoulder. Your arm will be quite weak at first, and it will probably be rather painful for a while, I'm sorry to say. Nevertheless, in time you'll be as good as new." Ross smiled briefly at the conclusion of this speech, but it was a purely professional smile, and Hope decided she would have preferred it if he hadn't smiled at her at all.

The other night, when he'd finished with his long-distance phone call, he had not come down the hall to the Fern Room, and since then the atmosphere between them had been decidedly cool. Surprisingly, though, he seemed to be around the house more than he had been previously. Except for the times when he was on call at the hospital, he spent a fair bit of time at home. He even swam twice a day in the pool, and Hope began to wish fervently that she could join him.

She'd told him that she wasn't much of a swimmer, and it had been out of the question, anyway, while she was using the shoulder harness. But now she wondered if it might be good for her to try. She was about to put the question to him when she stopped to think about what it would be like to be in the same pool with Ross Adair. It was all she could do to look at him in swim trunks without revealing the emotional impact this particular sight made on her.

Emotional? It was purely sensual, she knew. Sexual, for that matter. But she'd never before seen a man quite so flagrantly male as Ross, though he seemed quite unaware of this. He always wore either skintight black trunks or stark white ones, and she didn't know which were more disturbing.

He'd been swimming that morning before he came out to the terrace to tell her she could dispense with the shoulder harness. He had, in fact, helped her out of it. Then he'd repositioned the sling, but without the extra support Hope had felt quite strange. She soon realized, though, that the giddiness she was also feeling had nothing to do with the absence of her shoulder harness. Rather, Ross's touch upon her arm had set up a chain reaction that caused her to quiver, and she couldn't imagine that he wouldn't be aware of this.

If he was, though, he wasn't showing it. He'd changed into denim shorts and a matching shirt after his swim, and he went back into the kitchen and returned with two large mugs of coffee. Then he lowered himself into a deck lounger not far from the one Hope was using and looked across at her thoughtfully.

"I don't want you driving," he began, "but Wonder mentioned that Randy has said the two of you can use Betsy whenever you want to. I've no objection to your going on short excursions with Wonder occasionally, provided you exercise reasonable caution. Just don't try to go mountain climbing or anything like that, okay?"

Again he flashed her that professional smile, and she decided she thoroughly detested it, even though it made him look so handsome that all of his female patients must automatically fall in love with him. "Nor is there any reason why you shouldn't do some painting if you want to," he added. "Wonder could set up your easel for you, or I could—if you want to try something around the house here. Just don't attempt to do it yourself. You might inadvertently use your left arm, and the shoulder isn't ready for that sort of pressure."

"What about swimming?" Hope interjected despite her private qualms about this.

Ross frowned. "Not yet," he said. "After I've checked the next X ray and I'm satisfied that you're still healing well, I'd say that swimming—in moderation at first, of course—would be excellent therapy."

"Thank you very much, doctor," Hope said formally, and was rewarded by seeing him dart a decidedly suspicious look in her direction. But he was not to be baited.

After a moment he said, "What have you decided to do about your car? Randy said you were going to call him and let him have your decision, but that was a while ago. I gather the would-be purchaser is becoming impatient."

"I guess that's true," Hope conceded. "Wonder told me yesterday that Randy's asked her to persuade me to make a decision."

"But you haven't?"

"Well," she said hesitantly, "Randy pointed out that with the money I'd get I could easily buy another car. On the other hand, I'd really like to drive the Volvo back to Boston. It seems to me I could count on it to make one more long trip."

"Going on what Randy's said," Ross warned, "I doubt it. I'm sure it was an excellent machine in its day, but I'd say that that day is long gone. It would be ridiculous for you to attempt such an extensive drive in a car that old."

"It made it down here," Hope reminded him, "and I wouldn't have to push it on the way back. Anyway, it would be so much more convenient for me. It's occurred to me that it would be quite difficult to take all my painting gear on a plane, and the bus would be just as bad, if not worse."

"Your equipment could be shipped to you," Ross pointed out.

Hope didn't answer this at once. She knew, of

course, that her easel and paint boxes and all the rest of her gear could be sent on. But this would mean a further contact with Cherokee, and she had already resolved that once she left here she must put her time in these mountains behind her forever.

This conclusion had not been reached without considerable soul-searching, and already she was wondering if she could live up to her own resolve. She had become very fond not only of Wonder but of Loretta Wood, as well. Then there was Randy and Minerva Lightfoot and Penny Raincrow, who had stopped by to see her one day and was absolutely delightful.

And there was Stancil Owl. She hadn't heard from him since the day he'd left the pictures with her, but she knew he was depending upon her.

Now she remembered grimly that she'd had to search for those pictures. She hadn't been about to ask either Ross or his aunt what had happened to them. She had felt certain that Ross had done something with them, and she'd been right about that. She'd found them on the table in his study, where he'd thrust them to one side, but at least he hadn't tossed his books and research material on top of them.

She'd removed the paintings, taking them to the Fern Room, and she'd carefully placed them on a shelf in the closet. Nor had she said anything to Ross about this. And, rather surprisingly, he had said nothing to her, either, although he must have noticed that the paintings were gone.

She and Ross had not been communicating well

since the night he'd received that phone call from Boston. And in retrospect it seemed to Hope that too much—and not enough—had happened between them too soon. This sounded ambiguous, she knew, yet it described their dilemma quite accurately. Passion had swept them together, along with a physical demand that neither of them had been able to negate. They'd both been carried on a high, cresting wave, a wave of wanting that seemed doomed to surge on and on and would never be able to fulfill itself.

Passion unfulfilled. A seemingly trite sentiment, Hope thought, but not trite at all when it reached the point of tearing a person apart emotionally. She'd been completely torn apart by her need for Ross, and she was certain that he'd felt the same need for her. It was the last thing she'd expected. She'd never intended to give herself to another man after her hideous experience with Lewis, but the overwhelming thrust of her feeling for Ross had changed all that.

And there was the other problem. The problem of a love for him that went way beyond passion.

She sighed deeply, and Ross said in a voice laced with cynicism, "Excuse me, but I'm still here."

Hope glanced across at him quickly to see a smile from which all the professionalism had vanished. Now it was purely mocking.

"What do you mean?" she asked.

"What do I *mean*?" he echoed. "A number of minutes ago I asked you if it wouldn't be possible for us to send your things back north, if you opted to go home by bus or plane. And you immediately went into some sort of reverie, which has had you following a rather tortuous road, if the expressions that have been playing across your face are any indication. Do you have a lover back in Concord, Hope?''

The question came so swiftly that she was totally unprepared for it, and she overreacted. ''No!'' she said abruptly, feeling her cheeks begin to flame.

''Such vehemence,'' Ross drawled. ''No need for a show of outraged innocence, my dear. In our few brief encounters I've become thoroughly aware that there is nothing very 'innocent' about you at all.''

She stared at him. ''That's a rotten thing to say!'' she choked out, her voice hoarse with suppressed emotion.

''Please,'' Ross protested much too mildly. ''You're not trying to tell me, are you, that there's never been a man in your life—in the sense we're talking about?''

Hope felt herself grow cold. It was as if her heart had become a blackboard, and a giant eraser was wiping out love and substituting hate.

She got to her feet, trembling. ''I don't have to listen to this anymore!'' she managed to say, swallowing hard.

''No, you don't, do you?'' Ross agreed amiably, and stood up himself. ''Don't bother to make a calculated exit,'' he told her. ''I'm leaving myself. I have work to do.''

In another instant he was gone, and Hope sank back into the deck chair, her breath coming fast.

How absolutely awful he could be! She shuddered as she thought of his question about having a man in her life, and she realized she had condemned herself in his eyes by not answering it. She had no doubt at all he'd come to his own conclusions, and she could imagine the sort of mental picture he'd already painted of her—if, indeed, he hadn't long since completed that particular work of art.

Thinking of a painting reminded her of both Stancil Owl's work and her own. She regretted ever having become involved with Wonder's brother—not because she had obviously displeased Ross by doing so, but because the association was another link to Cherokee. She promised herself that once she'd found someone to refer him to, she'd sever her own connections with Stancil.

Thinking of her own work forced her to focus on something entirely different, a focus she badly needed at the moment. Ross had suggested that she try some painting if she wished to, adding that she should seek help in handling her easel.

Well, Hope thought defiantly, she'd be damned if she'd ask his help in anything, even if it were to save her life. She was perfectly able to manage the easel—and everything else—entirely on her own.

Suiting action to words, she decided to go for a walk on a path she'd noticed from the side of the terrace. It went on up the hillside, and although Ross had cautioned her about "climbing mountains," Hope didn't consider this in that category. From her vantage point she could see an alluring turn only a short distance away. This path was a mystery, and it seemed to beckon to her. She had no idea where it led to or what sort of vista it might expose.

There was a heady sense of freedom in going down the steps on the side of the terrace that faced the hillside and the woods after her long confinement in the house. She started out along her chosen path and soon felt herself immersed in a world that was entirely green and fragrant. And if the fragrance reminded her of Ross Adair she would simply have to get over it, she told herself sternly.

After a time, the path became steeper, and the going got harder. It came to the point where Hope didn't dare to continue any farther. The last thing in the world she wanted to do was suffer another fall and hinder her recovery.

She started back, pausing shortly to sit down on a large boulder that looked as if it had been upthrust from the earth especially for her convenience. Soon she became conscious of birds singing in the trees that surrounded her, and a chipmunk scurried across the path, almost brushing the toe of her sneaker.

The sun filtered through the greenery, casting a golden grid just beyond her. The air was soft and warm, and a gentle breeze stirred the leaves. She watched a delicate yellow butterfly soar across the path and disappear behind a pine tree, and she felt a pang of sharp regret that she would have to be leaving this beautiful place so soon. It was so lovely, so peaceful, and she was so lonely and heartsick.

Hope stood up. This was no time to become immersed in self-pity. Slowly she traced her way back to the house and found to her surprise that Wonder Owl was waiting on the terrace.

"Whew!" Wonder said. "I've been worried about you, but Ross said you could go for a walk if you wanted to."

"Ross?"

"He's working in his office," Wonder explained. "He was like a bear when I burst in on him because I couldn't find you. I think I'd better go and tell him you're back."

"No need," Ross Adair said. "I came to see for myself."

He was standing in the living-room doorway, holding his dark-rimmed glasses in one hand. Now he sauntered across the terrace and came to the very edge of the steps, so that Hope had to skirt around him in order to avoid a contact she wanted no part of.

"Enjoy yourself?" he asked dryly.

"Yes," she said, "I did. It's very beautiful up there."

Ross's lips tightened. "I thought I told you not to go around climbing mountains," he warned.

Wonder laughed. "That's hardly a mountain climb, Ross. Not until you get quite a way along, at least."

"It's too much of a climb for Hope at the moment," he insisted. "She should know enough to confine herself to flat surfaces."

"But there aren't any flat surfaces around here," Wonder pointed out.

"Oh, hell!" Ross exploded. "You, too, Wonder? I'll thank you to keep out of this."

"Keep out of what?" Wonder asked innocently. "I didn't know I was getting into anything."

Ross shook his head in mock despair. But then he flashed a smile at Wonder Owl that few women could resist. "How about making us some iced coffee?" he asked. "There's plenty in the percolator."

Wonder shook her own head in an equally mock despair, but nevertheless she set out to do as he'd asked. As soon as she'd disappeared inside the house Ross turned toward Hope, who was standing at the edge of the terrace looking out at the valley, which seemed especially green and gold and glorious today.

She was trying not to think of anything except how magnificent these Great Smoky Mountains were and how lush everything was. Above all, she was trying not to think about this man who had come to stand just behind her, much too close for comfort.

"Hope..." he began.

She stopped him before he could go on. "There's nothing to say, Ross," she told him firmly.

"On the contrary, there's a great deal to say. I've told you that we have many things to talk about, you and I. Those things haven't gone away, Hope. But before I can expect you to listen to me I realize I'm going to have to say I'm sorry once again. And I do apologize for some of my most recent stupid statements. I had no right to speak to you as I did a little while ago or to ask you such an intimate question."

She turned to face him, almost forgetting that powerful body next to her. "You've made similar apologies before, Ross," she reminded him.

"I know," he admitted ruefully, "but that doesn't mean this one is any less sincere. Every time I try to start following a new road with you I tend to go off track." He drew a long breath, then finished, "And...it becomes too much for me to handle."

Hope laughed out loud at this. "I don't think anything could really be too much for you to handle, Ross," she told him. "Especially anything involving a woman."

There was a dangerous glint in his jet eyes. "You think that, eh?" he asked, his voice soft, the Southern accent very pronounced.

"Shouldn't I?" she challenged.

"I don't know what you should do," Ross confessed, and then completely rocked her by asking, "What is it you want, Hope?"

How could she possibly answer that question? In desperation she sought the easiest refuge. "I don't understand what you mean," she countered.

"What do you want from me, Hope? Sometimes I think I'll go crazy if I don't find out soon. What do I mean to you? Do I mean anything at all to you?"

To this Hope could not even find her voice, let alone speak, and Ross laughed mirthlessly. "One thing is definite," he told her then. "Before you leave here, that's one avenue I intend to explore fully. You know what I'm talking about, Hope, and you can't deny that you've responded to me. Right now I could take you if I wanted to. *If* I wanted to? Hell, I want to so much I'd pay Wonder not to come back out here and I'd forget all about that shoulder of yours, which probably wouldn't be hurt anyway by a little honest passion. But I will never leave the way open so that later you can throw it in my face that I took you by force, Hope. And right now, judging by the look on your face, that's the way it would be. No, when our time comes I'm going to have you with the knowledge that you couldn't hold back for another second!''

"Our time will never come, Ross.'' It took all of Hope's inner stamina to force herself to say this, and even then her voice quivered.

His eloquent eyebrows tilted upward. "No?'' he asked mockingly. "I'll tell you right now that our time *will* come, Hope. It's written in the stars. Maybe even back at the beginning of time, when, according to the Cherokees, all living creatures made their home in the sky.''

"In Galun'lati,'' she murmured absently.

He frowned. "What did you say?''

"It doesn't matter,'' Hope hedged.

"All right,'' he agreed. "It doesn't matter. But what does matter is that our time will come—and sooner than you think.''

Hope drew herself together by sheer willpower. "Is that a threat, Ross?'' she demanded defiantly.

"No,'' he said, directing a bittersweet smile down at her that made her shiver. "It's a promise!''

When Wonder returned, Ross became a different person, laughing and chatting as he sipped his iced coffee. It seemed impossible to Hope that she'd actually felt mesmerized by him only minutes before. She told herself that he was like one of the chameleons who came to sun on the rocks along the edge of the terrace. He was able to change himself to suit the background and even the mood of the moment.

She was not so pliable. It was very difficult for her to try to hold up her part of the conversation under these circumstances, and she was glad when Ross finally left them, saying he had some long-distance telephoning to do.

She wondered if he was going to call the woman who had phoned him the other night, and she recognized the dull pain that came to twist inside her for exactly what it was—jealousy. Pure, unadulterated jealousy.

"Has something gone wrong between you and Ross?" Wonder asked perceptively.

About to invent an answer, Hope found herself saying instead, "Nothing ever went right, Wonder."

"I think," Wonder said slowly, "that he's fallen in love with you."

"No way," Hope stated. "Ross is primarily in love with Ross."

"But that's not true," Wonder protested hastily. "You don't really know Ross at all if you believe something like that. He's a very modest person, even self-demeaning at times, although he surely has no reason to be." She laughed. "In that way, he's a typical Cherokee male—young male, anyway. Our young men tend to be shy and difficult to get to know. They often hide their true feelings.''

''Ross isn't that young,'' Hope said shortly. ''And if you're defining a typical Cherokee characteristic, then I'll have to say that in my opinion he doesn't fit the mold at all.''

Wonder sighed. ''I had hoped that you...felt differently about him,'' she admitted. ''To tell you the truth, I think Aunt Loretta feels this way, too. Ross has been so different since you came here.''

''I know,'' Hope said grimly. ''I bring out the worst in him.''

''That wasn't what I was going to say,'' Wonder chided. ''Ross was very quiet until you came, and very serious. He kept to himself as much as possible, always up to his elbows in that work of his, or else over at the hospital helping out. He had no private life, no time to himself at all. I don't know how it is with him in Boston, of course, but that's the way he's always been here. At least, until you arrived. Before now he never would have thought of coming out on the terrace and having iced coffee like that. He never would have talked about all sorts of things and..., and....'' Wonder faltered.

''Wonder,'' Hope said softly. ''Don't try to make things up. If you're attempting to tell me that Ross was in a shell until I came here and I brought him out of it, you're only deluding both of us. If he was in a shell, and if that shell has cracked, I had nothing to do with it, believe me. Someone else did the Humpty Dumpty routine on him, not me.''

''What?''

"You remember the old nursery rhyme, don't you?" Hope said, and had to laugh at Wonder's mystified face. "Humpty Dumpty was a great big egg and he fell off the wall...and all the king's horses and all the king's men couldn't put Humpty together again."

Wonder said, "You're impossible!" But she was smiling. Then she added, "I can keep a secret, Hope, and I think maybe you need to tell one to someone. You love Ross, don't you?"

Hope looked across at the pretty Indian woman who was staring at her so solicitously, and something inside her gave a great lurch. Wonder was right. To save her own sanity she did, indeed, need to tell someone.

"Yes," she said, her voice so low that Wonder had to lean forward to hear her. "I do love him, Wonder. I love him with all my heart and all my soul. And...I'm afraid I always will."

CHAPTER FIFTEEN

WONDER CALLED THE NEXT AFTERNOON to ask Hope
if she'd like to go up to the Leisure Inn that evening
and hear the folksinger entertaining there. Hope
knew that this was a night when Ross would be on
emergency-room duty at the hospital, so the negative answer she expected she'd get from that quarter
would at least be avoided. She was sure that Mrs.
Wood would have no objection at all to her going
out. In fact, she imagined that Ross's aunt would be
pleased at the thought. The older woman had mentioned several times recently that Hope must be getting pretty bored, a remark that always drew an
angry glance from Ross if he happened to be
around.

Hope not only accepted Wonder's invitation but
felt a mounting sense of pleasure as she got ready to
go out that evening. Wonder, Randy and the young
man who worked at the Bureau of Indian Affairs to
whom Wonder had been wanting to introduce her
were to pick her up at nine o'clock.

She decided to wear her hyacinth caftan. Her arm
was still in a sling, and the loose flowing garment
was the most comfortable thing she had. She was
becoming more adept at fixing her light blond hair

with only one hand, and it looked quite pretty, brushed out and fluffed around her shoulders. She was adding some violet eye shadow and a pale pink lip gloss when Mrs. Wood appeared in the doorway of the Fern Room to say admiringly, "You look lovely, dear, but I thought you might want to borrow these, just for the fun of it."

Hope saw a glint of silver and realized Ross's aunt was holding out some jewelry, then saw that there was a necklace set with deep blue stones and matching drop earrings.

"Lapis," Mrs. Wood told her. "It comes from the mountains around here. My husband had an old silversmith make this set for me."

"It's absolutely beautiful," Hope said sincerely. "But I couldn't think of wearing them, Mrs. Wood. Suppose somehow I lost one of the earrings?"

"They're not doing any good gathering dust in my dresser drawer," Loretta Wood said firmly. "Here, let me help you put them on, and if they become you as much as I think they will I won't hear another word about it!"

Loretta Wood was right. The jewelry added the perfect finishing touch to Hope's costume and highlighted the color of her eyes, as well. A final glance in the mirror showed that her pretty, heart-shaped face looked healthier than it had in weeks. With a last-minute spray of her favorite perfume, Hope was ready to go anywhere.

The evening proved to be very pleasant. It was a bit strange to see Randy dressed up in beige slacks and a black-and-tan shirt, and Wonder looked particularly attractive in a green dress with a flounced skirt. Most noticeably, there was nothing strained between Randy and Wonder, and their carefree attitude set the pace.

Dave Ford, the young man from the Bureau of Indian Affairs, was in his late twenties, a pleasant, nice-looking person who finally confided to Hope, during a moment when Wonder and Randy were dancing, that he was engaged to a girl back in Dubuque.

This news further cleared the atmosphere so that Hope could enjoy herself all the more without having to fear any romantic advances later of a nature she certainly didn't want.

She didn't attempt dancing herself, so Wonder served as a partner for Randy first and then Dave, and she was breathless by the time they were ready to start home.

They had been drinking mock piña coladas, but Hope felt as if her drinks had gone to her head as if they'd been filled with double shots of rum. She hadn't realized how much tension she'd been under for a long, long time. First with her father, then with Lewis, then with her job, which she'd never truly enjoyed, and more recently, although in an entirely different way, with Ross. She'd forgotten that she was still young, with a lot of life yet to be lived. And the fact that she'd actually enjoyed herself tonight, without Ross, seemed a very positive thing to her.

Hope didn't expect to fall in love ever again. Nor could she imagine spending her life with a man other than Ross—and certainly she was going to have no chance of spending it with him. But there were other roads to travel, necessarily solitary a good bit of the time, she realized, but still worthy of pursuit.

She was in a cheerful frame of mind when Randy and Wonder dropped her off at the house, having previously left her escort at a house closer to town where he was renting a small apartment. She stopped in the kitchen for a glass of milk and a cookie and then continued down to the Fern Room, humming one of the songs that the folksinger had played a couple of times by request. She didn't know the name of it, but it had a catchy melody.

She was to stop singing very quickly, though. Inside the Fern Room she reached for a light switch, still humming, when suddenly the lamp by the side of the bed blazed into life, and Ross confronted her. He was lying back against the pillows, wearing pale gray pajamas that had a silvery sheen to them—and left absolutely nothing to the imagination. He got up slowly, his lazy, graceful movements enough on their own to start Hope's pulse racing.

Before she could move he came close to her and reached out to grab her right hand, as if to forestall anything she might do. His eyes glittered, and he looked as if he was in the grip of a fever. For a brief moment she wondered if he really was ill, but his first words dispelled that idea immediately.

"Where the hell have you been?" he hissed.

Hope's own anger rose instinctively to match his.

"That is none of your damned business!" she told him between clenched teeth.

"While you're in this house everything you do is my business," he informed her. "Were you with Stan?"

"Oh, for God's sake, no," Hope said impatiently. "I was with Wonder and Randy and a date they got for me, if you must know."

"A *date* they got for you?" He was acting as if he'd never heard the word "date" before.

"Yes. He works at the Bureau of Indian Affairs. A very nice person...."

"A white man?" Ross demanded scathingly.

"Yes, a white man. What's the matter with you, Ross?"

"Do you really need to ask that?" he growled, his voice low and dangerous.

"Please," Hope protested, trying to wriggle away from him, "you're hurting me!"

"I've had all I can take," he said grimly. "I've been sitting here waiting for you for the past three hours."

"Does your aunt know you're in here?"

"No, she doesn't know I'm in here," he said roughly. "She'd gone to bed by the time I got back."

"But you were supposed to be on duty at the hospital tonight," Hope said.

"They asked if I could switch to tomorrow night," Ross replied with an odd note of triumph. "So that's the story, is it, Hope? The old bit about the mouse playing while the cat's away?"

"Don't be absurd!"

"I have no intention of being absurd," he assured her, and there was a new note in his voice. She looked up at him quickly and tried to read the expression on his face, but he'd put his mask firmly back in place and was once again inscrutable. Only his eyes betrayed him, and Hope found it impossible to decide whether the sparkle that she saw in them sprang from derision—or desire.

She had her answer in another instant. Ross drew her against him, pressing her so close that even the fabric of her caftan and his pajama pants proved to be no barrier. She gasped as she felt him, the core of him, thrust against her thighs, and the full awareness of the hard power that was his manhood swept over her, growing more flagrantly tangible every second as he ground himself against her.

"Stop!" she commanded, but it was a pathetic cry and she was not surprised when she heard his derisive laugh. Nor did he waste any more time. He swept Hope up in his arms, sling and all, and carried her across to the bed, but there was gentleness in the way he laid her back against the pillows. The lamp he'd turned on had a white shade, and the light cast a pearly radiance across her pale skin. She watched him untie the sling and thrust it aside, and then he began to ease the caftan down over her shoulders. In this, at least, she could not fault his tenderness. The caftan had a low, scooped neck, so it was fairly easy to slip off, but Ross worked slowly and carefully until she was bare to the waist. Only then did he move back, surveying her with a kind of deliberation that made her bristle. There was no tenderness now. No tenderness at all. Nor was there any gentleness to his kiss when his mouth descended, plunging to claim her lips so searingly that Hope felt as if she'd been branded.

With his mouth still on hers, his tongue moving so tantalizingly that she squirmed beneath its quivering torture, Ross slowly drew down the rest of the caftan and then tossed it aside. Again he sat back to feast his eyes upon her body, his face still a mask of inscrutability but his eyes glowing with a fire that seemed to be consuming them.

Then he began to work on her as slowly, as deliberately as if he had fashioned a puppet out of clay and was about to breathe life into it. First he brushed her forehead with his lips while his hands began to caress her breasts in slow, circular strokes that gradually moved inward to reach her nipples. Then, when these had peaked to tautness, his moistened mouth came to tickle first one and then the other rosy tip. He used his tongue as if it was a paintbrush and each stroke was a splash of color on a canvas destined to become immortal.

"I've wanted you so badly, Hope," he said, his breath coming hot against her skin. "I've waited for you so long...."

Hearing him say this was a dream, a sensuous rift in reality, and Hope didn't even attempt to answer. She could only respond in sighs, and this she did with increasing fervor as she began to feel that her body was composed entirely of nerve ends, all of them exposed in ecstasy as he covered every inch of her with that blend of taste and touch that was supremely erotic, leaving a trail of fire in its wake.

This was a fire that would have to be quenched. It would have to be quenched by him, or its flame would burn until nothing was left of her but the ashes of unfulfillment. Hope knew that she was moaning, but she had no control over her own pleas, even as she heard his laugh, low and triumphant.

Suddenly Ross took his mouth away, her hands away, and all she could do was lie there bereft and consumed by a sensual grief beyond her coping. Then she opened her eyes to see that he'd stepped to the floor and was peeling off his pajama pants. He stood at the side of the bed, fully exposed before her.

She groaned aloud at the sight of him, the towering magnificence of him, and both arms stretched out involuntarily. And even though she felt a twinge in her shoulder as she did so, she was past the point of caring.

His hair was velvet under her touch, but her fingers didn't linger there. As if impelled by a force beyond her control they moved to follow the contours of his body, until sliding below his narrow waist they soon became involved in an intimacy that aroused her just as obviously as it did him.

She heard him groan, "Oh, my God, Hope," and then he was upon her, their urgency matching and their bodies meshed. She nearly screamed aloud as she received him, the sensation unlike anything she'd ever felt before, yet even in this moment of utter fruition she somehow stilled herself, as if knowing that this ultimate revelation would put her completely under his control.

Then she began to move with him, mounting rhythmically together to a height higher than the mountains that surrounded them. And as the pains of love blended with triumph, she fought to match his exploding passion.

Finally, their wave crested and broke, a tidal wave of infinite pleasure. And as the cascading glory of their lovemaking slowly subsided and the totality of true content washed over them, Hope drifted off on the tender wings of peace.

HOPE SLEPT—a sleep of pure exhaustion. And she awakened to find herself alone in the bed.

The light had been turned out, and the room was still dark. There was a moon that night, and its silver light slanting through the window highlighted something heaped on the floor. Hope leaned closer to see what it was and recognized her caftan.

Ross had tucked her into bed. She was still naked, but he'd drawn a sheet and a thin blanket over her. Then, she reasoned, he must have left her, but she had no idea when that might have been or where he might be now. Next door, perhaps, asleep in his own room? She resisted the temptation to go and see.

Glancing at the bedside clock she saw that it was four o'clock in the morning. No one would be up for another three hours at least, and she didn't think she could bear to be confined here that long.

Yet she had no wish to leave the room, because there was no telling with Ross. She could very well run into him in the hall or the kitchen or the living room or wherever she might go—and she had no wish to run into him at all.

There was nothing to do but suffer it out, and this she did until at last the sun appeared, a sliver of light above a distant peak. Then, and only then, did Hope get up and dress in denims and a loose-fitting blouse.

She opened her door very carefully and listened, and the heartening sound of dishes and pots being moved about came to her from the kitchen. She could only hope that the noises were being made by Loretta Wood rather than Ross. In any event, she couldn't stay in her room forever.

There had been an almost subliminal quality in last night's capitulation to him, nor did she try to negate this. But it had been a capitulation nevertheless, and she wasn't about to fool herself by attempting to rationalize what had happened between them. She had surrendered to him—oh, how she had surrendered to him! True, his passion had been equal to hers, his climax total. But she didn't delude herself into thinking that the same thing might not have happened between Ross and any number of other women. As a lover he was thoroughly experienced, and he had given her the full benefit of his skill, she thought dryly. The one thing he had not given her was a measure of love to go with it.

Well, he'd satisfied his desire, that much was certain, and in the process he'd also taught her a lesson—a very bitter lesson. He had been quite able to get up and abandon her at some point during the night without giving a thought to how she might feel when she awakened to find him gone.

In retrospect, this ultimate encounter between them, which could have been a miracle, became, instead, almost sordid, and Hope could not repress the feeling that she'd been soiled by it. Degraded by it. Ross had reduced her to a very low level.

Thinking this, she made her way noiselessly along the hall, determined to turn back at the kitchen door if she saw him in the room. Thankfully, it was Loretta Wood whom Hope found there. She'd been making muffins and was just taking them out of the oven. The air was redolent with their fresh-baked fragrance.

Mrs. Wood turned to greet her with a smile so warm, so sincere that the tears sprang to Hope's eyes. She turned hastily to pour herself a cup of coffee, intent upon hiding her own distress because she didn't want to get into a discussion just now about Ross or anything else that might relate to him.

Mrs. Wood asked, "Sleep well?" and Hope forced an affirmative nod.

"Ross left early," she volunteered then, and Hope thought silently, *I just bet he did!*

"He said he'd be home for dinner, though," the older woman finished, and added brightly, "That's your influence, Hope, and I must say I appreciate it. It was difficult to get him to settle down to much of anything before you came here."

There was nothing to say to this. Hope sat down

at the table, trying to fight back newfound thoughts. For the enormity of what she and Ross had done last night was just beginning to sweep over her. She and Ross had gone to bed together in the Fern Room. They had made love in Lamanda's bed, and despite herself Hope began to shake as if she was in the grip of a chill.

At once Mrs. Wood was hovering over her anxiously. "What is it, dear?" she asked, her face a mirror of concern. "Maybe you shouldn't have gone out with Wonder and Randy last night—maybe it was too much for you. I was pleased because I thought you needed the company of some other young people, but perhaps it was too soon."

"No," Hope managed, forcing herself to push back a veritable torrent of feelings, all so overpowering that she was in no way prepared to cope with any of them. "I enjoyed myself, actually," she said. "It's just that...well, I have a lot to think about."

"I can imagine," Mrs. Wood agreed. "Ross offers quite a challenge, doesn't he?"

This was the last question she'd expected Ross's aunt to ask her and she groped for an answer. But before she could find one, her hostess went on to say, her own voice quavering a bit, "Hope, I've been meaning to tell you about Lamanda."

This, at least, she could handle. She sat up straighter and said, "I don't want you to, Mrs. Wood. What I mean to say is, I don't want you to feel that you have to reopen old wounds because of me. I've had my own share of grief, and I know

there are some things that are better left unsaid.
Dwelling on them seems to do more harm than
good. So please don't feel that you have to tell me
anything.''

"I don't feel that I *have* to, dear—I want to."
Loretta Wood pulled out a chair and sat down, putting the coffee cup she had just refilled on the table
in front of her. "You already know that Ross and
Lamanda were married?''

"Yes," Hope replied.

"Well, it wasn't much of a marriage," Mrs.
Wood said ruefully. "Lamanda was already very
sick. She had a serious form of diabetes. That
Christmas, when Ross came home from college, her
eyesight had started to fail her, and we...we all
knew what was going to happen.''

"Please, Mrs. Wood," Hope protested.

"My dear, I want you to know this. I get the impression that Lamanda has become a stumbling
block between you and Ross, and he's too stubborn
to ever tell you the truth himself. You see, Lamanda
was several years younger than Ross. She'd idolized
him ever since I can remember. And...he was so
good to her. His father never had much time for
him, so Ross spent a lot of time at our house. He
and my husband were very close.''

"He's told me that," Hope admitted.

"Cal was more like a father to him than his own
father was," Mrs. Wood said reminiscently. "He
really loved the boy. I couldn't have any more children, so Ross was the son that Cal knew he'd never
have himself. To my mind, Lamanda was like a

younger sister. But she didn't look at it that way. She was totally infatuated with him.''

She sighed deeply and took a sip of coffee. Then she said, ''When Lamanda got sick, Ross began to pay special attention to her. But Lamanda took it the wrong way. She became convinced that he loved her as much as she loved him. And I'm speaking of romantic love, of course. He did love her just as much, but in an entirely different way. His was a brotherly kind of love.

''That last Christmas before she died, when Ross was here, I think he knew better than the rest of us that Lamanda didn't have long to live. I imagine it was Lamanda's idea that they elope, but Ross went along with it. Just then he would have done anything to please her. The day after Christmas they disappeared, and when they came back to us they were man and wife. Legally, anyway. For all that it matters or doesn't matter, I doubt very much that their marriage was ever consummated.''

Hope was so stunned that she could only listen, and sensing this, Mrs. Wood resumed.

''Not long after the New Year, Ross had to go back to school,'' she said. ''His studies demanded more and more of him, and he knew he couldn't get back here till summer. Meantime, he'd seen this house. It was for sale, and he told me he thought it would be the perfect home for all of us—my husband, me, Lamanda and himself.

''He knew—I knew, by then—that Lamanda was dying. But Ross wanted her to have a lovely place where she could spend the rest of her life, no matter how short that life threatened to be. He bought the house for us, and we added the ell with the Fern Room. Ross even told us exactly how he thought Lamanda would like it decorated, but by that time she was in the hospital, and that was where she remained. Lamanda never lived to see the Fern Room.''

Lamanda never lived to see the Fern Room. Lamanda had never actually occupied the Fern Room. She and Ross had never....

Hope bit back the thoughts that arose with this knowledge, and she didn't try to suppress the tears that came to fill her eyes.

"Ross came home for the funeral," Mrs. Wood continued, "but right afterward he had to go back to his schoolwork. There were exams and papers to finish, that sort of thing. And that's when he decided to specialize in the study and treatment of diabetes and to work with people who had the disease, as a sort of memorial to Lamanda.

"I'm not saying he didn't grieve. He did. But what I am saying is that he didn't grieve for her as a husband—because he couldn't have. He'd never been her husband in the true sense of that word, which means a lot more than many of the young people today seem to think it means," Mrs. Wood added firmly. "For myself, I felt that this was just one more sorrow for Ross, one more block to hurdle in a life that had already had more than its share of pain. Ross has had very little love in his life, and he needs a great deal of it. But he's much too proud to admit this."

Hope was trying to put the pieces together, trying to fill in the holes, and many things instantly came to nag her. "You say that Ross bought this house for you and your husband?" she began, wiping a tear from her eye.

"Yes, he did."

"I don't mean to pry, Mrs. Wood, but how could he afford to do something like that? After all, he was in college on a scholarship, wasn't he?"

"Ross?" Mrs. Wood queried, looking as puzzled as Hope felt. "No, my dear. There wasn't any scholarship. Ross paid his own way, just as he's always paid his own way—with his own money. He inherited a fortune from his grandmother's family. Didn't you know that?"

There was so much that she didn't know, Hope thought despondently. After a time Mrs. Wood started out for the Oconaluftee Village, where she would be doing beadwork. Left alone in the house, Hope tried to make an understandable continuity out of everything that Ross's aunt had told her. But her conclusion, in the end, was that although she knew a lot more about Ross's life than she'd known before, she knew less about the man himself.

She could understand his marriage to Lamanda. A chivalrous, boyish impulse, acted out in the face of tragedy. But it was more difficult to assimilate the fact that Ross Adair was a very wealthy young man, having inherited a fortune from a French grandmother.

Even this was not a happy story. According to Loretta Wood, Ross's grandfather, like his father, had been active in the affairs of the Cherokee tribe, and he'd made many trips to Washington for conferences with government officials. On one of these, he'd met the daughter of a high-ranking French dignitary who'd been on an official visit to the United States. They had fallen in love and eloped—eloping seemed to be a family act to follow, Hope thought dryly—and Ross's grandfather, a full-blooded Cherokee Indian, had taken his bride back to the village of his birth.

She had not fit in. Loretta, then a young girl herself, dimly remembered the impetuous Frenchwoman who had refused to bend in even the slightest way to the customs of the people she'd come to live among. Finally she had fled and returned to Paris, where she'd lived in solitary splendor until her death some thirty years before.

When she'd left Cherokee behind her she abandoned her son, also—a little boy then only two years old. Whether or not she had later rued this decision, no one was ever to know. Ross's father had grown up on the reservation, but he had gone on to college in Pennsylvania. Returning home, he had met a Cherokee girl who had also been away, pursuing her own education. They had married and tried to settle down, but this had proved impossible for her. And one night, when Ross was only a few months old, she had left her husband and child and run off with another man. They hadn't gone very far when their car skidded off a curve on the winding mountain road, and both had been killed instantly.

Eventually word of this had reached Ross's grandmother in France, and she in turn had made a strange gesture. She'd left her entire fortune to the little grandson who had been bereft of his mother...even as her own son had been bereft of her.

Hope had to concede that there was no doubt Ross had had a double dose of pain where women were concerned. His grandmother had run away, and so had his mother. Knowing these things about his past, Hope could begin to understand his cynicism, his arrogance and even some of the things he'd said to her. Was it any wonder that he had very little faith in the ability of a woman to remain loyal to a man?

Ross was part French, and there was no doubt that the blend of French and Cherokee made an exciting combination. But this was the least of Hope's concerns. What bothered her was the feeling that she had moved farther away from him than she'd ever been before. The mystery of him had been fully exposed to her, yet she didn't think she'd ever be able to solve it.

According to Lamanda's own mother, Ross had not loved his wife with the ardent sort of love that Hope would have expected. But then, Lamanda had been a very sick girl, and Ross had shown a total compassion where she was concerned.

Did this compassion extend into other areas of his life? Or with Lamanda's death had he turned it entirely toward medicine? Could he ever really *love* a woman, in the deepest sense of the word? Or had the factors that surrounded his relationships with women only caused him to become even more wary, so that where the opposite sex was concerned he limited his interest to sexual desire?

Ross was an innately sensual man and he could not deny his own nature. But last night there had been a streak of cruelty in what he had done to her, Hope thought. Although she admitted her capitulation to him—and could never stop being ashamed of it—she did hold him responsible for what had happened between them.

She stirred. The day stretched ahead of her, but she didn't think she could face it. In fact, she didn't think she could face any more days in a house that, to her chagrin, did not belong to Loretta Wood at all. No, Ross had bought this house for his aunt and uncle with Lamanda in mind, but essentially he still owned the place. Mrs. Wood had made that clear.

Ross was persuasive. There was no doubt of that, Hope thought bitterly. And it was easy to understand how simple it must be for him to twist his aunt around one long finger and how impossible it would be for her to refuse his wishes.

Hope doubted very much if, after the previous night, Ross still had any desire to twist *her* around his finger. Regardless, she was not about to take chances. Never again, she warned herself mirthlessly, could she afford to be trapped in his web.

CHAPTER SIXTEEN

ACTION WAS IMPERATIVE. Swift action. Hope knew very well that she couldn't afford to waste any more time.

First she phoned Randy Youngdeer.

"Randy, is the offer for the Volvo still on?" she asked.

She could sense Randy's relief even over the telephone. "Very much so," he said quickly.

"Then I've decided I'll take it."

"Great, Hope. That's good news."

"Yes," Hope agreed absently. "Listen, Randy. I almost hate to ask, but I was wondering...when can I have the money, do you think? I have quite a few debts to settle." This, she rationalized, was only a partial fib.

"No problem, Hope. It shouldn't take much time at all. The fellow said just to call him, and he's going to pay in cash."

"All right. You take your fifteen percent and—"

"No way," Randy interrupted.

"Randy, I've already told you. No commission, no sale."

Randy sighed. "You do know how to put a guy on the spot, Hope. But okay, if you absolutely insist."

"I absolutely insist."

"All right. I'll take my cut and bring you the rest of the money tonight, if that's okay with you. I'm sure this guy will come right down now, but I'm pretty tied up at the moment and I haven't got anyone to relieve me. As it is, I'm praying that I don't get any road calls."

"Tonight will be fine," Hope assured him. "And...thanks a lot, Randy. I really appreciate this."

Next, she dialed Wonder's number, but on the third ring it was a husky male voice that answered.

Stancil Owl!

"Is Wonder at home?" Hope asked rather meekly.

"Hey, Hope, how's it going?" Stan intoned, his voice friendly.

"Fine, Stan, fine. And yourself?"

He laughed sourly. "Hey, it goes, you know. Wonder's out in the yard hanging up the wash. Hold on a minute, and I'll go and get her."

"Wait, Stan," Hope said, hesitating. She had been planning to get in touch with Stancil Owl as soon as possible, so this provided an unexpected opportunity. "I'm glad I've got you on the line. I want you to do me a favor."

"I will if I can," he told her promptly.

"I'm sure you can. You have a car, don't you?"

"A pickup truck. It runs, that's about all I can say for it."

"I know this will sound crazy to you, but if I ask

you to do something will you keep my confidence, whether you can do it for me or not?''

"Sure, Hope. You have my word.''

"That includes not telling Wonder, okay? I wouldn't want her to know anything about this.''

"If you say so,'' he said doubtfully.

"I'm not asking anything wrong, Stan,'' Hope told him. "I'm just going to need transportation to Asheville, that's all.''

Stancil Owl laughed. "Wow! You kind of had me going there for a minute. I thought you were going to ask me to rob a bank or something.''

"Hardly,'' she said dryly.

"Where do you want to go in Asheville?'' Stan asked curiously.

"To a hotel. Any halfway decent hotel. But that's another thing you've got to promise me you won't tell anyone, just in case you're asked. What hotel I go to, that is.''

"Are you always this mysterious?'' Stan drawled.

"No,'' she answered a bit crossly. "But then I've never needed to be...until today.''

"Something happen with you and Adair?''

"I'm not in the mood to talk about whether anything did or not,'' Hope told him, then realized that she might just as well have said yes.

"It's okay,'' Stancil Owl assured her. "No problem, Hope. I'll meet you whenever you say and I'll run you into Asheville, and mum's the word. I hope you know what you're doing, though. Adair doesn't think much of me, and it's mutual. But

Wonder thinks the sun rises and sets in him, and Wonder's got pretty good judgment. I don't want to cause any trouble. As it is, Wonder seems to feel that Ross has really got something going for you. I guess what I mean is—''

"There's no need to explain yourself," Hope said. "Wonder is wrong this time." She paused, then added, "Anyway, Stan, there's something else."

"Yes?"

"Could you use an easel and some extra paints and sketch pads? All the things I brought down here with me, as a matter of fact. I don't want to bother trying to have them packed and shipped, so it would make me very happy if you'd take them for yourself."

"That stuff's expensive," Stancil Owl said cautiously.

"I know," Hope replied evenly. "I'm not suggesting that you buy a thing from me, though. I'd be very glad to give it all to you."

I'd be very glad to do anything that would help me get out of here with minimum fuss and maximum speed, Hope added silently.

There was a pause, then Stancil Owl asked roughly, "What's the catch, Hope?"

"There is no catch," she said, honestly puzzled.

"People don't just give away things like that for nothing!" he persisted.

It occurred to her that probably no one had ever given Stan Owl much of anything without attaching strings to the deal, and she said carefully, "That's not always true. If you can't use the paints, say so. I wouldn't want to burden you with them, but—''

''Of course I can use them,'' he cut in. ''It's just that....'' Wonder's brother paused, and Hope could sense his struggle for words. ''Hell, I've never met anyone like you before. If you give me all your stuff, though, where will that put you?''

''What do you mean?''

''I don't get the impression that you've got money growing on trees,'' he said dryly.

''I haven't. But I'll replace my equipment as the need for it arises. I can always borrow things like easels from the school. Anyway, for all the work of my own I've done these past couple of years it's a wonder my paint tubes haven't dried up.''

Stan Owl said slowly, ''You've seen my work. I'd kind of like to see some of your things.''

''Maybe someday that can be arranged,'' Hope promised. ''I don't have anything with me, though, and I haven't had a chance to do anything since I broke my shoulder....''

''I thought Wonder said Ross had given you the okay to try painting.''

''Yes, he did,'' Hope admitted. ''But it's difficult to manage lugging the things with only one good arm. Anyway...now I'm leaving.''

''And you're not going to tell Ross?''

''No,'' she said. ''I'm not going to tell Ross.''

Stan chuckled. ''There'll be a road to hell to pave when he finds out,'' he predicted, ''and I'll be up for the job when he realizes I was your ride, that's for sure.''

"You can be certain I won't tell him," Hope said.

"Doesn't make any difference," Stan replied. "It'll get back to him. Believe me, nothing—and I mean absolutely nothing—goes unseen around here."

Stan, Hope knew, was speaking from experience, and he was about to say more when the tenor of his voice suddenly changed. "Wonder's just starting in," he said in little more than a whisper. "I can see her through the window. What time do you want me to come for you?"

"I suppose midnight is as good a time as any," Hope decided, feeling ridiculously melodramatic about this.

"Midnight it is," Stancil Owl agreed. "I won't come up to the turnaround, though. I'll park down on the right by that lane that goes off into the woods. You know where I mean?"

Hope knew where he meant only too well. It was the path she had taken the afternoon Ross had ordered her off the property. "Yes," she said bitterly, "I know the spot."

"See you later then," Stan promised, and Hope had the feeling that he was enjoying this particular conspiracy. Then she heard him call out, "Wonder? Phone for you."

Wonder said, "Hope? How great of you to call. Nothing's wrong, is there?"

Hope yearned to answer yes and to confess that just about everything in her world was wrong at the moment, but she repressed the urge. "No," she said. "I just wondered if you might have some free time later, that's all."

"The whole afternoon," Wonder said ruefully. "And that's too bad for my pocketbook. I was going to fill in at the coffee shop at the Three Wigwams because one of the girls had a dental appointment. But it was postponed, so I'm free as the air. What did you have in mind?"

Hope knew that Wonder needed to bring money home to help out with her family's limited income, but for her own selfish reasons she was glad that Wonder didn't have a job to go to this afternoon. She said, "Mrs. Wood is working up at the village today, and I thought it might be fun if we could go and surprise her. I haven't been there yet, you know."

"That's a great idea!" Wonder said enthusiastically. "I'll borrow Betsy from Randy, and we'll go on a real expedition. Be sure you wear some flat, comfortable shoes, though. I'm not going to let you do anything strenuous, but we're bound to run into some uneven ground here and there. Come to think of it, maybe we should ask Ross if it's okay for you to do something like this."

Ross, yet again!

Hope said hastily, "No, we don't need to ask Ross. He's told me that I can be pretty active, within reason, of course."

"Well, if you say so," Wonder agreed. "I have a few more things to do around the house. Suppose I pick you up at two? That would give you time to get a little rest after lunch."

It was not quite ten o'clock, and the thought of waiting so long to go out made Hope immediately uncomfortable. Midnight, when Stancil Owl would be coming for her, seemed like the distant future, and she wondered how she could possibly get through all these hours and retain her sanity. The need to fill in time was one reason why she'd called Wonder. The other was that she was painfully conscious that this would be her last day in Cherokee, her last chance to see places like the Oconaluftee Village and to visit the friends she'd made. The important thing was not to give away the fact that she was actually saying goodbye.

Wonder asked again, "Is two o'clock okay, Hope?"

"Yes, of course," she answered. "I'll...I'll be ready."

With that Wonder hung up, and Hope wandered out onto the terrace. She was already restless, already seeking something to do. It was too early to start packing, and she still hadn't figured out how she was going to get her things out of the house without being noticed. She knew that she could manage to lug her suitcases down the road to the dirt lane if she took them one at a time. The problem was hiding them. She could probably find a bush that would camouflage them from sight sufficiently, but there was always the chance that Ross might come driving along and catch her in the act. He always seemed to appear at the most disturbing moments.

Finally she stretched out in a deck chair and tried

to put her escape plan into mental order so that nothing would go awry. Randy had told her he'd be bringing her cash from the sale of the Volvo, and it didn't really matter what time he stopped by, as long as it was before midnight. But what about her art supplies? She wondered if she dared leave a note saying that her paints, easels and everything else were to be given to Stancil Owl. Would Ross honor such a request, or would he merely toss her possessions on the nearest trash heap? It depended, she supposed, upon his mood.

Not only was Ross the moodiest person she'd ever met, Hope decided, he was also the most discerning, and Hope warned herself that she'd better not forget this. Mrs. Wood had said he would be coming home for dinner tonight, and just imagining sitting across the table from him began to make her jittery. The thought of those dark eyes watching her was completely unnerving.

At times it seemed as if he'd been able to read her mind, and she could only pray that he wouldn't display this facility tonight. If he guessed her intentions, it was highly unlikely that she'd ever make it down the road to keep her rendezvous with Stan.

She shook her head, amazed at all this. Until now her life had been relatively free of intrigue, unless one could describe the sort of politics that went on in a private school as such. Even so, because she always thought of her teaching post as a rather temporary job, she'd managed to keep herself remarkably apart from the power plays of her peers.

Hope smiled at her own naiveté. Among other

things, she had planned to build up a portfolio of her own paintings so that she might have the chance of being exhibited. She had hoped to do much more painting and gradually work her way into portraiture, which had a special fascination for her. She wanted to study, she wanted the chance to travel abroad and visit the great museums where the originals of the masters were reverently displayed. But so far she hadn't even managed a trip to New York, close to Boston though it was, with all of its marvelous museums and galleries.

True, she never missed Boston's Museum of Fine Arts or the beautiful Isabella Stewart Gardner Museum whenever she found herself in "The Hub" with a few hours to spare. Either that or she automatically gravitated toward the terrific galleries on Newbury Street in the Back Bay, places she could never get enough of.

The problem had been how to finance her travels, her studies and her pursuit of art for art's sake alone. And in this respect, Hope had never thought of marriage as a stepping-stone. The thought of finding a man who would make her his wife and then support her artistic habits had never appealed to her at all. In fact, the mere idea repulsed her.

She was much too independent ever to do anything like that. She had always known that when she married—or rather, *if* she married—it would be for love, and love alone. And now that she'd met Ross Adair and had fallen desperately in love with him, this was not about to ever happen to her.

Hope stirred restlessly at the thought of Ross and

got to her feet, moving to the edge of the terrace and staring out at the magnificent Great Smokies. As always, the mountains reminded her of the Cherokees and the respect they had for nature. The thought of taking another walk on the path came to tempt her, but she had no wish to do anything that might risk a fall. It would be foolish to take any chances. When Stancil Owl pulled into the lane at midnight she wanted to be ready and waiting for him.

She turned her attention to the problem of her personal belongings and went back to the Fern Room to figure out just how much she had with her. She'd brought two suitcases plus the art gear, though she had packed the suitcases lightly, thinking that she'd probably be adding a few souvenirs during the course of the summer.

Well, thus far she'd bought only two things, the woven bag and the beaded earrings, both from the Qualla Cooperative. She could use the bag as a handbag, and obviously the earrings didn't take up any space at all.

Finally, after surveying her clothes, makeup and a few other odds and ends, Hope decided that she'd limit what she was going to take to the things she could carefully stash in a canvas tote bag, and she'd abandon the suitcases. This meant that her main objective for the afternoon would be to buy such a bag at one of the local shops in Cherokee.

WONDER ARRIVED ON TIME, and Hope was so glad to get out of the house that she was down the steps and opening the door on Betsy's passenger side before her friend had a chance to get out of the car herself.

Wonder smiled sympathetically. "Slightly stir crazy?" she asked.

"Completely stir crazy," Hope affirmed, "lovely though the house is."

"Even a castle could be confining," Wonder said understandingly. "Okay, then. Now we'll do nothing for the next few hours except have fun!"

They drove to the Oconaluftee Village first, where Mrs. Wood was delighted and astonished to see them. She gave Hope a personal demonstration of the beautiful Indian beadwork she did and insisted on presenting her with a lovely necklace, one that she'd made herself.

It seemed that Wonder knew everyone who worked in the village, and they were all very friendly toward her "guest." Hope marveled at the skills the Cherokees displayed. She watched the basket workers weave strands of the native materials, which they had first gathered and dyed, and wished that she had time to linger and learn more about this particular Indian craft. It was an art form, as was the intricate "finger weaving," a true art that had almost been lost.

Next they visited a fascinating log cabin that was an exact replica of the kind of house the Cherokees had lived in before the time of the Trail of Tears. Then there was the seven-sided Council House, where a guide detailed highlights of Cherokee history as well as the customs and rituals practiced by the Indians.

Later, while they wandered through the herb garden and along the nature trail, Wonder elaborated a bit on what the guide had been talking about.

"In the old times," she informed Hope, "seven was a sacred number to the Cherokee people. That's why the Council House had seven sides. Also, there were seven clans among the Cherokees, as well as seven principal towns, and each town was a headquarters for one of the clans. The membership in a clan was inherited from one's mother, and you were not supposed to marry a member of your own clan. Now, of course, that has all changed. Most of us don't even know what clan we belong to!"

"What about medicine men?" Hope asked impulsively, as an unbidden image of her own "medicine man" came to trespass in her thoughts.

"Ah," Wonder responded, "that's something that has always intrigued me. We still had medicine men until very recently. In fact, I think the last of the medicine men—and that's what the people called him—may still be living in Cherokee. He'd be very old, though, if he's still alive. I can remember when you used to see him walking back into town with the herbs he'd gathered. His medicines were all made of herbs. They say he even went to a school in New England where he studied about them."

"In New England?" Hope echoed, surprised.

"That's right," Wonder told her. "And I've heard people swear to some of the cures he effected. Only a little while ago Ross said that modern medicine is borrowing from the old remedies much more frequently these days. Ross doesn't laugh at things like that, even though his viewpoint is obviously more sophisticated, scientifically at least.

"These herbs," Wonder went on, pointing out the different plants that were growing along the curving woodland path, "are all used for a variety of things. You'll find that Aunt Loretta keeps some of them right in her own cabinet."

"Actually, I'm not surprised to hear that," Hope commented. "In fact, it's a pleasant relief."

"I know what you mean," Wonder nodded. "There's comfort in old, familiar things and sometimes it's hard to know what's right and what's wrong. The old knowledge, the old ways start to disappear...and then they're gone forever. My generation, I know, doesn't do all it could to keep the culture alive." She laughed rather sadly. "As I've already told you, we want to be a part of the jet age like everybody else."

"Don't be too sure about wanting that, Wonder," Hope said softly. "Sometimes it's not all it's cracked up to be."

"That's what Ross says," Wonder admitted. "That's why he likes to come back here whenever he can. He says he returns to strengthen his roots and to remember who he really is. Sometimes I think that in spite of the fact he went away and became a doctor, he's more Cherokee at heart than many of the rest of us."

Hope didn't know what to say to this, and fortunately Wonder didn't seem to expect an answer. They made their way back to the village to see Mrs. Wood at work one more time and then drove back down the hillside and followed the Oconaluftee River toward Cherokee.

By mutual consent, they stopped at the Three Wigwams to have a snack in the coffee shop. Fresh peach pie was the featured dessert, and suspecting that it had been made by Minerva Lightfoot, Hope could not resist having a piece.

Penny Raincrow came to join them, and she was as friendly as she'd always been—and so much like her brother. They talked about everything from fashions to recipes, and it was the mention of the recipes, plus eating the peach pie, that made Hope remember she'd never had her lesson from Minerva Lightfoot on how to make bean bread.

As they left the Three Wigwams, she asked tentatively, "Do you suppose we could stop by and see Mrs. Lightfoot just for a minute?"

Wonder laughed. "Really doing the rounds today, aren't you?" she observed, and for an instant Hope wondered if Stan could possibly have betrayed her confidence. But she was sure that if this had happened Wonder would have blurted out something immediately—most likely her disapproval of Hope's impending action.

Hope's pretty Cherokee companion obligingly drove up a curving mountain road at the far end of town, and they soon came to a small house that overlooked Soco Creek.

There was no doubting Mrs. Lightfoot's pleasure when she saw the two lovely young women, and as they sat out on her wide front porch Hope complimented her on the mushroom soup

290 TWO WORLDS, ONE LOVE

and chestnut bread she'd given to Loretta Wood.

"Well," Mrs. Lightfoot said reflectively, "the chestnut bread isn't all that different from bean bread, at least in texture. The bean bread has a different flavor, and that depends on what kind of leaves you wrap it up in. Personally, I think I like the taste hickory leaves give it the best." She smiled. "It's kind of like olives, I guess. They say olives are an acquired taste, and I think maybe it's the same with bean bread—and some of the other Cherokee foods. We don't season things a lot, the way most other people do. For instance, we don't usually use very much salt, and I don't use it at all when I make bean bread. Salt makes the bread crumble."

Hope listened to all of this with interest, and when she and Wonder finally got up to leave, Mrs. Lightfoot pressed a foil-wrapped package in her hand. "The ramps," she said. "Don't refreeze them. They've already been parboiled, so you just add some grease and in this case maybe a little salt. Loretta will know what to do."

This simple gift threatened to bring tears to Hope's eyes, especially when she knew that this was the last time she'd ever see Minerva Lightfoot and that the bread-making lesson the gentle woman was still talking about would never come to pass.

It was late in the afternoon now, but there was still one more thing Hope had to do. "I've been wanting to get a tote bag, Wonder," she said casually, so as not to arouse her friend's suspicion.

"Something from Cherokee, you know? Could we stop off somewhere?"

"A tote bag?" Wonder echoed. "Whatever for?"

"It would be a convenient way to carry some of my paints around," Hope hedged.

Wonder seemed to accept this. She drove Betsy up to a shop on the main street where she said there was a good variety of native-made things to sell, and Hope quickly selected a tote bag designed with an Indian reminiscent of Ross standing against a setting sun. Wonder laughed when she saw it, and Hope said defensively, "Well, it was the cheapest of the lot," which happened to be the truth. She saw Wonder nod knowingly, and a faint pang of guilt poked at her conscience.

It was nearly six o'clock when they pulled up at Loretta Wood's house, and now that the moment of parting was upon her Hope didn't know what to say. She had already made up her mind that she was going to write a note to Wonder and also leave her everything that couldn't be stuffed into the tote bag. But Wonder, of course, had no way of knowing this, nor did she know that what they were facing was a real goodbye.

Again Hope could feel tears threatening, and as she turned to face Wonder across Betsy's big front seat she warned herself angrily that if she started crying now she would give herself away completely.

"This has been great, Wonder," she began nervously, groping for the right words. "I don't know how I...how I can ever...."

That was as far as she got. The sound of stampeding feet turned both their heads toward the house, and in the same instant they heard a familiar voice shout, ''Hang on there!''

Randy and Ross leaped down the terrace steps and came running across to the car. Randy looked as if the entire world had just fallen in on him.

Ross Adair, on the other hand, had never looked quite so furious.

CHAPTER SEVENTEEN

Wonder was out of the car first, her anxious eyes searching Randy's face.

"What's happened?" she demanded.

It was Ross Adair who answered. "Your brother has stolen the money Randy collected for Hope's car," he said icily.

Still awkward with the sling on her arm, Hope had just managed to climb out of the big red convertible and was closing the door behind her. She turned to face midnight eyes that scorched her with the essence of contempt. "I don't believe it!" she managed to say, horrified.

"Don't you, indeed?" Ross said, each word barbed. "Very interesting! You're not going to say that you arranged to have him pick up the money for you in Randy's office, are you? Without bothering to announce the fact?"

Randy, looking miserable, said, "Hope...he's right. There doesn't seem to be any doubt that Stan took it."

"Even if there were, you wouldn't allow for it, would you?" Wonder accused bitterly. "You've never given Stan the benefit of even the slightest amount of confidence. Neither one of you has!"

"That's not exactly fair of you, Wonder," Ross said, but although he was addressing Wonder his eyes remained fixed on Hope's face. "Stan's never done much to deserve a person's trust, wouldn't you say? Or is your sisterly love so blind that you can't see that?"

"Stan has been given very few chances," Wonder said evenly. "And because he's been in trouble before he's always the first one to be blamed when anything bad happens!"

Hope interposed. "Did you find the money on him?" she asked, facing up to Ross.

"No!" he exploded. "We didn't find the money on him! How stupid do you think he is, for God's sake? He obviously stashed it somewhere, with the intention of picking it up tonight before he comes to keep his midnight rendezvous with you!"

Hope could feel herself go weak and she actually swayed slightly, only to hear Ross say caustically, "This isn't the time to pull the fainting act, Hope. It would be as phony as Stan's alibi. You should be more careful in your selection of colleagues. While he was trying to make a case for himself he told us all about your little plan."

At this she turned away, feeling sick. She'd wanted to get away, yes. She'd been desperate to get away, but not for any of the reasons she was sure Ross must be thinking. He had been the motivation for her decision to leave Cherokee. He had been the problem, and he alone—this tall, dark, menacing man who was looking at her now as if he detested every bone and nerve in her body.

Wonder was saying in a small, hurt voice, "Is that true, Hope? Were you really going to run away with Stan?"

"Oh, my God!" she exclaimed. "No, I wasn't going to run away with Stan! He was going to drive me to Asheville as a favor, nothing more. He has a car, and I needed transportation. It was as simple as that."

"I have a car," Ross Adair pointed out coolly. "Why didn't you ask me?"

Her eyes blazed up at him. "I think you know the answer to that," she told him. "If I had asked you to drive me to Asheville tonight would you have agreed to?"

"No," he said shortly. "But you obviously never stopped to consider the fact that maybe it's because I have better things to do."

"Whatever you say," Hope said dully. "You know the truth. Or you should."

She was looking at him as she said this and she saw something flicker briefly in those jet eyes, but it died just as quickly. "*I* know the truth...about anything concerning you?" Ross asked bitterly. "I should be so fortunate! What is the truth, Hope? I'm not sure you know how to separate truth from fiction."

Randy said slowly, "Hey, Ross, come on. I told you Hope called me only this morning and said she'd decided to sell the Volvo. She wanted to get the money as soon as she could, but that seemed reasonable enough. Anyway, you'd said you'd already put the cash aside, just to have it on hand in case she suddenly made up her mind to—"

He stopped short when he saw the expression on Hope's face.

She turned toward Ross, having no idea that she'd gone white, and barely had enough voice left to demand, "You? It was you who bought my Volvo?"

She saw his jaw tense. Then he said in a voice totally without emotion, "I won't attempt to make you try to understand my reasoning. It would be useless."

"Hope," Randy put in, "Ross only did it because he couldn't stand the thought of you starting north in that car. It really is in pretty bad shape, you know—and I'm not saying that to offend you. Also, he said that it's going to be a while before that shoulder of yours is really strong again. He didn't want you running into some sort of trouble you couldn't handle, so—"

"I think he can speak for himself, Randy," Hope said abruptly. "Where is Mrs. Wood?"

Ross looked surprised at this question. "Aunt Loretta is talking on the phone to Wonder's mother," he answered.

Wonder's mother! Hope realized suddenly that she'd never met Wonder's mother, nor had Wonder ever invited her to their home, and she suspected this was partly out of pride. She sensed that Wonder's family had to struggle just to make ends meet, and Stancil, with his problems, had certainly not been much help along the way.

Wonder said ruefully, "Poor mom. She's not too well anyway. You know that, Ross."

"Yes, I know," he said quietly.

"Mom's one of the people Ross has been studying," Wonder said, turning to Hope. "She's diabetic, and he's been studying the effect that insulin has on her."

"I don't think Hope is interested in hearing about it," Ross said without looking at her.

She wanted to shake him. She wanted to shake him, she wanted somehow to strike out at him, yet more than anything else she wanted him to enfold her in his arms, even right in front of Wonder and Randy, and tell her that everything was all right.

She tried to keep her voice steady as she said, "Randy, would you give me a ride down to your gas station, please, so I can pick up my car?"

"Don't be a fool, Hope!" Ross barked.

"It is still my car—and when they find the money you can have it back," she told him. "Meantime, I haven't sold the Volvo, and I have a perfect right to go and get it. If you try to stop me I . . . I'll go to the Bureau of Indian Affairs!"

He laughed shortly. "So," he said, "you actually think it would take federal intervention to settle your claim." And he added cryptically, "My, we've come a long way from the peace pipe, haven't we?"

"Perhaps not far enough!" Hope countered.

Randy said, "Look, Hope, if you really want the car, Wonder can drive down to the station with me and bring it back up to the house."

Hope shook her head. "I won't be here," she said.

It was Wonder's turn to protest. "You can't start back tonight, Hope," she wailed.

"I don't intend to, Wonder. I noticed there's a vacancy sign out at the Three Wigwams and I'm sure Penny Raincrow will give me a room there—provided Dr. Adair doesn't call up and tell her not to."

Ross glared at her wickedly. "There's nothing I wouldn't stoop to, is that it?" he asked her.

"Very little, it would seem," she answered calmly.

"All right," he said. "I can't expect to change your opinion of me. I'll even go so far as to say that you have a right...to some of it. But if you leave here like this it isn't only me you'll be hurting. You'll be hurting my aunt very deeply, and I don't think she deserves that. She welcomed you into her home with open arms, and she's grown very...very fond of you," Ross finished, actually stumbling over this final phrase.

He had found her weak point and was pressing on it. Hope was sure he knew this, too, and would have no qualms about using his advantage even further. But before she could think of something suitably caustic to say to him Loretta Wood came to the edge of the terrace above them. "Must you hold a conference in the driveway?" she called down. "Certainly you'd be more comfortable in the house, and I think we could all use a drink!"

Randy and Wonder, both clearly relieved by Mrs. Wood's appearance, turned and started up the steps, and this left Hope standing there alone with Ross. He reached out to touch her right arm in a gesture that was actually imploring. "Look," he said, his voice husky, "I don't have the right to ask any favors of you. But please—don't rush off tonight, okay? Say that you'll stay, and I promise that I'll drive you to Asheville myself tomorrow and put you on a plane. I also promise that you'll be perfectly safe en route. I won't even attempt to...to touch you."

Day was beginning to arrange its meeting with dusk down in the narrow valley, and the sun's ebbing rays slanted across Ross's face, turning his skin to an enticing shade of copper. He looked as if he belonged in these hills, in these forests, in this country, which could become wild and mountainous as quickly as a bend in the road. And even though he also looked very tired, his weariness reflected in the sag of his shoulders, he seemed to Hope the most disturbingly alive man she had ever known. It shocked her to think how much she still wanted him, especially after the previous night.

Unavoidably, the memory of their lovemaking came to sear her once again, not only with the echo of passion's twisting pain but with the hurting sense of shame, because she had given herself to him so easily. Their union had been savage, almost primitive—there had been nothing tender about it at all. And she had gone along with him. She had followed him every frenzied step of the way.

If he had stayed with her afterward, it would have been different. If he had slept beside her and had turned to her in the quiet hours of the morning so that they could have come together in a different sort of culmination, a culmination edged with the promise of love, she would not feel so overwhelmingly humiliated. But he had not cared about this. No, he had left her in the darkness without a second thought as to how she'd feel when she finally woke up. . . alone.

She said thickly, "You're right, Ross. You really don't have the right to ask any favors of me." And with that she went up the steps, crossed the terrace and marched into the house.

Loretta Wood had already set up a tray on the coffee table in the living room. On it she'd positioned an assortment of glasses, ice, mixes and both sherry and bourbon.

"Tonight I'm going for bourbon," Randy said. "What about the rest of you?"

"I'll stick to ginger ale," Wonder told him. "Something tells me I'm going to need all my wits about me. You, Hope?"

"Sherry, please."

"You can make mine a double bourbon and go easy on the water," Ross told Randy. Then he turned to his aunt. "Is Mrs. Owl all right?" he asked.

"Yes," Loretta Wood answered. "Though naturally she's very upset. She told me she really thought in her heart that Stancil had learned his lesson."

"I think he has," Hope found herself saying, to her own surprise. "I think he's begun to realize there may be a whole new world out there waiting for him."

"I'd like to believe that's true, Hope," said Wonder. "Stan has seemed. . . well, different. . . since he met you. He was really excited about your praise for his artwork, but he swore that he wasn't going to let it go to his head, just in case nothing came of it. The important thing was that you showed you were really interested in him and felt he had real promise.''

Hope was aware of a sardonic glance from Ross when Wonder said the words "really interested," but she managed to ignore him and replied evenly, "He does have real promise, Wonder. And I made it absolutely clear to him that just because this is true, it doesn't guarantee that he'll ever make a cent from his art. I didn't gloss over how very hard it is to get anywhere in any creative field. Stan understood what I was telling him. He knows his chances are slim and that I don't have any great connections in the art world, but still. . . .''

"You had nothing to do with anything that happened so far as the money is concerned, Hope," Randy told her firmly. "So don't start blaming yourself for that. Remember I told you I was hoping I wouldn't get any road calls today? Well, in the middle of the afternoon I got one, so I had to leave the place unattended.

"Stan came in while I was gone and used one of the self-service pumps. The guy in the leather shop across the street saw him. I checked it out later on, and judging from the amount of the sale his pickup must have been just about empty.''

"But he would have done that anyway, Randy," Hope pointed out eagerly. "Don't you see? He was planning to drive—'' She froze. Looking apprehensively across at Mrs. Wood she said carefully, "He was planning to drive to Asheville tonight, and of necessity he was leaving at a very late hour. All the gas stations would have been closed by then."

She remembered that Stancil Owl had told her you couldn't do much around Cherokee without being noticed. "Did anyone see anything else?" she asked.

"No," Randy said. "When I got back to the station I decided I was going to call it quits. By then it had been quite a day. That's when I went in to get the Volvo money. Ross had given it to me in an envelope, which I'd stashed away in the file cabinet in the office. I thought I'd locked the drawer, but I guess a customer must have driven in about then so I never turned the key.

"I've always kept extra cash in that same drawer," Randy finished sadly, "and Stan knew this from when he worked for me. Most people wouldn't."

"But maybe some people would?" Hope suggested.

"There's always a possibility," Randy conceded glumly, "though in this case I'd say it's pretty slim."

"So . . . you simply decided to accuse Stan?" Hope challenged.

"Wait a minute!" Ross interrupted sharply. "Randy didn't accuse anybody of anything. If anyone accused Stan," he said, stressing the name, "you might as well say it was me. However, it was the police who made the arrest. If you have a grievance about it, I'd suggest you address it to them."

"Ross!" Mrs. Wood beseeched. "There's no need for you to speak to Hope like that."

"Isn't there?" he asked bleakly. "How would you have me speak to her, Aunt Loretta? No matter what tone I use, I can assure you she's not going to believe a word I say!"

"Who called the police?" It was Wonder who addressed the room now.

"I did, naturally, when I discovered the money was missing," Randy said miserably. "What the hell would you have had me do, Wonder? I had no idea Stan was involved. Matter of fact, though you probably won't believe this, either, I'd been doing some thinking lately and I was going to offer Stan another chance. I was going to tell him he could come back and work for me again if he wanted to."

Hope shook her head. "Your service station is great, Randy," she said, "but Stancil Owl should not be working there. I don't think you people have any idea of how talented an artist you have right in your midst."

"You really believe that, Hope?" Loretta Wood asked quietly.

"Yes," Hope said firmly. "I really believe it!"

She expected Ross to make some sort of snide comment, but he didn't. He was standing at the far side of the room, his glass of bourbon in hand, and she had the impression that he wanted to stay as far away from her as she did from him.

Unexpectedly, Mrs. Wood said, "Set the barbecue up on the terrace, will you please, Ross?"

Ross shook his head, seemingly unable to believe

the simplicity of such a request. "The barbecue?" he repeated dully.

"That's what I said. We'll grill some hamburgers and I'll open a few cans of beans. Wonder can make a salad, and there's ice cream for dessert," Mrs. Wood went on calmly, as if this were an ordinary summer day. "Randy, the charcoal's out in the back shed. Would you get it, please? It's a lovely evening, so we can eat right out there on the terrace. Perhaps you'd take out some forks and light some of the candles, Hope, while Wonder starts the salad. You might take out the ketchup and mustard, too, and I'll go and get my homemade relish."

It was all so prosaic that everyone seemed suddenly to snap to their senses. Hope was still slow at getting things together, though, and by the time she'd heaped the cutlery on a tray and taken it out to the terrace Ross already had the barbecue in place.

He looked at her across the chasm that had been carved between them and he seemed older and very weary. Then he said thoughtfully, "Thank you very much for not saying anything to Aunt Loretta about going to spend the night at the Three Wigwams. Do you want me to tell her you're leaving tomorrow?"

"No," Hope said stiffly. "I can speak for myself."

"I know that. I just thought I might be able to make it a little bit easier for her. It's kind of crazy, I know, but I think you've become more like a daughter to her than anyone's ever been before—

even Lamanda. Lamanda's diabetes was discovered when she was very young, and she had an exceptionally severe case of it. She always had to have special treatment, and I suppose that because she was a semi-invalid a good bit of her life we all tried to pamper her.

"If it hadn't been for that," he added carefully, "I would never have run off and married her. I knew that she couldn't ever really be...my wife. It was a question of doing anything to please her, because she had so little time left."

"Ross..." Hope began.

"No," he said roughly. "This is probably my last chance to tell you this. It occurred to me very early this morning that you might come to think that I...I'd taken you in the room that had been Lamanda's. That I'd made love to you in her bed, in fact. But that wasn't so. Lamanda never lived in the Fern Room."

"I know that," Hope said softly. "Your aunt told me the whole story."

"Perhaps, then," he said, speaking very carefully, "you can begin to see that for all the differences between us there are many things that could have been explained very simply. I told you all you had to do was ask me, but you never did."

"I couldn't," she said honestly.

"Because I was so difficult to approach?"

"Yes. At least, it seemed that way...to me."

She felt that Ross's eyes were coals upon her face and she would never forget their burning. Once again he was exerting that magical tug upon her that was so decidedly magnetic—a force Hope had already proved she was incapable of resisting.

She was saved from moving toward him by Randy, who came back to the terrace with the charcoal, and shortly afterward Mrs. Wood brought out a tray of hamburger patties. Hope finished her task of getting the condiments and paper plates and napkins, while Mrs. Wood went to fix pitchers of iced tea. Then, considering the dark circumstances surrounding their meeting, a surprisingly easy camaraderie developed among them. It could not have been called a party atmosphere, but the tension had definitely relaxed.

Hope was sipping iced coffee when she realized that Ross had left them. He had disappeared quietly without a word to anyone, and she kept expecting him to reappear, but time passed and he didn't. They'd all protested that they didn't have room for ice cream and had just begun to clear things away when Ross came back, bringing someone with him.

"Stan!" Wonder cried, springing to her feet and running across the terrace to embrace the tired-looking, disheveled man at Ross's side.

"I didn't do it, Wonder," Stancil Owl said. "So help me God, I didn't do it!"

"I never thought you did," his sister told him.

He looked across at Hope and grinned ruefully. "I'm sorry," he said. "I guess I've wrecked your plans."

Loretta Wood frowned at this. "What plans?" she demanded.

"I'm ashamed to have to tell you about it in this

way," Hope said unsteadily, "but Stan was going to drive to Asheville tonight—with me."

To her surprise, Mrs. Wood didn't look at all stricken by this. Instead, she glanced swiftly toward her nephew, her gaze accusatory. Then she said, "Have you eaten, Stancil?"

He grinned and nodded. "The jail food isn't half-bad," he conceded. "Better than some of the other lockups I've been in. Matter of fact, it's improved since the last time I was one of the customers there."

"That was a long while ago," Mrs. Wood reminded him. "And in this instance history shouldn't have repeated itself. Do you have any thoughts about who might have taken the money?"

"Some," Stan Owl admitted. "I stopped by to fill up with gas for the trip—well, the trip I thought I'd be making," he said wryly. "I owe you for that, Randy. Anyway, on my way out of the station, two motorcycles came by. I think they went on down over the river and up 441, but my guess is that once I was out of the way they swung back. I recognized one of the fellows. Sort of coppery red hair, dresses in black leather. He's from over near Bryson City, and he's done time for robbery."

He hesitated. "I told the chief this," he confessed, "and he got in touch with Bryson City. They're going to pull the guy in for questioning tomorrow. My guess is that if they keep to it they'll come up with the money, though God help me for being the one to accuse anybody else."

"Nevertheless," Mrs. Wood said, "you may be

right. Times have changed, Randy,'' she added. "Even here in the mountains life isn't as simple as it used to be. You should be more careful and not leave so much cash lying around. You should have a camouflaged wall safe at the least, I'd think, although the bank is the best place to put your money.''

Randy nodded glumly. "You're right,'' he agreed.

Loretta Wood turned to her nephew. "Is Stancil free?'' she asked. "Free to go where he wants to go, that is?''

Ross nodded. "Randy and I talked it over earlier, while you were all in the kitchen, and neither of us is going to prefer charges. Personally, I think you may be on to something, Stan. Maybe it was the fellow on the motorcycle from Bryson City. But there's a lesson here about jumping to conclusions. It's much too easy to do... about any number of things.''

Hope lowered her eyes when Ross said this, certain that he was looking at her. Then she raised them again when Mrs. Wood said, "Evidently you feel that you need to get back to Massachusetts, my dear. Is that right?''

Hope answered, her voice very small, "Yes, I really do.''

"Then,'' said Ross's aunt flatly, either not knowing or else not caring that she was dropping a small but very potent bombshell, "is there any reason why Stancil shouldn't drive you over to Asheville tomorrow?''

CHAPTER EIGHTEEN

HOPE SLEPT most of the way to Asheville, a sleep of pure exhaustion, and when she awakened it was only because something different had happened. Then she realized that they were no longer moving. Stan's pickup truck had come to a stop.

She sat up and blinked, then saw that Stan had parked in front of a roadside diner. He smiled across at her and said, "Going on eight o'clock. Thought it was about time we had something to eat."

Hope had never been less hungry. She wanted only to get to Asheville, book herself into a hotel room for the night and then take the first available flight back to Boston the following day. It had been a traumatic day, emotionally charged, heightened all the more by the fact that she hadn't seen Ross since he'd bade them all a cool good-night the evening before.

Loretta Wood had tried to apologize for him. "He had an emergency call very early this morning," she'd told Hope after arriving in Hope's room with a breakfast tray.

Hope had protested having the tray brought to her and had tried not to say anything at all about

Ross. But one look at the older woman's face warned her that she was not going to escape so easily. Without asking—although there was no real reason why she should ask, Hope conceded—Ross's aunt had pulled a chair up close to the bedside and sat down. Hope had tried to busy herself by pouring cream into her coffee and buttering the freshly baked bran muffin, but her gracious Cherokee hostess was not to be fooled. She gave Hope a long, level look and then said, "You love him, don't you, dear?"

The question stirred all the emotions Hope had been trying so hard to keep under control, and her eyes filled with tears.

"I shouldn't have asked," Mrs. Wood admitted. "But...I had to be sure, Hope. Ross has had so much sadness in his life. I don't suppose there's much I could do to prevent it, but I'm not sure I can stand to see his having to lose you."

This was too much. "He doesn't love me!" Hope said. "That's the fact of the matter. I attract him—but in an entirely different way. And that...that is...."

"Yes," Mrs. Wood said, the faintest of smiles flitting across her face, "I know what that is, my dear." She was quiet for a time, staring pensively into space, and when she spoke again it was to pursue an entirely different subject. "What are your plans, Hope?" she asked.

"I don't know," Hope admitted. "I have a house in Concord that's been in my father's family for a long time. I've thought of selling it, but it needs so much work that I wouldn't get a good price for it as it is now. The land is valuable, I suppose. In fact, it's worth almost more than the house,'' she added wryly. "Maybe I'll get the money to fix up the whole place someday. If not, well. . . who knows?''

"What about your job?'' Mrs. Wood persisted.

"Well. . . I'd hoped to be able to do something different after I got back,'' she said, "but now that I've had time to think it over I realize the only practical thing I can do is to go back and teach at the same school.'' To Hope this was tantamount to an admission of defeat, for this particular school offered her no challenge at all when it came to teaching art. The girls were almost all rich, and most of them were also more than a bit spoiled and not at all interested in art. What a joy it would be, she thought, to have a student with half the potential of Stancil Owl.

She forced a smile. "Maybe I'll have the chance to do some painting of my own,'' she said, "and one day I'll sell a few things. Then, if I can save enough money, I'll take a year off and go to Europe.''

Once, the thought of this would have made Hope's eyes sparkle with anticipatory delight. But now there was no zest at all in the thought of spending a year in Europe. . . alone. No, she knew only too well that visiting the Louvre or going to La Scala or seeing the magnificent white stallions perform at the Spanish Riding School in Vienna would all be very flat experiences without Ross Adair to share them with her.

Ross. All day long she found herself listening for the sound of his voice. It didn't seem possible that he would let her leave without saying goodbye. After a time, Mrs. Wood busied herself with chores around the house while Hope packed, and then Wonder came over. She seemed on the brink of tears throughout the entire afternoon because of Hope's imminent departure. Minerva Lightfoot stopped by briefly, having heard that she was leaving, and Penny Raincrow called to wish her well and to chide her for not having said something about going back north the previous day when they were having coffee at the Three Wigwams.

Only Ross remained absent.

Randy had really needed help at the service station that day, and Stan had asked Hope if she'd mind waiting until late afternoon to get started for Asheville so that he could lend a hand. Hope had been hard put to agree to this because more than anything else she wanted to put miles—safe miles—between herself and Cherokee. But she didn't want to do anything to jeopardize this newfound amity between Randy and Stan, so she'd swallowed her disappointment and said it would be all right.

It was nearly five-thirty when Stan had finally pulled up at the Wood house, and although Hope tried to keep the goodbyes brief they'd still seemed to take forever. Meantime, she'd kept waiting—anxiously at first and then in actual pain—for that devastating Cherokee to walk into the room and fix her with the enigmatic glance that she feared might destroy her soul. For all the trauma of their time together, she didn't know how she was going to be able to live without him.

But he hadn't come.

Now, parked in front of a diner at the side of the country highway, it was no wonder that Stan felt hungry. Hope was sure that he'd driven right through his supper hour, not wanting to disturb her nap.

Because she didn't want him to make a fuss over her, she ordered a grilled-cheese sandwich and a cup of tea and forced herself to eat while Stan wolfed down two cheeseburgers and a large order of french fries, then finished off with pecan pie topped with ice cream. After this, he ordered a second cup of coffee, then leaned back, lighting a slim dark cigarillo.

"Meant to tell you," he said after a moment, "Randy asked about the Volvo. Wanted to know what you want him to do with it. He said you told him that you won't sell it to Ross."

"That's right," Hope said levelly.

"Maybe it's dumb of me," Stan admitted, "but I can't figure out why. What difference does it make to you who buys it?"

"It doesn't make any difference, as long as it isn't Ross," she said. "I'm not being stubborn, Stan. Ross only wanted to buy it to keep me from driving it back north."

"And you're not doing that, are you?" Stan pointed out practically.

"True. So there's no reason at all for Ross to buy my car now. And...and even if there was, I wouldn't sell it to him!"

Stan shook his head, plainly puzzled by this. Then he said slowly, "Ross came by this afternoon. He said... well, he said to be real careful driving."

Hope suspected that Ross had said more than that, and after a long moment during which Stan was obviously pondering whether or not he should say anything more, her suspicions were confirmed.

"Ross said he was tied up at the hospital or he would have come to see you off," Stan said, then paused to take a puff of his cigar while she waited impatiently for whatever might be coming next. "I told him you'd given me your easel and your paints, but he didn't think much of that. He said there was no reason why you shouldn't have taken them along with you."

"Well, that's ridiculous!" she said sharply. "I couldn't possibly have managed to carry all those things on the plane."

Hope knew that probably she should have opted to travel on the bus, since the air ticket was going to devastate her remaining funds, but she'd decided that the most important thing was to get home as quickly as possible. How much would she really miss the few extra dollars it was costing her to fly? She'd simply follow the old New England thrift precept and eat codfish cakes and beans until her financial situation had stabilized, although even codfish and beans weren't especially cheap these days.

She smiled faintly, thinking about this, but then a thought crossed her mind that startled her so she actually jumped. "Stan!" she exclaimed, horrified. "Your paintings!"

He looked at her lazily through a wreath of smoke. "What about them?" he asked.

"I left them at the house. Oh, dear, I put them on a shelf in the closet in the Fern Room for safekeeping. Everything was so...so muddled today it went right out of my mind to wrap them in something sturdy enough for protection. Not to mention remembering to bring them along tonight."

"No big deal," Stancil Owl said equably. "I'm heading straight back to Cherokee after I get you settled. I'll tell Wonder, and she can go over tomorrow and get them. We'll send them along to you in the next couple of days."

Hope frowned. "I hate to trust them to the mails," she confessed, worried. "I really wanted to carry them back to Boston personally."

"Look," Stan said, "we'll insure each one for enough to break the U.S. mint, okay?"

"Okay," she agreed, as Stan's suggestion forced a little laugh out of her.

Stan wanted to pay the check, but in this instance Hope refused to let him do so. She knew that cash was a scarce commodity with the Owls, and even this inexpensive supper would most likely be a significant amount to Stan just now.

"One day when you're rich and famous you can buy me lobster and champagne," she smiled.

He grinned back at her confidently. "It's a date," he promised, "although I've never had either one of them. Lobsters look like big bugs to me, but I guess they aren't any stranger than coon or bear or yellow-jacket soup would be to some people."

"Yellow-jacket soup?" Hope asked faintly. "Do you mean what I think you mean?"

"Bees," Stan nodded. "What you do is take the whole comb. You pick out the yellow-jacket grubs and brown them up in the oven, and then you make the soup by putting them in a pot of water and adding some seasonings and a little grease. Geez, Hope, don't look like that! If it's made right, it's downright tasty."

"Maybe," she said doubtfully.

"Next time you come to Cherokee you'll have to get Minerva Lightfoot to make you up a pot. It goes quite well with bean dumplings."

"Bean dumplings?"

"Same thing as bean bread except for the shape and the way they're cooked," Stan said. "You know, Hope, the Indians have been around a long, long time. A good twenty thousand years here in North America. And back in the old days the Cherokees didn't have grocery stores and meat markets. They roamed, they hunted and they gathered things to eat. And not just meat, either. They collected fruits and vegetables...just about anything that grew. They had to take what they could get, obviously, but there was quite a lot to choose from."

"True."

Hope began to understand what Stancil Owl was saying, and she thought again of the injustices his people had suffered. They had been the indigenous population, after all, and America had been their land.

"Anyway," Stan continued, "when some of the tribes began to settle in villages they started to grow some of those wild crops in gardens, like corn and beans and sunflowers and squashes. The men would go out and hunt game like deer and bear—or anything else they could get with their bows and arrows or their blowguns and spears. But when it came to the cooking, it seems to me the first thing the women thought of was to make something healthy. Something nutritious, you know. They tried flavoring things up to make them taste good, and all those things like the yellow-jacket grubs were kind of delicacies. Birds' eggs and cicadas, too. It must seem strange to you, I know, but we still eat a lot of these foods today. My mother wouldn't think it was spring if she didn't go up in the mountains to get ramps."

"Mrs. Lightfoot said the same thing," Hope recalled.

"Well, it's not just my mother's generation speaking," Stan informed her. "Randy, Wonder, Ross, me...we were all brought up on that kind of food. You ask Ross what he thinks of it and I bet he'll tell you that everything the Cherokees eat is good for you," he concluded a bit defensively.

Hope said quickly, "I wasn't criticizing, Stan."

"I know," he told her amiably. "It's a matter of taste, that's all. Like lobster and some of the other stuff you probably like to eat. Chances are," he teased, "I just might turn my nose up at it!"

Back in the pickup truck again, Stan turned on the radio after asking Hope if she'd mind, and the air became filled with country-and-western music, which Stan obviously enjoyed immensely. Hope liked these particular tunes well enough herself and tried to get carried away by them, but she kept thinking of what Ross Adair must have been like when he was a boy growing up on the Qualla Boundary.

Earlier that day Loretta Wood had spoken again of Ross's family history. She had talked about his French grandmother, who hadn't been able to abide living on the reservation and had abandoned both her husband and son. Then there was Ross's mother, who had run away with someone else while Ross was still a baby.

Thinking about this, it was easy to see why Ross had become bitter about women. He had gone on to marry a girl who had died a short time after they'd eloped. But then, Hope reminded herself, he had known that Lamanda was dying. He had admitted that their marriage had been one of compassion on his part.

Anything to make Lamanda happy, he had said.

Was that entirely true? Or had he been so much in love with Lamanda that even the briefest sort of happiness had been worth snatching? Had he, perhaps, believed that love could triumph over anything, even death?

Finally they came to the city limits of Asheville. Stan seemed to know exactly where he was going, which surprised Hope. He'd mentioned earlier that he hadn't been to Asheville very often, yet now he drove through the city as if he knew it like the back of his hand, finally pulling up in front of a hotel that looked decidedly expensive.

Hope turned to him questioningly. "Why here?" she asked.

Stan's face was revealed by the light of the dashboard, and she saw that he was beaming. "It's the best!" he told her expansively.

Hope slowly shook her head. "Not for me," she said. "Stan, when I told you I'm traveling on a limited budget, I wasn't even thinking about the air fare I'm going to have to pay. I don't want to sound like an absolute miser, but...."

"You don't sound like a miser to me, Hope," he assured her. "Look, I'm used to pinching every penny until it squeaks."

"I'm getting used to it, too," Hope admitted. She didn't add that the main reason she was so low in funds right now was that she'd left two envelopes stuffed with most of her remaining cash with Wonder. Wonder, of course, didn't know what they contained or Hope was sure she wouldn't have undertaken to deliver them. One envelope was addressed to Loretta Wood. Hope had included a substantial amount of money along with a thank-you note in which she asked Mrs. Wood to please buy something for her lovely house on Hope's behalf. This was in lieu of rent, which she knew Ross's aunt would never accept from her.

The other envelope was addressed to Ross, and on a piece of paper torn off a scratch pad she had written only, "Will you please settle my bill at the hospital for me." She'd actually made a phone call to find out how much this came to and had been staggered. Even at that, they'd charged her only a bare minimum for the bed she'd occupied, since this was a government facility operated free for the Cherokees.

Had she not considered it an absolute necessity to leave behind the money for Mrs. Wood and Ross, Hope conceded now, she might even have considered spending just this one night in the establishment Stan had brought her to. Now, though, she said ruefully, "The thought's nice, Stan, but please...let's find someplace where there'll be enough left over for me to eat on until I sort things out after I get home."

Stan had pulled up just short of the imposing entrance, and he looked down at her with troubled eyes. "Listen, Hope," he told her, "a reservation's already been made for you here—and it won't cost you a thing!"

She stared at him. "You're not suggesting that you're going to pay for it?"

"You know better than that," he grinned. "I couldn't pay for one of the pillowcases in this place. It's been taken care of, that's all. So come along. Let me take your suitcases in for you and then you can get along to your room and enjoy!"

Hope's tone was cold. "Who is paying for it, Stan?"

As if I don't already know, she told herself bitterly.

"Hope...I promised," Stan pleaded. "You were just supposed to go along in and register, and then when you went to check out in the morning you'd find there was no bill."

"How very neat!" she complimented him dryly.

Stan frowned. "Hey, now. You're not mad at me, are you?"

"Of course not! But you can go back and tell Ross Adair that I'm capable of choosing my own hotels, and if he has to pay for the reservation anyway because I didn't show up that's his problem!"

"You really don't like him, do you?" Stan asked, watching her angry face with wide-open eyes.

There was an easy answer to this. It wasn't a question of *liking* Ross. The problem was that she loved him and always would.

"I'm sorry, Hope," Stan added quickly. "I guess I thought there was something going on between you and Ross. To tell you the truth, I more than half imagined he'd be meeting you here later tonight."

Hope's head spun. Was this what Ross Adair had in mind? Did he intend to appear somewhere toward the magic hour of midnight to spend the night with her in the same kind of intimacy that had occurred during that never-to-be-forgotten segment of time in the Fern Room? Did he really think that she was ready to give herself to him again as she had then? She still felt cheapened by the thought that he'd aroused her to the point where it literally had been impossible to resist him. Even thinking about his body taking possession of hers made her flame from head to toe and threatened to send her into emotional convulsions.

She sat dead still saying nothing, and finally Stan grumbled, "Hell, I didn't mean anything by that, Hope! I just thought—"

"You thought wrong, Stan," she interrupted.

"Okay, I thought wrong. I said I was sorry."

"Yes, you did, didn't you?" Hope managed, getting back her breath. "All right, then. Let's see if we can find someplace for me that's clean but reasonable. It doesn't have to be a parody of the Ritz!"

They drove through a variety of neighborhoods until finally Hope found the sort of place she was seeking. It was a pleasant little hotel, plain and tidy and inexpensive.

Stan carried both her suitcases into the lobby while she registered, and for a moment she thought that the desk clerk was going to question them. But when she requested a single room and then promptly brought out her wallet, he shrugged, and a moment later she was holding the room key.

Stan said, "I'm going up to make sure the room's all right, okay?"

Earlier Hope had taken the sling off for a few hours just to test out her arm and shoulder, but since their supper at the diner she'd been wearing it again. Nevertheless, she ached uncomfortably. She said wearily, "All right. I'd appreciate your carrying the bags for me, too. But I'm not up to much walking, Stan. I've had it for today."

He nodded, and once they'd creaked up three flights in an antique elevator and were at the door of her room he reached out and took the key from her, then insisted upon inspecting the place before he'd let her come in. She was touched and amused by Stan's protectiveness and somewhat relieved, as well, when he decided that although the hotel wasn't much to rave about, it would do for an overnight stay.

In the doorway he said, "Look, I can bunk down the street in the truck if you're worried about being alone here. I'm used to sleeping with one eye out for the cops, so I can move fast if I have to."

She laughed. "No need, Stan. I'll be fine, honestly. And by this time tomorrow night I'll be home, safe and sound." She tried to sound bright about what seemed a very dim prospect at the moment and hoped that Stan was finding this small act on her part convincing. Then she added, "Be sure you get Wonder to send your portfolio along. Meantime, paint as much as you can. You want to build up a collection so there will be plenty to show."

"I'll do that," he promised her, "although the gas station's going to cut into my time. I know you don't think much of my working for Randy, but I owe him one right now, and...I need the cash. Once I hear from you about the paintings I'll know where to go from there."

Hope had the sinking feeling that Stan was perhaps placing too much trust in her. She'd warned him that her connections in the art world weren't all that great. Still, she was prepared to forge her way into places on his behalf that she'd hesitate to approach for herself.

Finally they said goodbye, and it wasn't easy for

either of them. Hope could feel the tears brimming, because Stancil Owl was her last real link with Cherokee—and with Ross. She could see that he, too, was on the verge of becoming emotional.

He reached out and patted her on the shoulder. "Be seeing you, Hope," he said, then turned away. He didn't wait for the elevator and she could hear him clumping down the adjacent staircase.

Tired though she was, Hope found it almost impossible to get to sleep, and dawn was streaking across the eastern sky before she finally fell into a restless slumber. Immediately she plunged into a nightmare in which Ross was the principal character. When she awakened in a cold sweat, she knew only that in the dream Ross had been very angry at her and had put her in a pit in the middle of a Cherokee Council House. Then he'd ordered members of his clan to do a ceremonial dance around her.

Hope sat up alone in the strange bed, and the hotel room looked even more dingy in the first light of day than it had in the neon glow the previous night. She wished that she had a glass of milk to help her get back to sleep again, and she desperately missed the Fern Room. She missed the pretty kitchen at Loretta Wood's house, and she missed Mrs. Wood herself.

But most of all, she missed Dr. Ross Adair.

CHAPTER NINETEEN

THE END OF HOPE'S SAFARI was nearly as trouble filled as the beginning had been. She arrived at Boston's Logan Airport in the early afternoon to face the problem of getting out of Concord—not that far away, but still a hefty fare by either taxi or airport limousine.

She wished that she'd thought to call one of her friends to ask if they could meet her with a car. But the fact of the matter was that she hadn't really wanted to face anyone she knew. None of her own contemporaries, anyway. The sling on her arm alone would elicit curiosity, and those who knew Lorna Evans would have to be told about what had happened with the ill-fated Great Smokies painting trip. And naturally they would wonder where she'd been staying in the interim.

So in some ways she was glad she hadn't solicited help. Still, she couldn't face the thought of getting out to Concord by public transportation at this particular point in time. Finally she opted to share a cab with a pleasant couple who lived in Acton, the next town past Concord. Her share of the fare put another dent into her already strained financial situation, and as she paid the cab driver, after

thanking him for carrying her bags right to her front
door, she ruefully decided that the way things were
going she really would have to settle for beans—
without codfish cakes—for the next few weeks.

The cab drove off and the Acton couple waved at
her blithely through the window. Then, for the first
time, Hope really looked at her house, and the sight
of it was discouraging enough to bring stinging
tears to her eyes.

She should have arranged to have had the lawn
cut in her absence, for one thing. It was time she
remembered to take care of such practical details,
she thought dismally. But then, it wasn't that she'd
forgotten about them entirely. There was always
cost to be considered, especially since her father's
death, and so it had become a simple matter of
shrugging aside those things that were not literally
bumping her in the nose.

Well, the straggly grass would be bumping her in
the nose before very long if she didn't do something
about it, and as she fumbled in her handbag for her
key she wondered if she could handle the old power
mower with one arm still quite useless.

She tried not to notice the peeling paint along the
side of the house or the shabby front door. And this
was not the worst of it. Inside the spiders had been
having a field day. Cobwebs were draped lavishly
all over the place, making a perfect setting for a
horror movie. Hope pushed back threatening
laughter, which verged on hysteria.

Upstairs, matters were even more serious. The
roof had finally decided to spring some leaks, and

the stained plaster on the ceiling in her bedroom demonstrated graphically that rain had been an invader, probably more than once since she'd been gone.

Hope sat down on the edge of her bed and came close to giving in to total depression and letting herself cry. Yet she knew that even now what she really wanted to cry about wasn't the dilapidated condition of her house or her aching shoulder. It was Ross Adair.

"I've got to get over him," she told herself firmly, speaking the words out loud for emphasis. And the humor of this struck her.

"I'm going to be the kind of old maid who goes around talking to herself." She said this aloud, too, because the sound of her own voice was better at the moment than no sound at all.

A cup of tea was supposed to soothe the spirit in times of incipient crisis, so Hope went down to the kitchen and put the kettle on to boil. Opaque sunlight poured through the dirty window over the sink. To add to everything else, New England was in the grip of summer. The heat combined with humidity made the air really uncomfortable. Hope could not help but remember the cool breezes on Loretta Wood's terrace. She wondered what Loretta might be doing right now and if Wonder was working at the Qualla Cooperative. And she also wondered about Ross. She had a sudden vision of him bending over the desk in his improvised office, wearing those dark-rimmed glasses that only added to his air of authority, and she felt as if she was about to choke.

As she sipped her tea, she tried to convince herself that it was helpful, but she knew it wasn't. She told herself the thing to do was keep busy. Work was supposed to be a cure for virtually everything.

Putting her empty teacup in the sink she decided first to unpack and then to get out the vacuum cleaner and see if it still worked. Then she would check on her supply of detergents and other cleaning materials. There was also the matter of going to the supermarket and getting some groceries. At this thought Hope stopped short, appalled. Without the Volvo she had no transportation, and living where she did in Concord, a car was a necessity.

Well, she told herself resolutely, other people made do without cars, and so would she, for the present. Anyway, there was a small, independently owned market within walking distance. Normally she used it as infrequently as possible because the prices were considerably higher than those in the chain stores, but given the circumstances she'd have to make an exception to this. She'd simply have to shop on a daily basis and not buy so much at one time that it would be impossible to carry it home.

Keeping busy and trying to work out such mundane details as attending to shopping did prove to be a panacea of sorts as the afternoon wore on. Hope didn't have time to think very much about Ross. She made a supper of canned soup and toast, after which she showered and tumbled into bed.

Then, with night's shadows enfolding her, she was assailed by a string of bittersweet memories, going back to the time when she'd been a little girl.

This room had been hers for as long as she could remember, or almost as long. She'd moved to Concord with her parents the year she'd entered kindergarten.

In retrospect, her growing-up years had not been entirely unhappy. True, there had always been her father's "problem," something that had never been translated into words. For a long, long time, Hope had not known what it was that made him "sick." She had only realized that there were periods when her mother was especially tight-lipped with him and also inclined to be short with her. But even at his "sickest" her father had been kind and affectionate toward both of them, though sometimes this had been in a bumbling sort of way she hadn't been able to understand for a long time.

Nothing had seemed to help him. Hope suspected that at one point he'd tried Alcoholics Anonymous, but unfortunately it hadn't worked for him. Looking back, she could see how her mother constantly had been called upon to camouflage things, to cover up for her father. Otherwise he would have lost his job at the school.

Hope was only now beginning to realize what a strain it must have been for her mother all those years. Actually, it was a wonder that she hadn't left long before she did. But she'd stayed with her husband until close to the end. Then she'd left him, and Hope had been unforgiving about this. Even at his funeral, she and her mother had been like strangers—polite and cool.

Until now it had never occurred to Hope that her mother might have been cloaking her grief, just as she herself had been. She'd thought she was the only one in the world mourning her father, but now, finally, she could begin to grasp her mother's point of view. And, able to go that far, she could understand a number of things about a lot of other people. Even about her cousin, Emily Collingworth, who was really a lonely, embittered old lady.

This conclusion plunged Hope into a new sort of reverie, and she found herself speculating about what had happened in her life to make her definitely more...well, more tolerant than she had been before she'd started out on her ill-fated trip to the Great Smokies. The answer came to her like a sudden, jagged bolt of lightning.

Ross Adair.

Regardless of the way her stay in Cherokee had ended, Ross had forced her to open her eyes. She'd *had* to open up her eyes, in fact, in order to understand him at all. Probably without being aware of it, he had pointed up the differences between them, yet had also taught her that love could surmount differences and, more than anything else in the universe, achieve a true understanding between people.

Hope sobbed aloud, then turned her head into the pillows as the tears came. She didn't know how long she cried, but when she finally fell asleep her pillow was soaking wet. And her heart was thoroughly broken.

THERE WAS A ROSE GOLD QUALITY to the morning sunlight that warned of a hot day to come. Hope woke up early and made herself a cup of instant coffee, then tried to decide what to do first. She soon realized that the obvious was staring her right in the face, so she planned to spend the morning housecleaning. When she finished, she would take a shower, freshen up and do the essential shopping during the afternoon.

She tackled the windows, dusted and vacuumed, and all the while she tried to think things out, but her mind seemed clogged with little eddies of confusion. One thing, though, was certain. She had been forced to take a real look at her financial situation and her potential in that area. Thinking about this, she looked around her at some of the antiques she'd been dusting. There were Sandwich-glass candlesticks, an Amberina vase, a whole set of beautiful old Canton china in the dining room and early American wooden kitchen implements, which looked ancient but which she still used. All of these things, she knew, had considerable value, but she hated the thought of selling any of them. Nevertheless....

Hope was pondering this, glancing over some coin-silver spoons that had belonged to her great-grandmother, when the door bell rang. She groaned. She was not in the mood to see anyone this morning, and she looked a mess. It was hot, she felt as if her denim shorts and her old cotton shirt were glued to her and she knew that she had dust streaks on her face and probably a few cobwebs in her hair, as well.

She decided not to answer the bell's summons. Surely whoever it was would go away soon. But the buzzer was pushed again and again, and finally she couldn't ignore the irritating sound any longer.

Climbing down off her stepladder, she crossed the room impatiently and flung the front door open, only to shrink back in shock when she saw the woman who was standing inches away from her.

Eyes met eyes, a matching set. Then Barbara Standish managed a smile and said in a voice that shook only slightly, "Well, aren't you going to ask me to come in, Hope?"

"Mother!" Hope stammered, standing aside. "Yes, yes, of course." The next words came involuntarily. "I . . . I thought you were still in Europe."

Mrs. Standish shrugged. "I was going to spend a good bit of the summer at my friend Luiza's castle in the Algarve, as I think you know," she admitted. "But Luiza is recovering from emergency surgery, and I didn't think the moment was right for her to have a houseguest—and her husband, the count, agreed."

Glancing at her mother, Hope was painfully aware of the contrast in their appearance. Her mother was dressed in a stunning emerald green linen suit with pale green inset pleats, which spoke of haute couture. With it, she wore gray cobra pumps and carried a matching handbag.

Hope was also conscious of the state of the lawn outside and of the house itself, as well as of the dishevelment in the living room, where she was only partially through with her cleaning. Her mother, she knew, was used to having everything as perfect as things could be. When she'd lived here they'd had a full-time maid, and neither the house nor the grounds had ever been neglected. But then with her mother money was no object. And her father had never seemed to notice what state the things around him were in.

As her mother chose a tapestry-covered lounge chair that exuded a faint puff of dust as she sat down in it, Hope prepared herself for censure. But Barbara Standish, she saw, was looking at *her*, not the surroundings.

"How are you, Hope?" she asked, her eyes lingering on the sling. "Have you hurt yourself?"

"I fractured my clavicle while I was down in the Great Smokies," Hope said. "It's fine now, though. I'm just supposed to keep the sling on for a few more weeks. Sort of a... a precautionary measure."

"Should you be doing heavy cleaning, then?" There was no criticism in the voice, just polite interrogation.

"I'm not doing anything too heavy, mother," Hope said, ready to go on the defensive regardless. "I just got home from North Carolina last night and... well, as you can see, the place is in quite a mess."

Her mother nodded absently, and Hope had the feeling this didn't really matter to her, unbelievable though this seemed. Then she said, "Why don't you come and stay with me until your—what did you say it was—your clavicle has healed. Meantime, we can get someone to come in here and clean the house up for you."

"Thank you, but no," Hope said stiffly. "I can manage."

Barbara Standish sighed, and despite her faultless

grooming and the beautiful clothes she wore Hope noticed that she looked older. Older and quite fatigued, as well.

"I expected you to say that, dear," she said. "I know your independence. I even admire it... though at moments it has caused me considerable frustration. But the fact is...." She paused, then violet blue eyes stared at violet blue eyes directly. "The fact is I'm lonely. I miss you, Hope, and I'd like to have the chance to get to know you better," she finished simply.

Hope was flabbergasted. She sat very still. Odd thoughts came to filter through her mind like pieces of patchwork trying to force themselves into the pattern of a quilt. She could remember times when she'd been sick as a child and her mother had come to sit with her, to take care of her. Back then it hadn't been only her father who was kind and affectionate to her. Her mother had been a very loving person.

She could also remember going to her first dance, a prom at school. Her mother had gone with her to select just the right dress. It had been a soft pink that matched the color in her cheeks—their color back in those days, she amended wryly. And her mother's eyes had sparkled that night as she came upstairs while Hope finished dressing, bringing the rose-and-violet corsage her escort had brought for her to wear.

And there were other memories. They came flooding in, pushing out the negative ones, and Hope's voice was trembling as she said, "I appreciate what you're saying, mother. I... I really appreciate it very much. But I . . . well, just now I have to be here by myself, that's all.''

Barbara Standish nodded. ''I expected you to say that, too,'' she conceded. ''Darling, you didn't by any chance make coffee this morning, did you?''

''I made myself a cup of instant before I realized that there was still some fresh-ground left that I'd stashed away in the fridge,'' Hope said with a smile. ''But that was hours ago. Why don't I make us a pot?''

''That would be lovely,'' her mother nodded, but again she spoke absently and Hope suspected she had something else on her mind. She followed Hope out to the kitchen and sat down at the old oak table that had seen service in the Standish family for so many years. Surprisingly, she said, ''There's a stability to this house and the things in it, isn't there?''

Hope paused in the middle of measuring out a scoop of the fragrant grounds. ''I think so,'' she answered steadily.

''Even so, don't become too rooted to the past,'' her mother warned her. ''What I'm trying to say, I suppose, is that one should not avoid change.''

Hope frowned. It seemed to her that her mother was speaking obliquely, and very much so, for her mother, and she couldn't fathom what she was getting at. She sat down at the table while the coffeepot started to perk and pushed back a lock of straying blond hair.

Her mother, watching her, said rather wistfully, ''Your hair has never darkened at all, has it? Do you know...you've grown into a very beautiful young woman, Hope.''

Hope could feel herself flushing, and her mother added hastily, ''I'm sincere about that. Few people could look as lovely as you do just now with dirt on their face and—what is that, a cobweb in your hair? And an old shirt with a rip down the side!''

She laughed, then continued, ''Darling, I'm not being critical. I'm only admiring you. Most of us have to make a conscious effort if we're to pass inspection at all. Not you, though. And I think yours is the kind of beauty that will last forever.''

Hope didn't know what to say to this. She was, in fact, at a total loss for words. The pot had stopped gurgling, so she poured out two steaming mugs. Then she added a little evaporated milk—she'd found an unopened can in the cupboard—and a teaspoonful of sugar. Her mother, she saw, left her coffee black. Following Hope's glance, the older woman laughed again. ''If I didn't watch the calories I'd be a balloon in a month,'' she said.

''An exaggeration if I ever heard one,'' Hope teased, and was surprised at herself for doing so. She couldn't remember how long it had been since she'd said anything casual or lighthearted to her mother.

After a moment, Barbara Standish asked, ''What were you doing in the Great Smokies? Vacationing?''

''Not exactly,'' Hope said cautiously. But then she began to tell her mother about the troubles with the car, her fall and the aborted painting trip. Soon she was also telling her about Loretta Wood and some of the other people in Cherokee.

"How did you happen to stay with this Mrs. Wood?" her mother asked.

"Her nephew made the arrangements for me," Hope said rather cautiously.

"Her nephew? Is he a friend of yours?"

"No!" The protest came too quickly. "He's a doctor," Hope went on, trying to be calm about this. "He was on duty in the emergency room at the hospital on the reservation when I fell. I . . . I really didn't have any place to go and he suggested his aunt's home. He said she occasionally took in a boarder."

Thinking back, Hope realized that this had been just another prevarication on Ross Adair's part. She was almost sure that Loretta Wood had never before in her life taken a boarder into her home.

"How is it that this doctor had an aunt living on the reservation?" Barbara Standish asked.

"He's an Indian," Hope said flatly.

"Oh?" her mother questioned, her eyebrows arching.

"Three-quarters Cherokee, to be precise," Hope said. "One of his grandmothers was French. He. . . he is quite a remarkable person, actually. He was born and raised in Cherokee, but it's been a long while since he's lived there. Almost ten years, I think he said. The reason he's gone back now is that he has a grant to study the effect of diabetes among the Cherokees. It's a leading health problem with them, and that's his medical specialty. He also—"

"He does have a name, doesn't he?" Barbara
Standish cut in.

"Ross. . . Adair," Hope managed.

"Attractive?" her mother suggested.

Hope had not realized she'd been holding her
breath until she let it out. "Extremely attractive,"
she said then, adding hastily, "but older, of course.
He's a widower."

She hoped that with these two concise sentences
she'd given a picture of a rather elderly man, secure
in his profession and not at all the sort of person with
whom a woman would fall helplessly and hopelessly
in love. Evidently she succeeded, because her mother
turned the conversation to other things until eventually they arrived at the subject of money.

Then she said very gently, "It's the one thing I
have plenty of, Hope. And it hurts to think that you
won't let me help you when I can see you need help
so much. Pride can be a sin as well as a virtue, you
know. I don't need any instruction in that. It was
my pride that led me to leave your father. I. . . I
thought he had turned to someone else."

"What?"

"Don't look so incredulous, darling. For all his
weaknesses, your father was a very attractive
man—a man who had a great appeal to women.
There was a time when I thought he had returned
the feeling that one particular woman had for him,
and it was. . . well, it was more than I could bear. I
had put up with a fair bit—"

Barbara Standish stopped, then brushed her hand
in front of her face as if sweeping away a memory.

"That doesn't matter," she said firmly. "It's over and done with. Later, much later, I found out that I'd been mistaken, but I was too proud ever to go and tell him so. And then it was too late. The word came that he'd drowned on the cape, and I...." She shook her head. "Even now, I find I can't talk about it."

Hope leaned forward. "Mother," she said, "I had no idea...."

"No, of course you didn't. I was too proud ever to come and talk to you. Now...well, something's happened that has made me realize I had to make the first move toward you, Hope, dearest, and I can't tell you how happy I am that I've done so. Somehow I have to convince you that it's senseless for you to struggle when there is no need for it. Everything I have will be yours one day, anyway."

Hope could only sit there, stunned.

"Don't look so shocked," her mother resumed. "Didn't it ever occur to you that you're going to inherit my estate when I die? You are forewarned, though," she added, managing a faint smile, "that many in my family have lived a very long time, so that day may not be for a while yet."

"I wish you wouldn't even talk about it," Hope said uncomfortably. "I've never even given anything like that a second thought and...and I don't want to now." She glanced across at her mother, who looked as lovely and unruffled as ever, and it occurred to her wryly that she'd never seen her mother with her hair mussed. Yet for the first time since she could remember she felt something other than a sense of frustration and brimming resentment toward this perfectly groomed woman.

Her mother seemed to be aware of this, and Hope had the feeling that she intended to press the advantage. She leaned forward to say, "Please let me help you, Hope. It's clear that the house needs work, and you really should hire someone to help you with the yard work. It wouldn't do for you to undertake something like that yourself until you can take that sling off once and for all. You shouldn't be doing any of this work yet, for that matter," she remonstrated gently.

"Mother..." Hope began.

Once again Barbara Standish suggested, "Why not move into my apartment until your shoulder has healed fully?"

Hope shook her head slowly, not without regret. "It wouldn't do," she said honestly. "You know that, and so do I. We'd only be...."

"Rushing things?" her mother offered with a slight, sad smile. "You may be right. But at least let me give you enough to see you through the balance of the summer."

"Lend me enough," Hope corrected firmly.

"Very well, then, lend," her mother repeated. "From a grateful lady...to a gracious one."

The sum that her mother wished to advance her was ridiculously large in Hope's opinion. She refused, trying to match her mother's polished demeanor as she did so. Her mother had always had the ability to make her feel gauche, and it was difficult not to succumb to the old ways now.

Finally she agreed that they'd start out with what Mrs. Standish insisted was a moderate amount, with the proviso that Hope would keep in touch and let her know if she suddenly found herself running short.

"Also," her mother said, "I seldom use my car. There's no reason why you shouldn't borrow it until this friend of yours at the service station down in Cherokee sells yours for you and sends you the money. I'm going to be on Nantucket for the next six weeks, anyway," she finished. "So, if you change your mind, you can come and live in my apartment and have the place to yourself. I'll be at this lovely little cottage I've rented in Siasconset, and I'd love to have you come for a visit. It would be good for you, darling."

Hope finally agreed to all of this, and Barbara Standish made plans to drop the car off the day before she was to leave for Nantucket, adding that Hope could drive her back into Boston and join her for lunch.

After her mother had left, Hope sat quietly for a time trying to assimilate everything that had happened. There were still intangibles that she couldn't assess. But after the morning's unexpected meeting, she felt differently about her mother. It occurred to her that for the first time in her life her mother had treated her like a woman rather than a child.

It seemed incredible that her immediate problems had been solved so simply, in part because she'd been far more complaisant about accepting help than she would have been a few weeks ago. In her mind the money was still a loan, though even this didn't seem as important as it would have before her stay in Cherokee.

Hope mused about this. So many things had changed for her in Cherokee.

It was not until much later in the day, after she'd gone to the neighborhood grocer's and trudged back with a bagful of essentials, that Hope began to dwell a bit more on her mother's unexpected visit. In retrospect it gave her an odd feeling.

She'd never believed especially in the long arm of coincidence or the cliché about truth being stranger than fiction. Most things, she'd learned, had a logical explanation if one bothered to ferret it out. Yet it seemed almost too astonishing that her mother had appeared on her doorstep the very day after she got back from Cherokee, at a moment when she really needed help.

In fact, there was something about the whole encounter that had the touch of Ross Adair to it. But even as she thought this, Hope chided herself for becoming paranoid. It was ridiculous to entertain the fantastic notion that he could actually be attempting to arrange her life here in Concord.

There was a limit, she told herself, to even Ross Adair's range of influence.

CHAPTER TWENTY

By the time school started in September, Hope had long since discarded the sling, and her shoulder no longer bothered her at all. The loan from her mother had enabled her to fix up the house so that it didn't seem quite so shabby, although it still needed a new roof and an exterior paint job. But short of asking her mother to advance her some more money, she couldn't see how she was going to manage this before winter set in.

She'd found a retired man in the area who wanted to do something with his time and had been glad to take on the job of tending her yard. The old house no longer looked like an eyesore. With a little love and care, its charms had been revived.

Hope had also bought herself a new easel and an assortment of paints, and she'd used both fairly frequently during the last weeks of summer, trying her hand primarily at portraiture. Her progress had been satisfying, and inevitably she'd started a painting of Ross Adair. She'd been pleased with the result, which far exceeded her expectations. She'd needed no photographs to remind her of his features, and the final portrait was so striking that on an impulse she'd had it framed. Then she'd hung it in her bedroom, even though she knew there would be many times when it would hurt just to look at it. Yet Ross was still in her heart, and her heart still hurt, so it didn't make all that much difference.

Shortly after Labor Day she yielded to her mother's insistence that she go and charge a few fall-wardrobe items to one or more of Barbara Standish's accounts, these spanning all of the fashionable stores in Boston. Hope intended to pay her back, yet she could not negate the feeling of pleasure that came over her in giving in to her mother on this score. Barbara Standish had been almost pathetically pleased by Hope's acquiescence, and Hope sensed that her mother was trying to make up to her for a lot of things. These were things that could never be compensated for, but the important thing was to try to start anew. Hope was determined to do this, and she found herself becoming very fond of this woman who had been such a stranger to her for so long.

She didn't look forward to going back to teaching art, but having reconciled herself to the idea, she wasn't surprised to see that this year's students were replicas of last year's class.

September passed, and Hope managed to keep busy. It was not until late in the month, when it was announced that a distinguished art critic would be a guest lecturer at the school, that she was brought up short by the thought of Stancil Owl.

The portfolio of his paintings had never arrived, and when she finally realized this, Hope was horrified. How could she have let the matter lag for so long? She chastised herself for having been so pre-occupied with her own affairs and her heartache over Ross that she had been terribly selfish, to the point of forgetting a promise.

Shortly before school had opened, she'd bought a secondhand car. She'd been meaning to get in touch with Randy to suggest that he lower the price of the Volvo. She was willing to agree to anything that might ensure his getting rid of it. The day she heard about the art critic, though, it was the Owl house-hold that she phoned, hoping against hope that Wonder still had the paintings. If so, they could be sent to Concord by express, and Hope could bring Stancil's work to the attention of the visiting pro-fessional. She couldn't possibly make such a bold gesture using her own artwork, but she was deter-mined to do it for Stan Owl. His paintings, she recalled without envy, were fantastic. If only they could be shown....

Mrs. Owl answered the telephone. At first Hope didn't think the other woman even recognized her name. Then she revealed, somewhat grudgingly, that neither Wonder nor Stan was at home.

Hope nearly asked her about the portfolio, then decided it would be a useless question. Wonder had said her mother was artistic but had given the im-pression that Mrs. Owl didn't have the time or energy to think very much about Stan's work. Hope politely gave Mrs. Owl her number and suggested that either Stan or Wonder call her collect as soon as they returned home.

That evening she waited impatiently for the

phone to ring, but it was silent. As time passed, Hope grew increasingly restless, convinced that something must have happened to the portfolio or she would have heard from Stan by now.

Finally she couldn't bear it any longer and phoned Cherokee again, hoping that it wouldn't be Mrs. Owl who answered the phone this time.

It wasn't. It was Stan.

After only a moment of conversation, it was obvious that his mother had neglected to give him the message to call Concord, but he was so glad to hear from Hope that she didn't belabor the point.

Hearing his voice had a strange effect on her. He didn't sound like Ross at all, yet that soft Southern accent was enough to evoke a memory that set her pulse hammering.

"Wonder had just about given up on ever hearing from you," Stan commented, after asking Hope how her shoulder was doing. "She and Mrs. Wood keep checking with each other. You went off without leaving your address with anyone, you know. Guess you didn't realize that. But we figured you'd get in touch, soon as you had the chance. Then when Ross went back to Boston, Mrs. Wood said she was sure he'd figure out a way to find out where you were."

Hope's throat suddenly became parched, but she managed to ask, in close to a whisper, "Is Ross back in Boston now?"

"Sure. He went back the beginning of the month," Stan said cheerfully. "Said he might have to come down here again later in the fall to finish up his project, but I guess he didn't want to take any more time away from his hospital. He'd had a lot of calls, mostly from some woman up there."

"I can imagine," Hope replied, remembering all too well the phone calls from a woman in Boston.

"Haven't you ever run into him?" Stan asked.

"No, Stan," she told him. "Boston's a big place. Anyway, Concord is twenty miles west of the city, and I seldom get into town. Especially now that school has started again."

Hope paused and took a deep breath. Then she said, "Stan, about your paintings...."

"Yes?" he said, and Hope could sense the edge of excitement in his voice.

"You mailed them, didn't you?" she asked, beginning to feel rather sick. "Stan, I don't know how to tell you this, but...they never got here."

"No," Stan said. "I mean...no, we didn't mail them. I thought you'd packed them up and had them with you—"

"No, no," Hope interrupted frantically. "I didn't bring them with me, Stan. Remember, I told you I left them on the shelf in the Fern Room closet. I thought they'd be safe there. Are you sure Wonder didn't mail them for you?"

"They weren't there," Stan said flatly.

Hope was staggered. "They had to be there!" she contradicted him.

"Wonder went over the day after you left and looked," Stancil Owl reported. "There was nothing on the closet shelf at all. That's when we figured you must have taken them along yourself, and I'd missed noticing them when I dropped you off in Asheville.''

"Did you ask Mrs. Wood about them?"

"Didn't seem to be any need to do that," he admitted. "Wonder just figured you'd taken them, so I sat back to wait till I heard from you."

"Oh, Stan," Hope moaned, so distressed she could hardly speak. "Look, call Mrs. Wood right now, will you? And call me back collect. She must know something about this!"

Time seemed to halt entirely while Hope waited for the phone to ring again. When it finally did ring, it was Loretta Wood at the other end of the line.

"Hope," she said, and at the sound of that warm, familiar voice, it was all Hope could do not to break into tears. "Hope, dear, why haven't we heard from you?"

"I'm...I'm so sorry," Hope said, and she was sincere about this. "I feel ashamed, Mrs. Wood. When I left Cherokee, I tried...."

"To forget about us?"

"Not about you. Never about you. But I had to try to put everything—everyone—behind me in order to...."

"To get over Ross?" Mrs. Wood finished for her.

"Yes, Mrs. Wood. To get over Ross."

"And have you got over him, dear?"

"Please don't ask me that question," Hope pleaded.

"I think I can safely say that he hasn't got over

you,'' Ross's aunt told her. ''He was like an angry black bear after you left here. Impossible to live with. I was actually glad when he went back to Boston, and I hope he'll be in a better frame of mind when he comes back here to finish his work. As for Stancil Owl's paintings....''

''Yes?''

''I was with Wonder when she went into the Fern Room to look for them,'' Loretta Wood said. ''There was nothing on the shelf, Hope, just as Stancil told you.''

''But that's where I left the portfolio,'' Hope wailed. ''The whole thing. All that beautiful work he'd done.''

''I believe you, my dear. But there was someone else in the house at the time, you know.''

Hope digested this. Then she asked, appalled, ''Ross?''

''Ross *was* living here.''

''Mrs. Wood, you can't mean that Ross would actually do something to Stan's paintings. I know that he can be pretty arbitrary at times, but I think even he would have the sensitivity to recognize work with a touch of genius when he sees it.''

''Why don't you ask him?'' Loretta Wood suggested.

HOPE WOULD HAVE SWORN to anyone that the day would never come when she would telephone Ross Adair, nor did she do so at once. She spent a near-sleepless night after her conversation with Loretta Wood, thinking about Stancil Owl's portfolio and wondering if it were possible that Ross actually could have sabotaged his work.

Ross had made it plain enough that he'd never had much use for Stan Owl, yet he had been the one who'd left the barbecue that night to go and get Stan out of jail.

Although she knew that Ross had a towering temper when he was aroused, it didn't seem possible that he would have taken out his hostilities against her on someone as innocent as Stan had been in this instance.

Hope was irritable with her students the next day, brooking few of their excuses, and to her surprise she found that they actually worked better when she wasn't so pleasant to them. In a way, this was amusing. A lesson to be hoarded for the future, though she didn't especially relish the idea of sustaining such a mood just to get better teaching results.

Again, sleep was a stranger that night as she mulled over the matter of Stan's portfolio and Ross's possible part in effecting its disappearance. He must have had a hand in it somehow.

The next afternoon Hope went to the school library and found a copy of the Boston phone directory, but there was no Dr. Ross Adair listed in it. Frustrated, she gathered together the several volumes that constituted directories of Boston's suburban areas and spent a fair bit of time going through them, again without results.

Damn him, she thought savagely. His number must be unlisted! This meant that the one way she had of getting in touch with him was to call him at the Joslin Clinic.

She did this during her midmorning break the next day, only to be informed that Dr. Adair was in conference. The rather haughty voice at the other end of the wire suggested leaving a message, but this was the last thing Hope wanted to do.

After her fifth try, though, she was coming close to the end of her emotional rope. It was bad enough to have to be calling Ross at all, without having so many stumbling blocks put in her path.

She was a bit haughty herself the next time she phoned, but this got her nowhere. She hung up the receiver with the feeling that she'd been put firmly in her place. It had been made abundantly clear that one simply didn't reach a physician of Dr. Ross Adair's standing that easily...if ever, Hope decided cynically. On the other hand, his secretary or receptionist or whoever it was handling his calls again assured her that her call would be returned— if she would simply leave her name and number.

And again Hope refused to do so.

He must live somewhere, she told herself angrily as she hung up the phone for the eighth time in only a few hours. But since he kept his home number unlisted he obviously wanted privacy, so unless she could find out where his home was and go there and park on his curbstone, she couldn't expect to contact him.

By the next morning she was so upset about the situation that she did something she'd never done before. She called the school and said she was sick.

She knew that the Joslin Clinic was part of the New England Deaconess Hospital complex, but she wasn't prepared for the parking problem she ran into once she'd located the facility. It seemed to take forever before she finally slid into a parking space, and the meter was good for only one hour.

The clinic was a large, modern three-story building, and as Hope walked through the imposing glass entrance she felt very much like an intruder in an alien world. She expected the receptionist to be as haughty as the woman she'd spoken to on the phone, but this didn't prove to be the case. The matter of getting an immediate audience with Dr. Ross Adair was something else again, though.

"Possibly his secretary could help you," the receptionist began, but Hope shook her head firmly.

"Sorry," she said. "It isn't a medical matter, it's a personal matter. I'd rather not—"

And then it happened.

Hope, who had never believed in coincidences, looked to her right and saw a tall, dark man striding across the lobby. He was wearing a white coat, and there was an austerity to his bearing and a tilt of his head that made her want to cry out from the sharp, unexpected stab of pain that shot through her.

His back was to her, however, so her frustration was total. There was no way that she was about to start running down a hospital corridor after him. She could imagine the mockery in his smile and the unbearable arrogance of those dark, upraised eyebrows were she to do so.

Suddenly, though, he turned, and it was as if she had been a magnet tugging at him. He came to such a full stop that he literally rocked on his heels. Then, before he had time to don that inscrutable mask he kept so close at hand, Hope glimpsed the expression that swept over his face, and it was so revealing she gasped.

Ross Adair looked like a man in the throes of torture, his dark eyes afire with an inner agony. He started to raise his arms toward her but just as quickly dropped them to his sides, and as if by sheer force of will he kept them there, his fists clenched.

By the time he began to move in her direction, he'd gained control of himself, and he approached her as casually as if he'd seen her only yesterday. Politely he asked, "Hope! What are you doing here?"

"What do you think, Ross?" she returned evenly.

"I don't know," he said, displaying some vestige of uncertainty for a fraction of a second. "Visiting someone?"

"No. I've come to see you—and I certainly wouldn't call it a visit."

She was aware that the receptionist was looking at them curiously, and two nurses passed by and turned around to stare at them behind the lofty Dr. Adair's back.

"If you don't mind," Hope began, her words coming with difficulty, "you may be used to being at center stage, but I don't especially enjoy it.

Could we go somewhere a bit more private where I can talk to you? It won't take very long.''

He glanced at his watch. "I'm sorry," he said, sounding sincerely apologetic, "but I have a consultation in five minutes. That would hardly give us enough time. Would you... would you have dinner with me tonight?''

"No," she said shortly.

"Tomorrow, then?''

"Never," she assured him.

As she might have expected, his reaction to this was minimal. A very slight smile curved one corner of his mouth, and he said, "Obviously you wouldn't have come here if it wasn't important to you, Hope.''

"Obviously," Hope agreed coldly. "And unfortunately, something has come up I can't dismiss. I'm here about Stancil Owl's paintings.''

Again something flickered in those jet eyes. She wondered if he was imagining it or if it really was disappointment. But he said only, "I thought you'd want to know about them sooner or later.''

"Did you really?''

He had the grace to look uncomfortable—only slightly uncomfortable, to be sure, but at least it was a break in the facade. But before he could say anything the beeper he wore clipped to his belt sounded. Immediately he said, "Excuse me, will you please?''

He went to the receptionist's desk and Hope watched the woman fawn over him and then hand him one of the house phones. As if he couldn't manage to pick it up himself, Hope thought disgustedly. She also saw him bestow a brilliant smile on the receptionist and was sure that the woman considered this reward enough.

Chauvinist, Hope muttered silently.

A moment later, Ross was back at her side. "I'm really sorry, Hope, but I have to go," he told her. "An emergency. Give me your phone number and I'll call you later."

"No!" she said.

For the first time, the facade cracked visibly. "Listen!" Ross Adair told her testily, "You've come in on a very busy day."

"I guess every day is busy for you," she said, forcing herself to be casual about this.

"What do you mean by that?"

"I tried to get you by phone all day yesterday. I guess you don't speak to people on the telephone unless they've been cleared by your advance guard first."

He glared at her. "Why the hell didn't you leave a number where I could reach you?" he demanded.

Out of the corner of her eye, Hope saw a nurse hurrying down the corridor, zeroing in on them.

"Dr. Adair..." the nurse began nervously.

"Tell them I'll be right there, Helen," he said, nodding in her direction. Then he turned back to Hope. "Look, I want to see you. If you have one ounce of...of anything in that stubborn little head of yours, you must know that. If you won't have dinner with me will you at least meet me for a drink? I think we can be trusted in the middle of a crowd in broad daylight, don't you?"

"I know *I* can," Hope said sweetly.

"Don't be impossible, Hope!" Ross Adair said in little more than a whisper. "It only makes you more beautiful."

"Ross—"

"Stop protesting! There's a pleasant lounge just down Brookline Avenue. It's called Wayland's. I'll see you there at six, all right?"

With that he turned on his heel and walked away. There was nothing Hope could do except turn around and walk back into the golden September afternoon. But her emotions were so turbulent and so conflicting that she forgot all about her car. She had walked two blocks past where she was parked when she suddenly came back to something approaching reality.

Once inside the car, she sat behind the wheel and stared out at the traffic going by while she tried to decide what to do next. She could, of course, go back to the receptionist in the clinic and leave either a verbal message or a note for him, simply stating that she'd decided not to meet him. Not tonight. Not any night.

On the other hand, he acted as if he'd actually been expecting her to get in touch with him about Stancil Owl's art portfolio, damn him! She had no doubt at all that he either had it or knew where it was.

If she were to meet him, though, she had no illusions at all as to what might happen. The purely sexual attraction between Ross and her was very, very strong. Even if they both tried not to yield to it, she doubted they would succeed. For that matter, she wasn't sure he would even try. They could play the part of two strangers in a crowded cocktail lounge, true. But after a drink or two their inhibitions would lessen, and she could imagine herself agreeing, after all, to his invitation to go to dinner. Then, after dinner. . . .

"No way!" Hope spoke aloud so forcibly that a woman walking by the car turned around to look at her in astonishment.

Starting the car, Hope pulled out into the stream of traffic, but she didn't linger in Boston. Briefly she thought of stopping by her mother's, but she really didn't want to see her mother just now. She was feeling entirely too emotional, and although she and her mother were opening up to each other, they hadn't yet become close enough to share this kind of confidence.

The traffic was heavy, and by the time Hope had driven all the way back to Concord she had the rather dim satisfaction of knowing that even had she wanted to meet Ross at six o'clock at the rendezvous he'd appointed, she wouldn't have had nearly enough time to return to the city by then. She thought of bypassing the date entirely, but her basic upbringing had left her too well mannered to be that rude—even to Ross. After another minute of contemplation she dialed the cocktail lounge, ready to describe Ross Adair and ask that he be told when he arrived that the young woman who was to meet him there wouldn't be able to make it.

Hope soon discovered, though, that he was evidently a habitué of the place. He was certainly well-known to the point that she was assured "Dr. Ross" would be given her message the moment he arrived.

And as she hung up the phone, she could imagine what his reaction was apt to be.

CHAPTER TWENTY-ONE

THE FRONT DOOR BELL was ringing with an insistence
that couldn't be ignored. Hope, after poking at a
supper of scrambled eggs and toast, had tried to
escape into a television comedy, but the escape had
been successful only in that she'd finally fallen
asleep. She had welcomed sleep, though, because it
had blotted out thoughts of the traumatic encounter
with Ross that afternoon. She resented being awakened now, especially since her caller wasn't merely
pressing the door bell in the usual manner but was
evidently trying to wear it out.

Hope sat very still in the sanctuary of her living
room, its darkness relieved solely by the blue glare
of the television set. There was only one person she
knew who was quite so impatient, so demanding,
and who certainly would not go away until she'd
admitted him. But Ross Adair didn't know where
she lived.

Or did he? It came to her now that Ross had long
since developed an exceptional ability to find out
the things he really wanted to know.

She began to have the feeling that she'd been followed. *Don't be ridiculous,* she chided herself, but
she still made no move to get up.

When the tapping began on one of the windows, though, she was so startled that she leaped to her feet and nearly overturned the small table at her side. Fear came to send her pulse fluttering like a captive bird seeking release, even though she swiftly told herself there was no reason to be afraid. There was a man standing outside—Hope could see his tall form silhouetted through the window against the paler shade of night—but this man was hardly a stranger!

The window was at the back of the house. Ross obviously had made his way around to it in the dark. She heard him swear softly, then he raised his voice to command, "Hope, let me in, will you? I've cut myself on something!"

Hope's response was instinctive—and immediate. She ran to the kitchen door and threw it open. They nearly collided as Ross brushed by her. She wondered briefly if this might be a ruse on his part, but she saw he really was injured. He was pressing a handkerchief to his temple and she could see the blood welling through the thin fabric.

"Oh, my God!" she moaned. "I'll call the rescue squad!"

"That's hardly necessary," he snapped. "You have a refrigerator, don't you?"

"Of course—"

"Then get me some ice," he ordered.

Hope's fingers trembled as she fumbled with the ice tray, nor were her hands any steadier as she gave the frigid cubes to Ross and watched him slather the ice over the cut, which edged his forehead, going almost into that ebony velvet hair.

"Would you happen to have a hand mirror?" he asked her, dabbing at the cut with a clean dish towel Hope had somehow thought to hand him.

She left the room with an agonizing backward glance in his direction and didn't even remember getting to the top of the stairs, she scaled them so quickly. When she returned to the kitchen, Ross was sitting at the table, still holding the dish towel pressed tightly to his head.

She thrust her long-handled, pink-backed mirror out to him, an antique that had belonged to her great-grandmother, and watched as he lowered the dish towel and examined his forehead dispassionately.

"Would you happen to have a Band-Aid, Hope?"

"A Band-Aid? Surely that cut is going to require some stitches."

"I don't think so. Even small head wounds tend to bleed profusely."

Hope was not about to argue with him. Again she flew up the stairs, returning with a box of assorted Band-Aids from which he selected one after a careful inspection. Then, glancing at the mirror he held in one hand and the Band-Aid he was holding in the other, he said, "I think I'd better do this in your bathroom, provided you have a wall mirror there. I'll need both hands."

"Couldn't I . . . help you?" she ventured.

"No . . . thanks. I think I can really handle it best by myself."

Hope swallowed hard. Then she said, "The bathroom's upstairs, two doors down to the left."

Ross nodded, and Hope followed him into the hallway. She watched his long legs disappear up the staircase, then all of a sudden she was shaking uncontrollably. She groped her way to the nearest chair and sat down, queasy at the thought of the blood—his blood—she'd seen soaking the handkerchief. She wondered how she could possibly have managed if he'd been hurt seriously. She loved him so much!

Finally she went back out to the kitchen, where she set up the coffeepot. He'd need coffee, strong and hot and black. She was still shaky as she set out cups and saucers, instinctively choosing the hand-painted Limoges china that had always been used for very special guests.

Very special guests. Yes, she thought sadly, Ross Adair was indeed a very special guest, and this was probably the first and last time he'd ever appear under her roof. She could imagine that he was here only to express his annoyance at her for not having met him at the cocktail lounge. Once he'd finished saying what he had to say to her she was certain he'd take his leave and not come back. He was too proud a person to do anything else.

He came into the kitchen so noiselessly that Hope jumped when he said, "I left the rest of the Band-Aids in your medicine cabinet. I can't say much for your first-aid supplies, but at least you don't stock the assortment of worthless junk most people go for. A decent antiseptic and a bottle of aspirin wouldn't be such a great luxury, though, do you think?"

"No," Hope said meekly. "I...I'll do something about getting in some things like that." She stared across at him, feeling terribly inadequate. "Would you like some coffee?" she asked after a moment.

His eyes swept the counter where the coffeepot had already started its own form of communicating, but he shook his head. "No," he said bluntly, "I'd like a drink. If, that is, you keep anything alcoholic on your premises?"

There had been a time after her father's death when Hope had purposely avoided buying alcoholic beverages, but now she did keep a few bottles of wine and liquor on hand for those occasional times she entertained. "I believe I have brandy and vodka," she told him. "Which would you like?"

"Brandy," Ross answered, smiling wickedly. "It sounds more medicinal, don't you agree?"

Hope didn't answer. She hadn't intended to have a drink herself, but now she changed her mind and got out two old snifters, the glass from which they'd been made astonishingly thin and raindrop clear.

She poured carefully, her fingers trembling slightly, then handed one of the snifters to Ross. He took a hefty swig of the amber liquid and promptly looked surprised. "Very good," he commented.

"Thank you," Hope said, still not entirely steady. She swallowed some of the brandy herself and felt its fire warm her throat. Again, as there'd been so often in Cherokee, there was a sense of unreality to being with Ross Adair, to having him here in her house.

But if this is a dream, Hope told herself, *I don't want to wake up!*

Her eyes fastened on the white strip of bandage on his forehead, and she asked softly, "How did you cut yourself?"

"There's some kind of a projection sticking out of the back of your house by that window," Ross told her.

"It's a bracket for a hanging bird feeder."

"It's also a potentially lethal weapon!" He'd finished his brandy, and now he held out the empty snifter to her. "A refill, please," he suggested. "This time for sipping while you and I...talk about a lot of things."

Hope poured some more brandy for him but she avoided meeting his eyes as she gave it to him, saying carefully, "I don't think we have very much to talk about, Ross...."

"You don't?" he queried, managing to sound genuinely surprised by this. "Well, I do. For example, I think I'm entitled to a few explanations. You might tell me, to begin with, why you ran out on me in Cherokee."

"I didn't run out on you in Cherokee!" she protested. "You knew that I was planning to go. It... it was past the time for me to leave, anyway."

"I don't agree. And I'll bet you never had a follow-up X ray, did you? As you knew very well, I'd scheduled one at the hospital."

"My shoulder is fine," Hope hedged.

"Well, if you're plagued by aches and pains in your old age you can blame it on yourself," he told her, but he said this so lightly that Hope at once became suspicious. It wasn't like Ross to be light-hearted about many things. Furthermore, he was smiling as he said, "Aren't you going to ask *me* any questions, Hope?"

"About what?"

"About all sorts of things. Stan Owl's paintings, and how I came to find out where you lived, and...."

"And what?"

"I think that's more than enough."

"No," she shook her head. "You were going to say something else and I want to know what it is."

To her surprise, he looked away. Then, after a moment, he said slowly, "Why don't you just come out and ask me some of the things you want to know? You've never tried that."

It was impossible for Hope to make a quick response to this. Some of the things she wanted to know! There was so much she wanted to know about Ross Adair, Hope thought helplessly. She wanted to know everything there was to know about him. She wanted....

He said gently, "Would it help if I chose a start-ing point? You might begin by telling me why you resent me so much, despite the attraction we have for each other, which I, at least, think is...pretty powerful."

"But I don't resent you," Hope said, the words beginning to tumble over one another. "Not .. you. It's just that sometimes...."

"Yes?" he encouraged.

"You...take over," she said. "After my accident, for instance, I suddenly found myself living in your aunt's house. I appreciated your taking me there—I appreciated it very much. But then you left orders about everything I was to do. Your aunt practically wouldn't let me move without asking your permission. Neither would Wonder."

"And...."

"And then," Hope continued, warming to this, "you arranged it with Randy so that you'd actually buy my car. You knew you were cutting off my means of transportation by doing that. And when Stancil Owl drove me to Asheville you made a reservation at the hotel where you thought I should stay. How do you think that would have looked, if I'd actually gone in there and registered?"

"How would it have looked?" he asked mildly.

"People still do have reputations, Ross Adair, even in this supposedly enlightened day and age. It would have looked as if you were keeping me, that's how it would have looked. But you wouldn't care about that, would you!"

"Not very much," he agreed equably. "I've never been overly concerned with what strangers may think about me."

"All right, the worst of it is that somewhere along the way you stole Stan's paintings because you didn't want me to help him, and frankly I think that's...."

"Go ahead, Hope. Get it all out."

Hope looked at him, then shook her head. There

was not a trace of remorse on Ross Adair's face. "There's no use talking about it," she said.

Then she remembered something else. "How did you find out where I lived?" she demanded.

"Your mother told me," he said calmly.

"My *mother*?" Hope gasped, thoroughly shaken.

"Yes," Ross nodded. "She's on the board of directors at the New England Deaconess Hospital, and she's active in quite a number of other civic things around Boston. Last year, before I went back to Cherokee, I spoke to one of the groups she belongs to. They were interested in making a substantial contribution toward diabetic research, and they wanted to hear some of the latest facts. I was chosen to relate them."

"*Last year?*" Hope gasped.

"When I first saw you," he added slowly, "there seemed something strangely familiar about you. Now I realize that it's the eyes. Your eyes and your mother's eyes—they're very much alike, you know. Though to my prejudiced mind yours, of course, are much lovelier." He sighed. "I didn't really know your mother when I met you," he said. "But I was fully aware of who she was. And I admit it seemed wrong to me that you should be struggling with an old car and evidently have other financial problems, as well, when I knew how much she'd want to help you."

"And so you intervened?"

"Yes," he admitted, "and I suppose you'll never forgive me for that, either. But it seemed a logical thing to do. Your mother and I had a long talk over the phone before I told her anything about your accident—or about my own involvement with you.''

''I beg your pardon?'' Hope asked icily.

''Let me beg yours,'' he suggested, ''and rephrase that. Your mother and I had a long talk over the phone before I told her that . . . I love you.''

Ross Adair sat across from Hope at the old oak table in her kitchen, staring down at his leather loafers as he spoke. She gazed lovingly at the rugged profile and once again was forced to realize how devastatingly handsome he was. His clothes complemented his arresting color perfectly. His pale gray herringbone jacket was superbly hand tailored, and his gray flannel slacks contoured the lower half of his body beautifully, leaving little to her imagination. The yellow shirt and contrasting dark gray tie added a rather surprising note of high fashion. His clothes were in excellent taste, matching the natural dignity that was such an inherent part of him. And this man, this fantastically wonderful man, had just said. . . .

Hope shook her head as if trying to emerge from a daze.

Ross looked up at her, his gaze direct and darkly intent.

''I do love you, you know,'' he said simply. ''I think I fell in love with you in Randy's service station when you stared down at me as if I was the biggest clod in the world, and the mere idea of that kind of involvement terrified me.''

"Terrified you?"

He nodded. "The idea of ever really loving a woman has always... well, it's something I've never felt I could face up to, for fear of total disillusionment," he admitted. "Sometime I'll tell you why."

Hope already knew why. It went back to his mother, and to his grandmother even earlier. But she didn't tell him this now. It was more important to let him continue in his own way.

"By the time you loomed up in the woods below the house I was out of my mind over you and trying to shut you off, believe me," he told her. "The last thing I wanted in my life was a beautiful blond lady from New England. Then, everything I tried to do seemed to be wrong."

"Ross...."

"Look," he went on, and Hope had never before seen him quite so agitated, "about Stan Owl's paintings...I want to explain about that. After you'd left, I got to thinking about what you'd said about them, and I assumed you'd taken them with you. Then I went into the Fern Room...."

"Yes?"

Ross smiled wryly. "It seemed as close as I could get to you, being in there," he confessed. "I looked around, hoping that you'd left something—anything—behind so that I'd have some sort of...of tangible reminder of you. I opened the closet door and the portfolio was sticking out over the edge of the shelf. Naturally, I took it down. When I really looked at the paintings, I was astonished. I realized you were right in everything you'd said about Stan, and it was I who had been a prejudiced idiot.

"As it happens," he continued, "the owner of a very large art gallery in New York—one of the best—is a patient of mine. He comes to the Joslin for a checkup twice a year. I knew he'd be back in September, and I'd already decided to get back here myself by then. I couldn't concentrate on what I was doing in Cherokee once you left, so I thought it would be better to put the research aside for a couple of months and then get back to it with a fresh approach.

"Anyway, I brought the portfolio back to Boston with me, and I gave it my patient last week. He was as impressed as you had been and as I was. He'll be contacting Stan any day now, and I think by late fall we'll be seeing Stancil Owl's works in some of the best places."

"That's...wonderful," Hope managed. Then she couldn't refrain from adding, "But you had to practice one-upmanship even in that, didn't you?"

He seemed genuinely surprised. "What do you mean?"

"I think you knew very well that I wanted to do something for Stan myself," she pointed out.

"You'd mentioned that you didn't have any really good contacts in the art world yourself," he reminded her. "And my patient is—"

"I don't want to know who your patient is!" Hope retorted bitterly. Suddenly she felt very tired and totally unable to cope with the conflicting emotions waging war deep inside her.

She stood and said, her tone almost too polite, "If you don't mind, it's late. And I have to be at school early tomorrow morning."

"So," Ross said, raising his eyebrows eloquently, "you'd like me to leave?"

"Yes."

"And you have no intention, of course, of apologizing for not meeting me for a drink tonight, as you said you would?"

"I expressed my regrets when I phoned to cancel our appointment."

"How very proper of you," he returned. "But it isn't good enough, Hope. Where I come from, apologies don't count when you send them through an intermediary."

"This isn't where you come from!"

"No, it isn't, is it?" he agreed easily. "I'd say the Cherokees have much better manners. Better instinctive manners, certainly. As an example, no Cherokee would think of leaving an envelope full of money to be given to his hostess with the suggestion that she buy something she'd like for the house with it."

Hope stared at him, appalled. "I...I didn't mean to insult your aunt," she protested.

"Fortunately she wasn't insulted, because she knew you were upset. I also knew you were upset, so I'll overlook the way you left me money for paying your hospital bill. I'd already handled that anyway, so I gave your money to the Cherokee Historical Society as a donation. In your name, of course. You were so interested in the tribe I thought it would be appropriate."

He said this with such mockery that Hope could feel her cheeks beginning to sting.

"You also manage to forget friends very quickly," he went on. "It has hurt Wonder to think that you'd never bothered to get in touch with her. Not even a postcard. . . ."

"I spoke to her on the phone just the other day."

"Yes, I know, but you didn't call to talk to Wonder. You called because you were concerned about Stan's paintings."

"I can't win with you, can I?" Hope said dismally.

"It doesn't seem to me that you want to win with me," Ross told her. "To finish with all my explanations, though, I only wish to add that it seems to me the reason for my trying to buy your car behind your back was obvious, and the reason why I wanted to choose the place where you stayed in Asheville was equally so. It was my intention to join you there later that night for a long talk, which I'd hoped would. . .straighten things out between us. Then I found out you hadn't even checked in. . . ."

Ross stood now, dominating the room with his presence. "I notice that you still do seem interested in the Cherokees to the extent, at least, of displaying your literature."

He must, she knew, be referring to the antique pine cobbler's bench that served as a coffee table in the living room. On it she'd arranged the booklets she'd bought in the Cherokee Museum. Evidently he'd seen it on his way upstairs.

She said with a catch in her voice, "I will always

be interested in the Cherokees. I think your people have faced odds that would have vanquished lesser souls, and I might add that I'm not at all proud of the part my people played in any of it.''

Ross said gently, ''Your people, my people. We're all human, Hope. And that was a long time ago. You and I really had nothing to do with it, did we? The good or the bad. It's the way we handle ourselves today that counts.'' He paused, then said, ''I noticed that you have some material about Cherokee legends.''

''Yes.''

''Have you read them?''

''Yes, I have,'' Hope answered, her heart beginning to pound.

''So you know, then, that in the beginning all the people and all the animals lived in the vault in the sky.''

''In Galun'lati,'' she nodded.

''Have you read the part about the legend of the golden arrow?''

She shook her head.

''Well,'' Ross continued carefully, ''there are very few people left who hold to the original Cherokee religion today, but there are still stories of the earth, the moon, the sun and the stars, stories that are passed from generation to generation. And they tell of a time when the Cherokees believed in a supreme being whom they called Yowa. His name alone was so holy, so mystical, so completely sacred that only very privileged priests in the tribe were permitted to speak it aloud.''

There was a spellbinding quality in the deepness of Ross's voice, a quality that claimed Hope's total attention as he went on to say, "There were many religious ceremonies in the old times, and certain objects were sacred to the Cherokees. The number seven, for example. Fire and smoke, crystals of quartz, the sun and the moon, even corn. But very special among the sacred objects was the golden arrow.

"In each family in each clan the golden arrow was passed through the generations from eldest son to eldest son, to be cherished until he felt his heart pierced by true love. Then, and only then, did he place the arrow around the neck of his beloved, where she wore it until she, in turn, gave it to her eldest son when his heart became pierced as his father's had been."

As Hope watched, Ross reached into the pocket of his jacket and produced something slender and golden suspended from a thin, gleaming chain.

"This is my arrow," he said, "and it is for you, Hope. I never expected any woman to pierce my heart as you have. I never believed in such love because of experiences that happened in my own family. But now...even if you will not come to walk in the path made by my footsteps, I want you to have this."

Her eyes were glistening with tears as he fastened the slender chain around her neck, and her fingers reached for the smooth gold of the small arrow as she looked up at him.

"I saw the portrait in your bedroom, Hope," he

said quietly, his own voice shaking. "I didn't mean to spy, but I was upstairs...and I had to see where you slept. I...I was so shocked that...well, does the portrait mean...what I hope it means?"

It was the look in Hope's eyes that answered him.

In another instant Ross pulled her toward him and their lips met in a spirit of giving, a spirit that sent tremors of joy coursing through her body.

As she pressed herself close to him, Hope imagined for a moment that he'd brought the woods around his aunt's house with him. That piney fragrance she would always associate with him filled her nostrils and she swayed, knowing that her feelings were becoming so overpowering it was going to be impossible to restrain them. But she also knew that she didn't want to restrain them. Not now, nor ever again.

His hands caressed the contours of her body, leaving a trail of fire that spelled desire. And as Ross began to breathe more heavily, Hope's own passions enflamed. This was the moment she had yearned for, this was the man she wanted as she'd never wanted anyone else.

They stood in the kitchen, embracing as only lovers can embrace, until finally Ross said huskily, "Can we go upstairs, darling?"

She could only nod at him, unable to speak, but as they mounted step after step, so very close to each other that the warmth of their bodies seemed to be fusing, her anticipation surged. They came to her bedroom as naturally as if it belonged to both of them, and in the muted darkness of the moonlit fall night Ross began to undress her. When the last of her garments had slipped to the floor he picked her up with the gentleness that was such an integral part of him. Then, carrying her across the room to the old four-poster bed, he carefully lowered her into the softness of its sheets.

For a nebulous space of time she watched his silhouette as he undressed, tall, straight and...beautiful. Then he was beside her, nude and totally aroused.

Flesh touched flesh as they caressed each other in the most intimate of ways, exciting each other as they never had before, and Hope felt as if an earthquake of pure passion had come to shake her very core.

Then, when the urgency of their sexuality could no longer be repressed, he moved upon her until, in a transcending moment, he was inside her and they were truly one. Ecstasy was spelled out for Hope. Groaning with abandon, she and Ross conquered the heights of love together.

Theirs was a love of total possession and total giving, an equal and glorious union of two bodies and two minds. When finally their passion subsided, having added new colors to a rainbow all their own, Hope whispered, "I have been to Galun'lati, Ross. I've been to Galun'lati."

"As I have," he said.

He lay very still by her side, and for a long while neither of them spoke. Then, as she came slowly closer to reality, Hope sensed that something was troubling him.

Finally he turned to nudge her shoulder with that dark, velvet head, and he said in a voice that made him sound curiously young, "There's something you've never told me. You've...you've never said you love me."

"Oh, my darling," she said softly, staring into the dark pools of his eyes. "How could you even wonder about such a thing? I've loved you ever since you got out from under that car of yours at Randy's. I thought you were the most arrogant, insufferable person I'd ever met in my life...and I also knew my heart had stopped. Never doubt that I love you, Ross...or that I always will."

Ross looked back at her, his heart in his eyes, and she had the feeling that the mask of inscrutability that had so plagued her had been banished forever.

Then he said slowly, "There's something else we have to talk about. I think Randy and Wonder are going to get married before too much longer and I wondered if we—" He broke off, and Hope was amazed at his hesitation. Then he continued, "I know it might be a strange life for you...being married to me, that is. You got some idea of how demanding my profession can be when you came to the clinic today. The work never ends—the research, the patients—and even without it, I'd want to spend some time in Cherokee."

"And you think I wouldn't?"

"I don't know," he answered. "This house, Hope. This house is your heritage."

"And you object to that?"

"I don't think that's the right question," Ross

said. "I think it's whether or not your heritage will object to me."

It was Hope's turn to hesitate, then she said almost weakly, "In Cherokee, there was a woman who called you several times... from Boston."

He nodded. "My housekeeper," he reported, grinning. "She'd been on a brief holiday." Then he added teasingly, "She's sixty-five, darling, and she'd never leave South Boston for me!"

Hope's laugh rang with a new sound of freedom, for the last of her doubts were now resolved. Then she said, "Speaking of this house, Dr. Ross Adair... it needs a lot of fixing, but I'm very fond of it. Would you be willing to live in it?"

"I can't think of anything more wonderful than watching you have everything done to it that should be done, while we make it a home for both of us," Ross told her softly. "I do have an apartment in the city, but the thought of coming back here to you every night is almost too wonderful to think about. I... I'd like to give the apartment up."

Stinging tears burned Hope's eyes, for this had been an especially revealing statement on his part. She glanced at him through the darkness, just beginning to know how very proud he really was, how much of a loner he'd always been. But she, at least, would never let him down. She would love him forever.

"Hope?" he said suddenly.

"Yes, Ross?"

"I have one more confession to make. The legend of the golden arrow... was born in my dreams."

She darted a surprised glance at him, then asked carefully, "What about Galun'lati?"

"What about it, Hope, darling?"

"Do you suppose it's still there?"

"Well," Ross Adair said, reaching out to draw her close to him again, "we can always find out!"

About the author

This is Meg Hudson's sixth Superromance and the second of her multicultural series. If the backgrounds of her novels seem to sparkle with authentic detail that's because this author believes in setting out from her home on Cape Cod to explore locales for new stories. While working on *Two Worlds, One Love*, she and her husband spent considerable time in Cherokee, North Carolina, familiarizing themselves with the reservation and researching traditions, past and present, of Indian life. The author had an opportunity to talk with many of the residents of Cherokee, and it is this personal experience that shines through in her novel. We can look forward to her upcoming Superromance about San Francisco's Russian community, which will be published in the new year.

Harlequin Presents

ALL-TIME FAVORITE BESTSELLERS
...love stories that grow
more beautiful with time!

Now's your chance to discover the earlier great books in Harlequin Presents, the world's most popular romance-fiction series.

Choose from the following list.

Harlequin Presents

ALL-TIME FAVORITE BESTSELLERS

Complete and mail this coupon today!

Harlequin Reader Service

In the U.S.A.
P.O. Box 52040
Phoenix, Arizona 85072-9988

In Canada
649 Ontario Street
Stratford, Ontario N5A 6W2

Please send me the following Presents **ALL-TIME FAVORITE BESTSELLERS.** I am enclosing my check or money order for $1.75 for each copy ordered, plus 75¢ to cover postage and handling.

☐ #17	☐ #38	☐ #50	☐ #67	☐ #75
☐ #20	☐ #41	☐ #54	☐ #70	☐ #78
☐ #32	☐ #42	☐ #62	☐ #71	☐ #83
☐ #35	☐ #46	☐ #66	☐ #73	

Number of copies checked @ $1.75 each = $ _____
N.Y. and Ariz. residents add appropriate sales tax $ _____
Postage and handling $ ___.75___
TOTAL $ _____

I enclose _____
(Please send check or money order. We cannot be responsible for cash sent through the mail.)
Prices subject to change without notice.

NAME _____
(Please Print)

ADDRESS _____ APT. NO. _____

CITY _____

STATE/PROV. _____

ZIP/POSTAL CODE _____

Offer expires March 31, 1984

FAV-CB-2R

30956000000